IMMORTALS:

BOOK 3

THE

BRACADIAN

Published by: Wendiilou Publishing
                     Wendy Brown
Cover Artwork: © Chelsea Langdon
Line Art: © Andrew Munro
Pointillism drawings: © Theo Wright

To connect with the author, and for more information and resources visit

www.immortalsepic.com

For more copies contact the Publisher c/-
Glenburnie Homestead
212 Glenburnie Road
ROB ROY NSW 2360
Mobile: 0468 998 268
Email:wendiiloupublishing@gmail.com

A special thank you to Theo, Jono, and Luke

For critiquing my writing, and keeping it epic!

IMMORTALS: BOOK 3

THE BRACADIAN

Andrew Wratten

Wendülou Publishing

Prologue

Kraken relaxed against the railing at the skyship's prow. He drew deeply from the silver goblet he nursed, enjoying the scent and flavours of the mulled wine. Then, after swilling it around in his mouth and gulping, the immortal pirate slurred a deeply satisfied "aaaggghhhhh".

Not far from him, Morgan stood staring at the brigand and shaking his head.

"I should cast you over the bloody edge and let Ramthos finally have you. You will suffer a thousand deaths in his watery halls."

Kraken leaned over the balustrade to cast his gaze across the ocean far below and saluted the broad expanse with cup raised. Then, as he turned to face Morgan, he acquired a cheeky, mischievous grin.

"Ramthos and I have a bargain, Morgan. He'll not want me dead 'til I've delivered my end. So, throw me over if you care to. I'll see you soon enough in the next port. Toss the wine after me if you don't mind."

Morgan continued shaking his head. Testing the pirate's claims was tempting - be rid of his nuisance ramblings and mischief. It had been bold of the pirate to approach Morgan on his last visit to Dreban. As the emperor's ambassador, Morgan regretted his decision to let the miscreant accompany him. Not only would it put him offside with important allies such as Milan and his guild of merchants, but it was also becoming impossible to tolerate Kraken's disrespect for himself and his crew. The pirate acted as if he were irreproachable and untouchable.

"I'll be keeping the wine, Kraken."

Kraken snorted and shook his head as if Morgan were playing the fool. He peered into his goblet, which was disappointingly empty, then reached the cup up to Morgan's face and gave it a shake to indicate he needed more.

His temper ignited, Morgan reached down, grabbing Kraken by the belt. Then, with a great heave, he tossed the powerless man far out over the ship's edge. Two sailors busy nearby ran to the rails to watch the hapless pirate flail his arms as he plunged towards the sea far below. One of the sailors looked at Morgan incredulously, while the other laughed and called to his mates. Ignoring the commotion, Morgan turned and strode back towards his quarters. As he passed the skyship captain, who hurried to see what was happening, Morgan reached out and grabbed the man's arm.

"Change course for Charikon. I want to be well away from here, now!"

"Yes, Ambassador", was the quick reply. "Would that be the Charikon capital, sir?"

Morgan felt a tiny vestige of remorse for casting the old pirate to the ocean and almost certainly to his death. But Kraken was using him, and it wasn't for the first time, so it was a relief to be free of such a burden. The more profound truth was that the pirate stirred that part of Morgan that was an adventurer too, that was bold and unconventional, and who was only happy when faced with the unknown. Morgan served the emperor for fourteen years, consolidating the island colonies to the north and drafting the northern colonial divisions. When Morgan first headed to the islands, it raised his spirit to enter those new lands, but now his essence yearned for less-travelled destinations. Although he was the emperor's man, be it a man of alloys and magetech, he was beholden also to himself, and the emperor provided him absolute freedom to make his choices.

"Yes, to Ugol. Be to it."

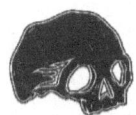

Even with the remarkable speed of the flying vessel, it was twelve long days before Morgan arrived at his destination. The journey gave him time to reflect on his actions and consider the future. He was more determined than ever to change his course, but at the same time, the more he remembered, the more he was drawn toward his past. With growing certainty, Morgan believed he must go back before he could go forward.

Ugol was an expansive city raised from the earth. Gigantic clay towers formed chaotic labyrinths, each pillar with its tribal markings and numerous entrances leading to a catacomb of homes and all types of industry or businesses. Smaller structures, all baked from the same earth, stretched to the ends of the rugged landscape, coloured with paints in randomness that could only be of orc design. As Morgan approached, he observed patrols of orcs and belg moving through the packed streets, enforcing good order. The skyship parked against one of the giant towers, alongside a rickety, seldom used dock, barely wide enough for the crew to disembark two abreast.

Morgan liked being in Ugol. The orcs here were civilised, yet they kept their old traditions and possessed an uncompromising culture. They were direct, ambitious, and, in Morgan's experience, very resourceful in getting things done. The Charikon were a happy race, and even in the overpopulated poor districts where the poverty and oppression often seemed overwhelming, the orcs were exuberant and celebrated life.

The ambassador did not desire politics or business on this trip. He deftly avoided unwanted petitioners by disguising himself in a long robe and joining those sailors headed for the brothel district. From there, Morgan made his way to Arta's, waiting patiently at her door for the big woman to return to her residence. As he stood in the darkness in the depths of a clay tower, he disliked the sense of being trapped and did not trust the integrity of the orcish design. He was relieved when Arta finally arrived, and her guards escorted them to an audience chamber.

As Morgan remembered her, Arta was large and grown fat in recent years, though she was still muscular across the shoulders, with fierce eyes and a tongue to match.

"Morgan, you look like a fucking ornament – all polished up and useful for nothing."

Morgan laughed. He was expecting the banter.

"You look younger, woman", he taunted. "Have you been exercising?"

Now Arta laughed too. The local orcs failed to understand sarcasm, glancing at each other but remaining silent. Arta now remembered why she was so fond of this metal man and his visits.

"Fuck you, Morgan. You useless metal man. Why are you here? What is the emperor's favourite trinket doing at the arse-end of this shithole?"

"Visiting a friend."

It was a simple truth, though Arta waved her large hand as if fanning away a foul stench. The big woman sat back on a cushioned chair, sagging into its folds, and wriggling to make herself comfortable. She looked about as if she had business to attend to, but instead, she focused back on her visitor after grunting to nobody.

"A friend indeed, Morgan."

A decade ago, Morgan assisted Arta in moving from Dreban to Ugol and setting up a small protection business. Now, Arta commanded a reputable ensemble of bodyguards and private enforcers. Since Morgan first journeyed to Bracadia, Arta remained his closest link back to the Eastern Colonies. He always enjoyed catching up with her, and it seemed they shared a common culture and humour that was refreshing in this foreign land. Today, however, was not a social visit.

"Arta, I miss the East. I miss the Blood Sea."

As he spoke, Morgan suddenly realised the essence of his melancholy, and with a sly grin, he shared his thinking with Arta.

"I miss Mannace. His leadership and his comradery. He is truly at the centre of events. But it is no secret that the Fates, the gods, and even the Four Hells poke at him and taunt him. He is their plaything, and they will never give him peace. So, Mannace will always be on the precipice, tiptoeing along the cliff's edge."

Arta began slowly shaking her head, not appreciating what Morgan was saying.

"You are full of shit, Morgan. The gods, seriously. The gods only care about the gods. The Fates are a fart in a storm, useless, like you are, Morgan. The Four Hells, what are you talking about, Morgan? You think the Four Hells give a fuck about that bad-tempered whores-arse. Fuck you! Don't feed me your pig shit!"

Morgan forgot that Arta and Mannace once crossed blades. It didn't matter; Morgan spent enough time with Mannace and the Oracle to understand that Mannace carried both a great blessing and a terrible curse, to rise higher and higher but never reach his ambition. But it was precisely that intrepid fortitude, the glorious insanity of striving against the impossible, that was pulling at Morgan. It was a blatant contrast to the mundane service that his life was becoming. While he adored and honoured the Bracadian emperor, he now realised that his old loyalties to Mannace, and their friendship, were more substantial.

"It is time for me to return east. I will find Mannace."

Arta was exasperated.

"Fuck you! Fuck off then and leave me to rot in this shithole!"

Morgan shrugged. They both knew that Arta was happy and at home amongst the orcs, more so than she had ever been amongst her kin. Morgan and Arta met each other's stare until Arta filled the looming silence.

"Whatever, blow wind up Mannace's arse if that makes you happy. Just don't ever trust that he has regard for anyone but himself."

With a sly look, the big woman leaned toward her guest, her tone becoming severe.

"Must you always follow, Morgan? Can you not be your own man!?"

Morgan flinched as much as a man of metal could. Arta's words hit low, knowing where Morgan was most vulnerable.

"You have become a bitch, Arta. Fuck you! Are you so proud to hide in this shithole and fill your purse with orc cock? I make things happen, Arta. Look about, I made this happen for you!"

Arta smirked, pleased with herself to have Morgan riled, to forget that he was so proper and important. In his temper, with his crude words, he stooped down to her level. She waved her hand again, this time to help the moment pass.

"Do as you will, and don't spare a thought for me, Morgan. I will be fine. I will die happy here, but remember me, Morgan. Everyone, even the lowest, should be remembered."

It was hard for Morgan to keep pace with Arta's conversation. It seemed that she moved from one drama to another, and he was amused more than annoyed that he let himself be so furious.

"Enough, Arta, don't play games with me. One day, I will return."

"No, you won't, Morgan, not in my lifetime."

Perhaps that was true, and Morgan did not have a response. Instead, he pulled his shoulders back to fortify himself, changing the subject.

"Do you need anything before I go?"

"Not from you! I have all that I need. All the orc cock a bitch could desire."

It amused Arta to stir Morgan with the words he had used in anger, though he did not cringe this time, and being an astute woman, Arta could see that their meeting was ending. She would have the last jibe.

"You are such a hero, Morgan. Go then and save Mannace. Save the whole, Hells-forsaken, fucking world!"

It felt to Morgan that visiting Arta marked the end of his time in Bracadia. It was odd that his farewells were to Arta and not the emperor, but strangely, that's where his deepest loyalties lay. Perhaps it was because the emperor was immortal like him, and time, for them, was not so much of the essence. But, ironically, now that he felt free of his obligations, he was in a hurry to be away.

In respect, Morgan bowed to his host, then he turned and traversed the tunnels until he exited into a busy market. He could see his skyship above through the bright canopies covering the food stalls. Though it had been his to command for fourteen years, the magnificent vessel belonged to the emperor, a borrowed possession, and Morgan knew he must leave it and all the other things he acquired behind. The revelation was oddly liberating, and until this moment, he did not realise how burdened he had become. Morgan was increasingly clear of purpose.

Lifting off the ground, Morgan hovered, ascending slowly above the canopies. He could hear the attention he was drawing from the market throng. It did not bother him. Over the years, he became more comfortable with his celebrity, the man of metal that could fly. Without further consideration, he sped now toward the heavens and then east. Below him, Charikon, the Dividing Ranges, and eventually, Bracadia, raced past. Morgan was proud to be a loyalist. Though he was leaving the imperial homeland and the emperor behind, the scene below reminded him that he would remain a patriot and an enduring symbol of what it meant to be Bracadian.

PART ONE:

The New Age

ANGOROK

Mannace, First General of the South, stared across the table at Vestig Gozer, Efate and Warlord of the North. It was audacious of his rival to trek his horde across the desolate demon wastes and knock in the night upon the gates of Angorok. Protecting the efate was heavy, black metal armour, from his wide feet up to his bull neck, finished off with a tall neck guard rimmed with gleaming white fur. Vestig's face was cruel, his lip turned up on one side in a permanent snigger, and his bright brown-green eyes were sharp and watchful. Deep lines on his forehead and creasing his eyes marked a permanent scowl. Matted blond locks fell loosely about Vestig's shoulders and down his broad back. Mannace recalled the efate leading the dreaded Hunga at the Mesah Long, fighting at their fore, so he was in no doubt that Vestig's sword arm was as savage as the murderous visage he portrayed.

Reygan, a supple and handsome man, stood behind the seated Vestig, and further back was the looming giant, Frain. Like Vestig, Frain was heavily armoured in the fashion of the Hunga, with bleached demon skulls strapped to his shoulders and arms, making him appear even broader and more menacing. His face was heavy set and his eyes dark, with a killer's cold stare.

It was Reygan that spoke. In a calm, charming voice befitting his handsome looks and occupation as Speaker, Reygan outlined the purpose of their visit.

"Vestig Gozer, celebrated Efate of Amon Murn, revered warlord of the North, acknowledges you, Mannace, as First General of the South and a rival of worth."

Reygan bowed deeply, rising slowly to show their host due respect. The Speaker threw his arms wide.

"We are in a new Age, gentlemen. An Age birthed of deceit and darkness."

Dramatically, Reygan clenched and shook his fists at the mention of deceit, as if he were personally afflicted. Then, leaning forward, his tone became even more tortured, carrying a purposeful bitterness.

"Events have changed all our fates, and prophecies were laid bare. At the Mesah Long, we were each denied an ending, cheated, cheated of our right to this new Age."

After a pause, the Speaker's shoulders slumped, and there was a deepening sadness in the man's eyes.

"The South was purged by the cursed dwarves and buried in snow. The North is wounded, infested by a demonic plague. But be assured that Amon Murn awakens, rising from the ruins, gathering its ancient strength, resurrecting what was lost, taking back its rightful lands."

In an even tone and looking directly at the first general, Reygan ended his brief discourse with what seemed a reasonable request.

"The efate would know of your plans, Mannace of the South."

All eyes shifted to Mannace, awaiting the first general's response. Mannace, however, remained silent. He understood his attendants were just as interested in hearing the answer. The first general was aware that many yearned to leave this forsaken place and return to their distant homes. Yet, he held them all here by strength of will and a stubborn resolve to keep the lands his armies fought so hard to take. Even with the civilians fled and the land amuck with demon spawn, he stayed true to his ambition to conquer the North. It was madness in him, and damn to the Hells this bloody Vestig for making him confront the reality that the time for conquest had passed.

As if Vestig heard Mannace's silent curse, the efate abruptly rose, and he looked down at Mannace, who was still seated. The efate's voice was like gravel scraping across glass. He possessed none of Regan's charisma or subtlety. He demanded an answer.

"Why do you stay in the North?"

For more than a decade, none of Mannace's advisors or retainers was so bold as to confront him with such a question. Mannace purposefully acted like the tyrant, putting himself above their wants and pleas. Vestig's challenge ignited the rage within him. It was a fury born of underlying frustration he could not justify nor explain. How could anybody understand being denied your destiny? Fourteen years ago, at the battle on the Mesah Long, his fate was ripped away and replaced with absolute emptiness that mercilessly devoured his being every day. Anger consumed the big man, and his seat clattered backwards as he rose abruptly to confront Vestig nose-to-nose, eye-to-eye. Mannace was taller than his adversary and looked no less murderous in his rage. Behind the first general, war priests rigged in their god armour inched forward, and the wizards behind them crackled with magic as they readied themselves to fight.

Though far outnumbered in this rival bastion, Vestig knew no fear. On the contrary, danger excited him so much that he purposefully lurched forward a hands-width, creating a brief panic, and raising tension that might quickly erupt into violence. Nevertheless, Vestig Gozer journeyed a long way to get answers.

"Why do you stay? There is nothing here for you but death."

As both men continued their fierce stare, Vestig could see the deep hate in Mannace's eyes. Good, he thought. The vicious glare spoke Vestig's language, and now he understood that Mannace, like him, had unfinished business. He no longer needed Mannace's response.

"If the demons do not kill you, I will!"

The threat suddenly awakened the voice in Mannace. He loomed over Vestig and releasing the full fury of his wrath; he consumed the room with his booming shout.

"GO BACK TO AMON MURN. THESE LANDS ARE NOT OF THE NORTH, NOR ARE THEY OF THE SOUTH. THESE LANDS ARE MINE. ANGOROK, THESE HALLS, MINE. ALL THAT WAS VELDAAN AND ISLAN, MINE. THE SARANG IS MINE. THE YOUNG KINGDOMS, MINE. MINE, ALL OF IT, DO YOU UNDERSTAND VESTIG? YOU TRESPASS ON MY LAND. LEAVE NOW, OR, BY THE HELLS, I SWEAR YOU WILL DIE."

Mannace pushed Vestig on the shoulder to start him on his way or invite him to strike back and conclude their rivalry here and now. Behind Vestig, who did not budge, Frain took a long stride forward, though the massive warrior was wise enough to draw to a halt as the room about them responded with a flurry of movement. More than ever, chaos and violence were a half-breath away. Some corners of the room darkened, and the rising sounds of battle were at the edge of hearing. It was the War God's presence, watching, anticipating, urging. Mannace was blind to it, only seeing the man before him.

"I WILL COME FOR YOU, VESTIG. BUILD YOUR NATION. RAISE YOUR ACCURSED ARMIES. WE WILL MEET IN BATTLE AS WE DID ON THE LONG, AND I WILL HAVE MY DESTINY FULFILLED."

Others might have counted Mannace mad, but Vestig grasped the First General's purpose. Though not as possessed or single-minded, he was afflicted with the same torment.

"As will I."

With that, the efate turned and led his retinue out of Angorok, and his hoard, under the safeguard of the eternal priesthood, started the long and dangerous march back to Amon Murn.

Mannace unleashed chaos with his words. Mayhem engulfed Angorok and weighed heavily upon the people of those lands he named. Crucially, the ill-spoken statements touched the ears of the eastern colonial leaders who were financing and resourcing Mannace's conflict against the demon hoards. By his proclamation, he shattered that tenuous tie to the past, and he could no longer count himself as the first general of the South. Instead, Mannace anointed himself ruler of his domain, independent of the South, and confirmed enemy of Amon Murn. He challenged everyone to either rebuke or rally to him. In his angry state, the big man did not care for politics. He felt liberated from that nonsense and wilfully embraced a reckoning. Damn them all.

Upon hearing of Mannace's declaration, Render hurried from Adash to Angorok. He was concerned for his friend. When he entered the main gates of the capital, the city was hectic as flying ships arrived and departed, ferrying away multitudes of troops. For years, it amazed Render that Mannace managed to retain such a large standing army in the North. In the ongoing defence against the demons that infested the surrounding lands, Angorok would desperately miss the departing soldiers.

Render sat with Mannace in the library, where they often relaxed. However, when his friend was in the mood he appeared in now, the sorcerer knew to match his meanness and be blunt.

"Mine, mine, mine! For Light's sake, are you ten years old? Is it a surprise the Eastern Colonies are pulling back their troops? You will lose the Muster, too, unless I rally them. Some I can make stay, and others will need to be convinced. We need the technomancers, so don't let them get on a ship. Shit Mannace, have you thought this through at all?"

Render could see that Mannace was not listening, caught up in his thoughts. Annoyed, the sorcerer sat back, taking a deep breath, and signalling a servant to bring wine.

When the estranged leader finally looked up at the sorcerer and spoke, he surprised Render. In a calm voice, Mannace's tone held none of the malice or forcefulness that Render was expecting.

"Yes, I was a madman, Render. The darkness in me controlled my words, and the light abandoned me as it did at Mesah Long. All that we have patiently built, I obliterated with my words. At least it may seem that way."

Mannace laughed at the confusion in the sorcerer's expression. He had more to explain.

"Why indeed are we still here when the North has no apparent value? At first, it was because we were saving people from demons. Then we killed demons in the North to not have to fight demons in the South. But, Render, no demon has attempted the snow in over a decade, and they do not travel beyond the lands they already infest. So, we have saved all that want saving. Those that remain here know the dangers and have adapted to a harsh existence."

Mannace reached out to steal a swig of the sorcerer's wine, swirling it around to wet his mouth before swallowing.

"I will let the soldiers go and any others who would follow them south. They deserve their peace, away from this torment. Let them be gone so that what is left are those who call this place home. That is our new beginning, Render, in this new Age."

With a rare exuberance, the big man leaned toward his friend.

"You will be surprised who will stay. You will stay, my friend. You will not leave what you have at Adash, and the Fallen will remain with you. Many of the war priests and their acolytes will persist. More of their kind will come, and followers of their God. It is a crusade for them. The Blood Legion will keep their base at Skon. Those are our bastions, Skon with its water barrier, Adash consumed with a sorcerer's darkness, and here at Angorok with the priesthood's warding."

Render was intrigued but with misgivings. Nevertheless, the truths were blatant, and Render's reply was matter of fact.

"The lands you claim are a wasteland of ruins and scattered bones. The garrisons are too few. The demons are too many. Staying in the North is insane, my friend."

"What kind of sorcerer are you to be so scared of demons and bones? Will they not bend to your will? Does the cult of the Fallen not count demons amongst their allies?"

Render scoffed. Mannace was making light of the seriousness of their situation.

"At Adash, we have no trouble with the demons that infest the lands, but the darkness, water, and warding will not be enough to shield us from the larger armies when they come. The departure of your soldiers will not go unnoticed by the Hell-spawn, and they will swoop soon enough. The full legions of the first Hell and their generals will soon be upon us."

Render chose another point to get off his chest.

"You should have made peace with Amon Murn. We do not need Vestig Gozer at our door."

"NO!" was the instant response. "War with Amon Murn is inevitable."

Mannace's look of determination was such that Render dared not dig deeper. Instead, he changed to a lighter subject on many people's minds.

"So, you have claimed these lands, this vast expanse. Mine, mine, mine! You have proclaimed yourself its leader. Have you a name for this glorious nation, Mannace? What title do you, as leader of this nation, claim?"

Mannace had thought on the subject and prepared his answer.

"We stand in Angorok. We will be known as Angorok, the city that became a nation. I am considering the title; King of Angorok."

Render laughed.

"We already have one mad king. One is enough!"

Render was right. While the Mad King was not present for the last fourteen years, it felt like the man owned the title of king, and Mannace was quick to jump to an alternative.

"Marshall then. It's military, and I am a better general than a ruler. Marshall of Angorok."

"Better."

Both men were pragmatists, and when Render left later that evening, he was motivated to do more. He was considering many ideas and intended to pursue them with renewed purpose. Some were ambitious, requiring others from the Muster for assistance. It amused Render that he travelled to Angorok to aid Mannace, but on reflection, he was surprised to be uplifted himself.

ADASH

"The Eternal Priesthood, the War Priests, the Light Bearers, perhaps even the Cult of the Fallen, they cannot be permitted to leave the Muster. It is essential; we must hold tight to religion to survive the demons."

It was the librarian, Elderlin, that responded.

"Kel, all the populace holds to the gods. They wear religion like they wear clothes. They crave hope, protection, and to save their souls when the end comes. To be godless in these lands is to walk naked into the Four Hells."

The elderly wizard took a moment to catch his breath before continuing. His audience of Asari and their apprentices were patient to hear the librarian's wisdom.

"The priests will not abandon Angorok. The fight against the Hells is a holy war for them, and their importance will increase as others of the Muster depart. Look closer. The Eternal Priesthood has prepared for this moment across countless generations, and their purpose is to help men survive the demons coming. They refer to this era as their ascension."

Some of the other wizards were nodding.

"The war priests will honour their pledge to Mannace, and many have risen in rank under his stewardship. They have experienced the War God's presence in the North. We all have, have we not?"

These things seemed so apparent to Elderlin. Perhaps it was because he spent more time than most with Mannace and possessed a listening ear for any of the Muster who came to him with ideas or sought his advice.

"The Light Bearer's purpose is to confront the darkness, and we neighbour Imazaran and the Holy Lands. So, they will stay. What choice do they have? And the Fallen have no home to return to, so they reside at Adash as long as Render stays there. Perhaps the question should be do we want the Fallen in Angorok?"

The value of the Fallen was a hot topic, and there was an eruption of voices and instant debate, with views supporting the Fallen as well as condemning them. Finally, Elderlin raised his hand and light emanated from it, consuming, and silencing the room with its brightness. As the light faded, the librarian continued.

"Yes, we do."

It was not like Elderlin to play games, and there were many frowns when he answered his own question. The ruse required an explanation.

"The Eternal Priesthood and the Fallen are not dissimilar; they each control demons. If we cannot defeat the Hell-spawn, if their numbers are too great to vanquish, perhaps there are ways that we can exist side-by-side, live amongst them."

Many present shook their heads or frowned. Finally, Elderlin, perturbed by the reaction, turned to glare at two apprentices bold enough to snigger.

"We summoned demons when needed, so we cannot place ourselves above such ideas."

Kel re-joined the conversation. His views reflected those of many others.

"Summoning demons always ended badly for us. Demons are a curse. The infestation upon these lands is a curse. The Fallen and their demonic allies are a curse."

Elderlin shrugged. He was not so invested in his opinions that he would discount others. He simply wanted the Asari and their apprentices to have open minds.

"Has Mannace not shown us that the combined talents of many can resolve problems that have seemed impossible? Has not the collaboration of the Muster led to possibilities that an individual working alone could never conceive? As unlikely as it seems, the Fallen might hold the secrets to our very salvation."

Kel shrugged too. Nothing in this Age was a certainty.

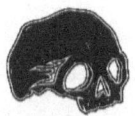

The Asari were closer to the truth than they realised. At Adash, a city engulfed in potent darkness, Render was already working closely with the Fallen. After defeating the rival sorcerer, Churgwarthos, Render made the fortress city his home, and during the last decade, the Fallen travelled to join him. They brought their demons, the great variety of dreamers summoned from the third Hell. To augment their flock, the cultists created sacred places where they lured and seduced the first Hell's rampaging soldiers.

Render walked through the unlit streets to assess the cultists' progress. Most alleys and buildings of Adash were crawling with demon spawn. Occasionally a shadowy creature flapped overhead or scampered across his path. Tens of thousands of fiends lurked in dark recesses, docile, restrained to watch and wait. They lived alongside the Fallen, who manipulated the darkness to subdue the demon's insatiable hunger and give them commands. At first, marauding demons came in packs to Adash as they did to other cities, hunting for blood. More recently, the cultists lured them with rituals, drawing them to the bastion like imps to a flame. Under the blanketing shadow of Adash, the amassed horde was an easily kept secret.

Although the cultists would not like it, Render arranged for the Eternal Priesthood to come to the city to share in the experiment. He was careful to choose priests he could work with and trust. The Eternal clergy were more familiar with the first Hell's denizens and were experts at harnessing such creatures.

As Render walked about Adash's narrow streets, zombies stood idle alongside some buildings, almost skeletal in appearance. Their stink was an assault on the senses, though not as bad as it had been in the early years. They were leftovers from the war against the North, another progeny of Churgwarthos that Render stole. Render's only original works were the stone gargoyles that scuttled about, often staying close to their master. The stone figurines were a prominent feature of the Adash architecture, and wherever Render discovered them, he would take the time to animate their forms. The animations were a potent defence and something he maintained absolute control over. Likewise, Fek, his protector, was nearby. The elite demon and his cultist followers lurked, almost invisible, in the deep shadows. They were proud of their role as the sorcerer's guards, considering themselves elevated by their association. There was nothing they would not do if Render asked it.

Render discovered a guest waiting for him at the citadel. Few people outside the cult would be brave enough to come here alone, with the nerve to walk in the darkness amongst the demons and undead. The sorcerer met with his visitor in the great hall, lit with fires along its walls, providing a flickering light.

"Jaal, why are you here? I thought you would have run far from these lands. Is the world so small that you must stay where you are unwanted?"

Render bore no personal malice for the dark elf, who was once a close friend. But Jaal picked the wrong allies too often, branding him as a renegade. Firstly, he aligned himself with the Mad King, who unleashed the demon hoards upon the North. Secondly, he served Eya, responsible for slaughtering the Elves of The Hand and driving the Alani into hiding. Jaal ignored the accusation, asking his own questions instead.

"Why is Mannace still here when the North is in ruins? Why are you at Adash, hiding in another sorcerer's shadow? Is this darkness not a reminder to you every day that your sorcery does not compare to his? He will return, Render; death will not hold him. Best you were far from this place."

Render laughed, turning his back on Jaal, drawing himself closer to one of the fires to be warm. Jaal moved to be beside him.

"What are you doing here in this doomed place, Render? You lower yourself to cower here."

"Who are you to say that? What have you become, Jaal? What have *you* achieved in the last decade?"

The dark elf did not feel the need to justify himself.

"Perhaps nothing. Mannace, you, and I; we carry the Oracle's curse of failed prophecy!"

Render turned to face the elf. He appeared angry.

"Failed prophecy! Do you understand the consequences, Jaal? Your damned king, the North is his mess. Your bitch queen, Eya, is at war with the elves. All elves Jaal, perhaps even your kin."

"I was not responsible for the actions of the Mad King. I seldom saw the man. Eya, yes, I was blind to her ambition, though I doubt she is at war with the dark elves – they are loyal to her, to the Order. Heed what I say."

"You are still blind to think such loyalty has any value. You were the Mad King's lackey. I am embarrassed for you, Jaal."

"Enough with the Mad King. I told you I had no part in that."

"And the Spider Mother?"

"Eya is single-minded, and she will take what she wants. I was wrong to trust her. But, Render, I cannot lie; the time I spent with Eya and the spiderkin is not something I regret. I regret only that the spiderkin, my children, are lost to me now. Roanna is lost to me too; I do not know where she is."

Render was thoughtful. The wizard stood silent for some time, focusing on the heat of the fire, and letting his mind clear.

"It is dangerous for you here. The elves have pathways to this place. They could appear at any time and take you. You would not enjoy their questioning!"

"I have spent time with the Alani. I was their prisoner for over twelve years, Render. Be sure there is no more I can tell the elves."

That was news to Render. It explained why Jaal did not come sooner, and the revelation immediately relaxed his animosity towards the dark elf. The sorcerer's thoughts quickly turned to how Jaal once saved him when he was impossibly trapped, and he felt guilty that he hadn't considered that Jaal might need his help. The culpability quickly became anger as he thought about all the time he spent with the Alani spellweavers at the Muster, and they never once hinted that Jaal was in their custody.

Render eventually turned to face Jaal.

"In truth, it will not be easy for the elves to travel the pathways to these halls. I have placed guardians against them and the spiders and demons as well. So, we will not be taken by surprise."

Render could see now that Jaal suffered. He was leaner and less toned. His spirit was wounded, dull compared to the brightness it radiated in the past. Render was sure the elves would be watching Jaal closely. Perhaps Adash was one of the few places their vision could not reach.

"The cultists can cook and fuck. They have many uses. You will stay here."

The companions turned to watch the flames and soak in the fire's warmth.

SKON

Casteel, commander of the Blood Legion, lay next to her lover, Shamal Shamas, commander of the Ravista. A sliver of sun from a narrow window fell across the bed. Casteel could see the dust their lovemaking had put into the air in the light. She slapped Shamal on his abdomen, causing him to sit upright in reflex.

"You would fuck me on a dusty bed. This place is disgusting; you let it fall to a shamble in my absence."

In truth, as Shammal looked around, the room was tidy and everything was in place. He let Casteel have her nonsense, not wanting to waste their time together on silly arguments. Shammal rolled atop Casteel, kissing her, and teasing her pointed nipples with his dextrous tongue. He enjoyed the closeness and her beauty. Eventually, he settled back next to her, caressing in long strokes from her neck down to her knees. Elven skin had a firmness he enjoyed. However, Shamal had more essential topics than housework on his mind.

"The Eastern Colonies are withdrawing their troops. Will the Blood Legion be departing with them?"

Casteel was expecting the question. To comfort him, she ran a hand down Shammal's arm, holding his hand.

"No, my Love. We have not finished our work here."

It was the answer Shamal wanted, and though he knew it was folly to seek greater detail, concern made him dig deeper.

"Did the order arrive for you to return?"

"Does it matter? The legion has three bases, here at Skon, in Dos Neran, and at Viletri. As commander of the legion, I can choose where we are most needed. I choose here."

Shamal knew it would not be that simple.

"More orders will come. They will be clearer about what they want. Will you go then?"

"No!"

Casteel held no desire to return to the bloody Blood Sea with its politics and drama. Her life was simple at Skon, yet meaningful. She spent most of her life seeking adventure, and now what she desired most was the routine she established in this isolated place. The legion operated three class A flying ships, and using Skon as a base, they supplied the safe havens scattered through the old lands of Islan, and where needed, they led away approaching demon swarms. The Blood Legion occasionally fought, but not if it put them in peril and only when they could make a difference - the last decade hardened Casteel to tough decisions and consequences. Through bitter experience, she learned the demons were far too many to take on in open warfare.

When Casteel was not on active patrol with her troops, she enjoyed her life in Skon with her handsome man.

"They can't make the legion return."

"They can, surely. The colonial leaders might consider the North lost, worth nothing to them, and would that be so wrong!?"

"No, not wrong at all. It is lost. Mannace has claimed these lands, and the Eastern Colonies will be relieved to rid themselves of the North and their first general. They can move on, without the burden of conscience or responsibility."

It was a pragmatic view, but Casteel was not ready to completely let the colonies off the hook.

"Unless Mannace fails in the North and the demons are left unchallenged. What if the legions of Hell, uncontested, cross the snow to enter Arenland? Then the Eastern Colonies will care about defence in the North! They will suddenly remember why conflict in the North is better than defence in the South!"

Shamal could see the rising passion in Casteel, though it was not a passion for the bed. To distract her, he moved atop her again and kissed her as she tried to talk. Casteel wriggled to be free, but Shamal would have none of it. Instead, he raised his torso and looked down at her pretty face. The Ravista leader's groin was pinning Casteel to the bed to suggest that sex was better than talk.

"Fuck me, if all you want from me is sex."

Shamal smiled.

"You only want to stay in Skon because the sex is so good."

Casteel's eyes narrowed, but before she could speak, Shamal's lips were again on hers, and she could feel below his spear hardening. The sexual contact made it impossible to think of a clever quip, and instead, she gave in to his advances, pulling his neck toward her so that their lips again touched. Shamal's kisses were the best kind of magic.

ANTIGOTH

The thriving city of Antigoth ruled over the Eastern Colonies of Bracadia. The colonies' distinguished Governor, Fitius Angelcry, prided himself as the model modern gentleman. As a revolutionist and industrialist, he drove himself to achieve incredible things. His ambition was for Antigoth to be the paramount centre of excellence for invention and innovation. To that end, he availed the colonial coffers to construct magnificent buildings and enticed the greatest minds and artisans to make Antigoth their place of residence. It was a prosperous time for Arenland and the other nations that comprised the colonies.

The war in the North was a stalemate. It was a relief to Fitius to have the soldiers of the Eastern Colonies returning so that he could forget Mannace and his legacy. It was one less impediment to moving boldly forward into this new Age.

Fitius deemed himself vital, as if the world were watching him, and that his decisions from his seat in Antigoth drove impacts that reached the farthest shores. Naturally, therefore, it was with utmost confidence that he addressed the Colonial Council.

"Leaders, ladies and gentlemen, friends of the Eastern Colonies of Bracadia, welcome to Antigoth. Welcome to the city of wonders."

There was a respectful clapping. Fitius looked back at the many rows of seated officials, meeting their stares with his infectious smile. His presence elevated the room so its inhabitants, like himself, were enthused by the prospect of the day's proceedings. Fitius ignored the frowns from the representatives of Yanth, Viletri, Attica, and Keshik, who he knew would be envious of the city that Antigoth had become.

"We embrace a gilded Age of harmony, modernism, fortune, and culture. We thank the gods for their blessings and the Emperor of Bracadia for his grace."

Though it might be a hard truth for the nations that were once his rivals to acknowledge, the Eastern Colonies took their instructions from Antigoth. As governor, Fitius' power was absolute. The manufactories of Ostoik, the marvels of Antigoth, and the flying fortresses of the God of War earned him that right. None could deny or oppose him, and it was in their best interests that he should lead them.

"I have a design, *The Reimagination*, for the future of the colonies, that today I will share."

Fitius watched the lord mayor of Yanth shift uncomfortably in his seat, but he and the bureaucrats accompanying him said nothing, not even a whisper. Why would they when there was no choice but to listen and follow?

"As I have promised, our invention and industry pave a golden road, a gilded Age. I will strengthen mining and manufacturing, enlarge the guilds and the unions, and expand commerce and markets in foreign lands."

Fitius gifted them a hint of what was to come.

"Twenty-two new colonial mines are planned. I will construct colonial manufactories in Karanthos, Loryan, The Footsteps, and The Ark. Macetown will have the first colonial paper mill. Labourers will come from Bracadia and Charikon. I have commissioned two thousand animated steel workers from Viletri. Twenty class B flying ships are being refitted for merchant and diplomatic duties to stretch our influence and trade far into distant lands. These projects are but a taste of what The Reimagination will deliver."

There was enthusiastic clapping. Fitius soaked it all in, enjoying the moment and excited for the week of intense debate and negotiations ahead.

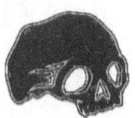

High above Antigoth, Milan's sleek flying ship passed between Arenland's new flying fortresses. The high priestess, Ahmeda, who was amongst Milan's party, marvelled at the two magnificent vessels, likening them to the mighty Harmsway, which was still the most powerful of the steel ships upon the sea. In truth, the fortresses were significantly more menacing, with their steel cannons protruding through portals on their sides, massive artillery visible on the main decks, and bursts of steam that hissed from outlets underneath. Aboard the imposing vessels, sailors and marines were immaculately dressed in their colonial blue uniforms, going about their business with the typical efficiency expected from the Arenlanders.

A military skyship intercepted Milan's craft to check their credentials and dutifully provided an escort.

Milan was late for the council meeting, so instead of docking against one of the many sky towers, he ordered the captain to set the ship down before the grand council chambers and lower the walkway. As the vessel descended, Milan's ship appeared tiny amidst the towering grandeur of the government buildings.

Undeniably, the spectacle was striking evidence of Fitius' investment in magnificent edifices and monuments to showcase the success of the burgeoning capital. All about them, on the streets and in the central square, people celebrated a week of festivities as was the tradition since the council's inauguration at Viletri decades ago.

It would have been proper to enter quietly from a side entrance, but not today. Instead, Milan ordered the main doors to the grand chamber opened, and he marched boldly in, entourage in tow. Fitius was at the podium addressing the council, and the governor at first appeared incensed by the disturbance, but his menacing look quickly turned to one of shock.

A young man amongst Milan's party walked forward. He was tall and handsome, with dark shoulder-length hair held back by a thin golden band. The mysterious gentleman wore a blue coat with golden buttons, white pants, and polished black boots. As he strolled towards the rows of benches and seats that reached back to the top of the hall, all eyes were on him, curious. A wave of whispers, started by those very few who had seen this man, cascaded through the throng. At first, some stood, then the others followed suit when they realised who was in their presence. Soon everybody was standing and leaning for a better view. Finally, the man had the full attention of all present, and he boldly met the stare of the excited crowd.

Fitius, who, like everyone else, was caught in the moment, recovered his wits enough to grab back the initiative.

"The council of the Eastern Colonies welcomes the Emperor of Bracadia. We are blessed and honoured by his presence."

Quickly assessing the others with Milan, Fitius recognised Ahmeda, who once led the priesthood at Ostoik, and several of the merchant guild masters that were regular council attendees. There was also a big belg, blonde-haired and curiously handsome for his race. The odd soldier was dressed finely in the red uniform of the Bracadian military.

"Welcome, Ahmeda, high priestess of war. We are doubly blessed."

There was no protocol for this. Fitius dutifully visited the emperor each year for the past fourteen years, but as far as he was aware, the emperor never travelled from his palace in the Blue Lands. As powerful as Fitius was, he was suddenly at the emperor's mercy. It was the most he could do not to panic or act rashly. Forcing a smile, Fitius anxiously waited for the Bracadian Emperor to reveal his intent.

Already, the emperor was engaging those in the front rows, asking questions and showing interest in the many different races and cultures. As he moved along the benches, tensions amongst the Councillors eased. Then, the ruler of the Madlands, known as The One, drew the emperor's attention with her green-scaled armour and wild red hair. Fitius could not hear their words, but the woman burst out in laughter and slapped her advisors on their backs. At length, the emperor turned, making his way to where Fitius stood.

"I am sorry to take you by surprise, Fitius, but I asked Milan to bring me east so that I could witness first-hand the distance and lands that separate us, and I wanted to experience the things you described in your visits. I can already tell you did not exaggerate, and the Eastern Colonies are more remarkable than I imagined."

"Thank you, Emperor."

The emperor seemed to have forgotten that there were others in the hall. He focused his attention on Fitius, and his voice was gentle and calm so that only Fitius, perhaps Ahmeda and the big belg who followed closely behind could hear.

"It is good that I have come here."

"We are blessed that you visit us, Emperor. I will show you Antigoth. You will be amazed."

"I am not so easily impressed by *things*. People intrigue me. I have said it to you at my palace; an empire is nothing if not its people."

The emperor's expression did not change. But his tone became noticeably more serious.

"Fitius, you have not been fully honest with me about what you do here and what you have achieved in the Eastern Colonies. I will be candid with you so that we do not have any pretence in our conversations to come. I can see that you covet what you have created and the authority you exert. More than a governor in your position should. It concerns me that you place your ambition above the needs of the empire."

Fitius was about to speak, but the emperor continued, cutting him off.

"I see greatness in you, Fitius, not in what you have built, but in you as a man that achieves what he sets out to do. You see beyond the obvious on a grand scale, and your mind will never be satisfied with the ordinary. It is you, Fitius, not the things you have created, that interests me."

The governor could not tell if he was being chastised or commended. The doubt left him without words to respond.

With the ground fertilised, the emperor planted a seed.

"With the learning and industry you have fostered here, what might we achieve on a grand scale across the empire, Fitius, if we plan and work together?"

Confused by events and confronted about his duplicity, Fitius was astute enough to keep his poise in front of the Council. The governor gestured to the emperor by extending an arm to recommend he address the wider audience.

The emperor surprised Fitius by making his way back to the crowd, where he manoeuvred amongst them, acquainting himself and sharing his thoughts or observations.

Meanwhile, Ahmeda moved to stand beside Fitius.

"It is a pleasure to see you again, governor, and good to visit Arenland. The God of War watches you with favour; you honour him with your dedication to the code and military preparations. The flying ships, the two steel monoliths above Antigoth, are impressive."

Not trusting the high priestess, Fitius kept it simple to avoid deeper conversation.

"How long will you be staying in Antigoth?"

"The emperor has been focused on the journey here and has not shared his intent beyond attending the council meeting. It would be best to prepare long-term accommodation."

After a few moments of silence, Ahmeda turned toward Fitius to give a warning and advice. With such an uncompromising tone, it may as well have been an instruction.

"And Fitius, it would be prudent to provide Milan's ship with a class A navigator for the emperor's return journey. He has become more knowledgeable about such things, so it is wise to think and act in the emperor's best interests, don't you think."

Fitius knew that he was indeed on the knife's edge. The emperor would have ascertained that Fitius provided the leader with a second-rate navigator in the knowledge that it prevented him from instantly travelling to the Eastern Colonies. Fourteen years ago, such a strategy seemed the best ploy, but the emperor eventually outsmarted him, and Fitius felt humbled and vulnerable. It was a stark contrast to the exuberance he felt when he awoke that morning.

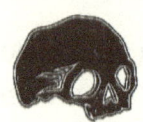

VILETRI

Morgan hovered high above Viletri. Below him, the city was bright and alive, though, in contrast, a wasteland of snow spread out from Viletri's walls and into the distance. Morgan hadn't seen the metropolis since the dwarves afflicted the lands with their blight, and it seemed to him that the city itself remained as bold and spectacular as ever.

Wasting no time, Morgan set down before the entrance to the Institute of Technology. It was the middle of the day, and students were coming and going. Most stopped to stare up as Morgan descended, and once he landed, they flocked to investigate closer.

Before he could engage with his audience, two shadows passed overhead, and when Morgan looked up, it was just in time to watch two other flying men descend to his position. Both forms were metallic like his own, though sleeker and silver in appearance. Morgan huffed, favouring his bulkier shape and black carapace. He laughed out loud at himself for making such a vain comparison. Each new arrival had a distinctive face, which Morgan assumed was the person's appearance before becoming a metal man. One looked familiar.

"Symin, is that you?"

"Yes sir, yes, Mr Cain, yes sir."

"Take me to the Architect Symin, now, please."

"Mr Cain, yes sir, yes Mr Cain."

As Symin escorted Morgan inside the building, a growing multitude of interested students filed in behind, and others

47

in the entry hall stopped their chatter to watch the newcomer. Symin led Morgan past the onlookers, through passages, until they came to a door, which he opened and entered. In the otherwise empty room, the tall, marble avatar of the Architect stood upright and stationary in the centre; his glistening silver mask with its accentuated features was expressionless. When Symin stood silently, waiting, as if this were a frequent ritual, Morgan did the same.

An hour later, six more silver forms entered the room. Morgan recognised two of them from the original SOTA, though he did not know if they still kept that tag for themselves. SOTA was an exciting collection of intellectual misfits, and even *animated* as they were now, the students still possessed that same sharp yet useless appearance. While the Architect remained stationary, one of the familiar students, Arlo, initiated a conversation.

"Welcome back to the institute, Master Cain. The Architect is travelling. It might be days or longer, in present time, that is, before he returns. Please make yourself comfortable."

Morgan snickered. As a man of metal, any position was as comfortable as another. He was fine enough to stand where he was, in front of the Architect's incarnation. Morgan remembered liking the young Arlo, who exhibited good energy and was exceptionally smart.

"When did you become men of metal?"

Arlo pulled his shoulders back and engaged Morgan with a purposeful stare.

"It was our idea; we wanted our devotion to the Architect and science to be heard and seen, as an example of achievement, like you are, Master Cain. We did it before the Muster drew the technomancers north, and Governor Angelcry summoned the magetechs to Antigoth."

Morgan was curious, "You were living men when I left Viletri."

"Sacrifices were necessary. We left our flesh and embraced the immortality of a new form. We are proud to embody what we believe and be a beacon to others seeking knowledge."

Arlo's glass-like eye glinted, reflecting his passion.

"We require the mini-gridstones and magetech for flight, but Symin is Class A, like the navigators. It is a marvel. Show him, Symin."

When all eyes turned on Symin, his metallic form instantly disappeared, as if he had never been in the room. After patiently waiting, when the student did not manifest, Morgan continued his questioning.

"What updates are available, Arlo? I have not upgraded to a new form for fifteen years."

Arlo looked at his comrades, who possessed blank stares. Arlo's response was apologetic.

"We don't do that anymore, sir. After SOTA transitioned, Governor Fitius and the Architect had a difference of opinion, and the Architect no longer collaborates with the guilds. The governor put us under the shadow, but he can't close us down. We are still doing amazing work. I will show you."

Morgan let himself be led away by Arlo, down several passageways and then ascending a steep set of stairs where they came to an internal balcony overlooking a hall. In the room was intricate machinery made of wood and metal. Students were at work, and he watched a group of young men and women making books. They collected pages that they were binding together with leather and glue. At least three other machines appeared to be putting words onto pages. Morgan once owned a book, but it was a rare artefact, and his knowledge of script did not extend far beyond what was on his charts and maps.

As they worked their way further through the Institute, of more interest to Morgan was a complex contraption of metal and glass through which a man could see vast distances. There were many uses for such a device, and Morgan congratulated Arlo and his crew for their ingenuity. However, Arlo could not accept the praise.

"As always, the Architect guides us, Master Cain. There are more than a thousand students that come to these halls. They learn, they create, and they share their expertise. The elbry-tube-glass was the idea of Elace Berry, a very clever woman, good with intricacies. She has several accreditations."

As interesting as the tour was, it was not what Morgan expected. After his last visit to the Institute with Mannace, which was at the peak of collaboration, he was disappointed on his return not to have found grander inventions, and he could not help but contemplate, where had the magic gone?

On exploring Viletri further, Morgan was relieved to see that the great city still had magic at its core; animation, clockwork, steamtech, magetech, enchantments, the green men grown by the Fesadi, and even the civil workforce of the undead. It was a magnificent clash of technologies and cultures, reflective of the diverse population that made the city their home. The liche, Kakos Agamos, still ruled over the city with utmost efficiency, which Morgan observed in the cleanliness of the streets and intricate detailing of the city's homes and businesses. It would be a brave man to place a blemish on the liche lord's coveted metropolis. The thought made Morgan smile.

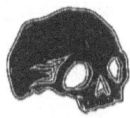

It was during a visit to the garrison commander, Titus Kane, where Morgan learned that Mannace was in the North, leading the defence against the demons. The news spurred Morgan to depart the city, but not before visiting the Oracle's estate to the west. When Morgan landed at the mansion's gates, familiar faces welcomed him. He laughed that they were unsurprised when he appeared; of course, they would know he was coming. A familiar face, but in a different form, approached him.

"Your room awaits, Morgan Cain. It is good to have you returned."

"Syprus, I am glad to see you freed of that terrible mirror. That never sat right with me. You must feel restored."

The Priest, in his statue form, nodded his head. His demeanour seemed heavy, and not because he was made of stone.

"You are a welcome relief here, Morgan, a glimmer of hope. We have commenced this new Age in the darkest of nights, and we must find the path again, Morgan, that leads us into the day. We will only be whole again when embraced by dawn's light."

"Indeed."

In truth, Morgan did not hold to the Light, nor would he want to seek it, but he trusted the magic of this place and the influence of the Oracle. Looking back, he could see that his time here constructing the estate calmed his spirit and shaped his path. It was a time of healing and clarity for him, which he hoped to recapture during this visit.

"I will rest here before travelling north. After that, I will join Mannace in Angorok."

"Indeed."

It was the priest's turn to sound cynical. Mannace hadn't delivered on the Oracle's vision, leaving many with a sense of loss and failure. Morgan could see that Syprus and his companions were humbled. The Fates stripped them of their confidence, and in some ways, it was pleasing to witness their arrogance checked. On the other hand, perhaps they descended too far, wearing depression like a beggar's rags.

"By the balls of Ramthos, Syprus, you easily abandon hope. Do not underestimate Mannace. You're an immortal, have patience; Mannace will prevail."

From the glimmer in some eyes, Morgan could see that these followers of the Oracle wanted to have optimism. Then, all of a sudden, Morgan realised the underlying issue.

"Has the Oracle abandoned you? Are you lost, Syprus?"

The stone man was quick to retort.

"I don't require a lecture from you, Morgan. It was a blow not to raise the Light in the North, to claim the Age as a new dawn for humanity. The Oracle is wounded, as are we all, and it will take time to recover. Many paths, not just the one

Mannace travelled, are lost to us. Morgan, this was no small catastrophe."

"Indeed."

This time Morgan spoke with compassion. He believed Syprus' loyalty to Mannace, even if the priest, in his despair, might think Mannace a relic of the past. So, he would give the stone man some grace to grieve his misfortune.

The emperor's ambassador took residence in a spare room, using the sanctuary to reset his mind and be ready for what lay ahead. On the fourth night at the estate, Morgan had a dream.

REGNORAK

Thag and Athose relaxed atop the wall tower in chairs they were accustomed to spending time in. Giants built the walls of Regnorak to accommodate their kin and men, providing a spectacular view across the ruins of the city behind them and the wrecked farms and orchards extending far outside the walls towards the foothills and mountains. After the razing of Regnorak by the demon hordes, the best and safest accommodation, claimed by the garrison, was within the wall towers themselves. Civilians took up residence amongst the ruins, with livestock and crops crammed into available spaces. Athose watched a group of colossi inside the city demolish and clear new areas for expansion. The colossi were tireless workers, and to Athose, they appeared to enjoy their role here at Regnorak. Initially only taking their commands from Athose, after a decade based at Regnorak, the impressive creatures now accepted instruction from the engineers in charge.

Regnorak was immense, taking three days to journey from its eastern districts to the distant western gates. Refugees from across the North took sanctuary in the city, though the safest parts were in the eastern cordon, nearest to the colossi and wyverns. A port was operating on the northern side of the haven. It would often fill Athose's day to make the journey across town to the harbours and markets, then return laden with fresh food before nightfall.

Athose guessed that hundreds of thousands of men and giants called Regnorak home. There was a sprinkling of other races, like orcs and the mysterious mole men. Regnorak was the only remaining stronghold in Amon

Murn, with little contact with survivors in neighbouring Churlamen and no communication from the devastated Markhon. However, the Mago seemed to have a knack for avoiding the rampaging demons and would sometimes visit. Altair was mostly unscathed in the frozen east, though few braved the journey to or from those distant lands. It was a desperate time, and the importance of the colossi and wyverns in defending Regnorak gave Athose a high standing amongst the Northerners. They considered him one of their captains.

Athose heard that Vestig Gozer and his army had returned to the city. However, seeing the efate and the giant Frain appear at the stairwell entrance was a surprise. Rather than approach Athose and Thag, the leader and his advisor went to the battlements, taking in the expansive view. Eventually, Frain turned, and he spoke to Thag.

"Brother, you were wrong about the South. They want war. They are determined to finish what they started. I worry for the fate of your kin."

Thag shifted uneasily in his seat. He trusted the South to give refuge to the Giants of Rockhome when he was desperate to find a haven for them. In such dreadful circumstances, a sanctuary in a distant land was preferable to facing the armies of the Abyss. He honestly thought that the war between North and South was put aside with demons as a common foe. It was certainly the case here at Regnorak, where Athose and the colossi were of the South, working alongside their Northern allies. Another example of collaboration was the people from the Havens. The tall Haven ships often docked at the harbour, sporting their trademark bright sails and flags. With them, the southern Wain, the first to establish markets and a semblance of trade in the recovering capital, lived and traded alongside the Haven folk. The presence of these people from the South flew in the face of what Frain was saying.

"We are all allies, brother, whether the Southerners want it or not. We fight demons, and we do what is needed to survive."

Frain laughed. It was not a pleasant sound; nothing about Frain had humour.

"Do you not understand men, brother? This Mannace, he has no allegiance or reason. On the contrary, madness and hate fill him. I saw his rage, brother. You cannot trust such a man except to know that he will be relentless in taking what he wants."

Thag shrugged. The news made him downcast.

"I understand nothing. There is little that I see that makes sense."

Frain shook his head at the giant's gloomy disposition. Amon Murn expected its soldiers to be resolute and fearless.

"Leave then. If you don't have the spine to stand tall and take pride in who you are. Sitting on a wall is serving you no purpose, brother. Better to feed the demons than spread your misery amongst those who would rise and defy the damned Hells."

Athose interjected, rising from his seat to stand between the giant champions.

"Yes, it is time to go. Thag and I have business that cannot wait. There is a ..."

Vestig turned, reacting instantly to Athose's declaration, speaking over the elf in his brutal way.

"The colossi and wyverns will stay. They are vital to the defence."

Athose spoke on instinct, a feeling in his gut that urged him to travel. He possessed no real plan, but what Vestig said was true; taking the colossi out of Regnorak would be dangerous for them and disastrous for the city. Moreover, the population would blame him for their downfall.

"It is a venture Thag and I must do alone. We will take a priest but leave the colossi. I cannot speak for the wyverns, as they do what they will."

Vestig nodded and turned back to stare out across the land. He put his hands on the crenelations and lifted himself to lean out to better survey the walls. The massive defence, reaching far down to the earth, and stretching east and west into the distance, nourished his pride, inspiring and reassuring Vestig that Amon Murn would stand firm and be powerful again. He would rebuild the nation as he wanted it, and like Mannace, who in a way was inspiring too, Vestig would shape this new Age to his vision.

Frain took a seat, then leaning forward, he drew his sword from its sheath and grabbed a whetstone from his belt. He spat on the stone to wet it and stroked the blade. He enjoyed the sharpness of the weapon. Caressing the razor edge helped him recall his favourite kills and lose himself in the memories. The others about him were silent too, all occupied with their thoughts.

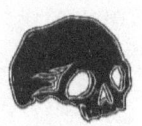

Athose led the way, scouting ahead of the group to spot potential danger, yet not so far that he would be isolated if discovered by demons. His lithe form stayed low to the ground as he kept to cover, moving in the terrain's shadow. Facial features that became more pointed with age gave Athose a distinctive angular appearance. His piercing eyes were so dark that their colour was sometimes indistinguishable, taking on bold hues in the light that shifted with his environment. The young elf carried his bow across his left shoulder, with two quivers of arrows over his right. His meagre possessions were in pouches at his belt.

With him was the dour Remman, Karack, who bore the tragic honour of being the last of his warrior kin. He was tall and robust, with a square face and dark, curly beard to match his short braids. Karack walked with a sword in hand and a heavy round shield on his arm. He and Thag were close, preferring the giant's company over Athose, who often annoyed the Remman with his juvenile or reckless behaviour.

Although young, Seb was a veteran of the Eternal Priesthood. He walked behind Karack with his head down and his hands in his robe pockets. He and Athose struck a friendship in Regnorak and often teamed up in various games against other city men. Like Athose, Seb was handsome, with a fit physique. He enjoyed the attention of young women, and the two often played and partied hard.

Thag walked to the rear of the small band. He wore fur over his leather armour to protect him from cold nights, but he sweated now under the morning sun. It was a significant risk to have the giant amongst the party, who stood out as they moved through the wilderness, but if they were to get into a fight, Thag would be a great asset. The giant kept a watchful vigil. As he looked up, he could see the specs of two wyverns that followed Athose.

Back at Regnorak, the wyverns kept to themselves, maintaining their private community amongst the ruins. Vestig ensured they ate well in return for their protection. Athose though, commanded their loyalty, and like the colossi, the creatures rallied to him, sharing an inexplicable bond that even Athose could not explain. The two circling above decided to join the travellers, only ever seen at a distance.

The group headed for Angorok, where it seemed likely they would split up. Athose had it in his mind to find his siblings, Vilera and Roanna. The others were unclear of purpose, though each preferred danger and adventure over another long year trapped in Regnorak.

They travelled a similar path to Vestig and his army through the Markhon, hoping the way was clear. However, it was not long before Seb sensed demons nearby, in large numbers. Twice Seb used priestly controls to order small packs of slithering demons to pass by them. Once a more significant swarm of flyers came close, but the wyverns dived low to scatter and divert them away. Not wanting to risk a more considerable encounter, where they might be overwhelmed, Athose hurried the group swiftly south. It took them towards the forests of the Mago, which Athose was interested in visiting. Thag and Karack did not share his enthusiasm.

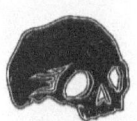

As they approached the Mago forests, the land was even more desolate than the devastated territories they'd already passed. Everything living, even the sparse grasslands and trees, was stripped bare. Bones of anything dead were scattered, and often rocks lay overturned.

There was a buzz in the air, inescapable and pervading every hollow. As the party drew closer to the Mago's forest, the sound became shriller, as if a warning to keep a distance. Athose signalled for the others to stay well back, where the shape of the land hid them, while he scouted carefully forward. Closer to the Mago's home, the green of the forest seemed alive, and inquisitively closer still, it became apparent that the trees were empty branches. What Athose had thought to be foliage was a great swarm of giant green insects, clinging to boughs and leaping rapidly between them. It was a living mass, frightening and unpredictable, and Athose did not dare draw closer. Above one part of the forest, a cloud of orange rose then descended: more insects. Was this the Mago's defence against the demons, a great swarm to fight a swarm? He had no way to know how they might react to seeing him, giving Athose no choice but to withdraw and for his party to depart. Avoiding the Mago required passing through The Gap, into Turbul and on to Islan. The Gap and Turbul were renowned as demon-infested, and nobody with good sense dared travel there.

PART TWO:

Age of Empire

THE EMPEROR'S APPRENTICE

The emperor liked Fitius since first meeting him in the Blue Land. The man was intelligent, infectious, ambitious, and thirsted for knowledge. The learning and understanding he already possessed, Fitius used in clever and insightful ways. Importantly, Fitius was born mortal but gifted with longevity. Only time would tell if he might indeed live forever. The emperor understood from speaking with Fitius that a demon's touch had blessed him and sustained him across worlds. It was a fascinating story and spoke much to Fitius' driven character.

"Your Reimagination is commendable, Fitius. It is a better strategy than the consolidation of the imperial colonies that I instigated. The Reimagination is astute, and it leverages the best you have. It delivers an achievable ground plan. I am very impressed."

Fitius appeared pleased with the praise. The emperor was genuinely optimistic.

"We can add to it, starting with manufactories in Vencia, Apello, Dreban, Antium, Ugol, Romas, Takini. Your steam and clockwork will spark innovation across all Bracadia. And your college for the arts, we must have one just like it in the Blue Lands."

The emperor made notes as he leafed through Fitius' documents. Then, after a time, he paused.

"I would like to see examples of magetech. You mention magetech here, but you don't give it the same consideration as other disciplines. You have dispersed valuable resources rather than encouraged them into a union or guild. Why is that Fitius?"

Fitius did not know how much the emperor discussed the topic of magetech with Milan, but it seemed to the governor that the emperor knew more than he was letting on. Fitius decided to be blatantly honest.

"Magic is lazy, emperor, and magetech is a product of that idleness."

Addressing the pitfalls of magic was a speech he was used to giving.

"We must invest our time and efforts into proper invention, through disciplines such as steam-tech, clockwork, metallurgy. Magic is not reliable, nor is it consistent. We must make real things for the physical world, things that we can control and are dependable. Magic is of an Age past, whereas our investment in technology and industry will spur us forward."

The emperor nodded to Fitius, though the leader's eyes seemed undecided. Then, with a slow, thoughtful movement, the emperor put down the documents he was holding and started a new conversation.

"Fitius, you will need to better understand the capitals and cities throughout Bracadia and the other colonies when you lead this revolution. It will be a grander scale than you can conceive. Grander, I believe, than anything anybody is used to."

The colonial governor wanted to cringe, and it took all his effort to remain straight-faced.

"Emperor, I can serve you best if I continue my work here. The more we innovate, and the more Antigoth is a centre for modernism, the more we will have to share with Bracadia. Perhaps Milan, who knows the empire well, is better suited to the task you require?"

"No, Fitius," the emperor was unusually terse. "You are the man I will have at my side."

The emperor could see that Fitius was struggling for words. The man seemed dispossessed as if the world were being taken away from him.

"Fitius, Antigoth is a pearl upon your palm. The Eastern Colonies, with all their nations put together, are a fist-full of precious gems. So, you already have great wealth and power in your grasp, and you can be proud of what you have accomplished."

The emperor held Fitius' gaze.

"Today, Fitius, I am offering you a much vaster treasure that would fill this room with precious jewels and the rooms beyond. I am offering you the world, Fitius. My consolidation of the empire was always a prelude to expansion. Think much bigger, not as governor, but as the controller of infinite resources. Fitius, together we will colonise and conquer all lands, and your modernism, industry, and idealistic vision will lead us into that future."

Fitius barely noticed that Ahmeda joined them. Instead, he was glued to the emperor's speech.

"I am not taking anything away from you, Fitius. Indeed, I am giving you everything. Everything, Fitius."

The emperor took Ahmeda's hand and held it gently as he smiled at the priestess. She returned the gesture, though her look possessed none of the same warmth. She seemed displeased. The emperor took a moment to turn back to his governor.

"Fitius, that is enough for today. Tomorrow there will be no more reluctance from you, and I expect my controller to focus on what we do next. Please leave us now."

In Ostoik, the emperor walked through the grand hall of the temple of war with Ahmeda. Their footsteps echoed in the eerie emptiness. Behind them, Claudius, the emperor's bodyguard, kept a respectful distance and constant vigil. As was his habit, the handsome belg held a hand on the pommel of his sheathed sword. Also tucked into his belt was a broad-barrelled pistol, with two larger versions of the weapon strapped to his back so he could access them quickly if needed. Yet, as capable as Claudius appeared, it seemed a meagre escort for a man of the emperor's importance.

At length, an acolyte came out of an adjoining chamber and approached them. Not recognising who they were, the young man made the mistake of looking down his nose at the commander of his order and the empire's leader. He barely mumbled three words before a hand gesture from Ahmeda, with the power of the War God behind it, tipped the man on his arse. Another flick and he tumbled across the floor, making enough racket that a priest and more acolytes came running.

The war priest, a swarthy man who Ahmeda recognised as Rugar, called the acolytes to order. When he saw it was Ahmeda, he immediately bowed to acknowledge her elevated status.

"High Priestess, your return is a great blessing."

Ahmeda, who recalled no fondness for Rugar, was incensed that the temple was a derelict shadow compared to when she had left it. Her tone was accusing.

"Where are the others, Rugar? Why is the War God not present here? What idleness has befallen this holiest of places?"

The war priest's sudden temper darkened his visage and words.

"We serve in the North. And we serve the new armada in the skies. The War God joins the fight against the demons in the Veldaan, in Angorok. We have not been idle, priestess."

Rugar puffed out his chest. Gone was the initial reverence he showed the high priestess, replaced with hostility, sufficient that Claudius put his free hand around the grip of his pistol.

"Are you so surprised to find the Temple empty, Ahmeda, when you led the war priests west, emptying the coffers to fund your ambition!"

"Then why are you here, Rugar?"

"I have spent time in the North, and I have done well by my God, Priestess. I am in Ostoik to recruit and ready new acolytes. In the Veldaan, they will be bloodied, and their training completed with a hammer in hand. Such is the way in a time of war."

Ahmeda seemed not to breathe as she reached into Rugar's soul to know his true intent. But, if she revealed any deception, she did not share it. Instead, she changed her line of questioning.

"Do the soldiers of the Eastern Colonies follow the code of war? Do they acknowledge the God of War and the emperor over all others?"

Rugar snorted, his nostrils flaring.

"Those that fight in the North are bound to the code. They know the War God, for they have witnessed his fury. The war and the War God are real. In the North, the armies follow Mannace. The emperor might as well be a myth."

"What do you mean?"

"How can you be in Arenland and not know? It is the news on all lips, that Mannace declared himself independent. He has named his nation Angorok."

Rugar snorted again. He looked down his nose at the visitors.

"War, in all its bloody glory, and the War God, are in Angorok. This pretty temple in Ostoik is just a building, surrounded by other worthless constructions, in a city neglected of faith. It means nothing."

Ahmeda leaned toward the Priest and spoke more slowly, caustically.

"Tell me, do the soldiers of the colonies follow the code, yes or no, Rugar."

"Ask them yourself."

The high priestess' eyes narrowed, and Rugar could hear the War God's presence return to the temple hall, the clash of battle from the alcoves, and dead eyes staring up from the glassy marble floor. The war priest, although riled, respected Ahmeda's powers enough to back down.

"Yes, they honour the code. But can you trust a soldier trained in a time of peace who has never faced death nor claimed a soul? The Eastern Colonies grow fat while there is fighting and famine and terror in the North. Bah, peace is a curse; it makes men useless."

When Ahmeda continued to stare, Rugar shrugged. Relaxing her stance, the high priestess stepped back to stand next to the others.

"Rugar, this is the Emperor of Bracadia."

The war priest's eyes went wide, and he could immediately see the truth. His arrogance evaporated, and he bowed low.

"Darkness pervades us. Glory to the God of War. Glory to the emperor. How may I serve?"

THE EMPEROR'S NEW ARMADA

There was no doubt that Fitius commissioned the most potent military force in the empire, and the emperor wasted no time taking command of the airborne armada. He immediately retrieved Admiral Jeylan Staronis from Bracadia and appointed the senior officer in charge of the flying fleet. As his first action, Staronis gathered the ship captains aboard one of the flying fortresses, addressing them.

"Stand up straight. As a professional soldier, pride in oneself is essential to commanding pride in others."

His order targeted one of the younger officers, who appeared relaxed, with one palm in his trouser pocket. The man straightened and clasped his hands rightfully behind his back. Some of the more experienced captains appreciated their new admiral's perspective, as shown by their broad smiles. As a rule, the Arenlanders who comprised most of the captains and crews, were orderly and immaculate in their appearance.

"Prepare your ships. Tomorrow, I will see them arrayed, and we will run through basic manoeuvres. Do you have a book of your tactics or a tactician?"

The captains stood silently until an older gentleman, anticipating the Admiral's line of questioning, offered his comment.

"Captain Rieck at your service, sir. No, sir, we do not have a tactician. About half of the captains here have returned from fighting in the north. For the most part, First General Mannace trusted the captains to execute his orders, but with the freedom to determine the how of it. He expected his leaders to show initiative and quickly adapt to any situation. In the North, our missions were mostly logistics, rescues, and diversions. Because of the risks of being overwhelmed, we only fought when there was no alternative."

The gentleman paused to check that the Admiral was interested. When Staronis gave him a nod, he continued.

"The other ships and crews are more recently deployed in Arenland, sir, and many have not seen action. Duties include patrols, transportation, and aiding with construction. At no time, sir, have the peacetime captains undertaken drills. Like in the north, they operate well independently, and all are competent with the subtleties of flight and manoeuvres. The capability of the Navigator often determines what tactics are possible."

When the officer finished, the admiral continued his questioning.

"Tell me about the Navigators?"

After no other officer volunteered, Captain Rieck answered the admiral's question.

"Each ship is dependent on a navigator for travel. The navigators manipulate a navigation stone aboard the vessel, enabling movement. Class A navigators are rare and can travel vast distances instantaneously, anywhere they have in memory. Class A and B navigators can move a ship; the speed and smoothness of travel are dependent on their ability. Class C navigators can move the ship, but in a limited capacity, typically in the direction and speed of a normal sailing vessel – they are limited to what their mind conceives as *real*. Sometimes, with experience, they can progress to Class B."

The captain paused again to ensure the admiral was interested, rewarded with another nod of approval.

"The fleet is limited by the number of navigators we can find and train. It is a rare mind, often a fragile mind, that can engage the stone and move the ship in space-time. The navigators are a special breed, sir, and a captain must have an intimate relationship with them – the vessel and crew depend wholly on their skill to move and survive. The mole men's conditioning can assist where behaviour is a problem, but First General Mannace preferred men to be of their proper wits. Can I arrange a tour of a craft for you, admiral, sir?

The admiral was quick to respond, seeming to be someone who confidently knew his mind.

"Yes, Captain Rieck. Over the next week, I will inspect every ship. Prepare my cabin aboard this fortress."

The admiral paused to ensure he had everyone's full attention and then raised his voice to be certain of being heard.

"This is a war-time armada, and you are immediately relieved of civil duties. Your deployment might be anywhere in Bracadia and on many frontiers. The empire rules the waves, and we will own the sky too. I have orders to expand the empire, and in addition to this fleet, we can enlist any resources we require, military or otherwise. These are momentous times, gentlemen, and there will be *no* tolerance of ill-discipline, idleness, or incompetence."

Admiral Staronis was glaring at the officer he reprimanded earlier to put the fear of the Hells into him.

"I expect perfection from my captains, and you must expect the same of your crews. So, prepare for the inspections, knowing I will hold you directly accountable for what I see. Perfection, gentlemen, forget that at your peril."

There was a look of nervousness and dread amongst some of the crowd. Staronis turned to his new Second.

"Dismiss the captains, Mr Rieck. Bring me a roster for inspections and make a time tomorrow for manoeuvres. I will meet the first crew within the hour. Make it so!"

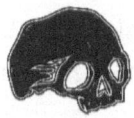

The admiral's flying fortress hovered near an abandoned citadel. The multi-tiered fort was a ruin in parts, and while squatters recently inhabited a section of it, it was vacant now and awaiting its doomed fate.

As Admiral Staronis watched from the deck, Captain Rieck pointed toward the sun so that with a hand shielding his eyes, the admiral could see black dots appearing and growing larger. Unpredictably, other flying ships appeared behind the citadel and immediately unleashed their broadsides into the abandoned defences. Four more salvos were rapidly delivered, crumbling once-proud structures, and leaving the scene strewn with rubble. Then, as quickly as they had appeared, the ships vanished.

The bombardment was a distraction, while the first vessels descending from the cover of sunlight positioned themselves above the fortress, angled so that their broadsides exploded against the citadel keep and inner buildings. Dust billowed from the devastation. The ships leaned the other way and a second volley added to the mayhem.

More craft passed by the main wall, blasting gashes into the primary defence, and sending stonework flying. These ships formed a chain, wheeling back from left to right to pass again so that there was a relentless and devastating barrage. Soon areas of the wall were collapsing, and the dreadful firepower added to the chaos already consuming the inner fort.

With the main wall defeated, the ships assaulting the outer defence withdrew towards the sun while the ships hovering above the fortress dived low into the dust amongst the broken buildings. A sharp hiss, heard as far as the admiral's vessel, accompanied a cloud of steam that erupted from the flying squad, enveloping the fortress, and spilling out over its ruined walls. Then, as the last airborne craft joined their retreating comrades, only the second flying fortress remained, hovering well back from the ruin. With great accuracy from the vessel's artillery, shots from an impossible distance hit and exploded around the area that was once the keep. Finally, the devastating performance was concluded with a single salvo from a great mortar at the rear of the admiral's ship. Landing behind the keep, perhaps not as accurately as intended, the massive shell exploded, throwing debris far into the air, and leaving a smouldering crater far more prominent than the admiral would have deemed possible.

The admiral could not conceal his delight, and he clapped appreciatively, nodding to those officers around him to congratulate them on the show of firepower. The manoeuvre was a great start. It showed Staronis that these captains of the Eastern Colonies knew their business, giving him a new respect for their prowess, and it exhibited the incredible capabilities of the navigators. His mind was abuzz with ideas and strategies.

After a final glance at the broken citadel, Staronis gave a last clap and ordered the captain to take them back to Antigoth. He was genuinely excited to share his observations and burgeoning ideas with the emperor. The thrill of watching the demonstration and knowing that these flying ships were his to command surpassed anything he experienced during his celebrated career on the sea.

THE EMPEROR'S INNER CIRCLE

When they first met, the emperor purposefully wooed Ahmeda for her Doctrine of War, in addition to her unparalleled beauty. He chose Milan for his commerce, Jeylan Staronis to command the fleets, and Fitius Angelcry for his industry. They were his inner circle, people he could work with who were ambitious and relentless in pursuing excellence in their fields. Morgan Cain was another - his ambassador. There was one more that he would have, one that would put the lion amongst the hounds.

With that in mind, the emperor arrived at Angorok aboard Milan's sleek craft. The new Navigator, Keppil, assigned to Milan's vessel, had travelled here before, so he could move them instantly to the remembered location. Again, the manoeuvre came with risk, with potential disaster if something else unexpectedly occupied that space, but catastrophe did not eventuate this time.

From a high vantage, the emperor could see that Angorok, set against the hills and backed by a deep ravine, was designed as a fortress with a citadel at its upper reach and a series of concentric walls protecting a great sprawl of residences and businesses. A solid military presence guarded the defences and moved about the streets. On closer inspection, some city areas seemed abandoned, though the emperor's assessment was abruptly cut short as the ship angled into a quick descent. At first, the emperor did not understand the sense of such urgent movement, but then a swarm of dark shapes appeared from above, matching the skyship's speed. The bat-winged monsters were screeching, a harsh, high-pitched noise that stabbed through flesh at the soul. Some of the creatures were close enough that the emperor could make out their night-black skin and elongated faces with jaws full of sharp fangs. They possessed legs and arms to balance themselves as they dived. It surprised the leader, seeing demons for the first time, that they had cocks and cunts too. The creatures were gone as suddenly as they appeared, angling away and then climbing into the skies. Protected by the city's enchantments, Keppil kept the ship low as he piloted his way to a nearby airbase

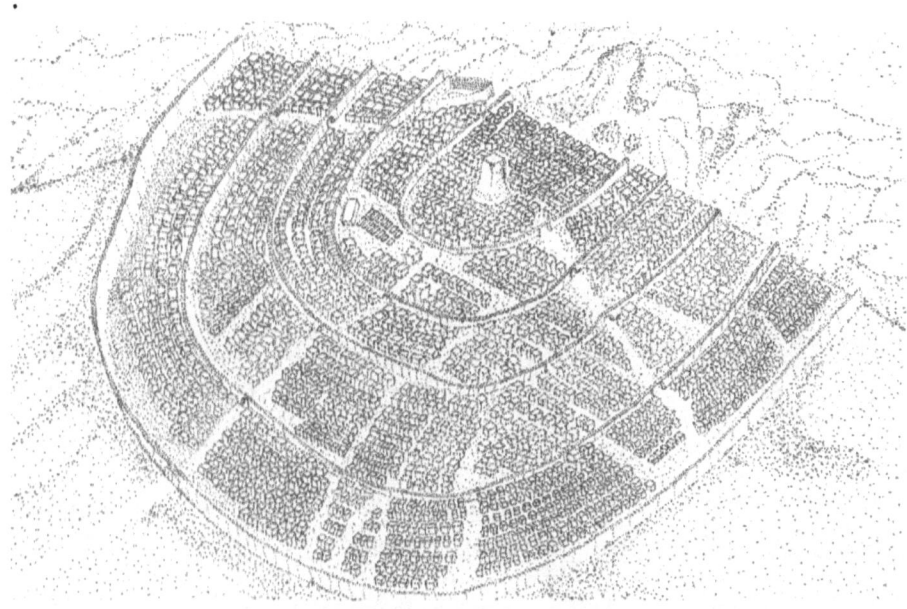

Soon after landing in a broad enclosure amongst other docked ships, a garrison troop arrived to inspect them. In addition to the regular halberdiers, some of the soldiers appeared carved from stone, and there was a tall clockwork man to their rear, pointing his ballistae skyward as he scanned for an aerial attack. When the emperor looked about, he was surprised by the various races and troops. The citizens and soldiers seemed relaxed but alert enough to jump to action at short notice.

Ahmeda and Milan knew the commander, who welcomed them to the city and quickly organised passage to the citadel. It wasn't long before the visitors were waiting in the war room, central to the citadel, where Elderlin the Librarian came to welcome them. Elderlin invited the guests to relax on the comfortable lounge chairs while he sent one of his apprentices for refreshments. Another apprentice set fires to heat the room, a feat accomplished with minor evocations. Soon they were all comfortable and warm, with drinks in hand.

Elderlin seated himself between Milan and the emperor, but his eyes were on Ahmeda, who relaxed opposite him.

"High Priestess, when you were here last, we were foes. You were at the forefront of the battle, and this city fell the next day. Many years later, the Asari, which I am a part, joined with the Alliance of the South. Dekon Ruel took your mantle when you departed, and he commands the Muster and the Priesthood of War."

Ahmeda had questions about Dekon Ruel but thought it best to introduce her companions first.

"Elderlin, this is Milan, who was also at the Siege of Angorok."

The priestess waited while the two men, remaining seated, gave each other a short bow.

"This is the Emperor of Bracadia."

Elderlin expressed a sudden look of panic, likely for being caught ill-prepared, but he recovered quickly, standing, and bowing deeply. He would never have been so bold as to seat himself next to a man of such magnitude. The situation seemed bizarre to him and almost unbelievable. Elderlin's gut, which always guided him, knew what Ahmeda said was the truth.

"Emperor, welcome to Angorok. I have sent word to the marshall that he has guests. I am sure he will be here soon."

Elderlin moved awkwardly to the side and spoke quietly to an apprentice who hurried from the hall. It was enough time for the emperor to rise from his seat and move to the table that dominated the centre of the room. A map carved into the tabletop had models placed upon it that represented locations and armies. Around the table were idle pieces, and shelves beneath held many more figurines. Elderlin came alongside the emperor at a respectful distance.

"There have been times, emperor, when the war room was full of clerks and generals, strategizing and issuing orders. Even today, a clerk will come to adjust the pieces when one of the captains or a scout returns with an update. Of course, scouting has become harder since the elves closed the Ways. Nevertheless, the marshall still spends time here most nights. It is where he does his thinking."

The emperor was an attentive listener.

"Thank you, Elderlin. Who are the Asari?"

"We are an order of wizards. We came together under the leadership of Tyriah, who commanded the Veldaan, and now we serve the Muster here at Angorok."

"What are the Ways, Elderlin?"

"They are portals between places, travelled by the elves and the spiders. However, since the Spider Mother declared war on the elves, the elves closed access to the Ways, and they are in hiding."

"Elderlin, who is the Spider Mother?"

Elderlin's response was interrupted by a noise at the door as two war priests bustled into the room, quickly followed by Dekon Ruel. Dekon instantly recognised Ahmeda and his brow deepened as he glared at her. The troubled high priest stomped across the room with resolve and purpose.

"Why are you here, Ahmeda? I am high priest, I speak for the God of War, I am the leader at Angorok."

Ahmeda rose from her seat, seeming small compared to the powerfully built elf confronting her, but she held a presence of authority that made Milan step behind his chair to shield himself if she might unleash. Dekon, though, was enraged, and he stepped closer.

"Dekon, don't make me show you who the War God favours."

"You left, Ahmeda. Why have you returned?"

"Because I crafted you, Dekon, I lifted you and showed you. I gave you authority, and I can take it back. You are what I made you, Dekon. You live by my grace. Remember that. Do you see it, Dekon? Do you see *me*?"

Others in the room were confused. To Dekon, however, Ahmeda's statements hit him like punches, and he reeled backwards. He seemed winded and speechless. Ahmeda, by comparison, was dominant, as if she held not just Dekon but all of them in her palm and might close her fist mercilessly. About the room, the fires flared, and cries of the dead swirled about in the dark corners.

The emperor passed between the two elves. In the flaring light, he saw something that interested him. A man was asleep on a chair in a side alcove. When the emperor bent over the man, it was as he expected, to see wax in his ears. It made the emperor smile. Upon returning to the war room, all eyes were upon him.

"Leave us now."

It was clear that he addressed everybody, and although not all present were his to command, they did as they were told.

When Mannace awoke in the dimly lit chamber, he was startled to see a man in the chair next to him. After a few moments to let his vision adjust, he took the wax from his ears and stretched while remaining seated. Mannace met many people under many circumstances and was observant enough to know that this was not all it seemed.

"Are you from the Aghan?"

"No, why do you ask?"

"I once met a man from there with a similar look."

"How similar?"

"Similar face, young and old at the same time. Your eyes were like the man's, as if you couldn't help but stare at them. And he was similar in his posture, confident."

"Did this man have a name?"

"No. The man was arrogant and dismissive. He had no time for others."

"I might know him. Can you take me there?"

"Where?"

"The Aghan?"

"Maybe. I will consider it."

Mannace was interested. The Aghan was a mystery that haunted him, and he hated not knowing what the region's sealed borders contained. This man who watched him sleeping was noteworthy, though he had no idea who he might be or his agenda.

"Did you have a look at the table?"

"Yes."

"What did you see?"

Now the emperor was intrigued. The question seemed like a challenge, a test.

"I see nothing."

Mannace looked disappointed. The emperor, though, was not finished.

"Nothing is happening. Not just on your table, but here in your war room. There is a war, but it is not what it seems."

"What do you mean?"

"I have been told that a mad king opened a portal to the Hells in Amon Murn and that demons constantly spew forth from it. My advisors tell me there are rampaging demon armies led by great monsters. Hell-spawn infests all the territories of the North, destroying everything. I have also been informed by more than one advisor that you, and your followers here in Angorok, will be overwhelmed and obliterated."

Mannace did not need to hear the obvious. However, the emperor surprised him.

"Where have the armies of Hell gone?"

"What do you mean?"

"They are not here besieging the gates of Angorok. They are not on your war table, at least not in the multitudes I expected. So where are they?"

"The North is vast, and the armies run amok. Tracking of all forces is not possible."

"I don't think so."

Mannace got up and strode to the map table. The emperor followed behind. After a while of staring at the models, the emperor asked.

"Have you any inkling where they have gone?"

Mannace was hesitant because he did not want to believe it, but he did have a thought.

"When the demons first appeared, their armies rampaged in all directions, but there was a number that headed directly for the Rift. They disappeared."

"This Rift is where they are then. Are more still travelling there?"

Mannace examined his map, and for his visitor's benefit, he used a long stick to draw a path from the portal in Amon Murn, through the lands of the North to the Rift. From what Mannace knew of the demon's strong points and movements over the last decade, it was indeed possible that monsters were still moving along that path. It was frustrating not to have reached that conclusion himself.

Perhaps this visitor knew more than he was sharing. Mannace's suspicion prompted him to explore further.

"So why do they move to the Rift?"

"Who lives here?"

The emperor was pointing to the vast expanse on the southern side of the Rift controlled by the dwarves. It was a surprise to Mannace that his guest did not know.

"The true dwarves. They are an enemy; we have no contact with them."

"What do the true dwarves have that the demons want?"

At first, it appeared a ludicrous question. The concept that the demons were more than a scourge bent on destroying and eating everything in their path challenged what Mannace understood. But then the small pieces of information he remembered suddenly came together, making him feel like a fool for not already knowing.

"The Core, they seek the Core."

"Why?"

"I don't know. The Core is a secret of the dwarves, shared once in confidence but not fully explained. It is a source of tremendous energy."

"Interesting. I think it is important to know the why."

Mannace was not used to being coached, and it suddenly irritated him. Was this man just another bloody mystery?

"Who the fuck are you?"

"I am the Emperor of Bracadia."

Mannace laughed. He did not doubt the truth of it, and it seemed ironic that after so many years of service to an emperor he had never seen, he was finally meeting him after denouncing the empire and claiming Angorok as his own.

"And why are you here, Emperor, at this time, alone?"

"I came with others, Ahmeda and Milan."

That immediately raised Mannace's spirits. He had not seen Milan for a long time and missed his friend. The emperor continued.

"Before we talk about why I am here, take me to the Aghan."

Mannace could tell by the emperor's serious look and insistence that it was important to him. The marshall was intrigued enough to agree despite the dangers.

"We will go in the light. I know a navigator that has travelled there."

A CONUNDRUM

Mannace stood next to the emperor. About them, rangers and musketmen scanned the countryside and horizon, ready to react to any sign of trouble. Two flying ships hovered close to the ground, their boarding platforms resting on the earth, prepared for rapid extraction.

Mounds of dead demons confronted the party. Ghastly piles marked the entire Aghan border, where the magic barrier surrounding the mystical territory claimed hundreds of thousands of their kin. Nothing living could pass the wardings and survive. When Mannace last travelled here, he tried to coax one of the mighty colossi to cross the enchantment, but the creature refused. However, the ordeal drew the attention of the Aghan's ancient and powerful resident, a man, young in appearance, who criticised and cursed him. At the time, it seemed to Mannace that the man possessed magic far beyond the sorcery of any other. Upon returning here, Mannace was increasingly confident of the similarity in appearance of the man and the emperor.

They waited to see if the man would reappear.

Though he warned the emperor of the warding, the leader seemed unafraid to walk up to the invisible barrier, assessing the carnage. The demon corpses were rotting, some partly eaten. Amongst them were creatures that once walked, others that slithered, some with wings, often mannish, but sometimes shapes that made no sense. They were black as the night and armed with spines, claws, and fangs.

There was a gap, free of demon bodies, where an ancient stone was embedded firmly into the earth. It had runes inscribed on its smooth surface and white rocks scattered in the grass around it. Without hesitation, the emperor stepped across the rune-stone and moved onto the grassland beyond. Two musketeers hurried to follow, but Mannace wisely urged them back. The emperor stooped to retrieve a loose white rock from the grass, before turning to Mannace to give a small wave. As he walked further away, his form faded until he completely disappeared.

"What are we meant to do now? We can't stay here."

It was one of Mannace's bodyguards, Jayne Azaryn, that spoke. He voiced what others were thinking; this was no place to be waiting for the emperor's return, and all were wary that the infested land would be crawling with Hell-spawn when evening approached. The dark elf looked to Mannace for direction.

Mannace was no longer as concerned with rank or protocol. It was more important to him that the troops remaining in Angorok did so of choice. They opted to reside in the city even though life was hard and dangerous. They revered Mannace, and he recognised that fact in how he treated them. Vestig's, and now the emperor's appearance at Angorok, was stirring something within Mannace; a realisation that he was broken and needed to remake himself to lead his followers into a better future. That would start today.

"Back to Angorok. We are not needed here."

Elderlin's apprentices ran the message service. They transferred and received written notes from Mannace's allies using magic boxes. Placing a notice in the box and closing the lid did the trick. When a letter appeared in the box, the contraption took on a dull glow. Mannace sent messages to the true dwarves for many years, but they seemed to ignore the correspondence, so he gave up. Today, Elderlin recovered the dwarves' box from storage. It glowed, and inside was a note scribed in the common language that he took to Mannace.

WE MUST STOP THE DEMONS. THE SITUATION IS DIRE.

Mannace recognised Logthar's scribble. But unfortunately, the box was in storage for more than eight years, and there was no way to tell when Logthar scribed the note or whether he wrote it of his own volition or under instruction.

"Send a reply. Say that we know the demons seek the Core. Ask for more information. Elderlin, add my seal."

The next day a new message arrived.

MANNACE I THOUGHT YOU WERE DEAD AND THE NORTH OVERRUN. THE DEMONS WILL SOON OVERCOME THE FINAL BASTIONS. IT WILL BE THE END FOR US ALL. I CAN'T SAY MORE, MANNACE. IT IS FORBIDDEN.

Mannace was relieved to have renewed communications with Logthar, though annoyed by the dwarves and their secrets. It seemed likely that Logthar, in desperation, sent the messages without the knowledge of his superiors. It created another impossible bloody predicament, where the problems of others became his to resolve.

"Elderlin, this will be a long night. Bring the box and parchment and join me in the war room."

The Muster were veterans of war. Like the soldiers in Angorok, this gathering of casters and clergy was casual in appearance but well-versed and professional in their purpose. They were an elite group. Most stayed in the North when the Southern armies departed Angorok, some because they promised allegiance to Mannace, most because they enjoyed how the Muster operated. When the Muster tackled an idea, conundrum, or problem, they would put their collective minds together, and solutions were quickly forthcoming. It was an alliance formed from desperation in a time of war and evolved to be a potent collaboration with the potential to be even more.

The Muster was vital to the defence of Angorok and the survival of civilians scattered about the lands, who they helped to hide and feed. Today, Dekon Ruel summoned them to their Muster Hall, warning that this would be their most formidable challenge yet. The urgent summons brought even the most reclusive members out of the shadows, so the hall was packed.

Dekon stood tall on the speaker's platform. He was adorned in his ceremonial armour, black like his skin and moulded to his muscular frame. His hair was oiled and tied, intertwined with demon bones as it cascaded down his back. The hairstyle was a custom amongst the War God's followers.

"The War God blesses this assembly."

As Dekon raised his arms, the War God's presence filled the room, and everybody drew energy and vitality from it. In places where the shadows grew and expanded, it seemed as if spectral soldiers stood amongst those gathered, staring up at Dekon but fading with the returning light.

Ahmeda moved through the crowd during the dedication and stepped up to the speaker's platform to stand beside Dekon. Her robe was of rare silk that shifted between deep purple and black as she glided. A spectacular diamond, carved to the shape of a hammer and hanging boldly between her ample breasts, amplified and reflected the room's light. Its radiance dazzled those close to the podium, and distracted Dekon, who turned to face the priestess. She glared at him, and the black of her silk robe issued forth a shadow, a living, writhing thing that cloaked Ahmeda and glared at Dekon menacingly with its thousand eyes. Then, with all attention focused on the high priestess, the hall darkened and became chill. Even the ceiling shadows gathered so that when the Muster looked up, it was into the night, with the War God himself, invisible yet tangible, black against black, looking down upon the crowd. The distant sounds of battle drew closer as the tension between the two dark elves increased.

By instinct, Dekon reached over his shoulder for his hammer, which was not there. The Muster was not a place for weapons, and this was not a fair contest. Had this been an arena or on the field of battle, Dekon's confidence would be justified. But here, without a weapon, or his god armour, Ahmeda could easily overpower him with her divine artifice. Dekon, with fists clenched and gritted teeth, backed down the steps, surrendering the room. Ahmeda relaxed her spell so that the shadow withdrew, hiding within the dark folds of her robe. Many of those present could still feel its eyes upon them. To those who had not met the high priestess, Ahmeda appeared as fierce as her reputation. As quickly as the room darkened, it returned to its regular appearance, and the unexpected drama seemingly ended.

"I am high priestess of the God of War. I am the patron of the War God in the Eastern Colonies. I am his voice throughout Bracadia. It was I who ushered the War God into the North. All devoted to the faith, obey me."

Ahmeda swivelled to take in everybody in the room. There were faces she recognised, deacons and war priests that acknowledged her with their temple salute.

"The Emperor of Bracadia is here in Angorok."

That statement caused a great commotion, much more than her performance.

"We are not of Bracadia. Angorok stands alone."

It was one of the animators that yelled out. Ahmeda was unused to such disrespect, and the Priestess could see by the man's meek appearance that he was not powerful. The defiance, though, gleaned support from others in the room. Ahmeda looked down at the insubordinate fool, knowing that if these were her halls, he would pay in blood for such rash words.

"Is that so!?"

After giving the Muster a moment to consider, Ahmeda offered them much more to contemplate.

"The fate of Angorok is insignificant. Insignificant! Is fighting demons in this wasteland the best use of your time? Are you winning this war?"

It was cruel, but it silenced them. Sometimes the truth was more potent than magic. One person who seemed unphased by the words was Elderlin. The Asari librarian climbed up to the podium too. Like Ahmeda, he was the leader of his order and demanded the same respect.

"We have important business, Ahmeda. So please step down if you wouldn't mind."

The Priestess went wide-eyed, but as easily as she had handled Decon, she too had little choice but to step back into the crowd. Elderlin spoke at length with authority about the true dwarves and the demons they fought. He covered the correspondence with Logthar and the concern for the little-understood, though vital, Dwarven Core.

"Members of the Muster, the emperor is indeed here. We cannot ignore such an important landmark, but that is the marshall's business. Our immediate focus must be the Core, what it is, what it will mean if the demons reach it, and what we can do to prevent a catastrophe."

With compassion, Elderlin reached a hand towards Dekon.

"Dekon, the floor is yours."

Dekon nodded at the gesture, though he was too furious to have clear thoughts. Slowly, to give himself time to reign in his wits, he ascended back to his position, and in a role he was familiar with, the high priest began to issue commands. Soon, groups of wizards and priests, animators and druids, weavers and cultists, were in robust discussion, arguing passionately as they often did, with some scuttling away to return with other experts or things. Ahmeda had never seen cooperation like this on such a scale, and the lack of hierarchy and proper order was disconcerting. The chaos had Mannace's influence all over it. Such bedlam was not for her, and Ahmeda watched for a time but did not participate. Nevertheless, there was an energy and excitement in the hall and its many chambers. Great minds and powers were at work.

GREAT MINDS

The Muster delivered a new pair of devices to Mannace. They put one in the communication box with instructions on its use and waited next to the other. The apparatus was a block of reddish alloy with a large white crystal embedded in the back, a smooth mirror-like face, and a glass-like sheen. There were, of course, intricate runes around the sides of the block. In addition, it had a varnish to give the thing cohesion and durability.

It was not long before the crystal came to life, glowing. A ghostly portrait appeared on the glassy face, not the dwarf Logthar, but some long-departed soul bound to the device. First, it looked around, then it spoke.

"Mannace, can you hear me?"

Mannace held the device. The words were clear, the voice pleasing to the ear.

"Logthar, I hear you, my friend. Is it safe to talk?"

"Indeed it is, Mannace. I will not be disturbed."

The Muster did well with the device, but it seemed strange to talk to somebody he could not see, and Mannace almost preferred sending the notes in the box. Such a process gave him time to be more selective with his words, and he did not want to scare Logthar away by saying the wrong thing. After so much bad blood over the last two decades, it would take the old friends time to rebuild their trust.

"I will be blunt, Logthar, what we can do is limited by what we know, and we waste time puzzling together a history of the true dwarves. We have a basic understanding of your religion and the principle of the Core. The Core is the world's forge; is that right, Logthar, at the centre of the world?"

When there was silence from the device, Mannace hoped that the thing was working, forging on.

"The core is fire, earth, water, and air. It is energy, and we have seen its storm upon the earth. It is the greatest treasure of the dwarves, and in history, this is not the first time enemies of your kin have coveted it."

At last, a reluctant response.

"Know that the dwarves are guardians. They safeguard the earth, which benefits all races."

Mannace almost choked on the mulled wine he was sipping. Sudden anger momentarily took hold of his tongue.

"Guardians! Huh! Tell that to the slaughtered Galandarians and the Roundmen. Shall I get Prince Malakai to come to my office, and you can tell him that the dwarves acted in the best interests of the horse clans? Or perhaps the ghosts of the Remman might find that fact interesting. Render too. The sorcerer might have some words to say on the topic."

Mannace abruptly realised he was ranting, which would not help him with his goal to coax better detail from the dwarf, so he took a deep breath to cut himself short. He mentally acknowledged the many others bitterly aggrieved at the genocide suffered at the hands of the dwarves.

"The true dwarves, and the grey dwarves too, Logthar, your kin, covet the core. They only have thoughts for their kind.

Don't insult me by saying you protect us, nor forget the grave darkness inflicted upon the South."

There was a long pause before Logthar replied.

"It might please you then that the dwarves are losing to the demons, that their realm is also in ruins. We are all wounded, and none have the patience or time to quibble."

"Then speak plainly, Logthar."

There was another long pause, and Mannace was determined not to fill the silence. This conversation was a reckoning for the dwarf. Trust must begin now if there were to be a partnership in this struggle against the Hells. Fortunately, Logthar seemed to be of a similar mind, and for the first time since their renewed contact, Logthar was candid.

"What the demons seek is deeper within the earth than you can imagine, and the elements run wilder the closer to the prize. Already, by ancient passages, or those they make, the fiends are most of the way there. The KinRa slow their progress, and there are those rare times when the generals stem the tide of reinforcements within the upper reaches. But each day, more dwarves die, and the demon generals get closer and closer."

Mannace was careful to use terms Logthar seemed comfortable with.

"What happens when they reach the prize?"

"It will be the new abyss, the first Hell rebirthed, or a new Fifth Hell. Demons will feed on it, and those with powers will revel in its unlimited charge."

"And?"

"And they will cover the world with their night. They will not stop killing and feasting until no morsel of life remains."

"Do you know this for a fact, Logthar?"

"It is what the dwarves believe. It is what the KinRa tell us."

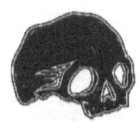

From a great height, Morgan Cain surveyed the lands once belonging to the South but now ruins buried in snow. He crisscrossed what was once the Northern Young Kingdoms, Veldaan, Sarang, and Islan so that he better understood the devastation of those nations by the legions of Hell. Morgan witnessed a demon horde moving through Islan, like a swarm, scavenging off the already barren land. He pitied the survivors, if any were to be found. Countless smaller swarms infested the wounded landscape, rampaging and destroying.

Morgan passed over Adash, covered in darkness, which he assumed to be a demon stronghold. He saw Skon, too, a rare bastion of humanity amongst these lost lands. Now the Bracadian ambassador landed before Angorok, cautious of magical defences as he descended from the skies. After entering through the main gates, soldiers escorted him to the citadel, where he finally reunited with his friend.

"Mannace, it is excellent to see you. So much has changed. I have seen the North from the skies. It appears to be a desperate time, my friend."

"Truly, Morgan, it is a great boon to have you returned. It seems we are always in desperate times; it is just the foe at our door that keeps changing."

Both men laughed, for it was true, putting their current circumstances in perspective. Mannace knew little of Morgan's time in Bracadia, but he wondered if it was a coincidence that the emperor was here.

"Did you know the emperor is here, Morgan, in the North, at the Aghan?"

Morgan was shocked by that. It gave him mixed feelings.

"No, my friend, I did not. Honestly, I journeyed here partly to be away from the emperor. He is a great man, but sometimes I feel trapped in his service. I have never been so free as I have in these last days, studying the lands of the Great Continent. It is good to be here, Mannace. I am glad to see you."

Mannace could tell that Morgan meant what he said. Nevertheless, he resented that Morgan shifted his allegiance to the empire many years ago. It was a fact that he could not let pass.

"I missed you, Morgan. I needed you here. Not just for your sword arm."

The marshall did not know how to better put into words that he needed their friendship, though Morgan knew its gist.

"I could not stay away, Mannace."

Morgan was uneasy, and it seemed unbelievable that the emperor might be here. It did not make sense.

"Why is the emperor here? He has never left his palace in Bracadia. There is nothing here but desolation and death."

"He has not shared his purpose. It surprised me, too, except that he has already influenced our path. He is very observant, or he knows more than he is revealing. Perhaps he is more than he seems. In that regard, he reminds me of the Mad King."

"He is very astute, Mannace. I think more so than the Mad King. He deduces much from little said. But, except for that, I have never witnessed anything to suggest he is more than a man. Moreover, he is exceptionally long-lived."

Mannace shrugged, then smiled.

"Milan is here too, and Render is on his way. It will be like times past."

Mannace, Morgan, Milan, Render, and Jaal sat on comfortable chairs in the War Room. They jovially pulled the seats in front of a fireplace to stare into the flames and enjoy the warmth. It felt like decades since they were all together, and although they were each immortal, they could see changes in one another. Jaal, an unexpected guest, smiled as he taunted their host.

"You are getting fat, Mannace. I am surprised you can find enough scraps to get so big in this desolate wasteland."

The companions laughed. Mannace retorted.

"You are too thin; the Alani should have treated you better. The pantry has beef and gravy; we'll put some meat back on those bones."

They hadn't eaten since sitting down some hours ago, and Mannace called for servants to bring food and more wine. When he turned to shout his instructions, he was surprised to see the emperor standing behind them. As the others shifted to see what alarmed Mannace, the emperor first waited for Mannace to complete the orders to his staff, then he stepped closer and calmly pre-empted their questions.

"I returned using the Ways. Such travel was new to me, and my friend said the way to this location had been closed. So, he opened it, and here I am."

Morgan respectfully made his seat available to the emperor, moving to stand by the fireside. The companions were uneasy, unsure of the protocol, but Mannace was unperturbed. Instead, he was impatient to learn about the Aghan.

"What of the Aghan, what of your friend, I need to know?"

If Mannace's brash style affronted the emperor, he did not show it. Instead, the leader took a moment to accept a cup of wine offered by Milan and carefully studied the companions. The emperor remained upright at the edge of the seat as if he did not know how to relax.

"Of course, Mannace, you are owed an explanation. Are you a wizard?"

The question was directed at Render, taking the sorcerer by surprise. Laughing, he replied.

"Indeed, Emperor, I am a wizard."

"My friend told me that magic was invented for the young races."

Render previously investigated the topic, and he summarised what he knew.

"It was a gift of the Ancients, first to the elves and dwarves, and then to men."

"My friend said there is a difference between powers used by the Ancients and the magic that is touted today."

Mannace was frustrated. It was not his habit to have patience, and it seemed the emperor was avoiding his question.

"For fucks sake, answer my question. The Aghan and your friend, what are they?"

With any pretence of protocol cast aside, the emperor seemed uncertain what to say. Awkwardly, he sighed deeply twice as he searched for a measured response.

"Know that my friend is very private, for a good reason. There is a limit to what I will share."

The room was silent while the emperor selected his words. Then, when he was ready, he looked at them, speaking directly to his host.

"The Aghan is, as the land was, before the Ancients. The land and my friend are timeless, born before any Age, and will outlast the final Age. Within the Aghan is nothing, and everything, creation, and oblivion."

The emperor was finished, but those in the room were smart enough not to fill the void with their own words. Reluctantly, the emperor continued.

"My friend has no name or race. He has a purpose, but that is his to know. He will not interfere in what happens in the lands of men. He is adamant about that. My friend is neither your friend nor foe."

Mannace was unsatisfied with the information. To encourage the emperor, he decided to confront something more tangible.

"And what of you, Emperor? If you cannot talk about your friend, surely you can talk about you!"

Nobody had ever been so audacious as Mannace was now. The emperor glared at his host, reaching past the man and into his soul. He assessed his very being. Only the cracking of wood in the fireplace broke the pervading quiet.

"Mannace, you are too bold."

"I think not."

The stare of the two men did not soften as more time passed. Such blatant confrontation was new for the emperor, not controlling the dialogue and having his hand so brutally twisted. He came here to enlist Mannace, and the situation he found himself in made him uncertain of his choice, or perhaps it was somebody of Mannace's character that he needed most. When the emperor finally decided to share, so many millennia had passed, and the leader was uncertain what to say.

"I am the creation of my friend, an exemplar for the design of man."

After expressing those first sentiments, other words came more easily.

"Though it was the design of my friend, it was the Ancients that birthed and fostered humanity, to serve, not just them, but also to aid their creations; the elves, the dwarves, the Dragu, and others. That is what passed, as my friend explained it. I did not witness such things."

The emperor looked down at his feet. Saying these things was humbling. Then, after taking a moment to let the thoughts pass, he looked up again to meet the group's gaze, then focused his attention back on Mannace.

"My first memories are of being amongst other men. Like you, I toiled, and I was elevated so that eventually, the empire that is Bracadia formed around me. As generations come and go, Bracadia expands and evolves, while I remain at the centre, constant."

The leader sat back, thoughtful.

"This region of the Eastern Colonies is significant, especially here in the North. The Ancients began here. The lesser races began here too. Magic emanated from these lands; now, your science is the new revolution. Even the gods and their faith are tangible here in the North; I had not expected that."

Render interrupted, but it was a question on all lips.

"Why are you here, Emperor, at Angorok?"

The emperor acknowledged the question with a slight nod as he continued to meet Mannace's stare.

"I want you to be my general, Mannace. I want you to lead the armies of Bracadia. Together we will conquer the world."

Mannace laughed a cold, sarcastic chuckle. He had no time for nonsense.

"War is not so simple. People are not so simple. I'll tell you what, Emperor, when you help me conquer the North, I will help you conquer the world."

It was not something said in seriousness, but the emperor replied, "Agreed."

Both men stared at each other while the others in the room shuffled in their seats, making small remarks that went unheard against the deafening silence between the two men. Then, after a short time, the emperor expounded.

"I expected no less. First, I will help you to end the conflict here. Then you will help me."

Milan was shaking his head, and Morgan voiced his concern.

"Emperor, at what cost? The war in the North is much more than it seems; you have just said as much yourself. The empire could fail here."

"If we cannot prevail in this small pocket of the world, how can we aspire that all the world will be Bracadian?"

Render and Jaal both looked at the emperor as if he were mad. Mannace was unsure how to take the proclamation or even if it was what he wanted. He was glad to be distracted by servants arriving at the door with food. It seemed a convenient time to draw the discussion to an end.

"I will consider your offer further when I have a full stomach. So, let's eat, my friends."

A GIFT

Render was furious. The Muster instructed one of the Fallen, a cultist amongst their number, to bring them the Staff of JolRek-AsnakTorWervak. Hells knew what it took to sway the man's loyalty, but the fool would regret it a thousand-fold when Render or the Fallen got hold of him. The Muster knew Render would not release the staff, so they circumvented him and stole the divine artefact from Adash. Mannace was aware of the subterfuge.

"Are you fucking insane, Mannace? Who the fuck do you think you are to steal from me!"

"It must be this way."

"Fuck you. Do you know how powerful that staff is?"

"It's just a staff."

"It's the greatest source of power ever conceived. A channel of fucking energy your fucking pig brain can't possibly understand!"

"That's why we must return the staff to the dwarves. They need it. Have you ever used the staff, Render?"

"Fuck you. When was the last time you used your cock, Mannace? How would you feel if somebody stole your cock in the night? It's nice to know it's there when you need it. Pretty damn fucking important when you want to fuck somebody over. Like Churgwarthos, I used the staff when I fought him!"

Render paused to breathe, but his finger was still pointing and waving. Ironically, it was the same digit he lost in the duel against the dwarven wizard whom the staff was taken from, regrown by the Fesadi menders. The artificial digit comprised many tiny vines, intricately interwoven, as alive and functional as the flesh and blood it replaced.

"What's going to happen if bloody Churgwarthos returns, or any other ancient fucker, Mannace? When I need the bloody staff, when things are desperate, we'll all be fucked. Fuck you, Mannace. Fuck you, and fuck bloody Angorok."

Render turned and stormed away. Mannace's ranger guards scampered to be out of the sorcerer's way, while others ran ahead to ensure his path out of the citadel and Angorok was clear. Mannace misjudged how incensed Render would become, and the Muster's argument seemed less compelling in retrospect. Regardless, it was too late now; the deception required them to act decisively, take the staff, and put it out of Render's reach, out of everybody's reach.

After the confrontation, as Mannace walked back to his quarters, his limbs never felt heavier, and the silent chambers where he slept were never emptier. Pragmatism to do what was needed drove him, but today the price was too high. He slowly realised that Render, the most loyal to him and his steadfast supporter, might no longer trust or respect him. To make it worse, Render's words that his bed might be empty were valid, and it hurt that Render and others might discuss such things. It had been a stressful day, a low point, and the marshall of Angorak felt very alone. But, most importantly, the confrontation with his friend shattered his resolve, and what was happening around him, even the Oracle's unfulfilled prophecy, suddenly seemed of little consequence.

As Mannace lay on his bed, still clothed, he became inspired to embrace what the emperor offered him and use the promise of Bracadian support to stomp his authority over the North. Decisively and on his terms. And not as an end, but as a beginning to more extraordinary things. Mannace abruptly realised the North was not the prize. It felt as if his old self, the ferocious, relentless leader he somehow misplaced, was reasserting control. Today, he was ashamed of the shell of a man he had become, and Mannace was determined to be proud of his future actions. To make his father and Rakor, both looking down at him from the War God's Halls, proud. He let the bloody Muster decide his actions when it should have been him pushing them. For Render and their friendship, he should have found a better way. Without realising it, Mannace sat up, rose, and started walking back to the war room where he always did his best thinking. His pace was quickening, and already he had ideas.

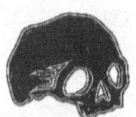

Morgan held the Staff of Jol, as the Muster referred to it, close to his chest. He was high above the IceSleepers and following Logthar's directions. Next to him, Symin kept pace. Morgan brought the young man on this mission as a witness and messenger if needed. The land below them was spectacular, with colossal mountain peaks and cavernous valleys layered in deep ice and snow.

On a mountain was a fortress carved from bedrock. The construction was ancient, crude, ill-maintained, and yet majestic for its lofty position amongst the peaks. And, as Logthar warned, there were dwarves along the battlements resplendent in their battle armour. The soldiers wore fluttering purple cloaks and generous hoods shading their eyes.

Morgan looked about for the KinRa-KluerKinBar. The KinRa, with their elemental magics, could destroy the duo as they drew close. Descending slowly, Morgan and Symin landed in a courtyard behind the primary defence, placing themselves at the mercy of the true dwarves. Logthar, the grey dwarf, appeared from the ranks to greet Morgan, and together the old acquaintances made their way into passages leading deep into the mountain. Symin followed obediently behind. The paths to the outworld were sealed behind them, and his fate with it, if the dwarves possessed no honour.

Morgan Cain, ambassador of Bracadia, stood before EaJa-KulAmani, BruEkNa and queen of the true dwarves. Symin waited nervously behind him with the other spectators. The Dwarven leader was broad-shouldered and commanding as Morgan expected, and a dwarf he recognised as SinKayLas was beside the queen. SinKayLas was tall and heavily bearded, dressed in red robes and peaked hat. His eyes were white and pupilless, but he glared at Morgan all the same. In their communications, Logthar explained that SinKayLas forfeited the Staff of Jol to Render when they battled at Viletri.

Many other dwarves were present in the large hall, but in the very dim light, Morgan perceived little detail. When the queen spoke, Logthar quickly replied and provided Morgan with an interpretation.

"The BruEkNa accepts you into her realm, and you have her protection. I accepted the invitation."

Morgan bowed to acknowledge the welcome.

"Tell the Queen, the Emperor of Bracadia seeks alliance against our common enemy, the Four Hells. The emperor asks that the queen accept a Bracadian embassy in her capital. He invites the delegates of the true dwarves to establish themselves at his palace, in the Blue Lands."

Logthar spoke the words as asked, though the translation was lengthy, and Morgan worried that the dwarf added other things. SinKayLas and other dwarves hidden in the shadows became involved in the conversation, escalating it to a heated debate. The discord continued until the queen raised her hand to command silence, issuing Logthar her instruction. The grey dwarf listened intently and interpreted once more.

"You will have your alliance and embassy, lad. The BruEkNa will keep to her word, but they don't trust you with the staff. Most here believe you to be a powerful magician, and with the staff of JolRek-AsnakTorWervak in your hands, they fear retribution. So best do what you came for."

The Staff of Jol was a tremendous gift, and Morgan held it in front of him, at arm's length, gripped tightly in both hands. He looked the queen in the eye, his face stern, in respect to the moment's importance. However, SinKayLas, not the queen, stepped forth to receive the artifact. In the brief moment when both sets of hands were upon the relic, Morgan could feel a surge of energy, intense heat, and passion, underpinned by an eagerness of the staff and KinRa to be reunited. Morgan let go and put his arms at his side.

Immediately SinKaylas turned, slapping his fist to his chest in respect to the queen, then shuffling away with others of the KinRa. The wizards bustled past the crowd and away from the gathering. There was a sense of relief from those that remained.

The queen looked Morgan up and down and spoke at length to Logthar. When she departed, with others quickly following suit, only Logthar, Symin, and Morgan remained.

"You and your companion will be the BruEkNa's guests here, lad. I will show you to your chambers. She is indebted to have the staff returned and obliged to discuss Bracadia; you will not be wasting your time. As I told Milan and Mannace, the BruEkNa will reciprocate your gift, as compelled by our customs."

"Thank you, Logthar. I will be honest that if I were a man of flesh, you would see sweat upon my brow and panic in my eyes. I swear that inside the guts of this mountain is no place to live, buried deep in stone. Perhaps you can convince your queen that conversation is better in the fresh air, under the stars."

"Perhaps, Morgan, we will soon see."

A PROCLAMATION

With help from Admiral Staronis' clerks and Milan's chief cartographer, Fitius pieced together what he hoped was a comprehensive map of Bracadia. It astounded him that such a thing did not already exist until he undertook the task and began to understand how immense and fragmented the empire was. Of course, it was not a perfect or complete representation, but the assembly hall floor was carpeted with broad tiles, each with geography etched into its surface. The massive map was filled with wooden tokens representing cities or other places of consequence. All the time, Fitius' staff assigned more tokens and recorded information about each location. Volumes of such data were starting to fill the shelves Fitius installed against the north and eastern walls. The emperor was impressed.

"Fitius, I commend your efforts. How will you use all this information?"

Fitius could not contain his excitement.

"This is just the beginning, Emperor. It is the data we need to understand and plan. How have you managed such a vast empire?"

"Mostly, it has managed itself, Fitius. Each region has a governor, even the Blue Lands, who can do as they see fit."

When Fitius appeared doubtful, the emperor explained more.

"All I ask is that the governors act in the interests of the empire. There are admirals and generals too, who abide by the same rules. The governors and military leaders appoint their successors, so the tradition of government and empire grows over the generations. With coaxing and patience, the empire expands. It's about the people, Fitius, as I have always said."

The emperor was taking in the map as they talked, and he had an observation.

"I can see that the tokens marked blue are the Capitals. There are only thirty-eight. Two are missing."

Fitius, who took pride in his attention to detail, was shaking his head. The map was masterly, so he expected the emperor had miscalculated. The emperor, though, was clear of thought.

"The R'Gayle in the Western Ocean, and Angorok."

His expression showed that Fitius did not like the answer, so the emperor at first skirted the anticipated issue.

"The R'Gayle are seafarers. Their vessels shelter in the fjords along the jagged Sapphire Coast in the harsh winter."

The emperor pointed to a coastal area on Fitius' map, at the edge of a large land mass.

"The ships have a box shape, allowing them to draw together, forming platforms and districts. When assembled, they are entire cities. Their capital during those months is R'Gayle Soonwea. The Western Ocean and Sapphire Coast governor is Ka'a Unguwae, who has visited the Blue Lands twice. He brought paintings of R'Gayle Soonwea and the Togwame, the floating island. You may have seen them at my palace."

Fitius had not paid attention to many things at the emperor's palace, as they were primarily relics of the past or curiosities with no real purpose. He shook his head, speaking his mind.

"What consequence is Angorok?"

"None for the moment, but these lands you call the North, they will need to be governed, like all others. Let's not be limited to what we can see now. I have learned that the young races, and even magic, began in the North. It will always be a place of significance."

"And Mannace would be your governor?"

"No, I would have Mannace as my general."

Fitius was still shaking his head. He'd only just freed himself of Mannace and his doom.

"Beware that man, Emperor. He is turmoil and chaos incarnate, he will follow his ambition at any cost, and his loyalty may shift with it. He has already denounced you once."

"I do not know your history with Mannace, Fitius, but you wear your animosity against him like a shield. Free your mind of its fiends, as they serve no purpose except to cloud your reason."

Head still shaking, Fitius appeared defiant or non-believing. The emperor did not need such discord amongst those he would have at his side.

"I have met the man and know his character. You are not in *his* thoughts, Fitius, and you bear no consequence to him. Therefore, treat Mannace with the same indifference, and do not let your grudges decide your course. It is a flaw in you, Fitius, in your confidence and character. Address it."

Fitius let his chin fall to his chest, seemingly deflated.

"I held Mannace in the highest regard, Emperor. I adored the man, and I followed him. I strived for him."

When Fitius looked up, there was steel in his eyes.

"He struck me down. He has no respect, and there is terrible darkness behind his guise of light. You cannot trust such a man, and Mannace would also strike you down in his rage. Therefore, Emperor, I do indeed hold a shield before that man so that I will not be cast down again, and as your loyal servant, I will raise that same defence for you. I will not permit his darkness to harm you or the empire."

The emperor eyed Fitius warily. Although the passion was misplaced, it was good to see the man's spine, and that he could stand up for himself and what he believed.

"I will be mindful of what we have discussed, Fitius, and I ask that you do the same."

The conversation ended with good timing as workers entered the hall carrying trays laden with figurines. Claudius was at the main door, eyeing the servants warily but not delaying their work. The new figures included manufactories, shipyards, and other distinctive buildings.

Fitius was excited as he hurried to greet the arrivals and peruse their craft. The emperor smiled but did not appear to share the same enthusiasm. Instead, the leader joined Claudius, and together they exited the complex. Soldiers waiting on the street formed a more substantial guard around the leader as he set his course for the sky tower where Admiral Staronis awaited him.

As the elevator slowly ascended the tower's many levels, The emperor took a moment to survey the city of Antigoth. He was becoming more familiar with its districts and interesting places, ever more impressed with its people and culture. The emperor realised that Fitius and all Arenlanders were a race that challenged themselves and achieved remarkable things. At the top of the tower, Admiral Staronis disembarked his warship to greet the emperor and escort him aboard. Soon they were at the helm, just beneath the top deck and looking out through the thick glass at the sky fleet. Finally, the admiral dismissed his aides so that he and the emperor were alone.

"I have completed the relay. All Class A navigators are now familiar with every critical location. They have started moving troops into Angorok, but it will take time."

"And what of the ships in the sky above Antigoth, the Class B's and C's?"

"They might serve many purposes, Emperor. Fitius has sent me a schedule that would see most of them assigned civil tasks, all important. If it is what you want, I will do as he asks and send the remainder to Angorok to supply and run missions in the North."

"Send *all* ships that are here to the North. Go with them; as I have said before, this is your fleet now. Take what else you need for the war effort. Know that Bracadia is at your service, I proclaim it, and I will write you papers to that effect. Work with Mannace to secure the North and start preparations for a war that will take you much further afield. Put the word to the other admirals to expand, explore, and raise our banner upon new lands. You will command the seas and the skies, Admiral. All this I will proclaim."

The emperor was unaccustomed to incorporating magic into his strategies, but he gleaned what wizardry might accomplish.

"I have witnessed devices used by the Asari at Angorok that can communicate across vast distances. Talk to Mannace about it. Talk to him about many things, Admiral, and become familiar with the man and his ways. As you are my admiral, he will be my general."

The emperor issued one other instruction.

"When you are in the North, talk to the wizard named Render. Ask him about immortality. You will not see the world conquered in a mortal's lifetime."

Admiral Staronis seemed uneasy, but he bowed low.

"It will be done, my emperor."

THE BLOOD LEGION

With great luck, one of the flying ships of the Blood Legion, the *Gull*, spotted Athose and his small troop. The *Gull's* crew were tracking the movements of a demon army as it moved through The Gap towards Islan. While they always looked for survivors in the army's path, they were amazed to see Thag and others. With precision, the Legionnaires swooped in and executed their rescue just in time as flying demons attracted by the craft swarmed over the area and tried to grab the ship's rails. With Athose and others on board, the navigator instantly transported them to Skon and safety. A legionnaire with a repeating crossbow shot several bolts through a demon clinging to the carved gull's head that extended from the bow. At the last moment, the snarling creature tried to launch itself free, but as the bolts impaled its torso, the demon's wings went limp, and it spiralled out of sight into the Skon forest below.

Athose knew many of the legionnaire crew, and he was thrilled to be reunited with Rey and Agro. The experienced belg and orc were likewise excited to see the elf, and Rey lifted Athose above his head, declaring to the crew that the champion had returned. While Athose still appeared a young man, Rey and Agro were markedly older since he last saw them, sparking a sadness in the elf. However, it also sparked more profound memories of the arena and its contests.

"Are there games in Skon?"

Rey laughed, "Sometimes, but games are for boys. You will like the parties. The Islani are mad, they drink, and they fuck, and they have no limits."

Agro was smiling. The huge orc poked Athose in his ribs, making the elf squirm.

"We have a game to celebrate your return. We butt heads and break faces."

Rey looked across the deck at Athose's new companions. The giant was sitting cross-legged in the centre of the deck while the others enjoyed the view over the ship's railings.

"Why were you travelling through The Gap, Athose? You are lucky we rescued you."

Agro added, "Know giant, he Rockhome Chief. He came to the Wengo. See Games."

Athose watched the group too. He knew Thag and Seb would be apprehensive about being amongst the Southerners. Karack was likely indifferent, as he was to everything.

"I want to find Roanna and Vilera. Seb knows how to ward off the demons, and he would have gotten us through The Gap."

Rey and Agro both laughed. One priest against an army was like trying to hold back an avalanche with your hands. Rey and Agro witnessed a lot of tragedy over the last decade, and they had no patience for gibberish. Rey slapped Athose hard on the side of his head.

"Wake up, boy. You cannot rely on your luck all the time."

Athose reeled at the slap, his vision momentarily blurred, his head down.

"I am still here, am I not, Rey? Do you not see an elf before your eyes? I know how to survive."

"There is always chaos in your wake. You are not safe to be around."

Athose was stunned, as much by the words as the blow. He was unused to being criticised, and he didn't much care for it.

"I am no boy, Rey. I have led orcs and men."

"To their doom, I am sure. You carry the Mad King's curse."

"The colossi follow me. They will follow nobody else."

Athose suddenly remembered the two wyverns. They would have lost sight of him when The Gull transported him here. They might be in danger if they panicked. He looked up at the sky while Rey talked.

"Even the invincible colossi die too. We will die if you stay with the legion."

"Athose stay. He *wonder boy*."

The beleaguered elf appreciated the support from Agro, but it was many years since the orcs at the city of Colossus called him by that name.

"I am no boy and no wonder."

Rey shrugged and left for the lower deck. Agro smiled and slapped the elf across the other side of his head. Athose wasn't expecting it, recoiling again.

"You get slow, boy, to let Rey hit you. Yuriki here, you remember her?"

Athose indeed remembered her fondly. They spent time together on the Palainth when they competed in the regimental games. Yuriki touched his body and soul, unlike any other he had lain with. Just the thought of her made him forget what he was going to say and even why he was here.

"Where will I find her?"

"Where you least expect me."

Agro was used to the Vostovian's sudden appearance, but Athose had forgotten how elusive and mysterious Yuriki could be. As he turned, she seemed to always stay on his shoulder, teasing him. Then, when he turned the other way, she was, in his face, a quick kiss as a reminder of intimate times.

"I am here, and I am there. I will catch you unaware."

She kissed him again, but from across his shoulder so that Athose could feel the young woman's hands on his back. It made him dizzy the way she was everywhere at once. He closed his eyes to focus.

"I have missed you."

When Athose opened his eyes, she was gone. Yuriki hadn't changed since Athose first met her; dark-skinned and slight, delicate, and beautiful, with large, mesmerising eyes. Her white robe hugged her slender form, as he remembered and since dreamed. Athose took a step towards the entrance to the lower deck, but Agro pulled him back.

"We'll be on ground soon. Fuck later."

Athose tried to push the orcs hand away. However, Agro knew the elf's character, so he kept a firm grip.

"Rules. You follow rules. Remember rules."

Athose shook his arm harder until Agro let go. Then, instead of continuing towards the lower deck, Athose made his way over to his companions, leaning over the railing to look down upon Skon. It was a bustling, beautiful city with tall buildings and busy streets. A high wall skirted the town, and a river flowed around it. Seb, who stood next to the elf, was glued to the scene. In particular, a beast with the appearance of a gigantic lion but with a mannish head and barbed tail was flexing its massive wings in a city square. It pranced in a circle before disappearing into a side street.

"I have heard of the Manticore but never imagined seeing it. It is miraculous in these dark times, Athose, to see a place like Skon that is so full of life."

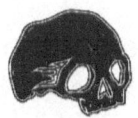

Athose accompanied the captain, who was delivering his report to Casteel. The commander of the Blood Legion looked concerned.

"Take the *Gull* and leave word for the other captains to lead the demons south through Islan and the Sarang. I will send word to Mannace. Did you have time to assess their numbers?"

"It was a smaller force, possibly three to four hundred thousand. We could only see the one general, a big brute, not a flyer at least."

Casteel was nodding.

"South then. Let me know if they deviate."

As the captain left, Athose stepped forward. Just half a step, though, as he saw the stern look on Casteel's face and stopped.

"Athose, why are you here!?"

It was not the warm greeting he was expecting. It seemed the war changed everyone.

"Where should I be?"

The cheeky reply made Casteel smirk. She remembered why she liked this young elf, though it was many years since he was counted amongst the legion.

"Far, far from these lands, Athose. You know that the Spider Mother has declared war on the elves. She has eyes everywhere in the North, and you are in great danger even inside the walls of Skon. Her hunters will find you."

"I didn't know about the spiders. What of you, Casteel? Why are you here then? Why do the spiders not come for you?"

Casteel shrugged. Herself and Athose were perhaps the only elves that remained in the North. That realization softened her mood toward her visitor.

"I won't return to the Blood Sea. I would rather face Eya and her brood. But that is not the business of a boy."

Athose felt the same way about returning to the colonies. He let the quip about his age slide.

"There is no going back. The only direction is forward."

Casteel did not intend to be so candid, especially to Athose, who she never confided in before, nor thought to have any degree of wisdom or intuition.

"And there is no staying still. We cannot languish here. We must reach beyond the North."

Athose was nodding, and in this conversation with Casteel, he could drop the pretence of searching for his sisters.

"Is it normal to feel such a thing, this need to travel?"

Casteel tilted her head and raised her brow enough as if to say maybe. She was also young by Elven standards and still with much to learn about her kin and their ways. Nevertheless, the elves believed strongly in destiny and their critical part in important events, and Castell knew it was more than arrogance that gave them that view.

"We could consult Antiel, the Light Bearer, if we can find him."

Athose nodded, though he'd never heard of the Light Bearer, assuming it was an Alani thing. The pull to travel further north seemed tangible and stronger over recent years. To have Casteel endorse what he sensed was a relief that he was not going mad.

"Who is Antiel?"

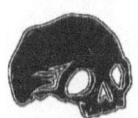

Casteel reassigned the *Gull* from its intended duties, and now the vessel hovered in the sky above the mountain ranges that comprised Rockhome. It was a vast territory to survey, even with the advantage of a flying ship. Thag was with the captain and navigator.

"Follow that ridge. Then angle across the valley to the right. There are nests on both sides of the vale. It is a hunting ground for them."

Before the ship reached the valley, the crew could see rocs launch from their mountain perches and climb quickly to be above the *Gull*, observing their approach. At least six of the enormous birds were visible, some brown like the scrub lands far below, others grey like the mountain face. The captain ordered the ship to slow, and then as the valley came in sight, he ordered a complete halt. The magnificent creatures doubled in number.

From a ravine between two tall peaks, a white roc caught an updraft that lifted it quickly to the same height as the *Gull*. Then, with mighty wings, the majestic bird flew closer until the crew could see its yellow eyes as it circled and observed them. Casteel, who knew Antiel before he transformed into a roc, stood at the foredeck in plain sight, returning the bird's stare.

"Casteel, why have you come to the mountains?"

The voice was in her head, calm yet commanding as Casteel remembered the Elven Elder. Then, not knowing how to cast her voice with her mind, she shouted a reply.

"We are here, Antiel, because Athose and I feel the pull to travel north, beyond the North. The sensation grows stronger as time passes."

"Then go north. I sense it too. It is illuminated, born of the Light. It is a summons, Casteel. Others will know it for what it is, and they will travel. All elves will travel."

"Will you go north, Antiel? Will you bear the Light to lead our way?"

"SQWAAARRRK"

The white roc continued to circle the *Gull*. After a time, the voice of Antiel returned.

"No child. It is not time for me yet."

Antiel circled once more before angling away to join other rocs that kept a more distant vigil.

Casteel stood for a time watching the scene. Finally, Athose, who stood back with his companions, moved to be next to the commander. There was a tear on her cheek as she stared into the distance. Eventually, Casteel turned to shout a command to the captain.

"Set a course north, Captain."

There was a reluctance in the captain's posture as if he were struggling to do as ordered. Others amongst the crew were murmuring, and Thag, who made plans to travel south, carried a deep frown. They all heard Casteel call out to the white roc, so they understood the intent of her order. The crew were wholly loyal and trusting but travelling north into the unknown and unprepared was much to ask. Casteel knew she owed them more explanation, but they kept a communication box on board, and the navigator could always return them instantly to known lands. She could not explain to her crew that she could not face Shamal, whom Casteel loved deeply, and who she was so abruptly leaving behind. Castell did not know if she would ever return.

Steeling her mind for what lay ahead, Casteel let the sadness pass, and she embraced her traveller. It was an Elven trait to know and follow your calling.

"North, Captain, at speed. Be to it."

As Athose stood at the prow, he was distracted by two dots in the distant sky. They were much higher than the roc's and almost indistinct, but Athose knew by the way they circled that the wyverns had found him. It was reassuring to know they were there.

Athose turned to Casteel, who caught his movement out of the corner of her eye, looking to where Athose pointed.

"My friends, the wyverns."

"You are full of surprises, Athose. Brief me later in my quarters."

"Yes, Commander."

Amongst Casteel's possessions was a device gifted to her by the Fogmir Druids, which she recovered from her bags that morning. The apparatus allowed her to communicate with the Fogmir Elves, Ahmeda, and her Alani elders. However, once alone in her quarters, Casteel put the device aside. Later at night, she wrapped it in cloth and placed it back amongst her belongings. To herself, she made a promise.

"I own my decisions. *I* command my hand."

RISE OF THE FALLEN

The fortified city of Tarnac, like Adash, was engulfed in darkness summoned by the ancient sorcerer Churgwarthos. And like Adash, Render was able to manipulate the sinister enchantment to give him influence over any demons or undead that might occupy it. It felt as if the darkness were an expansion of his consciousness. For now, Tarnac was vacant, but for a few lost souls, ghosts that haunted the city well before any sorcerer devoured it. Render used the city to set a trap. It was risky, but his frustration and anger at the Muster's and Mannace's deception encouraged him to be reckless, making him care less for the consequences. Render surveyed the surrounding terrain while Jaal, next to him, looked up.

"Do you think the demons will follow the sky globes?"

"I do. Can you not see that it is already working?"

Jaal squinted. Certainly, he could make out shadows flitting about the globes, like bugs to a streetlamp.

"It is just local swarms. The numbers are too few."

"Look closer at the lights farthest away. They are disappearing, are they not."

"Yes."

Jaal suddenly understood what Render meant. It was as if a great cloud were coming, black against the night, so any movement seemed like a trick on the eyes.

"Are you sure of your plan?"

Render laughed, though it was more of a menacing cackle, darker even than their surroundings. The master wizard raised another light globe brighter than the others into the night. Although it was consumed partly by the enchanted darkness, it was enough for Jaal to see cultists and priests lining the walls and streets. Jaal knew many others were spread out behind the city's defences and throughout its districts. The gathering brought their rituals to a climax.

"We will soon see if we will live or die."

Behind Render, living statues stood in their tortured poses. The obsidian animations hosted power for Render's spells. With a quickness to his step, Render and his entourage descended from the fort to join others in the courtyard at the city gates. The darkness was more tangible here, suffocating to those who didn't understand its properties and how to manipulate them. Demons loyal to the cultists, summoned from the Dark Dreaming, were in the shadows or on balconies and roofs. Some were powerful, and the darkness multiplied their strength. It was dangerous to bring them here, but Render had to trust the bond the cultists and dreamers forged.

Suddenly, the noise of the approaching demons, their flapping and screeching, could be heard. Just moments later, the first of the flyers appeared overhead. They were black and humanish with bat-like wings and fierce animalistic heads. Some swooped low, while others darted high over the city. Where they saw the cultists or priests, they shrieked and dived, ravenous and craving blood.

Render felt the sorcerous darkness that enveloped Tarnac swell, making his skin tingle and the hairs on his body stand on end. The collective casting of the cultists and priests, combined with the servant darkness, quickly subdued the foe. Everywhere, bewildered demons settled on buildings or lay on the streets, their mad frenzy defused.

A few of the priests retreated towards the centre of the city. As they barked commands, entranced demons scuttled like rats across the cobbles or over the buildings to follow new masters, becoming needed soldiers for the defence.

As Render gazed skyward, eyes appeared atop the city walls, a multitude of red dots staring down into the streets and courtyards. It took a moment to discern the dark forms in the blackness, many with human traits, some slithering like snakes or lizards, and others monstrous and atrocious. Some demons clung to the stonework while others dropped over the walls or leapt down stone stairs to where the cultists and priests waited. Then, a distant horrifying roar sounded outside the defence. In response, the trickle of appearing creatures became legions of scampering forms, screeching, and clambering over each other as they descended. In the overwhelming turmoil, Render lost sense of how his allies fared along the wall or in the town proper. But, like him, they raised their defences, and most were veterans of demonic battles.

Mannish things, long-legged and claws extended, threw themselves at Render, bouncing back off invisible barriers. More of the creatures, one larger with tall spikes down its shoulders and back, bustled around or over their stunned pack-mates. Murder and hunger drove them feverishly toward the wizard, requiring all his concentration to hold them at bay. To Render's right, a cluster of enemies suddenly froze in place, taking on an obsidian sheen, the work of the dreamer, Ruu. In another wave of dreamer magic, more attackers met the same fate. The growing tangle of statues made it harder for other devils to reach him, gifting Render the moments he needed to strike. Drawing on the sorcerous darkness, Render seized control of the swarm, turning demon against demon, biting, and rending each other with their powerful claws.

Fek and the Drutha lurked nearby, though Render could not distinguish the dreamers from the battling throng in the gloom. Their close presence gave him confidence that he was protected, and with more time bought, Render used his reserve of souls to feed the pervading oblivion that engulfed Tarnac, fuelling the rituals of the priests and cultists as they laboured to subdue and control the attacking hoard.

Jaal was crouched within the sorcerer's protection, his blades in hand, ready to defend. To the dark elf, the odds appeared against them, and under his breath, he cursed Render's arrogance.

At the front gate, an entire section of the fort suddenly shuddered, impacted by a colossal blow. A second mighty thump collapsed the building inward, taking the whole gatehouse with it, and mercilessly crushing demons and cultists beneath the tumbling rubble. A great beast stomped across the debris out of the dust and gloom. It was part man, part animal, with shoulders and chest like an Ox, stomping on all fours. The gargantuan brute bellowed as it shook its horned head. Jaal never imagined a creature could be so physically powerful.

Eyes closed and with a hand over his gut, Render entered a trance, collecting his power. As his defences slacked, demons launched themselves at the sorcerer. Jaal responded with a flurry of blades - slowing time and moving amongst the enemy with unprecedented speed, cutting and stabbing with an assassin's deadly precision. Fek appeared atop one demon, ripping its head from its shoulders, before pouncing upon another. He was fast, and his sharp claws sprayed blood as he tore wildly at the enemy. Together, the raging dreamer and Jaal kept the Hell-spawn from Render's throat.

Render's eyes opened wide as he raised his hands dramatically above his head. Then, boldly turning towards the unstoppable beast as it crashed through the city streets, Render thrust his arms forward. A stream of crimson light emanated from his fingertips, arcing across the ruin, and striking the colossal creature. Flame erupted across the monster's side and back. In response, the freakish brute raised itself upright, towering above Tarnac and screaming into the night. Painfully it turned, staring back down the punishing beam to seek out its originator. Roaring with rage, the beast charged toward the caster.

As Render frantically collected and concentrated his energies, animated statues that stored his reserve power, cracked, and disintegrated. One exploded, showering the allies with sharp debris. Close-by, demons, enemies, and allies, shrivelled into husks, their life force syphoned. Incredibly, as the sorcerer incanted, Jaal sensed Tarnac's darkness wane. Beside him, Render blazed red, a magnificent beacon, his hair lit with mystical flames. From the sorcerers glowing arms, the crimson ray split into many parts, all striking the great beast as it charged. Render unleashed his fury, dominating the wild energies with his ego, commanding the arcane forces to entirely consume the gargantuan creature in blistering fire.

Jaal desperately fought frenzied demons and black hounds that converged on their location. Out the corner of his eye, he could see the burning monster stumble and then topple. After turning to dispatch another of the leaping dogs, Jaal looked back again to see the gigantic beast's body slide across the rubble, scattering stonework, and burying unwitting combatants. Finally, as its momentum ceased, the charred head hit the ground, its great horns dramatically coming to rest close enough for Jaal to reach out and touch.

The rising dust from the wreckage and sudden stench of burning flesh was as suffocating as the city's darkness. Utterly exhausted, Render lowered his hands and put his chin on his chest. He coughed, entirely spent, using his remnant of strength to remain standing.

Without Render, it was up to the priests, cultists, and their dreamers to subjugate the remaining foe. Jaal pulled the sorcerer into a shelter, to keep him safe. Nearby, enemies were bursting into flame, meaning Gax, another dreamer, was close too.

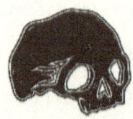

Their triumph elevated the Fallen and Eternal Priesthood. Tarnac joined Adash as a second city under their dominion, filled with demons from The Abyss and the Dark Dreaming. Moreover, their achievement motivated them to lure other swarms to the cities.

Their Master, Render, left them to their business. He thought he might have a chance to bring the greater of the demons under his control, but when the devilish beast assaulted Tarnac, its will, like its bulk, was unassailable. Render was fortunate to have defeated the creature, cursing Mannace again for stealing the Staff of Jol, when its limitless power would have dominated the swarm and its general. But that was if he dared wield the staff, for he sensed that the artefact possessed a will of its own. Mannace and the Muster need never know that.

Not to be entirely undone, Render imbued new life to the great beast he slew, preserving it with rituals and spells. Now he worked to give the enormous form sentience he could control. Animation of the flesh was experimental for him, using the soul of a cultist who was grievously wounded, gifting the woman a second chance to serve. Much of the spell-craft needed was second nature to the sorcerer now, but the massive bulk of the creature and the unknown composition of its form were differences that required him to adapt and innovate. Render relished the challenge, knowing the monster would make a fine centrepiece for his expanding army. The sorcerer drew on an old artefact Mannace once gifted him named the Essence of Life. Interwoven with his restorative magic, a small amount of the substance resulted in an animation resembling a living being.

Render progressed other plans, too, to connect Adash and Tarnac to the portals already at his holdings in Viletri and Vlustoven. He would invest time to make travel through them safer, through the timeless domain of the dead. Adash would be his home, his throne. Tarnac and the surrounding regions of Sompher Gris and Yan were his gifts to the Fallen and the Eternal Priesthood. It made Render laugh to think Mannace was not the only one to make bold claims on the lands of the North and proclaim himself sovereign. He would eventually forgive Mannace, but he would never again serve the man.

THE EMPEROR'S NORTH

Bracadian divisions constantly arrived at Angorok, enough that the city buildings were becoming full. The professional soldiers were smartly dressed in their red uniforms and well equipped with rifles or muskets. These troops were the emperor's standing army. Mannace and Admiral Staronis were in the war room, surveying the table filled with figurines representing the allied operation and known enemy deployments in the North. Mannace looked up at his counterpart.

"Jeylan, we are tracking eight demon armies active in the North, plus an unknown number in Amon Murn and Churlamen. The portal to the Abyss is in Amon Murn. After securing the lands we know well, safeguarding the portal must be our next goal."

Mannace was holding a long stick which he tapped on the figurine of a city.

"Regnorak will fall after that."

Sweeping the stick over other parts of the northwest, Mannace coolly added, "The rest will follow."

The admiral tried to keep a calm demeanour, but he shifted uneasily, and Mannace could see his poorly disguised angst.

"Do you have concerns, Jeylan?"

"It all seems a bit simple. War is more complex than toys on a table."

Mannace laughed.

"I am giving you an overview, Admiral, of the land and the task ahead. Do not think me a fool. We will return here with our scout commanders and clerks, and you will have all the details you desire. Every element will have a place and plan before we act."

As the admiral relaxed his stance, Mannace raised a query.

"Already, there must be a million Bracadians in Angorok. How big is the army you are bringing?"

"Well, you must forgive me too for lack of detail. When the time is right, I will also come to your table with my chief officers and staff. When I have completed the transportation, the soldiers will be yours to command."

As he thought deeply, the admiral put his head down and his hand up to request silence.

"You are right; about one million of the emperor's standing army have already arrived, and another five hundred thousand are preparing for transit. I expect six hundred thousand from the colonies north of Bracadia and just two hundred thousand Charikon soldiers. Once they are here, half of the flying fleet will keep the forces in supply. The other half will be battle-ready."

While Mannace should have been excited by such vast numbers of well-appointed troops, the marshall felt uneasy, evident in his cold silence. Jeylan suspected why.

"You are Bracadian now, Marshall. When you look out your balcony, you will see Bracadian troops in your streets and Bracadian ships in your skies. It is the emperor's banner that they will hold high as they march into battle. The Emperor will be the people's hero when the demons are purged from this land."

Mannace shrugged as if it were not significant, though his frown told a different tale.

"We harboured a mad king who was like the emperor, who expected the world and people to fit neatly to his design. He was a master manipulator, and we were all pieces in his games."

"The emperor has given you what you asked for, Marshall. That is all that he has done. In return, you promised him your service. Are you having second thoughts?"

"No! Before the emperor arrived, conquering the North was my whole ambition. Now it is just the beginning. It will take me some time to adjust my thinking and decide my purpose."

"Nicely said. I feel the same. The emperor chose us, and I can see it is for a good reason. Does that mean that we share his vision or that it is our passion to expand Bracadia and devour the world? I expect that I am like you; that I will wait, and I will learn, and I will see."

Both men nodded. After their talk, Mannace appreciated and respected Jeylan, and he suspected the feeling was mutual.

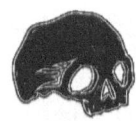

Mannace did not need to wait for the whole Bracadian contingent to arrive to commence his campaign. Using leaders and scouts familiar with the local lands and enemy, the Bracadians deployed to make safe the lands Mannace claimed as his nation of Angorok. They quickly dealt with the marauding demons. None of the greater demons were in the locale, and it seemed a simple assignment until a commander of the brula hurried to Mannace's office.

The brula officer wore black leather pants and a black shirt with dark skin and reddish lines painted on his cheeks and arms denoting his rank. Like most of his kin, long hair was beaded and tied in a top-knot. The commander folded his wings behind his back.

"Marshall, Sir."

"Yes, Commander."

"We made a discovery, Sir."

"Yes, Commander."

"It is the first time it has been safe to scout the Rift, Sir, properly. There was no way we could have seen it before, Sir."

"Yes, Commander, your scouts put their lives at risk daily. However, their efforts are vital to the war effort."

"The Rift is bottomless in places, and we cannot access many locations."

Mannace's interest peaked. The Rift was a vast chasm that separated the North from the South. For many generations, the North and South fought across it. More recently, the southern side was buried in snow and claimed by the dwarves.

"I understand *the Rift,* Commander. What was your discovery?"

The commander was still apprehensive, but Mannace could see in his eyes that he was ready to disclose what he knew. The marshall further encouraged the officer with an impatient wave of his hand.

"The Rift is crammed with demons, Marshall, Sir, masses of them. There are few flyers, but there are generals and great beasts. They are dormant, as if they're waiting."

The report immediately made sense to Mannace as it fitted the conclusion he came to with the emperor. He had assumed, though, that the demons were still fighting the dwarves. Perhaps not all journeyed underground, or maybe the dwarves expelled them. Regardless, it was a major worry.

"Thank you, commander, please report to my clerks and give them details. I will need an indication of numbers and where they are along the Rift. Keep gathering information. I will send word to the generals to keep their distance."

For good measure, Mannace added, "I don't want any more surprises, Commander."

"Yes, Sir."

"Jeylan, we must learn if the flying ships can kill the greater demons."

Jeylan nodded. It was a growing concern that the generals of The Abyss might be unbeatable. In past battles, only the colossi were their match, and previously, flying ships fired on the beasts but with little impact. Rumours abounded that Render defeated one, but the sorcerer was estranged, and for now, Mannace would let him be. He used other means.

"The war priests are blessing the ammunition."

"Huh, religion will not guide a cannonball or pierce the impenetrable. Mannace, our best option is the artillery. The battleships can destroy the generals without getting close."

"Against a normal foe, not against these creatures. Trust me; we have been fighting demons for fifteen years."

The admiral folded his arms as if he were immovable in his thinking. Mannace knew it was essential to convince him of his intent, but he could see that words were insufficient. Instead, the marshall excused himself, returning with a cannonball in hand. He passed the object to the admiral.

"What do you think?"

Jeylan was surprised by the cold touch and polish on the steel. The ball was smooth, and his fingers glided across it. He was shocked to see a face on the mirror surface staring back at him. The admiral dropped the ammunition and stepped back, looking at Mannace as if the marshall had handed him a bag of spiders.

"A blessing is not a trivial thing, Jeylan. The war priests, the priests of The Light, the Eternal, and others make life in the North possible. The gods and the powers of their priests are undeniable."

"The emperor has decreed that we shall follow the God of War and his doctrine. However, I confidently tell you that there is no god to guide your bullet on the battlefield. There are no halls after death for the valiant. They are stories to give soldiers hope and to command their loyalty."

"That may be so in the heartland of Bracadia, in the safety of your barracks, but you will soon learn that the gods are real here in the North, on the field of war, and without them, we would all be lost. I will let Dekon explain it to you.

He will show you the power of his God, and you will not dare mock him."

Mannace spoke with such confidence that Jeylan was silent. Then, he carefully turned the cannonball over with his foot until the face reappeared. It faded then came back stronger, staring up at him.

"This is madness, shooting ghosts at demons. My peers would laugh at me in Bracadia for suggesting such nonsense. How many of these do you have?"

Mannace laughed, and he slapped Jeylan on the arm. The Marshall of Angorok poured some wine and invited his guest to sit.

"We must be patient and trust the Muster. Jeylan, tell me more about Bracadia?"

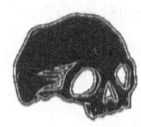

FITIUS

Fitius was infuriated that the emperor gave away his flying fleet, leaving him just five diplomatic craft in service, that he kept hidden away from Antigoth. He secreted them well out of the emperor's reach. The upset governor expected to share the ships on his terms, but to lose his prize possessions flabbergasted him. With the help of his staff, Fitius found the emperor and Ahmeda at *Saska's* in the city. The top-end brothel was a place where he had spent time in the past, but he was surprised to discover the emperor there. Claudius and the soldiers at the door would not let him enter, so he waited until the couple emerged.

On seeing Fitius, the emperor detected impatience and angst in his twisted features. Usually a gentle and sensible man, Fitius seemed like he might launch into an attack.

"Fitius, you would be amazed at what I have discovered."

When his controller did not enquire further, the emperor explained anyway.

"It was your own immortality that gave me a clue. Did you know that Saska has an apprentice?"

"No", even in his rage, Fitius couldn't help but be interested.

"Jesephine. She will be meeting the admiral. I believe they will make a good coupling, don't you think?"

It was Saska and her ability to drain life from others and gift it to those who followed her that extended Fitius' life. The connection affected him still, even though Saska was a world away. Fitius was aware that the emperor was purposefully distracting him, so he brought the conversation back to his agenda, unconcerned that others would hear.

"I need the flying ships. I need them returned to administer the empire. I can't *control* what I can't reach. Without consulting me, you have gone too far to give the fleet to Staronis!"

The emperor, always calm, uncharacteristically flinched. Ahmeda could see it immediately, and she glared at Fitius to make him stop, but the controller continued his complaining.

"The ships are wasted in the North. The campaign to dominate the world will not begin with victory in the North. Conquest will start in the manufactories, in the production of arms, and in equipping the armies of Bracadia with the best technology. You are sacrificing the future, for what, to serve one man's vanity."

That was its crux; Fitius' hatred of Mannace contorted his features. The emperor was quiet for a time, looking at Fitius while he contemplated his response. Everybody was silent, except for Fitius, who again felt the urge to expel the thoughts that consumed him.

"The flying ships are mine. It was my efforts that put them in the sky. It is my efforts that have built everything here that you can see. If you want Bracadia to be like Antigoth, you need me, and I need my ships."

"I don't need you, Fitius."

"What!"

"You are a barrier to progress."

Fitius was dumbfounded.

"My whole life, I have dedicated myself to progress. Nobody else could have achieved what I have in such a short time. You are not making sense. Look around you. Antigoth is everything to aspire to."

The emperor stared directly at Fitius as he delivered his response.

"I have learned that many technologies you profess as your own are inventions of The Architect, whom you have ostracized. Even clockwork that you are so proud of is the brainchild of the dwarves. I understand that the magetechs, Fitius, are forbidden to do more than the simplest things, for you have no respect for their craft. The guild masters I have spoken to are frustrated by your single mindedness as if you only have ears for your own ideas."

The emperor raised his voice.

"I know, Fitius, that you cherish Antigoth at the expense of other cities of the Eastern Colonies, and you place the needs of Arenland above those of colony and empire. It is blatant that you keep your competitors humble so that your greatness can shine. You don't play nicely with others, Fitius."

"People need strong leadership, and leadership requires a resolute mind and hardened hand. I cannot be replaced, Emperor, and the irrefutable progress you see everywhere about you is proof of that. I challenge you to find a better controller!"

Fitius was growing in boldness, puffing himself up with his own words.

"Bracadia will not reach its potential without me!"

"You have deceived me in the past. I do not trust you, Fitius."

The emperor hesitated only a moment before turning to Claudius, raising his eyebrows, and motioning with a subtle flick of his head towards Fitius. There was an understanding in the look between them. Fitius took a step backwards, astute enough even in his arrogance, to sense imminent danger. He suddenly looked like he might run.

With practised speed, Claudius drew his pistol from his belt, and with a loud crack, he shot Fitius in the chest, hurling the man back onto the ground. Then, while everyone else froze, shocked, Claudius moved over the body and nudged it with his foot. There was no response except for a whir and twitch from the controller's clockwork arm. The belg was confident from the gaping hole the bullet left that Fitius had drawn his final breath.

The emperor sighed, and he turned to Ahmeda.

"I was wrong to have chosen him."

The high priestess nodded.

"I liked him as a younger man when he was with Saska. She helped him to have ambition and spine. His family will be outraged at his death."

"I once liked him too. He tries to be confident, but he lacks self-belief. It is a sadness to be undone by such a simple thing."

The emperor wanted his controller to be immortal and from the region of the Blood Sea, where innovation and industry were revolutionary. The recruitment took him to new places. He met with the Slave King in Gormoth and Kakos Agamos the Liche Lord at Viletri. They were not who he would trust to run his empire. The Viletri elder, Shepherd, was a good diplomat but not an administrator. He liked another Viletri elder, Althea Kane, whom Mannace recommended as intelligent and sensible, but in their first meeting, she did not impress him for the position. He considered giving Milan the role, but though the merchant was gifted at making money, he was not the right person to build the industry and economy. Fitius had been the best fit.

The dilemma required different thinking, and a discussion with Ahmeda helped. They were in bed, and the slender dark elf was sitting on his cock, moving back and forth gently, almost absentmindedly, as they talked.

"What if I worked with the guilds directly? They are, in a sense, immortal. They will persist until they are no longer needed."

Ahmeda raised slightly and moved her hips in a round motion, massaging the tip of the emperor's spear. She settled back onto the length, making him gasp.

"The Guild Masters bicker; they're like children. How would you keep them focused? How would you make them collaborate?"

Running his hands down Ahmeda's side and back up to her breasts, the emperor enjoyed the firmness of the tits in his hands. The high priestess leaned down and kissed him, then moved a breast so that the emperor might suck the nipple. He ran his tongue around it before placing it in his mouth. The dark elf responded with a moan, and she tightened about his spear. He fucked her back with slow strokes, both enjoying the motion.

"You are right; it still needs somebody to be in charge. It will require someone to manage the guilds. So, it comes back again to an individual."

"A strong individual, but not necessarily an administrator."

The emperor pulled Ahmeda close, embracing her and then rolling them both over so that he was on top. Now he fucked her, and she responded by holding his arse and encouraging him deeper. They looked at each other, and he leaned down to kiss her. Before their lips met, he shared a thought.

"I like Althea."

Ahmeda laughed, momentarily breaking their rhythm. He could feel her nails bite into his arse and claw down his back.

"Is that something you should say when we are fucking."

The pain was somehow exhilarating, and he thrust deeper, holding his spear inside her for a breath in time, the way she liked it, relishing the soft flesh of Ahmeda's loins, and his stomach pushed against hers. The emperor relaxed his arms so that the dark elf's breasts were against his chest, her hard nipples caressing his skin. They kissed passionately. Fucking and kissing, Ahmeda's magic pulsated as her senses heightened, with all thought of other things suddenly gone.

PART THREE:

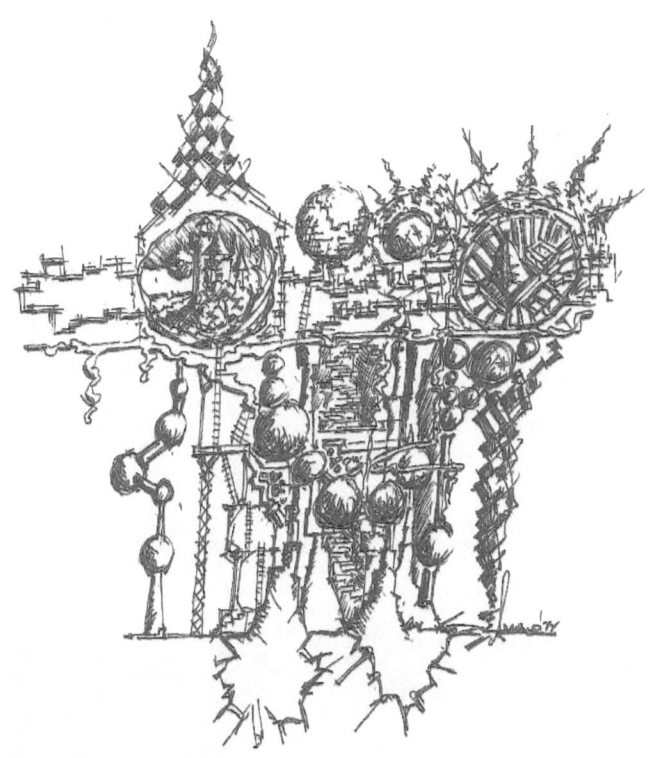

The Rise of the Sorcerers

ALTHEA

The emperor shifted his residence to Viletri, where he seconded Mannace's home in the city and the two villas next to it for his retinue of staff and guards. It was six months since Fitius was found wanting and executed, and in a courtyard at the rear of the property, the leader of Bracadia sat at a small table opposite his new controller, Althea Kane.

"What have you achieved, Althea?"

Even sitting, Althea placed her hands on her broad hips. The stern woman eyed the emperor warily.

"Not a lot, Emperor. Progress will take considerable time."

"Of course. But we have time, Althea, to do what is needed."

Althea relaxed, putting her arms on the table, and leaning towards the Bracadian leader.

"As we agreed, I will focus on the people's wellbeing first. I am passionate about having a quality of life for even the poorest."

The emperor nodded, encouraging Althea to say more.

"Right. As I understand it, there are thirty-nine capitals, plus Angorok. I am working with the Fesadi to build at least one Healer's Temple in each. The larger capitals will require two. Finding and training menders and surgeons will take time, but there will already be healing arts practitioners in most places. The Fesadi are travelling with papers, and I expect all governors to give their support. If they don't, I will need you to clarify that this work is a priority."

"They will do as you ask, Althea. I have proclaimed that your instructions are to be obeyed."

Althea cringed at the word *obeyed*. Then, taking a deep breath, she continued.

"Attached to the temples will be the controller's offices. I am selecting my staff carefully. I want a controller in each capital who can assess what is needed there and arrange the right contracts. Already, the industrial guild masters understand your desire to build manufactories throughout Bracadia."

"They will be welcomed, Althea. What of the other guilds?"

"They will take their trades and wares to the capitals too. But I assume Bracadia has its guilds, and they will need to compete."

"Indeed, that seems a reasonable approach. Milan can help you; he knows more than anyone about business and has contacts throughout Bracadia. What else?"

"SOTA, the Students of The Architect. They are the best placed to recruit navigators. It will take time, but if we create learning centres like the Institute of Technology here at Viletri, it will foster an environment to attract and identify worthy candidates. We can share what we know and study other cultures. SOTA, the magetechs, animators, wizards, and priests, can all teach and recruit. I am working with them to get it started."

For the first time, the emperor leaned back as if he didn't like what he heard.

"I like it all, Althea, except for the priests. I have had bad experiences with religion, where its followers have been problematic. Nevertheless, I have embraced the War God, for it serves the empire's purpose. One religion is enough."

Althea shook her head, not because she was an advocate for religion but because her views were widely known regarding the futility of war.

"Of the gods to pick, why the God of War?"

The question was rhetorical, and Althea continued without waiting for an answer.

"I'll not be building your war machine, Emperor. That can be another's business, and I'm not impressed by flying warships and all that sort of nonsense when the technology can be used in much better ways."

The emperor was curious, "What ways?"

It was a reasonable question, and Althea put her elbow on the small table and a hand on her chin as she contemplated her answer. She watched how Fitius used the flying ships, which seemed silly when better solutions were apparent.

"A ship is just a shape. It makes sense on the sea, but what use is a ship in the sky?"

The emperor was leaning forward. Althea continued.

"I saw the crews of flying ships using ropes to lift stones to add to the constructions in Antigoth. Wouldn't a flying platform with cranes like those at the dock be better suited to the task?"

"Yes, that's a good point."

"And flying ships are used to transport people and goods. Well, you can't fit many people on a ship built for war, but you can fit many people in a building. So why not make a flying building? Or why does it even need to fly, when you can transport it immediately from location to location. Why can't we have buildings that move between cities? It's obvious."

"It is now when you say it, Althea."

The emperor smiled. He liked his new controller.

"I understand your reluctance to support the coming conflict, but I will need our learning centres to include military studies, like the School of War in Viletri. And I must have more navigators for the admiral's fleet. Expansion is part of our plan, and the flying fleet will significantly affect our success. War, where we encounter resistance, will play a factor."

"I'll tell you what's ridiculous; it takes the same navigator to fly a rowboat as a battleship. The admiral can use what he has much better; he needs to replace the little ships with bigger ones. He can talk to the guilds about that himself. I'm not doing it."

"Althea, I will be frank. The navigators are a rare commodity, and we require more to expand. So, I need you to help me with this."

Althea, ordinarily unflappable, was huffing and throwing her hands about as she thought through her response. Aiding the admiral to expand his war fleet was not something she wanted to consider. At last, she calmed and put her hands back on her hips.

"When we find somebody with the skills to be a navigator, we will let them choose their role. It is for the best. No more slave conditioning for those who don't comply or express their free will. Positive changes, Emperor, for the benefit of the people."

"I accept that approach. For the people, Althea."

The turn of conversation reminded Althea of other concerns she had.

"Not all technology is good."

The emperor was curious, turning his head a degree to suggest he needed more explanation.

"Thog is a curse, and Nyx, and Near-dust. It makes people stupid; you can see it on the streets in the poor districts, and it's spreading just as fast behind closed gates in the wealthy neighbourhoods. It scrambles the brain and makes good people do bad things. Ban such concoctions, Emperor, before its darkness spreads beyond reach."

The emperor had not seen evidence of such things, but he nodded as if knowing. Althea moved quickly on.

"And the damned mollies. There are only a few in the Madlands and at Gormoth, plus the half-castes at The Ark. They use dark arts and science to take your mind away and mock the human form. I don't want a part in spreading that foolishness."

The emperor nodded, though his eyes possessed a gleam that Althea did not trust. The leader suddenly looked up from his thinking as Althea prodded him with a finger. He had never been touched uninvited before.

"I know that look. The mole men will only take you down a dark path."

"That is narrow thinking, Althea. You can do better."

"I know where the shadow is cast."

The emperor stared at his controller, who defiantly crossed her arms.

"I inquired about the mole men when I was in Gormoth. Did you know that as a race, they call themselves the Dragu and their alchemy is as old as the Ancients? It seems that what they can do to the body and mind might interest a healer. Are you not a healer, Althea?"

"Did you see the slaves at Gormoth, the mollies take away their humanity and mutate their bodies? It is cruelty and horror. I'll not abide by their nonsense."

"I have witnessed your Fesadi surgeons take away a man's leg."

Althea looked sideways at the emperor, knowing it was not a fair example. But, as a privilege of rank, the emperor claimed the last word."

"I am observing that the ways of the Dragu, like those of the Fesadi, might be misconstrued. Have you investigated if their potions might have other uses? Uses you might approve of. Never close your mind to possibilities; turn the adverse to your advantage where you can. If you don't like what you see, recast the Dragu in an image that pleases you, or take their secrets and be done with them. It's up to you. You are an intelligent and powerful woman, Althea, so act like it."

It was not a finger, but Althea nonetheless felt as if the emperor poked her, prodding where it hurt the most.

"Hmmm."

CHURLAMEN

Demmal stood at the hill's crest to see across the border from Churlamen into Amon Murn. A chill wind blew from the west, while the sun in the northern sky was hot against his face. The war priest was dressed like those around him, in a steel breastplate over a leather shirt and studded leather pants. His cloak was deer hide and wolf fur, wrapping around his body as protection from the cold weather. On the back of his hands and face were tattoos of runes and complex shapes to safeguard against other things.

Ahead, the hill sank into a swampy marshland and a great plain beyond that. Mountains were barely noticeable on the horizon. To Demmal's left and right, a long line of men stood vigil along the crest, surveying the same scene. Behind them, a horde of undead waited while others of their kind, skeletal and stinking of death, shambled up the long slope. Keepers and their guards, all dressed in colourful robes, starkly contrasted with the decay and tatters around them. One keeper waved his bone staff, and as he chanted, a corpse lifted itself from the ground, shoving aside the partially covering dirt. The skeleton was bleached bones, with dirty stretched skin across its chest and face. The eyes were gone, but the empty sockets now glowed with a dull, blue light.

Further back, as far as Demmal could see, other keepers, with their undead packs, made their way to the same place. Not all undead were once human; giant and bestial shapes were amongst them. There were groups of the War God's followers, too, like the warriors already with Demmal.

Once together on the hill, the collection of men and undead were a formidable host.

A spectral form coalesced in front of Demmal, looking across at Amon Murn, then turning to face the war priest.

"Wait here. It will take time to gather the dead."

The spectre quickly faded, leaving Demmal frustrated, with questions not asked or answered. Then, shaking his head, he turned to the man on his right.

"Spread the word to make camp. Get Hallard's men to scout the marsh; we need to know the best paths to cross. Tell Rulf to organise foragers."

The man immediately moved to relay Demmal's instructions. Another man to Demmal's left, dressed in purple robes decorated with ivory trinkets, leaned on a plain staff crafted from a long, narrow bone. His beard was white, though he bore the physique of a young man. Demmal tapped his knuckles to the staff to ensure he had the man's attention.

"Make your defences along the ridge to protect the living. The Devoted and the keepers will camp together. If the gifted arrive, bring them to me, I need the vision of what lies ahead."

When the man did not move, Demmal continued with an explanation.

"Who knows how long we will camp here? If we must wait for every corpse across Xu, Daras, the Dead Wastes, and Churlamen to join us, we will be here past the new moon, perhaps the one after."

Finally, the man spoke, his voice gentle but deep.

"When will the Belarch and Churgwarthos arrive?"

"The Belarch, soon I hope, we need them if the Hell-spawn assail us with their full strength. I do not expect Churgwarthos until he is needed, or we reach Regnorak. Before you ask, the High Keeper is another who has not shared her plans. For now, we have what you see."

"It will be cold up here at night."

"But at least we will see an enemy coming."

"I will gather the others. Then, we will set defences."

Demmal shrugged, if only to satisfy himself that there was little to do but wait. He called out to those not already involved in preparations, "Make camp. Be vigilant. The God of War watches."

It was only a few days before the first of the Belarch arrived. The three young sorcerers, accompanied by six Dragu, set up their camp at the foot of the hill amongst the standing undead. When Demmal descended the slope to visit them, it was at a time when the Dragu were administering their concoctions that would gradually bolster the Belarch's physique. Demmal experienced the torturous treatment himself, making an unpleasant memory. There was no choice but to wait until the Dragu finished and their patients recovered. Finally, after most of the day passed, one of the Belarch stood and led Demmal aside from the shady canopy to give him instruction.

"You will stay camped here until the third full moon."

The young man's voice was far deeper and more commanding than his age. Demmal, a fearless champion of his God, who commanded the Devoted, and was general of the undead horde, felt a chill up his spine and uneasiness upon his soul. While knowing the Belarch were in a fledgling form, reborn and gradually regaining their power - already they were terrifying and formidable, perhaps more so because their host forms were so deceiving.

"And then where will we go?"

"We will cross Amon Murn, where that nation's dead will also rise to serve."

"And when we have amassed all the dead that we can, what then?"

The Belarch glared at Demmal, but rather than answer his question, the young man turned away and strode back to re-join his companions. He seated himself next to them, and like the others, the Belarch rubbed his arms and legs as if soothing away some aching pain or discomfort.

He stood amongst the undead, contemplating the Belarch's instruction. In a rare respite, when the wind died away, Demmal felt suffocated by the pervasive stench of mould and rot. Uncomfortable and displeased with his orders, Demmal pushed past the skeletons to make his way back to the ridge.

Beyond the marsh, a demon host appeared during the night, settling over a large area of the plains. When Demmal compared it to the growing horde behind him, the demon host was perhaps half the size but included two enormous creatures he assumed were the generals. It was fortunate that Demmal kept his army hidden behind the ridge.

In the daylight, the demons mainly rested, though small groups roamed. A cluster of flyers was getting dangerously close to the range where Demmal's forces hid. Eventually, they roamed near enough that Demmal sent runners with instructions for the commanders to prepare their troops and to summon the Belarch. When the Belarch arrived and observed the scene, one of them moved over the ridge and, for reasons it did not share, cast a spell at the flyers as they swooped along the hillside. There was a series of sharp snapping sounds, and the demons fell from the sky, landing heavily and screeching.

On the plains, the sleeping demon host came to life. One of the generals, a bulbous giant, waved its arms, and its thunderous hooting carried the great distance on the wind to where Demmal watched. In response to the general's call, dark creatures scurried towards the hill. Some already entered the marsh at its base, wading, or scampering where they could find dryer ground.

The other demonic general, also gigantic but serpent-like, lifted itself so that its sleek body reached skyward, not stopping until it stood impossibly tall, like a staff, with only the tip of its tail remaining grounded. Then, from a reptilian head, green light rays emanated towards the Belarch caster. All three Belarch sorcerers raised their hands, and an invisible barrier deflected the beams down the slope, where the ground exploded in a spectacular shower of debris.

Almost too late, Demmal noticed movement in the tall grass halfway up the hill. Sleek creatures were hugging the ground, speedily ascending the incline. With a thunderous roar to draw attention, Demmal shouted for the undead to top the crest and charge down the other side. Immediately, the keepers spurred their flock into action, and skeletal soldiers charged past the Devoted, descending the slope into Amon Murn. The animated dead were driven by the keepers' chanting, sprinting and leaping down the hill, quickly engaging with Hell-spawn that rose out of the grass. The first ranks of skeletons drowned in a slithering sea of dark, slippery shapes, like a tidal wave of enormous eels, enveloping and crushing their prey, biting, and snapping bone. At first, the creatures' momentum continued their surge up the slope, but the attack was thwarted by thousands of undead swarming over the hilltop, hacking and bashing with their improvised weapons. With the increasing press of numbers, the demon forerunners recoiled downhill, some crushed underfoot.

Once committed to an attack, Demmal could not restrain the horde from continuing its charge down the slope and into the marsh. Fighting was everywhere. Neither the undead nor demons possessed any concept of strategy, driven by more primal instincts to kill or feed. At the ridgeline, the Devoted kept vigil while the keepers chanted to sustain the fury of the undead. Alongside them, the Belarch were content to observe and be wards against diabolic magic.

As the battle pushed onward from the marsh onto the plains, it was clear that the undead horde was ascendent over the less numerous enemy. The Snake general, sensing defeat, cast a final light blast before lowering itself and quickly retreating. Its bulbous counterpart bellowed defiantly but soon followed. In their wake, the demon thralls defended fanatically, and as dusk brought its shadow over the land, followed by the blanket of night, the fighting continued, desperate and fierce.

From the ridge, Demmal patiently watched. The faint blue glow of necromancy pinpointed his troop's movements in the darkness. By their erratic actions, he could tell they were chasing the last of their foes.

By dawn, the demons were destroyed or gone, and the skeleton horde was scattered. The undead were again dormant, and the keepers with their guards moved down the hill to organise them. The Devoted did not wait for Demmal's order, moving back to their camps, not needed in the fight or retrieval. Scanning behind him into the lands of Churlamen, Demmal could see a constant procession of keepers and their undead flocks arriving. From the direction of the capital, a train of larger skeletal forms approached: elephants. He had seen them before their deaths when the demons first appeared. They were part of the capital garrison, which perhaps meant that Churgwarthos might soon make his appearance.

COLOSSUS

Fire and billowing smoke rose from many districts of the city of Colossus, but rather than commiserating the destruction, the orcs and goblins that lived there were celebrating their triumph. For a second time, the might of the abyss laid its assault upon the capital of the Wengo. But again, the orcs were victorious. When the demons swarmed through the mountain passes, the Wengo harassed them, luring the Hell-spawn into traps or ambushing them under the shadow cloaks of the allied Iron Jaw. Knowing the beasts' fear of water, engineers broke clay dams set back in the valleys, drowning many of the creatures. Even one of the greater beasts perished in the deluge. Four more of the demon generals and a great host of their soldiers lay dead in the streets of Colossus, strewn amongst the bodies of brave orc defenders. It was a brawl on an epic scale. The colossi that defended the city all carried wounds from claws and bites and the magic of the powerful generals, but none perished. All knew the importance of the colossi's survival, who could not breed, unlike the prolific orcs and goblins. The Champions Stadium, the much-honoured showpiece of the metropolis, was intact. There was indeed much to celebrate.

During the last hour of the battle, ten flying ships from Angorok came to their assistance, helping dispatch one of the generals and clear the skies. Not long after, as the city's clean-up began, Mannace paid a personal visit to the chief of Colossus. Amongst the Wengo chief's entourage were an orc war priest, still in his war rig, and a shaman of the Iron Jaw, reminders that the orcs were now a united tribe.

"Congratulations on your victory, Urglis. Nobody has defeated a demon army with five generals before."

"Orcs smart. Colossi orc friends strong."

Urglis, like all Wengo Chiefs, was a large orc, heavily muscled and with a long jaw that slurred his speech. After the battle, he was still in his bloodied armour, and his exhaustion from the fighting further hampered his words. Mannace paused to make sure he was interpreting the chief correctly.

"The Wengo are mighty and clever warriors. We honour our alliance."

"No alliance, Mannace. Orcs united. North gone. South gone. Wengo strong. Urglis, no alliance. Other chiefs, no alliance."

"Yes, the Wengo are strong, and Angorok is strong too. Together, Urglis, we can take the North. First, we will purge the demons and march into Amon Murn. Then, we will take Regnorak, as we planned."

"Wengo strong in mountains. Not care Amon Murn. Orcs no need die for Mannace."

Mannace was taken aback by the chief's bluntness. In truth, many Wengo had perished under his military command, and as he contemplated their sacrifice, Mannace could not think of a justification for such large-scale losses. He was not to blame, though, for how the Age ended. That was the Mad King's doing.

"The war between North and South ended badly for everyone. We all have suffered, victims of the Mad King's treachery. The colossi are of the South. They are needed in the conflict to come."

"King friend to Wengo. Colossi, not mine command. Not your's command. Colossi follow king. He gone. Colossi, choose stay."

The chief's nostrils flared.

"No more talk. Mannace go."

When Mannace made no effort to move and looked like he might resume the conversation, the chief's agitation peaked, and he growled through his teeth and tusks.

"Wengo used. No more. Wengo smart. Look after Wengo. Mannace, go!"

As Mannace reluctantly departed aboard his flagship, *The Bracadian*, he watched sea-borne vessels returning to the city's harbour. Amongst them were trading ships of types he recognised from the Blood Sea and Bracadia. The Wengo were allied with those countries, which meant that the rejection he was shown was not political. It was personal. Urglis was rejecting ties with *him*. It annoyed Mannace that the chief of Colossus might hold him accountable for the peril that befell the land.

Angorok was secured, and the imperial divisions brought relief and order to the remnants of bordering nations. Those lands on the eastern coast, parts of the Young Cities, Kampatan, Churos, Anglan and Ulo, retained a semblance of their governments. Still, they welcomed the Bracadian soldiers and embraced the empire as protector. However, the goblin nation of Greshnak suffered less at the hands of the demons by hiding underground. Luring the goblins into the open or securing a meeting with their council of chiefs proved impossible.

To the west of Angorok, Granash was an example of how the demons could infiltrate underground when motivated to do so. That orc nation was obliterated, as were the bordering human lands of Turbul and The Gap. Demon armies frequently traversed these regions, and it was here that Mannace focused his attention. More than one million troops cleared lower Turbul of nuisance swarms, and now they waited for a more prominent host to arrive. It was not long before Brula scouts reported a legion of the abyss approaching from Makhon, descending through The Gap, that would soon cross their path in Turbul. Reports suggested the rampaging Hell-spawn would equal or better the Bracadian's number. Mannace rushed reinforcements to assist.

With the blessed ammunition successfully used in battle at the city of Colossus, Admiral Jeylan Staronis was ready to confront the demon generals. He realised that half measures would not suffice, and his captains understood what to expect and do. The fleet climbed skyward, high over the Bracadian position so that the long patchwork of trenches and palisades far below looked like scratch marks made by some great dragon across the earth.

When demons appeared, they were a blackness, enveloping the greens and browns of the landscape like a great flood. As the surge drew closer to the Bracadian earthworks, its pace hastened, which Staronis expected was the flyers launching their attack. Multiple dots of colour against the black told him the artillery was at work. Then, as the black collided with the defences, the lines of trenches were lit with white musket and cannon fire. It was too early for the flying fleet to reveal themselves, and the admiral trusted that the prepared Bracadians would not be overwhelmed. His heart was racing.

It was time. The fleet quickly descended on the admiral's signal. Forming into lines, the ships dived toward the demon generals, who were easily distinguishable by their immense size. As the vessels drew closer, they passed the first of the flying demons, many of which were more significant than the bat-winged creatures they usually fought. Some of these were monstrous, all teeth and claws. One that passed by Staronis' windows was serpent-like, with a head like a cock, its single eye staring at him through the glass. His flagship suddenly jolted as it collided with a large cluster of the enemy, disappearing for a moment into the airborne swarm. Once on the other side, the admiral heard the scuttling and screeching of creatures that attached themselves to the hull, and one slid across his window before flapping away. At the captain's order, the admiral's ship turned, shuddering as it delivered its first broadside. Then, as the craft swung around to bring its other guns to bear, Staronis caught a glimpse of the horrific target, an impossibly long monster with insect-like legs down its side. The creature lifted its fore section to reveal armoured plates on its underbelly. They were an inadequate shield, full of holes, and some of the creature's legs were missing. Its roar reverberated through the ship, and there was a cracking of wood as something large impacted the vessel's underbelly. The view was quickly gone, and the ship again shuddered as the second broadside found its target.

Abruptly transported to be well above the battle, and while looking anxiously down on the chaos, Staronis could hear fighting. He assumed the commotion was flyers still clinging to the ship, engaging with the crew. Out his window, other Class A ships were appearing close by. Staronis turned to those behind him.

"Captain, turn so we can see the others."

As the captain worked with the navigator, the ship wheeled allowing Staronis to check that the other ships were safe. Only one appeared damaged, with its rear section crushed and steam escaping in a great cloud.

Tilting to give a better view of the Class B vessels, Staronis watched them ascend quickly after delivering their salvos. They were hard-pressed, some covered in demons and others with swarms in pursuit. At the edge of his vision, two ships were still near the ground. One became lost to the blackness that consumed it, while the other exploded in a flash of red, with a boom he could hear from his lofty vantage.

"Order all marines on deck. Assist the Class B's when they arrive."

It was too early to know if their tactic was successful, though Staronis was optimistic.

"Well-executed gentlemen. Captain, I want confirmation that the targets were destroyed."

"Yes, Admiral."

The emperor visited Angorok, and after eating a succulent lunch prepared by Jayne Azaryn, he and Mannace were soon bent over the map table in the war room, discussing how the campaign to secure the North progressed.

The emperor circled a large area with his hand, where there was a significant collection of figurines depicting demonic forces.

"What is this region, and why is it important?"

Mannace shifted around the table to be next to the emperor. He used a long rod to point as he talked.

"These were once the nations of Eros, May, Sarville, and Markhon. Strategically they are not important, except that the demons are there, and we will purge them before they roam further south. Once these lands are secured, it leaves only The Hand and Adras. The Brula reported that Adras is mostly untouched by the demons, and many refugees from other lands gather there."

The emperor was aware of Adras.

"The navy from the Eastern Colonies is aiding the people of Adras to migrate. Many of those displaced are making their homes amongst the islands of the Scurry. Althea is supplying them."

Mannace nodded.

The Hand of Fengal was an immense forest that took up a large map section. Both men studied it now. There was only one figure over it, which was in the likeness of Eya, the Spider Mother. Mannace shared his analysis.

"The forest was home to the elves of The Hand, the spiders, and the Fen. We are certain the elves are gone, and the Fen may be destroyed. The Fen are of no consequence."

"What do you mean by *no consequence*?"

Mannace looked up from the table to meet the emperor's gaze.

"They are a race that keeps to themselves. If they were gone, they would not be missed."

The emperor frowned, though he kept his thoughts private.

"And what of Eya and the spiders?"

"Eya betrayed the Southern Alliance when she attacked the elves of The Hand and the Alani. However, since the demons' arrival, she has been fighting them, as we all have. Several armies of Hell-spawn entered the forest, never to re-emerge. It is not her purpose, but by defeating that foe, she protects Adras. We can deal with Eya later."

The emperor was shaking his head.

"Is dealing with the Spider Mother not of utmost importance, Mannace? You are taking a great risk to leave Eya unchecked."

Mannace was direct, "I can't afford to make Eya my foremost enemy."

When the emperor raised his eyebrows, Mannace explained.

"Eya is focused on killing elves. Through the Ways, her hunters strike wherever the elves congregate. We have little defence against it, and the elves have fled. If we send our armies into the forest, I know she will send her hunters to seek out our generals. We are not ready for that."

"So, you would forgive the execution of the elves?"

"No! But I don't have the means to protect against Eya's assassins, nor the forces to fight her in her domain. So, I will leave her and The Hand until I have defeated the demons. Eya can bloody wait!"

Both men were quiet for some time, returning to staring at the figures on the table. Mannace broke the silence.

"What do you see, Emperor? What advice do you have?"

The emperor looked over the map and took his time before responding. He was across the table from Mannace when he looked up to address him.

"My advice is not what you want to hear, Mannace. My guidance is to leave the North and let it be what it is; a disruption of powers, fates, and struggles with no end. The North will not be tamed. You will never have peace here as you seek it."

Now Mannace was shaking his head.

"I will solve the problem of the North. When starting any endeavour, always tackle the toughest parts first. If you can't be successful with them, what is the point of the rest of the work."

Mannace's voice remained calm, bringing his thoughts into a perspective the emperor would appreciate.

"You want to control all lands and for Bracadia to be omnipotent. The campaign begins in the North. It is the key to unlocking all other conquests."

The emperor shrugged rather than respond. Then, switching focus back to the conflict in front of them, he shared another piece of advice.

"It is unwise to ignore the Fen. Understanding their fate, or what they know, is important. They may be your eyes in the forest."

Before Mannace could respond, Elderlin appeared at the doorway, waving for them to follow him. They did so, arriving at a balcony overlooking the Temple of Healing and other buildings fitted out to treat the wounded. Flying ships descended on a square where they unloaded injured soldiers. Mannace called out to marines on board a vessel that hovered nearby.

"Did we defeat the demons?"

"Aye, Marshall. It was a victory of sorts, bought at a high cost."

Mannace could see what the marine meant. As the leader paid closer attention, he saw that even those unwounded men appeared tired and battered. Across the decks of the ships that were close, injured soldiers lay in stretchers, or perched up against the railings, crowded for space. Guild healers and Fesadi menders moved amongst them, applying their skills. On the ground, stretcher-bearers were running between the ships and buildings, and helpers arrived from nearby districts. From the different orders, priests were also rallying to assist the dying.

Claudius stepped onto the balcony, Jayne behind him, checking that the leaders were safe. Claudius' jaw dropped as he watched the horrific procession of the wounded.

"Glory to Bracadia. Welcome back to our heroes," he bellowed. He held his fist out, a gesture returned by the marines and some of the wounded that heard him.

THE SORCERERS

Demmal and his host stopped at the desolate city of Egerth in Amon Murn. It was once a significant metropolis until the demons devoured it. Now the keepers were busy scouring the districts and raising the murdered population to their service. It would take time to uncover and raise hundreds of thousands of recruits.

Churgwarthos arrived with his horde under the cover of a summoned darkness. Within the sorcerous shroud, the undead grew in awareness, becoming more like their former selves, alert, and observant. Unfortunately, Demmal was unable to confer with the sorcerer, who privately held counsel with the Belarch. The undead that made up his army appeared ancient and with great variety; creatures and types of troops born of different millennia. There were spectres and phantoms amongst them and other ethereal beings. To Demmal, it seemed a ghastlier collection of nightmare creatures than the cursed Hell-spawn they fought. The following night, Churgwarthos departed Egerth, taking his army and much of Demmal's horde with him.

Two days later, the High Keeper arrived. She brought reinforcements, including the remaining keepers, their colourful guards, and the multitude of skeletons they collected from the ransacked lands. Her legion of mummies raised from the tombs of the Dead Wastes assumed pride of place as her guards, while giant vultures circled high above the immense hoard. More of the Devoted arrived with them, reporting to Demmal for new orders.

The High Keeper took up residence in an abandoned temple, and the next day she summoned Demmal to the location. Grengal was human-like, tall and feminine, though her greyish skin seemed stretched and rubbery, with transparency that showed through to sinew and flesh. She was hairless, naked, and though her form was strangely toned and elegant, it emanated a stench of rot. To Demmal, who stood before her, the smell was overpowering, and it took his entire constitution not to choke and vomit. Flies buzzed about her.

"Demmal, is your War God with us?"

"Yes, Keeper."

Demmal raised his arms and let the War God's presence flow into him and through the room. The handful of keepers and devoted gathered in the great chamber felt the energy surging around them, and some of the Devoted raised their arms to add their prayer to the blessing. Grengal appeared to greedily soak the energy in, then throwing her arms wide, a swarm of flies emanated from the pits of her arms, expanding, and swarming to consume the room. Demmal could not stay a moment longer and retreated as best he could with such poor vision. Exiting to the street, he looked back to see a cloud of flies pour through the temple exits and windows, spreading out to permeate the city and settle everywhere upon the undead. Demmal watched one land on a zombie standing idly next to him, burrowing into its decaying flesh. He did not understand or need to know the nature of such horrific witchery.

An undead host gathered outside the walls of Regnorak. As vast as the city was, the horde encompassed all the surrounding land. Vestig estimated possibly tens of millions of the resurrected soldiers and civilians besieging the capital. Along the sections of the wall where there were not enough priests to defend, ghosts and other spectral things were already inside the defence, lurking amongst the ruins. At the western gate, sorcerous darkness shrouded the enemy. He knew this to be the army of Churlamen and its sorcerer, Churgwarthos. Therefore, he was not surprised when a gathering of young wizards revealed themselves at the entrance where he waited.

On the battlements alongside Vestig were the casters of the Wurn, and below, ready to burst through the gates if needed, were the elite Hunga led by Frain.

Further back, colossi collected, and Vestig was grateful for their show of support. Likewise, wyverns ascended above the city, with the few that dived low adding their significant presence. All other soldiers and priests manned the towering walls. Then, at Vestig's command, The speaker, Reygan, called out to those confronting them.

"Wizards of Churlamen, we welcome our ancient allies and applaud your show of strength."

Reygan extended his hands towards Vestig, who stood upon a chair so that he was clearly visible above the wall's crenulations.

"Vestig Gozer, Effate and Warlord of Amon Murn, gives his blessing to yourselves and your hoard."

With no response and having no patience, Vestig yelled down in his gravelly voice.

"Will you fight or talk?"

One of the young wizards called back, "Open your gates. First, we will talk, and then we will decide if we fight."

Vestig ordered the gates opened. As they swung outwards and the portcullis rose, Vestig knew this would be the wizards' first glance at the colossi that waited beyond. The inspiring creatures would make any attacker think twice about their plans. The thought made the efate grin as he descended to the ground and exited the entrance. Frain strode forward to join him, so the two warriors confronted the horde alone.

"Tell your sorcerer that the Efate of Amon Murn will speak with him."

A young wizard smiled and came forward. His eyes glowed blue, similar to the undead horde surrounding them. The mesmerising gaze was like Vestig remembered when he met Churgwarthos at the time of the Sleeper's awakening.

"I am the sorcerer, Vestig. I am regenerated, as are the Belarch. Do you understand so little?"

The insult made Vestig sure of the claim; who else would dare curse him in such an off-hand way? This bold youngster was indeed Churgwathos incarnate.

"So, you were defeated then. Is that why you were not at the battle on the Long?"

"Do I look defeated, Vestig? Look about Regnorak. Are you not surrounded by my horde?"

Frain could not restrain himself.

"You look like a boy. And these others are children. Your horde …"

Vestig cut the giant short by raising his hand, and then he removed his helmet so that he might match the sorcerer's stare.

"Why are you here?"

"Because the North belongs to the dead and the darkness. It is no longer a place for mortal men. See what lies outside your walls; death, of the type that will devour you."

"So what! Undead or demons. It is much the same thing!"

There was a silence that Vestig eventually filled.

"Will you fight us?"

In the ensuing quiet, Vestig noticed Churgwarthos look past him at the colossi and up at the wyverns now circling lower. With its high walls, Regnorak would not be an easy conquest. Vestig could see the sorcerer rolling all those thoughts over in his mind.

"Your army will break upon Regnorak's walls."

"Stay within your walls then, Vestig. These lands outside your gates are forbidden; enter them, and I will put darkness upon Regnorak and cast you into the void."

"If you were able, you would have done it already."

"As your giant companion so cleverly put it, I am but a child, Vestig. What harm can a child do? That will change when you next see me. From now, you are Efate of Regnorak and no more."

Like the sorcerer, Vestig had his limitations. If he were to successfully attack Churgwarthos' army, he would need the colossi and wyverns to lead the assault, but they acted of their own will and were not his to command. The truth of it was that Regnorak was currently the extent of his control anyway. It was a humbling point, but Vestig's pragmatism was more significant than his pride. The Efate signalled to Frain, and they both walked away. The city gates closed as they passed, the steel portcullis slamming into place. Vestig was grinning again.

"Let Mannace deal with Churgwarthos. We are better off within these walls."

Frain laughed.

"Where did the demons go? Perhaps Churgwarthos will take care of them too. He seemed very helpful."

Now Vestig laughed at the sarcasm, though the gravel in his voice confused the chuckle with something much more sinister.

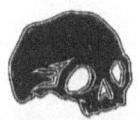

Grengal's horde doubled as it passed through the ruined cities of Juwon and Juwal on its trek across Amon Murn. The terrible slaughter that occurred there a decade ago at the hands of the demons was reaping a reward now as the city's skeletons rose to the keeper's call, following them in an impossibly long procession. After weeks of travelling, the host of skeletal soldiers was many times its original size. Along the journey, Demmal confronted two more demon armies, crushing them, and three of the defeated demon generals now marched alongside the undead. They were not dead themselves, nor wholly alive. Instead, they were half-dead, sustained by Grengal's diabolic magic, shambling and dazed, a tortured shadow of their former selves. Each carried the same stench as their new mistress, and their tormented bodies were infested with flies and maggots.

Once Amon Murn was cleansed and harvested of its dead, the destination of Imbor was within easy reach. At Imbor, crumbled ruins of temples on the slope above where the city once stood were a sad reminder of its former prestige. Where there had once been a town was a massive hole, impossibly deep, and a portal into the abyss. Demons scuttled about the pit, and a general, one of the fantastic beasts of Hell, presided over it. As Grengal's horde approached from all sides, the beast lifted itself on massive wings so that it hovered and looked down on its foe. A gigantic third eye on its broad chest pulsed white then red, in time with the creature's heart. Grengal sent her swarms of flies against it, but in a wave of force, her spell was blown aside, and skeletons caught in the blast disintegrated. The extinguished undead became dust on a hissing wind that lashed Grengal and her army. Then, at the magnificent beast's summons, flying demons swarmed from the abyss and blanketed nearby undead with overwhelming numbers and unbridled fury. All around the pit entrance and for a great distance, the two forces wrestled, fearless and ferocious. Beyond that, with most of her horde intact, Grengal retreated.

Fearing further retribution, the keepers pushed the horde west towards the Makhon, where Churgwarthos and his army were waiting.

A RECKONING

The emperor stood back to watch Mannace interrogate the emissaries gathered in the war room. As the marshall looked over his papers, Admiral Staronis appeared out of an adjacent chamber, joining the emperor. Soon after, Ahmeda entered the room, seating herself to one side, seemingly disinterested in the proceedings.

The first emissary to speak was one of Milan's men, Evatus, a well-dressed merchant who held his nose high, which gave the impression that he was looking down on those about him.

"Marshall, the guild master instructed me to give an account of our trade with the North. First, I must say that the merchant's guild has always maintained neutrality in politics and conflict. I will keep my report at a high level, which I believe will cover what you need to know."

The man paused, and Mannace nodded for him to continue.

"Firstly, the nation of Kandor that occupies a large island north of Amon Murn is untouched by the conflict with the demons and has swelled in population with refugees from the North. The Twin Cities from the mainland migrated from Amon Murn to Kandor early in the conflict and re-established their base and government there. Between Kandor and the Twin Cities, they have a significant army and navy, at least four hundred ships, some with iron sides."

Again, the man paused until Mannace indicated for him to go on.

"Some trade passes through Regnorak, but most merchants avoid contact with the mainland. Likewise, during the summer and autumn, there is river trade to Altair, another nation brimming with troops and civilians fleeing from Amon Murn. A lot of giants there, I am told."

Almost forgetting, the merchant added a point he knew Mannace would find interesting.

"Since fleeing the dwarves, ships from the Havens use Regnorak as a base, and other southerners can be found there too, including colossi. Apparently, old animosities were put aside when the demons invaded the North. I have heard it said that they share a common interest to survive."

"What else!?" Mannace hurried the conversation on.

"There is some export to Adras and The Scurry, but they are a desperate lot, more likely to seek passage than trade; many migrate to better lands. The city of Colossus off the Wengo coast is a richer port. I believe that you already have a good understanding of that location and the ones south of there."

"And ..."

"And I don't have other information, Marshall. Some of the traders in the North are not from familiar lands. I have not spoken to any."

Mannace's nostrils flared, clearly exasperated.

"Evatus, I expect details of the military capability at Regnorak, and I want to know all about these foreign traders. Everything! If you are Milan's man, you will make it your business to have that information back to me before the next cycle. Damn your neutrality, we are at bloody war, and your trade aids our enemy. Best you prove good at your spying. Else you are more harm than help."

The merchant seemed startled to have such a burden placed upon him, but he bowed and withdrew. Then, wasting no time, Mannace nodded towards the captain of his flagship. It was the only flying vessel still under his direct command.

"Captain, what news?"

"Sir, my reports for Eros, Sarville, and May regions are unchanged. Three demon armies remain. They are most certainly combining into a single host. It's hard to get close, but at least three million spawns, eight confirmed generals, possibly others."

Another captain stepped forward, who once reported to Mannace but was now one of the admiral's men.

"Sir, bands of undead appear in Markhon. There is a darkness over the border to Amon Murn - it could be disguising other troop movements."

Mannace glared at the admiral, as the presence of undead was new information.

"I have only just received this news myself, Mannace. I have sent ships to investigate and to travel further east. We should know what this darkness is soon enough."

"I know what it bloody is, Jeylan. It's vengeance. It's bloody Churgwarthos, and I'll bet he's heading for Adash. He'll want Render's head on a spear and skew the rest of us for good measure."

"Who is Churgwarthos?"

Mannace put his hands on his hips and drew a deep breath.

"From the time of the Ancients, a sorcerer. He ruled over Churlamen, and he was defeated by Render and the elves when the Sleeper awakened."

"Render will defeat him again then. The Muster will help him."

"The elves who helped Render have gone, Jeylan; they are all travelling north. Churgwarthos is powerful, with magic that destroys whole cities. The Muster may not be enough, and Churgwarthos will have allies too. Render must be warned."

Jaylan Staronis looked away from Mannace toward the emperor.

"These lands will be the death of us. Let the North have the North."

The Admiral did not get the support he wanted from the ruler; his gaze met with a blank stare. Sighing deeply, Staronis turned back to the emissaries.

"Any other surprises?"

A ranger stepped forward. He was a lean man with a stern disposition.

"We could not find the Fen, Admiral, Marshall, but we did discover demons in the forest. They were dormant, like they were sleeping. We were lucky not to be ambushed and dared not delve deeper. The forest of The Hand might be full of spawn."

Mannace felt the pressure upon his shoulders, bearing him down. He dreaded to ask, "Dormant, like when they are controlled, like when the Eternal cast their prayers?"

"Yes, Sir."

The emperor moved to be closer. Decisively, he drew a deep breath and turned to his leaders.

"Mannace, this war is not what you thought it was."

The tension was palpable.

"Will you keep to your word, Emperor?"

"You have the resources of Bracadia at your command. However, the ultimate goal is not to take the North but to conquer all lands and unite them. We have time, Mannace. Perhaps this moment is not ours."

Mannace huffed, clearly in turmoil over his course of action. Turning away from his colleagues, the big man leaned over an armchair, gripping the back of it until his knuckles went white. Then, after several deep breaths and stretching to relieve his tension, he turned to face the admiral and emperor.

"It is premature to decide if we will stay and fight or if we will leave the North. While we wait for scouts to bring more information, preparations for both possibilities will commence. We can act earlier if the situation escalates."

The marshall met the emperor's gaze. They both held expectations of the other that would be tested by what happened next. Mannace did not like the sense of being judged.

"We have faced the impossible many times, Emperor. Yet, we are still here."

"Why have the dark elves not answered the summons to travel North?"

Render did not typically interrogate Jaal, but he tried to understand the reasoning behind the elf's plan.

"I do not sense any summons. It is the Alani and Fogmir elves that answer the call. Dekon is still at Angorok, and so are other dark elf priests. Whoever welcomes the elves north, those of the shadow are not on the invite list."

Render's scowl showed he was unconvinced, so Jaal continued.

"Jayne Azaryn and Ahmeda are others who have stayed. Ahmeda will know more. Render, I don't even know what a summons would feel like."

"And no dark elf has been hunted by Eya?"

"No. It would never happen."

"Why is that? Why are the dark elves immune to her wrath?"

"There is an order to things, Render. Eya understands that, and the dark elves know it. I cannot share more than that, but it is why I can travel safely to The Hand."

"And you think Eya will welcome you, and aid me against Churgwarthos, as the elves did? How would she do that when the Alani already sealed access to the Ways?"

"Eya is more familiar with the Ways than the Alani. Never underestimate her, Render."

Jaal reached up and tapped on a small cage sitting on a shelf. The large spider trapped inside moved, raising its forelegs, and silently staring at the dark elf. There were two other cages around the hall that Jaal placed there. Elsewhere, spiders and their webs abounded about the citadel of Adash. They were all the Spider Mother's agents.

"Care for the spiders, Render. These eyes are how Eya will know when to act. She has been watching and will already expect my arrival at The Hand. Be certain she has forewarning of what I will ask. If I am right that she will aid us, she will be ready when Churgwarthos comes."

"How can you be certain, Jaal, of your plan and Eya's cooperation? I trust you, but I'll not put my fate entirely in Eya's hands. Not while I still breathe. Don't underestimate me, Jaal."

Jaal shrugged, "Make your contingencies then. Nothing is ever a certainty, Render."

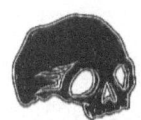

Symin appeared in the teleportation chamber at Angorok. It was a particular room set aside for just him as a safe place to travel. Immediately, the student was hurried by Elderlin to see Mannace, who was inspecting the corpse of a cat-like demon. A priest struggled to hold the dead weight upright and let it drop to the ground when Mannace turned away to face his visitor.

"Symin, what news of Morgan and the dwarves?"

Symin looked like he might start his sentence, but his eyes closed, and he snorted. Finally, words poured out in a great flood of information on his fourth attempt.

"Safe. We are safe. Morgan says the dwarves are winning. With the staff. They are winning with the staff. Because they have it. Expelled the demons. Not all of them. Many of them. He says to *watch out*. Watch the Rift. Morgan says to watch it. The Rift. Watch the demons."

Once said, Symin disappeared. Mannace could only assume he returned to Morgan's side or at least to a location within the Dwarven domain. Mannace looked at Elderlin.

"It aligns with the messages from Logthar. What do you think we should do?"

The elderly wizard frowned, his tone serious.

"The unexpected."

Elderlin clasped his hands behind his back; something Mannace watched him do numerous times when he was about to share his mind. The leader waited patiently and was not disappointed.

"Mannace, everybody expects you to fight. They believe you will fight fist and foot to hold Angorok, and they all know your vow to defeat Vestig and Amon Murn. Your stubbornness is legendary; it is why men who should leave the North stay; they believe you will persist and ultimately prevail. Your pig-headedness drives you to bring people together and achieve amazing things. It is why I stay, when I know it is wise to leave."

Mannace was attentive, so Elderlin continued.

"Doesn't it seem ironic to have the might of Bracadia to command? Millions of troops. Yet the fates still cast a shadow over your enterprise. Perhaps you are not meant to be victorious here as the emperor said, not at this moment, at least. But honestly, I feel anxious for all that are here."

"I rely on you for logic, Elderlin. What is your *mind* telling you?"

"To flee to survive. But wisdom is not of the mind, Mannace. It comes from the gut. My gut is telling me that the North is lost. My innards are screaming to be gone from this place. I don't say that lightly, for Angorok has been my home for an age. I was here before the Veldaan was founded and the first stone of Angorok was laid. I want to fight, but I am not ready to die. Certainly not at Churgwarthos' hand, to be tortured by that bastard for eternity."

It was not like Elderlin to curse. And strangely, it lightened Mannace's spirit to see a different side of the Asari mage.

"I will do the unexpected then, Elderlin, for the sake of your old soul."

ALLIES

Reports soon arrived detailing the vastness of Churgwarthos' horde and another great host of undead marching across Amon Murn, seemingly to combine forces. At least Churgwarthos waiting for his allies was buying time for Mannace to prepare.

With help from the Blood Legion, Mannace attempted to lure the massive demon army that lurked in the Sarville into the path of the undead. With Casteel's departure, Khing came from Attica to take command of the manoeuvre, and now he appeared in Angorok to report the outcomes directly to the marshall. The muscular warrior was adorned in battle armour, with a greatsword in a sheath across his back. His hair was matted as if he had forgotten how to use a comb. It was a style gaining popularity amongst the Blood Legion, who did not adhere to the rules of other military divisions.

They were alone in the war room.

"Khing, it is good to have you returned."

The warrior looked severe, and his tone was confronting.

"You are fighting with demon-spawn and the dead over scraps of land that no sane man would settle. What is happening here, Mannace?"

"I don't need to hear that from you, Khing. What I want is your loyalty and support. You must tell me that the demons are moving south and will soon clash with the undead."

Khing was shaking his head.

"The Fates are not with you, Mannace. You will have no such easy escape. The demon generals hold their host firm, and they organise them. It's not safe to persist with the same tactics."

Khing straightened his back, and he stared Mannace in the eye.

"The Legion has only two ships, but at least they are Class A. We have begun an evacuation of Skon. We need assistance from the fleet."

"You are running!"

"We are protecting the people of Skon, as we have done for many years. But, even if we can defend the demons and undead, how do you defend against Churgwarthos? Would you have Skon consumed by sorcery like Adash and Tarnac? Nobody wants to leave, Mannace, but they don't want to die either."

Mannace was quiet. Khing could not read his expression.

"We will take the people to Attica and give them land to rebuild."

"Go then. You will need to ask the admiral if you want his ships. What of the survivors not in Skon, who live on the land, who rely on the legion for help?"

Khing ignored the question.

"You should go too. You should gather all these men loyal to you, and the Bracadians, and you should flee. We have seen it before when good men die fighting a foe already dead, and then they rise to swell the enemy's ranks. And for what? What do you gain?"

Mannace was exasperated and struck the wall beside him.

"I did not think I would need to convince you of your loyalty, Khing, or earn your trust. We have fought side by side, feasted together, and shared triumphs where the odds seemed impossible. Do you think I am so blind or stupid that I give no thought to those we serve or protect?"

The marshall's hand braced against the wall as if he took strength from the cold stonework.

"It all began in the North. Everything was birthed here. Everything! The North is the world's womb. The Core that the dwarves covet is the world's heart. When the North bathes in light, that light will shine over the world. If the North falls to darkness, it will be the harbinger of night, a great doom. The fate of the North will be the fate of all. The outcome we fight for here will define the Age, if it will be one of darkness or light, not just for us, but for all."

Khing shrugged, and both men were silent. Then, after an awkward time, Khing turned and left.

As Mannace stood silently, deflated, a figure appeared from a side alcove. The marshall was surprised.

"Render!"

The sorcerer took a deep breath and flexed his shoulders as if shaking off some invisible burden. Then another breath, followed by a sigh and a slight head shake. To Mannace, it seemed overly dramatic, but he waited for his estranged friend to speak.

"I had not looked at it that way."

It was Mannace's turn to shrug.

"The pieces keep coming together, Render. Even the emperor is from the North, and his maker is within the Aghan. If the demons held the North and secured the core, the world would become their Hell. If Churgwarthos holds the North, the world will die."

"And if the emperor commands the North?"

"The world will be Bracadian. It is a better future than other possibilities."

"I prefer a world where we can all make our choices, Mannace. I know you believe the same. You finally cast aside the shackles of the empire, and then a heartbeat later, you are suddenly its champion. Is it truly your destiny to be the emperor's lackey?"

"Destiny! You would pick at that wound, Render. Every fibre of my being yearns to take the North, though I know that time has passed and our destiny with it. The Oracle's blessing has become a curse. Do you not feel it too?"

"The Oracle had different plans for you and me. So, I can let that destiny pass."

"Lucky you", Mannace laughed. He was more isolated and tormented than ever. "I will never have such peace."

"Then have patience. You are immortal, Mannace. Let time be your ally. Why is it so important to have the North today?"

"It was always my ambition to unite the South and the North. But it seems the time is past that nations will follow me. Perhaps, as the emperor's agent, I have a second chance to unify the lands. Do you think that is possible?"

"It would not be the same. The emperor's unification will cast all nations in *his* ordained image. Is that what you want?"

"Perhaps that is how it needs to be, to manage a vast empire. The emperor is a pragmatic man like I am, embracing progress as do I. He will give me a free hand."

"We will see, then, won't we?"

Sensing that Render might turn to leave and not wanting the conversation to end, Mannace quickly changed the topic.

"Will you face Churgwarthos? He will be coming for you. He will also want his vengeance against the elves, but you will be the one occupying his thoughts. He will have a plan for how you will die."

"Fucks sake, you would have my guts cast across Adash, and my soul kept in a jar to play with at night. Churgwarthos is my unfinished business. We all have our challenges to face."

"Is that why you are here, Render? Are you gathering allies for the fight?"

While Render considered his answer, Mannace turned the conversation further on its head.

"Everybody questions why I am still here. So now I am asking why *you* are still here when Churgwarthos and his Belarch are coming for *you*? It's not me he wants, Render, it's you who faces his fury! Perhaps you are not being honest with yourself that destiny has its claws in you too."

"Huh, ego maybe, more than destiny. I cannot be *the sorcerer* if I remain under Churgwarthos' shadow."

Render stepped closer, and his voice was soft as if he shared a secret.

"But there is more to it; I defeated Churgwarthos at Adash, and his body was destroyed. Only his soul escaped, and it will take him time to attain his full presence and powers. The Belarch, too, will be weak. I don't know their resurrection process, but it is better to face Churgwarthos now before he has his full powers. Unlike you, my best time is the present."

Mannace nodded.

"Take what you need. You are our best hope to defeat the Ancient and take control of his horde as you did before. You will have the resources of Angorok at your disposal. I will let the officers and Dekon know."

The estranged friends glared at one another, leaving much unsaid for the sake of a familiar foe. Finally, Mannace turned and left the wizard to his skulking.

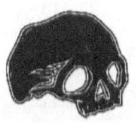

After his talk with Render, Mannace no longer felt overwhelmed by the tens of millions of undead and demons on his doorstep. That was just numbers, and he always beat those. He was the Marshall of Angorok and First General of Bracadia, and he best act like it. He felt mad and foolish for constantly needing to bolster himself, but no one else would do that for him, not Render nor the emperor. Perhaps, Morgan, had he been there. Mannace's blood was racing; it was time to lead.

After giving orders to his commanders and with little time to waste, Mannace boarded the *Bracadian*. It was the only ship in the armada with two navigators, one who knew the destinations throughout the North and another who could pilot amongst the Eastern Colonies and to Bracadia itself. Mannace directed the captain to set course for Zetarach, the capital of the Rhalec. It was a location he had never visited, and the divine Atek was the recluse leader he had never met.

Zetarach was within the dense rainforest of the Fogmir. The mighty Achna river originated there, bubbling slowly up from the ground over a broad expanse and snaking its way through the forest and swamp. From above, small lakes and clearings were visible through the canopy, and ziggurats poked through the foliage. A great pyramid rose skyward, its foundation amongst the trees. Near the mighty structure, rhalec warriors guarded a landing platform, adorned in their traditional shell armour and gleaming steel blades. Most wore feather headdresses, and the commander carried a tall staff with long teeth embedded as a sign of rank. On closer inspection, as they approached, Mannace observed that one of the soldiers had a clockwork crossbow and another a shard gun; examples that the Rhalec embraced modern technologies.

The crocodile people were a secretive society, but today, through his interpreter, who made formal introductions, Mannace was clear about his intentions.

"I honour the Rhalec. I am here to speak with Atek, to give thanks for the enterprise of the crocodile people and ask for aid. My need is urgent, and I must leave before dark."

Mannace was led into the pyramid and through a long series of tunnels. Once deep underground, their escort changed to be soldiers and priests, more traditionally armed with jagged swords. Their grey-scaled leader was primaeval in appearance, with a look of granite, and he blinked in slow motion. The group did not move on until he finished inspecting Mannace and his entourage, giving a glacial nod of approval for Mannace but indicating the others to remain behind.

The subterranean world they moved through was nothing like Mannace had ever seen. They passed through caverns, around lakes and past expansive communities lit by light globes. When they descended deeper, all form of light was gone, and Mannace stumbled through the pitch black. It seemed an eternity before he arrived at their destination. The hands that led him withdrew, and after a time in the darkness, Mannace sensed he was alone. Then the darkness was abruptly consumed with something much more significant, a creature that created a breeze with its movements, and the sound of breathing echoed about him. The sense of danger and dread was suffocating.

"Atek, I applaud the enterprise of the Rhalec during the conflict in the North. I am thankful. The Rhalec and the portal saved millions from the wrath of Churgwarthos and the demon spawn that followed."

Mannace continued to address the silence.

"I ask for aid against Churgwarthos again. He has returned with a vast host of the dead to support him."

A voice whispered in Mannace's ear. Though a whisper, it had a depth and resonance suggesting it came from a creature of immense proportions.

"Did you know that the Rhalec serve the Order? They are loyal to the old ways."

Mannace did not know that. He knew, from his talks with Jaal, that the dark elves followed an Order, but like many secretive societies, Jaal never shared the intimate details. Nevertheless, Mannace was wise enough to ascertain that he was in the presence of an Ancient, or at least a creature born of that past Age.

"The Rhalec understand service."

"Indeed."

Mannace took a deep breath of the cool air through his nose, but there was no hint of scent to help him understand who or what he faced.

"The rhalec towers are a steadfast defence. The portal will facilitate a retreat if the situation in the North becomes hopeless. The rhalec warriors are strong and fearless. These are the things that I need."

"And what of my needs, Mannace of the True Men?"

Mannace stood tall, staring into the blackness. He possessed no appreciation of Atek's motivation or the price for cooperation. He remained silent to let Atek answer the question.

"My price is the sun, stars, and the wind across my face. Small things, don't you think."

Mannace's mind raced as the answer was more of a riddle and raised many questions.

"Those are things easily attained. Are you trapped?"

There was a flurry of movement about him and a noise as if something heavy dragged across the stone. The ensuing echo was disorienting. Then, unexpectedly, the voice was against his other ear.

"The colossi are free. The Kraken is free. It has been too long in the dark."

It was the Mad King and the Bell that released the ancient creatures. Mannace did not know the whereabouts of either and did not have the time to chase mysteries. How much did Atek know? It would not go well for him to be caught in a lie, but he needed the Rhalec and their magic.

"I will do everything I can to release you from this prison."

"Now!"

"It will take time. I will free you. I give you my word."

"Words. They have great power. I bind you by your word, Mannace of the True Men."

Before Mannace was permitted to leave Zetarach, an official came to him to organise what he needed. During the discussion, a stocky Rhalec, dressed in a crimson robe adorned with bright feathers and a glistening shell, stood beside Mannace. The priest clasped a great tooth, as long as his arm, rimmed with gold and encrusted with jewels. When Mannace and the official finished, the priest addressed the marshall in the common tongue.

"My name is Uz. I will be by your ssside, Mannisss of True Men, until your promisss isss fulfilled. I will ensure that you honour your word."

The city of Colossus enjoyed a day of games, and the stadium was packed well beyond its capacity with roaring orcs and goblins passionately supporting their favourite teams. In the confines of the arena, more than a hundred orcs fought to be the last orc standing. Already those defeated were limping or being dragged to the side. A maddened Two-Face competitor rampaged, bowling over his competitors in a berserk rage and dishonouring the rule of no Thog. Officials with crossbows were manoeuvring for a clear shot to put the big fighter down.

Suddenly, the sky darkened, filled with ships and others swooping in from above. The majority of vessels hovered menacingly over the stadium while the two largest, the gigantic battleships of Bracadia, descended into the Arena. Cannons were visible through open portals. On the decks, organised lines of Bracadian riflemen aimed their guns at the astonished crowd. Finally, one of the warships pulled close to Urglis' podium. The ship's hull scraped an area of seating, scattering the crowd and crushing those that were too slow. The roar of angry orcs became deafening as the stadium looked to Urglis for direction.

The riled leader puffed out his chest and came forward a step to confront his foe. From the deck of the ship, Mannace and Admiral Staronis stared back. Mannace was adorned in armour, with his sword slung over his back. He slapped the rails and leaned to shout out to the orc. Urglis waved his arms to silence the crowd, though Mannace's voice boomed above all others.

"WE GO TO WAR. WILL THE WENGO FIGHT WITH US?"

Urglis looked about at the orcs who stared expectantly at him, and he glanced up at the might of the war fleet with their weapons pointed. The grand spectacle fired his blood and made him forget why he hated Mannace and his weakness. It called to his warrior being.

"RRRRAAAAGGGGHHHH", he yelled back, and the spectators erupted in kind, waving fists, and hooting their battle cries.

Leaving Staronis to work with the Wengo, Mannace arrived at Viletri. Once, this city meant everything to him, after raising it from ruins and blessing it with vibrant life. That sentiment was gone as he descended the sky tower and went through the streets to the Undead Dormitory. It was late in the evening, and he remembered enough of Kakos' habits to know he would find the liche lord there. As Mannace strode purposefully, Jayne and the ever-present Uz scurried to keep up with him.

Kakos was in his office. He appeared displeased to see Mannace, indicating with a wave for his entourage to remain outside the door. There were papers on the lord's desk, stacked neatly, and shelves of other documents and books also in good order. Kakos' eyes were heavy, and his skin was grey.

"I am leaving here with you, Kakos. I need your help, and Render needs your help. Look around you at what we have accomplished. And yet there are always challenges that sometimes we face alone, and other times we must come together. We face Churgwarthos and his undead horde. It will take us all to defeat him, and Kakos, you most of all, have the talents to end his curse."

When the liche stared maliciously at him, Mannace matched his gaze and stepped forward.

"Churgwarthos died and was rebirthed. Render expects the sorcerer will recoup all his powers over time. But, it made me think, there may be a way for you to be rebirthed."

"No. Render explained it to me. Once your soul reaches the Domain of the Dead, only un-life will restore it, but true life is denied. So, sorcerers protect their soul from entering the domain and prepare an alternative host. It is too late for me."

Mannace was glad to have captured Kakos' interest. It was better than the blunt refusal he received from the liche the last time he asked for help.

"The Muster represents many disciplines and aeons of knowledge. They will investigate possibilities. You may be surprised at what they can achieve."

"Why would they help?"

"It is what they do for one another. The Muster would welcome you as a peer."

"I stand alone. It is sufficient."

There was only one more argument Mannace possessed that might sway Kakos to help him. To hide his desperation, he purposefully calmed his tone and spoke in a clear, confident voice.

"We will defeat Churgwarthos and his Belarch. You will capture their souls when we do."

After a pause, the liche responded, "To what end?"

"What might you do with the soul of an Ancient, Kakos? There is great potential in such a gift, and each Belarch is a potent sorcerer. Can you see possibilities, Kakos?"

There was a very long silence before Kakos came forward to be inches away from Mannace, close enough that the marshall was mesmerised by the swirling shapes in the liche's eyes.

"I will help you for the prize of Churgwarthos' soul."

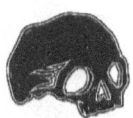

Mannace's last preparation was one that he could not accomplish himself. Instead, he talked with Logthar over the new device and sent the dwarf a note to share with Morgan. Mannace trusted the metal man's diplomacy enough to ask Staronis to send a ship into the IceSleepers. All of his pieces were in play, and just in time, with reports coming to him of undead surging through The Gap into Turbul. Soon they would flood into Islan and overwhelm Skon. Mannace was glad of Khing's instinct to evacuate that bastion. With no time left, it required the kindness of the fates to be ready when the enemy reached Angorok and for Render to gather his strength in Adash.

THE HAND

Jaal hadn't expected The Hand to be teaming with demons. But, like Adash, where he was familiar walking amongst their kind, they were also dormant, and their bloodlust controlled. Despite his discomfort, he knew he was safe if he was careful not to approach too close. Initially, caution slowed his progress, but when he crossed into the areas guarded by webs, Jaal quickened his pace along the paths used by the spiders and spiderkin. Here spiders of all sizes lurked above in the trees or amongst the clusters of webs, but they knew him as Father and sensed the mother awaited his return.

Spiderkin appeared ahead of Jaal, leading him through the trees, then underground into the mother's lair. He knew where she would be waiting and hurried to undress and enter her private abode. The utter darkness and dimensions of the silky chambers were familiar.

Jaal expected Eya's caress, so he was not alarmed when her hand passed over his chest and across his buttocks. With anticipation, he reached out, feeling his way up Eya's arm, to move his hand over her shoulder. With his other arm, he drew her close. Now his fingers could explore more freely to caress Eya's curves, and his spear, already hard, pressed against her thigh. In response, Jaal sensed the Spider Mother's breath on his neck as the supple Ancient caressed his back and gripped his ass. She drew him even closer so that their bodies pressed against one another.

Eya turned, keeping body contact, to allow Jaal to massage her breasts. He took a gulp of air as his spear slid between the cheeks. Then, as Eya bent forward, Jaal guided his spear inside her, moving it slowly to savour the penetration. With his cock in place, Eya leaned upright, allowing Jaal to run his digits over her smooth stomach while his other hand roughly grabbed her tit. The dark elf nestled his nose into Eya's neck for a moment, before biting her shoulder hard enough to make her flinch. Moving his hand from the breast, Jaal gathered Eya's hair in his fist, clasping it firmly, as he quickened his rhythm. It was some time since he tasted these fruits, and his blood raced.

Another body, naked, pressed up against Jaal from behind. Breasts with their firm nipples pushed against his back, and a woman's thighs leaned against his arse, forcing him to slow his movements. Long fingernails teased as they moved up Jaal's sides, then dug under his arms with a pinch of pain. As his pulse raced, an inner presence was also imposing further pressure on Jaal's heart, burrowing mercilessly into his soul. It linked with him, taking control over the life forces that sustained him. He knew who this was, and his mind would have questioned why if he were not utterly lost in the drunkenness of the coupling.

In the aftermath, as Jaal lay helpless, alone in the blackness, he could not remember if one or both of the women took his seed. He would not have given it if he were in his senses, but both matriarchs possessed powers to give and take. His body and mind were euphoric. His life, though, was on a thin thread. So much so that barely a spec of sanity and shallowest of breaths separated him from death.

Small movements in the silky floor, made Jaal aware that the spider mother loomed over him. Even in his incapacitated state, he understood her desire to devour him. However, he was incapable of defending himself, still far too intoxicated and exhausted to move. After a long wait, there was another shift of movement in the darkness that Jaal recognized as Eya changing her form. Then a gush of liquid, piss from the scent of it, splashed across his stomach and chest. More movement of the web so that Jaal sensed Eya moving away. In a brief moment of clarity, Jaal remembered his purpose, and in a small voice that used all his fleeting energy, he uttered, "Eya, I implore you, help Render."

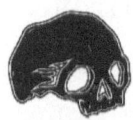

Many Fen perished under the terrifying assault of the demons, just as other races fared. The communities of survivors were secreted away in the most tangled areas of the forest, hidden amongst the undergrowth and roots. Roanna, the Dark Druid, and daughter to Ahmeda and Jaal, was their protector. With her were two mystical Ra Anu, a doe and a young crow that stood as tall as her thigh. Together, they shaped the forest and secreted the Fen from prying eyes, setting vigilant guardian vines and spores.

At first, other Elven druids and wardens aided her, but in recent years, they answered the call to travel north. Perhaps because she was a dark elf, Roanna did not have the same impulse, though she expected that her compassion for the Fen fuelled a greater purpose. She was teaching the forest people druidic skills, for which they showed an affinity. Some possessed the natural talent to assimilate with the forest, rewarded with its protection and bounty.

As the Ra Anu matured, so too did the influence of Fengal upon the Fen's domain. Such forces aided the alliance between beast and men, so the Fen were affiliating themselves with the nobler of creatures. Commonly, they lived, travelled, hunted, and foraged together.

With more forest creatures taking refuge in the safe areas, it was becoming harder to remain hidden, and in fact, the growing flocks of birds were often like beacons to the demons. Even in their dormant state, some Hell-spawn roamed into the Fen's sanctuary, and their limp, decaying forms were hanging from the trees where the spores and vines ensnared them.

As Fengal's champion, Roanna planned to retake the forest and eventually recover The Hand. The reclamation soon became the primary occupation of the Fen, so that together, their shrunken domain gradually expanded.

THE BASTION OF ANGOROK

The fear for Angorok was that Churgwarthos might consume it in darkness, as he did at Adash and Tarnac, where the populace of those cities vanished. The ancient sorcerer's legacy of terror caused panic and left Mannace guessing his tactics. But, for now, brula scouts reported that the enemy split into two main forces and that Churgwarthos headed with one of the hosts towards Adash. The other horde was almost upon Angorok. It was close enough that their numbers were already visible as a shadow on the horizon.

Mannace relied on the Bracadian infantry. However, after experimenting with undead lent to him by Render, it was as he feared, that the rifles and muskets were mostly ineffectual against the undead. It often required headshots, lucky enough to shatter the skull, to bring them down. So Mannace set his soldiers to work fortifying buildings within the city and setting wires to confound flying foes. It was fortunate that orcs from the Wengo were arriving. They were deployed to the walls, joining Mannace's loyalists as the main line of defence.

Almost at the last minute, two divisions of rhalec warriors entered through the gates of Angorok. They came from the plain of Palainth, where the mystical rhalec portal reappeared. But, unfortunately, rhalec towers, so effective in the war against Amon Murn, were too cumbersome and slow to be in time for the imminent siege. Mannace hoped that some might reach Adash in time.

Notably, the Rhalec arriving at Angorok brought priests who joined other clergies as the backbone of the defence. The war priests, Light Bearers from the Holy Lands, orc

Shaman, and few Eternal that were not with Render blessed the fortifications and troops. It would be their role to turn back the most potent spirits and keep a firm resolve in the face of such a terrifying foe. In their favour were the High Satar's blessings over the capital, set to ward against demons but useful against any unnatural enemy. Dekon Ruel led them, and the Muster aided them with their potent magic and animations. Mannace was standing with Dekon at the front wall when the signal came from the admiral's flagship hovering above for the artillery to commence firing. The boom of the mighty guns from positions behind the main walls and from the battleships above was frightening. Flashes of fire and billowing dust clouds were seen in the distance. Dekon shouted to Mannace above the din.

"That barrage would break any mortal force. Can you imagine being struck with such devastation before putting eyes upon your foe? They will suffer grievously and not a sword raised."

"We will run out of ammunition, Dekon, long before they run out of undead. They will get wiser of our capabilities, and their generals will adjust."

"You think they have generals?"

"Of course, they will know their capabilities much better than we do. They will likely expend the weaker creatures to test our strength, and we will see their veterans and elite after. It is too early in the battle for them to worry about attrition when their numbers are so vast."

Dekon shifted in his rig so that the gears whirred, and there was a small puff of steam as he stretched up to his full height to better view the distant explosions.

"They still move slowly. It would make more sense to charge. The undead do not tire."

"Perhaps they are not all undead."

Along the walls, some men and orcs were hooting and roaring, starting their rituals in preparation for the fighting. The men loyal to Mannace were a ragtag of nationalities and types, but they were all proven and brave.

"I am proud of the men of Angorok. I wish only that the Remman stood alongside them."

Dekon nodded, "The Wengo orcs are well equipped. I have seen some with pistols or clockwork crossbows – of orc design, much bulkier than those of the Arenlanders. The orcs have war priests too, and they possess training in the Rage. There is much to be proud of Mannace. The War God will look down on us with favour."

Mannace pointed to a tower further along. "Ahmeda has joined us."

"Huh, a change from being the emperor's whore. We will see if she has left her spine in the bed chamber."

Both men watched as the enemy shambled closer. They now saw that the undead carried burdens: rocks, branches, even the broken bodies of their fallen hoard. As they drew closer, the loud bangs of Aren mortars joined the Bracadian artillery's thunder. It was too noisy to converse, and the two leaders watched as undead reached the walls of Angorok, cast their loads of debris against the stone, and then stepped back to stare up at the defenders. Soon, the ground before Angorok was teeming with the undead that bustled forward adding debris to the growing pile.

Meanwhile, other enemies clambered up the hills and into the valleys flanking Angorok to surround the fortress city. The tall gates and walls of the defence were enough to prevent direct assault. Still, as the pile of refuse slowly accumulated, the undead's plan to construct a great ramp along the entire front facing of Angorok was blatant.

Mannace turned to one of his runners, "Order the artillery to cease fire. Tell the captains to save ammunition. Go, soldier."

Dekon nodded towards a wizard who released a gush of flame into the mass below him. Occasionally a bowman would loose a bolt, but it was insignificant in the context of the standoff.

"They are calming their nerves. Let them have their practice. One way or another, we have a lot of undead to kill."

To himself, Mannace uttered, "This is madness to wait."

Uz, who stood behind Mannace, rarely spoke, but now he was grating his sharp teeth and placed the ancient tooth he always carried against his chest.

"Give usss ssstrength, Atek, that we may ssserve with honour."

The Rhalec raised the tooth above his head, and although there was no fanfare or spark, the Rhalec nearby opened their jaws wide and gave a repeating noise like a bark. The crocodile people looked fearsome with their teeth displayed, and they grew in stature as they howled and danced. Some of the orc shamans joined with their tinkering and movements, inspiring their troops to hoot and wave their arms. The display extended along the wall as more warriors joined the ritual. Typically, a dour character, Dekon grinned.

"It looks like a damned festival. We will have a party while the enemy scales our walls."

"Sometimes there is magic in simple things", Mannace replied. "That is a lesson the Mad King taught me."

The undead worked tirelessly throughout the day and night to build their ramp. Sometimes the artillery, a spell, or oil poured from pots and set alight would disrupt them. But there was no endless supply of such things, so the defenders carefully conserved their resources. On the second day, Mannace rotated rifle battalions and musketmen into positions where they could fire at the skeletons. It was good practice and further hampered their progress. Uz was getting bolder in discussing matters with Mannace.

"What will you do when the enemy finissshesss their ramp?"

Uz had been present for all the discussions with Mannace's officers.

"Have you not listened, Uz. We stand upon the first wall, which is the tallest and sturdiest. Look behind you; there are five layers to the defences, then the citadel. We will fight and retreat to the next wall and fight again."

Because the Rhalec was attentive, Mannace continued.

"On the third wall, we will hold them. It is a smaller defence, and we will use the animations crafted in

Angorok by the Muster, plus others are arriving from Viletri. The animations are tireless opponents, like the undead we face. By the third wall, the enemy will be feeling their attrition. They may appear endless in numbers now, but they have finite resources too. Angorok will defeat them; they will break against its walls."

"The Bracadiansss are not good sssoldiersss againsssst the ssskelletonsss."

"True, but they are needed against the demons when they come. The Bracadians are deadly against the Hell-spawn."

"How do you know the demonsss will come?"

"They will wait until there is a winner here, then they will come to fight the weakened victor and claim the spoils. If I am wrong and they do not come right away, I am certain they will come for Angorok in time, and we will be fighting demons soon enough. If there is a break in the fighting, we will reinforce with rhalec towers from the Palainth."

Uz nodded enthusiastically at the last point.

On the fourth day, the first of the undead clambered high enough to swing their rusty weapons at the defenders, and some attempted to scramble over the crenulations. At first, the garrison made easy work of them, but as the ramp increased in breadth and height, the skeleton throng was relentless, and their numbers would soon become overwhelming.

Mannace was at the front wall with Uz and Jayne by his side. Rangers and loyal Viletri elite fought around him. At the same time, Dekon stomped along a section of the battlements he alone claimed, sweeping away the undead with his divine magics and smashing skeletons as they struggled for a foothold.

There was blue fire powering the undead that blazed in their eyes, and as they drew close, their passivity was replaced with frenzy, driving them at the defenders like crazed berserkers. Some of the walking dead hefted weapons but most improvised with sticks or anything else they could wield. Tattered armour was draped over those enemies that were once soldiers. Worryingly, larger frames of giants posed more brutal threats amongst the human-sized foes. At first, the skill and tactics of the defenders easily kept their position, but as the day progressed, the number of undead clambering over the ramparts became an avalanche of animated bones and rotting flesh, relentlessly continuing into the night.

Mannace ordered the artillery to resume their barrage to provide relief, and the admiral made swooping attacks with the flying ships to blast the ramps and distract the swarming attackers. As the defence became more desperate, Mannace hacked and slashed alongside the soldiers. Where he fought, there were undead on the walls and others leaning over the crenulations to strike or to pull themselves across. Mannace hoped he had not left it too late to retreat. His limbs were tired from hefting his two-handed sword, and adrenaline and desperation fuelled his strikes, blow after blow. Next to him, Jayne was bleeding down one arm, and there were increasing casualties amongst those fighting nearby. As a flying galley passed close to the wall, its incredible hulk scraped across the makeshift rampart, stemming the tide of undead momentarily. It was enough for Mannace's command group to clear their area of the battlements and for

Mannace to signal retreat. Jayne yelled the message along the lines, and orange smoke rose from fires on the wall behind. As rehearsed, everywhere they could, defenders backed down the steps and hurried to the gates. Flying ships and waiting escorts of riflemen covered them as they abandoned the outer wall, and the next tier of defences, the fourth wall, became the new front. Where the retreat was thwarted, Staronis' fleet lowered ropes and nets to rescue stranded soldiers. The defenders watched the tide of undead pouring into the outer city, and it was not long before the districts in that part of Angorok were teeming with them.

As Mannace scrutinised his enemy, he saw a man amongst the skeletons, moving along the rampart. It was a fleeting glimpse, too far and the light too poor to tell who it might be, but it was the first sign that the undead were not acting alone. Oil and straw were stacked against the buildings between the outer and fourth walls, and fire arrows arched across the night, starting small blazes where they found their targets. Soon, the fires spread, and it was not long before the outer districts were ablaze. Some undead collapsed, while the tumbling buildings crushed others. However, fire and destruction did not deter them. Already some were placing debris against the base of the fourth wall. Within the bastion, wizards did their best to blow the suffocating smoke away, while most residents and military took shelter until the inferno abated. Fatigued soldiers who fought to the limits of endurance rested while the Bracadians kept vigil on the walls.

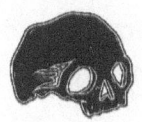

THE DEFENCE OF ADASH.

At Adash, Render waited. The horde of Churgwarthos was still days away, and he collected all the allies that he could rally or that Mannace arranged on his behalf. Kakos was always close. Render's apprentices and supporters from the Muster gathered in the citadel to make their preparations. Then, unexpectedly, Morgan arrived aboard a flying ship with Logthar and the KinRa. The dwarf, SinKayLas, who Render previously battled, was amongst them, bearing the staff of Jol. That seemed ironic, almost insulting. Regardless, the dwarves were given quarters where they kept to themselves.

Render was sleepless these nights, and as he often did, he laboured in the throne hall on his spell-craft and defences. He knew in his gut that Churgwarthos would want to settle their score here, where Render and the elves defeated him. Approaching footsteps distracted Render from his work, though he often caught Kakos wandering the halls while others were resting.

"Kakos, do something useful."

"Like what?"

"Prepare. Churgwarthos and the Belarch will be here within days."

"These halls, this darkness, it is preparation enough. What more preparation do you need?"

Render dismissed the comment, but then he remembered the liche's nature and knew to delve deeper.

"What about these halls and darkness prepares us, Kakos?"

The liche crossed the floor to where Render stood, looking into the wizard's eyes as if searching for truth.

"You don't see it, the life in the darkness?"

Render was surprised. Of course he could see the darkness, feel its potency. Within its dark shroud, night creatures thrived, and dark magic was easily cast. He wondered what Kakos might sense that he could not. As if reading Render's thoughts, Kakos elaborated.

"The darkness is life. It is the essence of those consumed by sorcery here at Adash. It lives and breathes and watches."

As if to demonstrate, Kakos held out his arms and breathed in deeply, connecting to the darkness that engulfed the city. Suddenly his eyes were wide, and he looked urgently at his host.

"Churgwarthos is here!"

Render needed no further warning. Instantly he raised his shields and sent a mental summons so that his apprentices were abruptly aware of the danger. Then, all about the citadel, wizards leapt to action and called a warning to others.

A cold breeze blew through the hall. Three cultists, Render's guards who lurked invisible in the corners of the room, revealed themselves, staggering as if drunk and collapsing to the floor. Their lifeless forms instantly decayed as if they had been lying there dead for decades.

At the same time, humanish silhouettes appeared at the main doorway, and other phantom shapes coalesced amongst the shadows of the ceiling, descending towards Render and Kakos.

Kakos' command of the undead easily dispersed the floating spirits but could not stop soldiers, wrapped in ancient cloth, from rushing through the entrance to secure the room. Two of them charged to their left, seemingly at nothing, until Fek appeared and leapt at them. One of the mummies' blades caught the demon on the shoulder, but Fek ducked under the swing of the other and dug his claws into the creature's side, tearing free tatters of cloth and dust. More cultists appeared from their hiding places in adjoining chambers to confront the invaders, but the ferocious mummies quickly drove the defenders back.

As the darkness swelled, black-robed figures appeared out of the night and strode boldly into the hall. They were young in appearance but marched forward with the type of arrogance born of supreme confidence.

As Render planned it, the great hall itself came to life; every type of gargoyle unfurled and leapt at the invaders. It was an avalanche of stone, sweeping aside those fighting on the outskirts and threatening to roll over the robed figures in the room's centre. Only blasts of force and fire held them back. With so many magi, the magic-lit room was consumed simultaneously by waves of darkness and annihilating forces.

The sorcerous duel began in earnest, with all vision lost in the crescendo of powers and spells. Both sides came fully prepared and held nothing back. Within a heartbeat, Render was on the defensive, his spells not dominant enough to penetrate his enemies' protection. The combined might of Churgwarthos and the Balarch was rapidly overpowering him, breaking down his defences with assaults of force and psychic domination. Beside Render, Kakos was bent at the knee, also outclassed, and humiliated by the ancient magi's superior mastery.

The first of Render's allies emerged from the passageways. The new arrivals immediately launched blasts of fire and ice at the enemy, until a turning Belarch scattered the wizards with a fierce bombardment of darkspears. Only the relentless surge of gargoyles threatened the enemy, who shielded themselves and blasted the scurrying creatures back. One Belarch, a fatal lapse in his concentration, succumbed to the relentless animations, buried under a heap of thrashing, clawing stone.

Increasingly desperate, Render's mind sought out the nearby Staff of Jol. Hastily and uncaring of the dangers, Render accessed its powers through a key secreted within the device's sentience. He called on the artefact's primeval magic; the pure, untamed essence of the Core. Channelled through the sorcerous darkness that filled Adash, Render frantically sucked the energy into himself, bolstering his defences and fuelling his magical strikes. When Render's reinforced spells pierced his enemy shields, a Belarch, caught off-guard, screamed as he was thrown on his back. Blue flame ate his face and flesh. A gargoyle leapt on the magi's chest, swiftly joined by a host of its swarming mates.

But the Adash darkness was of Churgwarthos' making, and as quickly as the energy manifested, the ancient sorcerer also drew on its strength. He wielded it like a colossal fist, thumping down on Render, draining his defence, and threatening to crush him against the stone floor. The Belarch, too, soaked in the Core's magic and released it against defenders that rushed into the throne hall.

Awakened by the Core's vast powers, the life that was within the darkness, the lost citizens of Adash, writhed and screamed at Churwarthos' beckoning. The tortured screeching of thousands of the damned, ruthlessly filled Render's consciousness, the noise and pitch of the cries overwhelming all other senses. It assaulted Render's sanity and clawed at his very being, stripping away all rational thought, so that he yanked wildly, single-mindedly, at the Core; his attention only able to focus on this one calamitous thing. Out of control, the rapidly escalating sorcery, fed by the world's forge and which ensnared even Churgwarthos with its omnipotence, threatened to devour the whole of Adash and mercilessly obliterate them all.

Then, as abruptly as it started, the escalation ceased. The sentience key was broken and access to the Core was gone. SinKayLas, who held the Staff of Jol, opened his eyes and savagely banged the staff's tip on the ground. He looked fiercely at the dwarves gathered around him, too overwhelmed with anger and emotion to speak.

In the throne hall, both sorcerers and the Belarch sucked in air. They had each been lost in the elation of unbridled energies, madly prepared to embrace oblivion, but a vestige of sense was returning. The wizards and priests that rushed to Render's aid were gone, cruelly sucked into the darkness that now completely turned against Render. Through it, Churgwarthos was imperious, his stern features replaced with a thin, arrogant smile. In the absence of other magic, his granite will bore down on Render like a vice, squeezing the life from him. Exhausted, Render's vision went black, and he fell to his knees next to the bent liche. The ego that sustained Render's magic was broken, yet he defied Churgwarthos with every fibre of his being.

Still blinded by the manifestation of powers assaulting him, Render sensed a dramatic shift in momentum. Unexpected magical aid was forthcoming, a great surge of spells and energy, though by whom he could not tell. It was not the same unbridled power as the Core, but it was significant, ancient, and usurped the remnant energies of those present. With no choice and desperate abandon, Render disregarded his defence and projected the little power he possessed and the great well of strength he could borrow from his new allies towards the centre of the room. As he channelled the force, his mind shaped a spell; something new that would circumvent the defences and strike down his foes. The sorcery drew on all that he had learned in this battle, and it threw caution to the wind. It was his final heroic act, genius in its design, and utterly reckless. If he were going to die, he would leave his mark on the world and take the bastard ancient with him. Fuck Churgwarthos! Fuck the Belarch! Fuck them all!

The cataclysmic explosion threw Render off his feet, spinning him as he skidded across the floor. The left side of Render's body felt like it was on fire, and with his vision restored, he looked down at his right arm, which had disintegrated to the bone. Though agony consumed him, the sorcerer risked a desperate glance back across the room. His enemies were gone; annihilated. Through glazed vision, beyond the rubble, he saw the silhouette of four figures, feminine. Behind them, other shapes moved, but the scene quickly became a blur, and with a remnant of energies, Render slipped into near-space. His screaming eventually abated, replaced at first with numbness of mind and then the terrifying uncertainty of unconsciousness, or was this in fact his final breath?

Kakos ignored what was occurring in the physical world. Instead, his mind hunted the realm between the living and the dead. In this space, he had no equal, and he scooped up the bewildered Belarch as he found them. Then, when Churgwarthos appeared, he enveloped the stunned essence of the ancient before it might escape, trapping and securing it as he was so used to doing. He was not disappointed; the immortal soul had a sentience and purpose unlike any other before it. First, he sensed the terror of being trapped, then the anger, and finally a plea for mercy. It was Kakos' turn to smile.

The wizard, Amnicles, rushed into the wrecked hall. Some others that beat him there were already combing the rubble in search of clues to what had occurred. Splattered blood and guts covered the floors, with broken gargoyles scattered from wall to wall. The pungent stink of acid and burning filled the air, causing Amnicles to cough.

In one corner, a priest and cultist were helping Kakos to his feet. The liche appeared battered, and there was a sword poking through his chest, which the cultist extracted with a hefty tug. Outside the citadel, in the city streets, Amnicles heard fighting, but soon the indistinct noise died away. The wizard could not ascertain the outcome in the room, though it was evident by the residue of power and magic that an epic duel had transpired. Once other wizards arrived at a run, he gathered them together, giving each instruction to begin the search for Render. He could see that Kakos was dazed, but he went to the liche anyway.

"What happened here, Kakos? Does Render live?"

"You know Render is alive. Has he not set it so you will lose your powers if he were dead?"

It was true that Render set a key upon the minds of his apprentices so that if he died, they would lose access to their craft. It was an assurance of their loyalty, and the liche's reminder added further angst to Amnicle's worried visage.

"Yes. This is not the first time Render has disappeared when his life is in peril. The last time he was grievously wounded, he withdrew to near-space, and only Fek or the Drutha could follow him there. So, his fate may be in their hands."

"Let's hope they, too, are interested in keeping their master alive."

"Did Churgwathos come? Was he defeated?"

Kakos pushed a loose piece of flesh on his arm back into place and dusted his jacket, pulling it by the tail to settle it back into place.

"He was defeated, of that I am certain."

"How can you be sure?"

Kakos ignored the question, instead patting the top of his pants. His left ear fell from the side of his head and dropped behind his shoulder. He seemed oblivious.

"My job here is done. I will return to Viletri. Bring me a ship."

Amnicles was not about to let Kakos depart without a complete account of events.

"It will take time to organise transport. There is still much to be done here. There is still a horde at our doorstep. You are needed."

"As you wish."

Unbeknownst to Amnicles, Render had shown Kakos the secret portal he made between Adash and Viletri, going as far as providing instruction on how to use it. They discussed what it might mean for Kakos to pass through the inter-dimensional gateway and traverse the domain of the dead. It seemed possible that the trove of souls that Kakos possessed within his being might attract the attention of the lords of that realm or their sinister goddess. Would the dead welcome him, or would they look to trap him? Might they set the souls he carried free? Kakos was surprised Render shared such a secret with him, and it seemed reckless to Kakos to tempt him with such a risky proposition. Possibly Render did it purposefully, for his experimentation or amusement. Or perhaps Render knew more than he had revealed, a devilish trap. Unwilling to meet Amnicles' demands, it was time to discover the truth.

Grengal did not expect to come west and switch allegiances as she had, but like her collaborators, she believed there would be no better time to end Churgwarthos and his cursed Belarch. As fledglings, the sorcerer and his servants were powerful but not as potent as they would be if left to regain their full capabilities. After the fight and her betrayal of Churgwarthos, Grengal didn't dally to learn if she, too, would be deceived. Instead, she escaped upon the swarm as only she could, and was soon back amongst her familiar horde. The Ancient would know soon enough if her new allies would be true to their word.

THE GAME

An elated Morgan arrived at Angorok with news of Churgwarthos' demise. The KinRa travelled upon the vessel with him. SinKayLas remained angry at Render's subterfuge, yet the dwarves were considerably indebted to Bracadia and would dutifully assist in the defence of Angorok. They were quick to put their feet back on land and preferred the citadel as a platform to cast their magic rather than the metal deck of the flying ship. From the citadel's balconies, the KinRa manipulated the elements until an angry storm gathered over the besieged city. SinKayLas fed the summoning with the energy of The Core, and the rising tempest sparked and rumbled in anticipation. When at last, the dwarves were ready, they unleashed a barrage of elemental forces against the undead that besieged the third wall. SinKayLas sent more forks of lightning to harass the enemy further back and out of sight. The thunderous bolts blew apart bone and decaying flesh, causing grievous carnage, and blasting apart makeshift ramps. In some places, the elements swirled, forming briefly into elementals that swept aside the undead with battering blows. The furious storm was not enough to ultimately stem the tireless assault, but it pounded the enemy back and delayed the advancing siege.

On the ground, Mannace committed everything to the shrinking defence. The stone and clockwork guards were islands of stubborn resistance in the sea of chaos. The animated creatures bashed and stabbed with relentless efficiency, while their hardy bodies easily deflected the undead attacks. Still, after catching sight of some forms as large as the colossi amongst the undead reserves, well back from the action, Mannace was concerned. His scouts told him the newcomers resembled the demon generals, and it was not long before they advanced to the front, alongside giant skeletons, to assist and protect the ramp builders. While the lumbering demons were large and formidable, they were a shadow of their true selves, without ferocity or magic. However, fronted by the massive brutes who jostled with the defenders on the wall, the undead progressed their ramps.

Orcs and humans worked the walls in shifts to give time for rest and to heal minor wounds. With the help from the dwarves, it seemed at first that the defence of the third wall might hold, but the enemy committed more reserves, and it was now that they showed their full capability. In the night, ghostly apparitions moved through the walls and struck terror into those they confronted, while other spectres wailed and decayed anything they touched. Some of the phantoms possessed magic, while others blended with shadow. The priests confronted those they could see and put wardings in place to deal with others.

From above, giant vultures dropped zombies from a great height. On regaining their feet, the infiltrators hunted the living. Some lurked in buildings to ambush the unwary.

Logthar directed the KinRa. He stood on a high balcony with two dwarven mages, pointing to the areas where they should focus their storm-work. Mannace came from a passageway to stand next to him, watching the dwarves invoking their spells. Riflemen followed the leader, moving out to secure the balcony and keep vigil over the skies. They could see other squads of Bracadians taking up positions elsewhere about the citadel to shoot at the vultures or falling dead. Uz lurked back in the corridor, and next to Mannace, Jayne was also ever-present. Mannace placed a hand on Logthar's shoulder.

"From one trial to another, my friend, the North will give us no peace."

Logthar gave a wry smile and absentmindedly groomed his beard with his hands. He seemed at ease, even with the drama playing out about him. The dwarf pointed at flamers on a distant wall who cleared the parapets of swarming enemies. Amongst the flames, a stone man continued to hack at the burning undead.

"It has always been so, lad. It is the fate of all races to move from one war to another and onto the next. It is the game that the fates and gods play." Then, changing the topic, he added, "I see you have replicated the flamers; well done."

"You know Arenlanders. They excel in stealing others' ideas."

The dwarf's smile lengthened as he remembered the rivalry between Viletri and Arenland.

"So much more is accomplished in times of peace. This war in the North serves no purpose. Why do you persist here when even the dead want you gone?"

Mannace frowned at his estranged friend.

"Logthar, what will happen if we leave the North to the demons and the dead?"

When the dwarf shrugged, Mannace continued.

"They will not be satisfied. The demons will renew their attacks against the dwarves and The Core. The undead will cross the snow into Arenland, forever seeking to expand and devour."

"Mannace, you don't know that for certain. Perhaps they will be content with the North. Why do you care so much for this place?"

Mannace rolled his eyes. He was tired of the same questions from those he felt should understand his purpose. He was weary of defending his actions.

"Fuck's sake, Logthar. Would you hide in your hole and pretend that your problems will disappear? Who will confront this darkness if not us, here, at this moment?"

Mannace sighed profoundly and drew a second deeper breath as if to heal his soul. He did not want to share the words on his lips, as they contradicted everything he felt in his gut and soul.

"It does not matter anyway. It appears our emperor does not share my belief. Ahmeda has brought instructions that the Bracadians are to evacuate immediately. They will depart Angorok and the North."

Logthar's brow furrowed as if the reality of such news made him consider the repercussions for his kin and others in the region.

"That may herald greater darkness, more than we have already endured."

"It will be an *Age* of darkness, Logthar. Can you see the truth of it now? Do you see why the North is so important?"

Admiral Staronis ordered the flying fleet to gather near Angorok, out of harm's way of the dwarven storm. While the ship's crews and marines remained vigilant for the giant vultures, the Admiral briefed the captains on his plan. It was audacious, but it seemed reasonable that desperate measures were required to evacuate the Bracadian troops before Angorok succumbed to the horde. The situation appeared dire from above the city, seeing the enemy masses stretched across the Veldaan plains and into the hills. To escape, the ravine and valley behind Angorok formed a passage that eventually led through other passes into Rockhome. From there, a road wound its way east to the mountains of the Wengo and the city of Colossus. It was a well-travelled route with sturdy highways and bridges.

When all was ready, the garrison opened the back door to Angorok. Staronis and his fleet swooped low to support the exiting troops as they charged through the great gates and down the steep paths into the valley and waiting enemies. Bursts of steam and the boom of cannons and artillery blasted a route for the escaping soldiers. Explosions drove the undead back and confused them. For half a day, the assault continued until the fleet's ammunition was spent, and the admiral had no more to give. Thankfully, the flotilla successfully secured passage for most of the Bracadian divisions, with only a few caught in the resurgence of the undead who swarmed to reclaim the lost ground. Despite his efforts, some Bracadians remained trapped in the city as the gates slammed closed.

From the northern side of the citadel, which commanded a view of the rear gate, Mannace watched as the horde overran the stragglers and gave chase to the others, knowing they would hound the Bracadians all the way to the coast. They might even overtake them, though once the sky fleet resupplied, Staronis' navy would help them to safety.

The citadel's once crowded inner districts seemed empty about without the bulk of Bracadian troops. Yet, despite the loss of the allied infantry, the plight of Angorok was little affected. With the noise and spectacle of the fleet's assault abated, the flashes and thunderclaps of the dwarven magic again dominated the approaching twilight. Mannace turned to Jayne, who stood behind him with three other rangers.

"It will be night soon, and we will join the defence at the wall. I will talk with the officers of the Bracadian troops remaining here. It is time they joined the wall too."

Jayne nodded. Mannace noticed the dark elf hesitate, and then he looked directly at his commander as if assessing him. It was a moment that quickly passed, but it left Mannace curious.

"Jayne, what is on your mind?"

"You have not eaten. I will pack food to eat at the wall."

"Is there anything else you want to tell me?"

Jayne was astute enough to know Mannace read his demeanour. It was not typical of Jayne to express anything but the calmest manner, nor was his mind ever so conflicted. He decided to share his thoughts.

"We should leave Angorok."

"And how will we do that? We have my ship, Milan's ship that Ahmeda arrived on, and Morgan's. There are still a million soldiers and civilians within these walls. So, we will stay, Jayne, until we can exit the front gate unimpeded."

Jayne nodded again. He excused himself to fetch supplies for the night ahead. Mannace watched him leave, still unsure what this change in character meant. However, for now, there were many other things to be concerned about.

The emperor arrived unexpectedly at Angorok and made his way immediately towards the war room, where he knew he would find Mannace or his clerks. Claudius strode confidently behind him, and a troop of elite riflemen filed behind. It was not typical of the emperor to travel with such a large entourage.

As he marched down a wide corridor, Ahmeda, Dekon, and three other dark elves appeared from a side passage. The two groups approached until they stood an arm's length apart.

"What have you done, Ahmeda?"

"We should discuss this in private, Emperor. You will see the wisdom of my actions. Do you doubt my vision?"

The emperor looked hard at the high priestess. His normally unflappable character evaporated, replaced with an agitated stance and angry eyes.

"I know your character, Ahmeda, I have eyes and ears, and I will not be manipulated. Nor will I stand aside and watch my work undone. I can see the pieces coming together, not for the benefit of Bracadia, and it is your hand that shifts them into place."

"God before emperor. Even emperors must humble themselves to the divine."

"Do not hide behind your religion. Ahmeda, I applaud your ambition, but you have gone too far."

The high priestess relaxed as if a shroud were lifted, and now that her scheming was exposed, she no longer needed to maintain a pretence of servitude. Lifting her chin and looking down her nose at the man before her, her voice was dark and powerful.

"I serve the Order, the Darkness, and I am the voice and fist of the God of War."

Throwing her hands in the air, a great wave of force accompanied the swift action, hurling the emperor and his men back across the stone floor. Some of the riflemen who raised their guns in anticipation of a fight fired hasty shots. A dark elf reeled backwards with a wound to his hip. Dekon, too, clasped his shoulder, shocked, though the bullet ricocheted off his armour. Of the Bracadians, only Claudius remained on his feet, sliding backwards, and keeping his balance long enough for a quick draw and hip shot aimed at Ahmeda's head. The boom of the large pistol echoed through the chamber, and the bullet sped to end the high priestess' life.

Miraculously, the projectile stopped a thumbs breadth before Ahmeda's nose, a fraction from killing her. For a moment, time paused, then as speedily as the bullet had travelled towards her, it sped back at the big belg, taking him squarely in the jaw. Conjured dark-spears followed the blast of force, skewering Claudius and those riflemen behind him. Ahmeda and Dekon both advanced, unleashing their malevolent wrath. As Ahmeda scanned those tossed to the floor, she could not see the emperor amongst them. Panic suddenly took hold. While the high priestess desperately searched, two dark elves with repeating crossbows kept a lookout for any Bracadians that might still be alive. The citadel garrison would soon appear.

Dekon turned to Ahmeda.

"Where is he?"

"I killed him. He took the brunt of the force, and I saw his chest and throat caved in." She was sure, though his body and the proof had disappeared. "It is a mystery that will need to wait. None of you will speak of it."

After waving for the others to step back, Ahmeda focused her power on the stonework so that the rock warped and melted. As the structure collapsed, rubble cascaded into the passages, which would delay any investigator's work.

"Go." The dark elves dispersed at the order, helping their wounded comrade, and leaving the high priestess to explain what had unfolded. Already she looked distraught, and with her magic, Ahmeda desperately cast broken stone aside as if searching. Others came running, Dekon amongst them, and they assisted as best they could.

PART FOUR:

The Darkness

THE PACT

Jaal tensed then relaxed some of his muscles, though the effort exhausted him. Dutifully, Vilera and another of the spiderkin helped Jaal to his feet to practice moving about the chamber. He was given water in a tall cup, which he sipped. Jaal didn't realise how parched he was until the cool liquid awakened his mouth and senses. It gave him the strength to gulp the water greedily and address his helpers.

"Where are you taking me, daughter?"

"The mother would see you. We will clean and feed you. You will need your strength."

After being led, and sometimes dragged, through the dark tunnels, Jaal was fed meat and fruit, forced into him by unfriendly hands. It all added to his humiliation. The water they used to wash him down was bitterly cold, so his mind and wits became fully alert. Eventually, he stretched to ease his muscles, allowing Jaal more control over the simple movements that were previously denied him. He was resilient, returning quickly to life with the small aid from his children.

Led through passages he was familiar with to a sizeable lit chamber, Jaal stood before the three women so intimately entwined in his life.

"Kneel." It was Eya that commanded him. She was always direct, but this was different, said in a tone that demanded his servitude. When he did not comply, Ahmeda held up her arm and tightened her fist. Unseen energy gripped Jaal's gut, and he crumpled helplessly to the floor. The dark elf struggled against the agony to raise himself on his arms, staring defiantly at the women who would humble him. Saska came closer, and with a savage kick, she took Jaal's arms from beneath him so that his face hit the stone floor hard. His nose felt strangely numb from the impact, and blood dripped from it onto the floor. He wanted to rise, but Ahmeda's divine forces held his chest against the stone. Eya moved to stand alongside Saska, looking down at the pitiful elf.

"Know your place. Ahmeda and Saska are second in Order, and you will obey their commands. You will have no other loyalties, no freedom to decide your fate. Darkness is rising. Regain your strength, for tomorrow you will command the spiderkin. Understand your purpose, Jaal. There is nothing else for you, only obedience."

As he looked up, Eya and Saska were naked. Even under such shameful circumstances, his lust was on fire, blinding him to thought and reason. It was a hold Saska had over him, amplified by her growing powers, and used to control his desires. As much as he comprehended the demoness' ability, Jaal was entirely at her mercy, and his cock hardened. The errant erection did not go unnoticed, and Ahmeda laughed cruelly. Saska, who was just as much at the mercy of her magic, purred. Eya, bored of the play, turned to the spiderkin who were waiting.

"Take him."

When the spiderkin and Jaal departed, Eya turned to the other women.

"It is time. Grengal is ready. Everything is in place."

Ahmeda was apprehensive. She saw their alliance as a collaboration, but it was becoming apparent that Eya, as patron of the Order, commanded the plan. For so long, the Order hierarchy advantaged the high priestess, who rallied the dark elves to her service. But now, the Order demanded her servitude and sacrifice.

"Eya, I must have an assurance that when this is done, I will be free to continue my work in the War God's service. It will take me away from the North."

Saska smiled. For her, the Order was convenient, and her loyalty would last only as long as it served *her* purpose. Ahmeda's angst amused the succubus. Eya, however, appeared deadly serious, and the predator that lurked within the spider mother seemed as if it might leap and consume the high priestess.

"Do you not trust the old ways, Ahmeda? Would you rebel like the others, or will you stay true to your kin and oaths? Is it not enough for you to serve? Are your ambitions more important than the will of the Order?"

"This is an alliance of The Darkness. The Order, as it has always been, is a tool to command the devotion of others. I have shown my loyalty to that Order. It has been my life purpose to protect the old ways, but I am not a slave to them, nor to you, Eya."

Eya's small frame seemed to expand as if she would burst out of her skin. Her eyes multiplied, all staring at the high priestess malevolently. Ahmeda was not going to back down.

"Do you think Saska is loyal to the Order? She will walk away when it no longer suits her purpose."

Saska stiffened at the accusation. She was not expecting to be called out, which awakened the predator in her. She knew in the moment that she would side with Ahmeda if her hand were forced. Her eyes were on Eya, judging her movements and preparing her defences. Fearless, Ahmeda took a step toward the spider mother as she spoke.

"See this partnership for what it is, Eya. Do *you* command the God of War? Do *you* command the demons? Do *you* command the dead? Do you command the dark elves without my help? The Age of the Ancients has passed, and the old ways must adapt to survive. We need loyalty amongst sisters, Eya, to end the rule of men."

At the last point, Eya flinched, and a spec of clarity appeared to take hold. The fearsome visage eased, and Eya paced the room as if that helped to release the burden of anger that consumed her.

"Sisters!"

Ahmeda nodded. Saska was still tense. Not as intuitive as the others, she remained ready to pounce. Eya walked up to her and looked the succubus up and down, examining and judging her.

"You are a child!"

It was the high priestess that came to Saska's defence, "And yet she commands the armies of Hell. We are a potent alliance, Eya!"

Eya swung about to face Ahmeda, subjecting the high priestess to the same scrutiny, locking eyes. Then, after a time, she spoke with words of power.

"The Order forever binds you to my service. Only when I grant it, may you leave the North to follow the War God's purpose." Quickly turning back to Saska, she reiterated. "You, Saska, are bound to the Order and my service. You will *never* be free."

Saska gave a small laugh as if the conversation were nonsense, earning her Eya's diabolic glare. Unphased, the succubus lashed back.

"I not be caged." Insolently, Saska walked around Eya, using the fingernails of her right hand to gently caress over the spider mother's hip and across her buttocks. Then, sidling closer, their thighs touched, and the Succubus' lips caressed the spider mother's ear. "It you needs me."

"Do your job," was the blunt reply.

Admiral Staronis felt vital and energised, as if he were a much younger man. The emperor was correct that Jesephine would gift him life, and he felt it coursing throughout his being. His mind was sharp enough to know the cost of the gift, though he did not have the will to resist Jesephine's instructions or the dire consequences. However, it was with angst that he pulled the fleet away from the conflict, ordering all the navigators aboard his mighty flagship. He called it a conference of minds, required to convey a vital revelation regarding their expertise. The high priestess came in person to ensure proceedings went smoothly, with the mighty war priests stomping about in their riggs, entrusted with the navigators' protection. Ahmeda's presence gave the Aren captains confidence that their new admiral would not place them in peril.

In the sky above the Ryde, the ships deployed in a protective sphere, with weapons aimed outwards. Their captains were nervous about being without their ability to manoeuvre. In the centre of the defensive formation, the admiral's battleship, with the navigators collected together, took centre stage. When the flagship suddenly disappeared and all the navigators with it, the stunned fleet panicked. Those suspicious of the admiral's intent immediately denounced the betrayal for what it was, and they cursed the fates. Then, as if to affirm their worst fears, a demonic swarm manifested in the sky to the west, becoming black and immense, like thunderclouds gathering and angling closer on a strong wind.

Above the Ryde, flying demons hung to the ships' sides or crowded on the decks, tearing relentlessly at the metal hulls. Atop one vessel, a many-headed demon flapped its wings as it ripped great chunks of steel and wood from the hull with its massive beaks. Where it could see inside the ship, it poked its heads into the holes to search out prey. Musket shots rang out, but the demon was unperturbed.

After a day and night of intermittent fighting, the noise of cannon fire and hissing of steam had wholly abated, and the disarmed fleet succumbed to its attackers. Demons that could find no room to perch, flew wide circles about the fleet, while others soared over the plains, scanning for anything alive. Far below the ships, on the Rhyde, demon dead were piled, with other Hell-spawn scrambling over them, feasting on the foul flesh, or gnawing at bones.

One ship appeared above the others, looking down at the odd siege. Saska leaned over a deck rail to watch her army at work. The two dark elves standing beside her seemed impatient, and one who wore the trappings of a war priest spoke out.

"It will take the demons weeks to complete this task. Ahmeda was clear that there must be no survivors. We should descend and get this over quickly."

"Ahmeda not in charge here. Hydra command when we gone. Will come back, make home. Saska powerful sorcerer. Live in sky."

The war priest shook his head. "Anything might happen if we leave the demons to finish this task. The Hydra is a beast of chaos and could lead the swarm away. You risk too much if you let this siege linger."

Saska prickled at being challenged, turning to face her accuser. The pupils in her eyes flared red, and the war priest flinched as if his gut ached. He was sturdy, though, and he possessed magic too, which he used to ease the discomfort and defend against further aggression. "Keep your tricks, Woman. I am a Deacon of the God of War, do not trifle with me. I am here as your advisor. Listen to what I say!"

"You doubt ability command? You think Hydra not obey?"

Saska did not wait for a response. Instead, she turned to the other elf and indicated the ships below with a slight turn of her head.

"Fly."

The elf lifted himself to stand on the rail without hesitation. Then, bending his legs and drawing a sword from his scabbard, which he held outwards, he looked back at the succubus with a grin, and then he launched himself out and away from the ship, arms outstretched. It looked like he might soar, but within moments he was tumbling downwards towards the ground far below.

The war priest slammed a hand on the rail. Then, with a gruff "hmmph", he turned away from Saska and strode towards the ship's bow. After another grunt, he gripped the side rails with both hands and bent his head in prayer. Saska watched him, unafraid of what his God might tell him, curious if he would turn against her. It would be at his peril.

THE PROPHET

Mannace was surprised to see the prophet of Kampatan at the entrance to his bed-chamber. Nobody came uninvited to his quarters, yet this odd man in his orange robes and holding his orange hat awoke him from a deep slumber. Mannace was still dressed in his uniform and breastplate, which he started to take off as he sat up.

"Where is Jayne? Why did my guards let you pass?"

The prophet shrugged. He was well known in Angorok and passed by the guards without questions asked.

"Bring me a drink." The marshall pointed at a jug on a table.

The prophet could not see a cup, so he passed the jug to Mannace as instructed, then he stood back and waited patiently for Mannace to slurp his fill. As Mannace continued to undress, the prophet cleared his throat and addressed the leader in a calm voice. "Angorok will fall. It will be soon."

"When exactly?"

"A day. Days perhaps. When the others arrive."

"What others? Don't make me draw the whole story out of you. By the Four Hells, man, tell me in detail what you know."

The prophet frowned, taking a moment to organise his thoughts. After an unsuccessful attempt to begin a sentence, he raised his arms instead, and an image appeared between his hands. As the hands spread wide, the vision expanded so that Mannace felt emerged within it. He looked down upon Angorok as if he were on a ship above the metropolis. It was night, and as usual, the undead assaulted the third wall. When Mannace peered closer, his focus drew him to an area of the defence where men fought against men, barbarians leading the undead against the familiar forces of humans and orcs. When Mannace thought he had seen what he needed, black shapes passed by, so real that he swatted at the air. Demons! Soon he could see that they were everywhere in a great flock, then just as suddenly, they were behind him. The vision faded, and the prophet dropped his hands.

"Some of it I just know; that the defence will fail. The enemy will take Angorok."

"Don't be another to tell me I must leave."

The prophet seemed perplexed, "How would you do that? There are a million people still within the city. The numbers of the enemy surrounding Angorok appear endless."

Mannace laughed, "By the gods, we are doomed. We must make our own miracle if we are to survive. Tell me, Prophet, what miracles do you bring?"

"The earth will give you sanctuary." When Mannace looked to the prophet for more, the man again shrugged, "It is just a sense of things."

"Yes, they can work with earth and stone, but they cannot do what you ask. They cannot transport all the people here at Angorok through the earth to safety. So be reasonable, Mannace. You ask to raise a mountain in a day."

As Mannace sat across the small table from Logthar, the dwarven wizards gathered in a circle around them. Some were conversing. SinKayLas suddenly loomed over Logthar and they spoke with profound seriousness in their dwarven language.

Further back, Elderlin, Jayne, and Uz watched proceedings. Finally, after a time, Elderlin came forward, "Mannace, the Alani can make a city disappear. They can use the Ways to travel."

Mannace slapped the arm of his chair, and he raised his voice to the elderly wizard. "Where are the fucking elves, Elderlin." Then, seeing the shock on Elderlin's face and pausing for a moment to put his sudden anger aside, the leader spoke in a more even tone. "Apologies, my friend, I am annoyed with myself for not looking at possibilities earlier, and we have no time for anything except desperate measures. What you have just said makes sense, but we do not have the means."

Interrupting Logthar's conversation, Mannace asked the dwarf to discuss what Elderlin raised, and a raucous debate amongst the KinRa ensued. Meanwhile, Mannace pulled Elderlin aside, "Gather the Muster. All of them."

To Jayne, who Mannace summoned with a wave of his hand, he added, "Fetch Ahmeda and Morgan to the war room. Tell me when they have arrived."

Ahmeda was hard to find. It required the dark elves to search for her. Eventually, Mannace met with the high priestess and Morgan as night fell.

"It seems clear from the evidence that the emperor is dead or captured. We can't wait for the admiral's return before we act. There is no time. It falls to the two of you as his agents to take the news of the emperor's demise to the colonies and Bracadia,"

Ahmeda seemed impatient as if she had other things to attend to. It was quickly pissing Mannace off. "Am I boring you, Ahmeda? I would have thought this was of utmost importance to you."

The high priestess bristled at the half-accusation but relaxed her stance after eyeing both men in a calculating fashion. "What is it you want, Mannace?"

"You have the emperor's ship. Take it now while you can."

Ahmeda huffed. "You cannot order us, Mannace. You do not have that authority."

"It is a gift. To free you from the fate of Angorok."

"I will stay. I will leave when I am ready."

Mannace's gut tightened, and his mind was racing as he began questioning the high priestess' motives. "There is something you are not sharing with us, Ahmeda. Tell us what that is." Morgan remained silent, but he appeared as interested as Mannace to hear the priestess' answer, watching her intently.

"The emperor is gone, Mannace. I am the voice of the God of War, and I am needed here, where the soldiers of the War God fight. Therefore, I will honour him as his hand in battle, and I will leave when Angorok is secure."

Mannace shook his head, "You have changed, Ahmeda. It is time for you to leave Angorok. Immediately."

The priestess' eyes narrowed, and she appeared to rise in stature. Before she could act, however, Morgan took a tight grip on her arm. "Ahmeda, we will leave now. I will escort you." Then, to Mannace, Morgan added, "I will return, my friend."

Ahmeda stood at the entrance to the emperor's palace, at the heart of the Blue Land. She was furious with Morgan, who dumped her here in Bracadia and departed. He would sorely regret such drastic action. On the other hand, it would give her time to organise before he returned.

Morgan's act abruptly ended her part in the Northern conflict, and despite being at the centre of the Bracadian empire, she could not have felt more isolated. While her elaborate plans seemed ruined, she already did enough to firmly seal the fate of Mannace and those others under his care.

STONE AND STEEL

Mannace ordered the third wall abandoned, and the defence of the second wall commenced. Knowing it was a task he could not delay, the marshall went to Dekon, who rested with his priests in their barracks. The building's halls and rooms, usually pristine, were cluttered and dirty, with no time or motivation for the acolytes to grab a mop. Jayne, who was at Mannace's side, ran a finger over a dirty tabletop as they passed, huffing with disdain at the trail his print left in the grime.

Dekon led Mannace to an altar room, where they sat on an extended bench. Both leaders prayed to the God of War, and Mannace felt a weight off his shoulders and strength in his tired bones.

"Dekon, you are high priest once more. Ahmeda will not be returning. I must know that the priesthood and the dark elves will be loyal."

Dekon looked hard at Mannace, risking a glance towards Jayne, who remained straight-faced. The bodyguard didn't like games or the politics of his kin.

"I serve the God of War." As he said it, Dekon could feel the War God's presence in the room, and he heard a voice booming from his gut, "GLORY EVEN IN DEFEAT". It was the first time his God spoke to him directly, leaving him shaken as if he might suddenly weep.

Sucking in a deep breath and puffing out his chest, Dekon looked fixedly at Mannace, who returned the intense stare, "Glory, even in defeat. The War God is with us this night."

"I had a vision, Dekon, that the enemy overran the third wall tonight. So, I have withdrawn our forces to the second wall to confound the enemy's plans and buy us more time. It will take them days to build new ramps. We will use that time to manufacture a miracle, for that is what we will need, and it is what the Muster will deliver us. Lead the Muster, Dekon; they will rally for you."

Dekon nodded, but he was still reeling, still momentarily broken, and humbled by the voice of God. "I must pray tonight. Then I will command the Muster."

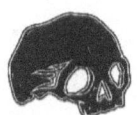

The Citadel was enormous, befitting a city the size of Angorok, and the extensive network of cellars and armouries below the complex were likewise impressive. Its architects designed it to withstand the direst of sieges. It could accommodate a multitude of civilians and soldiers, though it was still not big enough nor defensible against the horrors Mannace expected.

"It must be strong enough to turn back the demon generals with their sinister magic. One hole in the defence will let in a flood of ..."

"Stop yourself there, lad," interrupted Logthar. "Would you tell a dwarf how to grow a beard? The KinRa know their business, Mannace, and they won't appreciate your babble."

Mannace laughed. Logthar talked over the top of that too.

"We're sealing it up. These halls will never again see the light of day. Follow me, and I'll show you."

The dwarf led the Marshall of Angorok through a series of familiar passageways to an area where a dwarven wizard was at work, aided by conclave members. Mannace immediately observed that the ancient blockwork had lost all of its cracks. Where there had been a narrow window, now the gap was filled and seamless as the other masonry. A Maven was there, casting her magic to augment the dwarven craft, strengthening the stone to give it a hardness like steel. Three priests of different faiths added warding against the demons and undead. Mannace stepped aside as two magetechs came in carrying lighting strips, followed by one of the Fesadi who placed plants at the edge of the room. The strange vine reached out to the stonework and stretched itself a meter up the wall. When the plant relaxed, leaves unfolded, and buds were already appearing. One tendril stretched a little further and was still again. On noticing Mannace's interest, the Fesadi commented, "When it is fully grown, in about a week, it will cover this wall and help with the air. Its berries are sour but edible."

"Is that how we will breathe?"

"No, Lad," interrupted Logthar. "The KinRa will handle that. Clean air is the first thing you must consider when your home is beneath the earth. There are many other matters, but it's all in hand. So, relax, Mannace, put your attention to something you understand."

Again, Mannace laughed. This time Logthar frowned, not seeing the humour. One of the dwarven wizards spoke to Logthar in their language, reminding the grey dwarf of other details to share with the marshall.

"Most KinRa are in the lower reaches, burrowing beneath the citadel and into the hill. In the depths, there are some existing wells, but they won't suffice, so the KinRa are widening them. And most importantly, more room is needed to fit everybody. Stone and earth are the essences of the Core, Mannace. It won't be fancy, but the dwarves will deliver what you need."

As Mannace made his way through more corridors to one of the few remaining balconies, Jayne and Uz joined him. With Jayne present, his other ranger guards departed.

The three men looked out over the city. Below, many of the populace were already making their way into the citadel, dragging their essential belongings. It would take time to squeeze them all in, and Mannace gave a silent prayer to the War God that they would have the capacity for the soldiers as well. On the second wall, warriors maintained their vigil, and with the elemental storm dissipated, they were enjoying the warm day. Beyond that, the enemy horde swarmed about the city and quickly built their ramps using the city dwellings which they tore apart. It was happening much quicker than Mannace would have liked. Further afield, the enemy numbers remained endless.

"Jayne, have word sent to the Arenlanders to use the remaining mortar ammunition. It's too damn quiet. Let's remind everybody that there's a battle to be fought."

Just before Jayne disappeared down the passage, Mannace called out. "Jayne. Send a messenger to have the bulls and brula search for the admiral. Let us survey the land, a final look before we hide away."

The dark elf nodded. Mannace turned back to stare up at the circling vultures. The giant birds were slow but sending his scouts into the wilderness was risky. Nonetheless, perhaps it was better for the flyers to be free rather than trapped beneath the earth.

The KinRa finished crafting an immense cavern beneath Angorok, where Mannace's flagship appeared, then was quickly gone on its next mission. The underground port would be a vital link in supplying the defence and keeping contact with their dwindling allies at Adash, Colossus, and amongst the Eastern Colonies. Mannace hoped for more ships, but the Blood Legion did not return from Attica, and Admiral Staronis appeared to have abandoned them. Even Morgan did not return, though rumour placed him at Colossus, where the Bracadian army was now regrouping and awaiting transport home.

To avoid combat as the enemies' ramps drew closer to the crenulations of the second wall, Mannace ordered the retreat to the first wall, his final bastion, which the soldiers achieved in good order. But, as the citadel filled, it became more apparent that there would not be sufficient room for all his troops. A final battle seemed inevitable.

Dire news arrived that Adash had fallen, and the surviving Rhalec and allies fled towards the Palainth. Render was still absent, and the whereabouts of Jaal was also unknown. Mannace could feel his influence shrinking so that soon, the citadel of Angorok would be his whole world, caught in a hopeless trap and waiting for the end. It made him laugh at himself and the Fates.

At last, a spec of hope; a message in one of the magic boxes from Colossus, from Morgan, that help was coming. Then

Morgan's empty ship arrived at Angorok, and Mannace borrowed it so that he could command two vessels. With increased urgency, he transported civilians to Attica, where Khing made them welcome.

THE FALL OF ANGOROK

An Iron Jaw orc, one of the revered bull riders, brought news to Mannace that he witnessed the fate of the admiral's dead fleet. It was good that the orc possessed the sense not to spread such a terrible omen more widely. Another rider came with the news that colossi were marching from the city of Colossus towards Angorok and that Morgan Cain was with them. Mannace kept this secret too, except for his most senior commanders. Aside from that, none of the other scouts returned.

The dwarven wizards, bar one who chose to stay, returned to the IceSleepers aboard Morgan's ship. Logthar, who was leaving with them, offered some final advice for Mannace.

"Lad, forget about the colonies, Bracadia, and even the North. You are not indebted to any of them. You are a free man."

Mannace dipped his head.

"Logthar, why did the dwarven wizard choose to stay?"

"UnRey, he is the youngest amongst them. It was not his choice, lad, SinKayLas ordered him. I do not know the why of it. They will not likely see such reasoning as my business."

The line of questioning raised a thought in the dwarf.

"The queen's mastersmith, GarRamMon. His teams make the earth-breakers and drills for the VengTan-AsTenRey. I have worked alongside him. If you survive this siege, lad, I can work with the engineers to get you what you need to expand deeper into the earth. It is not so bad to be underground."

Mannace put a hand on the dwarf's shoulder, and his eyes were shiny as if holding back a tear. "Logthar, I am broken. I truly appreciate you as a friend."

Logthar put his hand on Mannace's shoulder too. He did not know what words to share. Instead, the dwarf nodded his head, and he turned to board the waiting vessel.

As the marshall returned to the upper citadel, Elderlin intercepted him. The wizard seemed excited, leading Mannace through passageways to a small room. It was one of the outer chambers, where the wall facing the citadel exterior had been transformed into glass. The transparent section was perhaps the depth of a tall man.

"The Asari worked on it with the techsmiths. They say it is tougher than the walls around it, merging with the stone so it can't be poked out. Unfortunately, there is too much else to do to create more, but it is a blessing nonetheless, a light in the void, so to speak."

Mannace understood what the wizard meant. His spirit lifted to see natural light in the darkness. The citadel suddenly felt less like a trap. Eager, the marshall stepped up to the glass and looked at the sky and city. Almost immediately, his optimism was replaced with a tightening lump in his gut. A flight of demons passed high above. Their blackness and erratic formation gave away their identity, even at a great distance.

"The Hells come together against us, Elderlin. They give us no peace."

"There has never been peace, Mannace."

The logistics and maths were not working for the marshall. By his calculation, the citadel and extensive catacombs would accommodate half a million civilians and warriors. While it seemed a significant number, it was half what he needed. To make the situation worse, news of the colossi making their way to Angorok leaked to the general populace. Those uncomfortable about locking themselves away in the dark were clinging to the hope of rescue. Mannace was certain such thinking was folly, but he did not have the means to enact a better plan. His fatalistic views were such that he dared not engage further with the prophet of Kampatan; lest his predictions eroded his remaining resolve. Instead, the leader took his fate into his hands, summoning his staff and generals to prepare a final defence and retreat.

As Mannace looked over the roster of his armies before the meeting, he realised what an elite force they had become. In particular, the loyalists stuck with him over the decades of warfare in the North. Five divisions of these soldiers were from across the Eastern Colonies, with all types of armaments and capabilities. Mannace was immensely proud of these men and women, and he knew they would stay with him at Angorok no matter how dire the circumstance. Many of them spent their whole adult life here, and some were born in the region.

With his officers gathered, Mannace banged on a table to get everybody's attention, and then he started with what they already knew. "Five Angorok divisions. Eighteen divisions of Bracadians, including artillery, and nineteen divisions of orcs. Two rhalec divisions. Eight hundred stone animations, steel workers, and the Muster of magicians, priests, and animators. Over half a million civilians."

It was time to confirm to them the rumours and the intent. "Morgan Cain will arrive within the day with the colossi. When he arrives, the orcs, Bracadians, and those civilians waiting for rescue will join him. Then, they will return to Colossus."

One of the generals of Mannace's Angorok forces called out the thought that was instantly on many lips.

"With the colossi, we should fight. We will push the enemy back from Angorok."

Mannace needed to be firm.

"The colossi are loyal to the city of Colossus, not Angorok. These colossi have not fought our battles nor marched with our armies. They are not ours to command, and they are not invincible. They come to take the Wengo home. It will not be an easy escape."

The orc generals seemed uneasy. Finally, one of them raised his voice.

"Wengo orcs colossus friend. Angorok lost. Wengo go."

One of the Angorok commanders was unconvinced, "Churgwarthos is dead. There is nothing here to give the colossi a challenge. They can clear the walls and target the enemy command."

Others were nodding. Mannace was sure in his gut that they were wrong, but he did not have arguments that would convince these men. He could command them, and they would obey, but doubt would make them stupid and put the defence at risk. Reluctantly, Mannace called for the prophet of Kampatan, and the strange man, dressed in his distinctive orange robes, was soon standing before them.

The prophet was agitated at being summoned and asked for time to prepare, which he was allowed. As the others in the room stood with their arms folded or leaning against the walls, the prophet closed his eyes and gradually emptied his mind, allowing the void to be filled with knowledge and visions. He knew the question on the lips of the generals, so he let the answer reveal itself, then be released. His arms outstretched, the projection of his knowledge manifested between his palms, then expanded to fill the room. All the commanders flinched or ducked as imaginary demons swarmed about them. Beyond the lesser creatures, the demon generals loomed, hurling their diabolic magic. As the vision lifted skyward, the commanders in the room looked back at the demon host and undead horde side-by-side as they swarmed over Angorok. Potent magic issued from both armies, washing over the citadel, and assaulting the impregnable defence. As the vision faded, the exhausted prophet collapsed into a chair, and the room was utterly silent. Victory was impossible, and at best, the citadel preparations would provide a desperate refuge against an overwhelming onslaught. Even Mannace felt he was watching his doom, though he was not utterly defeated yet.

"Our time will come to rise again. Without Angorok as an enemy, these undead and demons will turn to war upon one another or other rivals. Through alliances, we will regather our host and our strength, and it will be our enemies that crumble. That is how it is, my friends, that we will rise from the earth to reclaim what has been lost. We will stamp our authority irrevocably on the North."

His audience wanted to believe Mannace, and the words helped them to see past the great peril in front of them, to gift them a spec of hope. It was no secret that the Fates and Gods gave Mannace no peace. It was why the adventurous of heart flocked to him.

"Be proud that you are at the centre of the world, and the gods stand here with you. Your ancestors and your future generations stand with you. The North is no ordinary land, and you are not living an ordinary life. Rejoice that we are the light in the darkness. As champions, we raise our swords against the enemy of all mortal races."

It was as if the enemy knew Morgan would arrive soon with the colossi, increasingly determined to complete their work before he appeared. Multitudes of flying demons circled above Angorok. The flyers were always a precursor to the arrival of more significant forces. In this case, Mannace was expecting the formidable demon army that collected in Sarville to soon appear from the west.

The undead laboured tirelessly, driven hard by unseen masters, to complete their ramps, and they were already assailing the last defence with sporadic surges. There was a great sense of impending calamity, and Mannace walked the wall to rally his troops and keep them steadfast. They all knew the importance of holding the final bastion until Morgan arrived.

Human adversaries appeared on the walls the enemy previously captured. It was the first time the necromancers in their bright robes revealed themselves. Similarly adorned in colourful clothes, their guards and other sentinels watched and waited. Units of organised dead, more aware and capable than the rabble they fought so far, marshalled in preparation for an attack. Barbaric warriors made their way towards the ramps through the throng, spurring Mannace to call his reserves to action.

The walls were packed with orcs and faithful Angorok fighters. Behind the defence, the forsaken Bracadians formed their units, and Angorok crossbowmen looked out from buildings. Dispersed were the priests, vital to holding back the undead and demons, backed by the many stone and steel animations.

A roar started amongst the barbarians, culminating in a great rattling of bones and shouts from the living, as the enemy host surged forward. First to come over the ramparts were the swarm of skeletal undead, frenzied and throwing themselves upon the defenders. Their attack was furious but easily contained. Mannace, who stood between Jayne and Dekon, was pleased with the ferocity of his troops, who fought with skill and savagery.

"Fuck these undead and their bastard masters. They will need to throw more than bones across these walls to give us a challenge."

As if the enemy heard him, the first barbarian stepped onto the crenelations, leaping at the trio with a yell. Behind the fierce-looking warrior, three others pushed past the clambering undead. When the musketmen below fired up at one of the fighters, the tattoos covering their target writhed, and the bullets ricocheted harmlessly off his skin.

Mannace drew his long blade but let Dekon and Jayne step in front of him. Dekon in his war rig was an incredible sight, and the god hammer he wielded swept aside the undead and collided with a barbarian's axe in a flash of sparks and power. Both combatants staggered back, unused to giving ground. Seeing that the barbarians possessed magic, Jayne backed away from his adversary and swapped his swords for the bone bow on his back. Like the bullets, his arrows struck the fierce enemy but caused him no harm. Wisely, the elf and Mannace retreated down steps towards the inner-city streets. Angorok soldiers, including a stone man, ran past them towards the battlements and to Dekon's aid.

Ghostly spectres of long-dead heroes appeared above Mannace on the battlements, fighting the living and dead, and some struck at each other. What was happening seemed obvious to Mannace.

"Jayne, the barbarians are the War God's champions too." To runners who awaited his orders, Mannace shouted, "Put up the green smoke. It is all in now."

A brula latched high on the outside of the citadel launched itself, speeding down to Mannace's position. In a shrill voice, the creature told Mannace what he feared most.

"Demons west. Undead move south."

Mannace was out of tricks, out of luck. He watched Dekon, who was joined by another deacon of his order, as they unleashed god's wrath on their opponents. Skirmishes abounded on the battlements around them as the rabble undead were replaced with more sinister foes; well-armoured skeletons that were agile and skilled, and ghostly banshees that forced men back with their high-pitched screams. One of the barbarians leapt amongst a group of halberdiers, cleaving one and then sending others scampering with a titanic swing of his broad axe. The burly warrior bellowed, his war cry audible above the noise of battle, before throwing himself into combat in a crazed frenzy. On the street next to Mannace, more Bracadians gathered, their regiment firing into the melee but with limited effect. Horses pulling an artillery piece cantered past, coming to a halt in an area with more room to set up. The artillerymen quickly arranged their equipment.

In a magical blast of tremendous force, Dekon was lifted off his feet and spiralled through the air. Although Mannace could not see it, he could hear the war priests rig smash into the roof of the building above him. From the noise of splintering timbers that followed, Dekon was still alive and breaking himself free. The artillery fired a shell into the battlements, where the enemy rushed in large numbers. The explosion sent stone and skeletons flying, showering those on the street below with debris. One of the targeted barbarians landed near Mannace and Jayne, and Jayne stabbed a killing blow at the stunned and battered man. Though the dark elf's blade poked out the barbarians back, the enemy raised himself onto his haunches and rose slowly to his feet. It wasn't until a brave rifleman ran to put his gun to the barbarian's head and pull his trigger that the fighter, his skull shattered, slumped lifeless to the cobbles.

Uz appeared at Mannace's side, having rushed from the citadel to witness events. The Rhalec carried his horn above his head, and it glowed as if it were the sun. Under its bright rays, the enemy's ghosts and the War God's spirits all faded, leaving only the living to wrestle and cleave. Another artillery shot brought down more debris, and Jayne pulled at Mannace to withdraw. Together they moved past the big guns to an area where the defence was more intact. Uz and a gathering force of rangers followed. In their wake, Dekon burst through the wall of a building and joined orc reinforcements as they ran up the stairs to re-enter the wall melee.

It seemed to Mannace that these new undead came with more flies that buzzed and bit. It was a nuisance that added to his sense of dread.

CHOICES

Demmal clambered over the makeshift ramp and lifted himself onto the battlements. He joined four of the Devoted and the necromancer who had captured the position. The necromancer stayed where there was cover, and as he waved his staff, the undead responded by surging in a great mob around him and over the wall. Where they could not reach steps, the rabble of skeletons and zombies leapt at the enemy that waited below, uncaring if they plummeted to their doom. In such numbers and with their fanaticism, the skeletons were a lot for the tiring soldiers of Angorok to defend. The advantage gave Demmal time to survey the deployments. He sent two of the Devoted west along the wall towards a defended tower, with a contingent of the Tomb Guard on their heels. Then, Demmal turned to the other two barbarians.

"Fanger, hold this section of wall. Call more Tomb Guards onto the battlements and send a unit to take and hold those buildings. Vikas, come with me."

With his orders given, Demmal took a step and leapt after the skeletons, raising his axe so that when he landed heavily amongst the fighting, he swung the weapon in a wide arc, causing bloody mayhem. The leader of the Devoted summoned a prayer of fearsome visage, and to his opponents, Demmal appeared to grow and loom over them, his axe brushing orc warriors aside. In a glance, he saw Vikas land further down the street, cleaving the hapless enemy. Ghosts of wolves gathered about Vikas to feast off the dead and leap at the living. With the space in the street created by the Devoted's attacks, more undead landed, most rising to rush at the stalwart defenders. It gave Demmal another moment to step back and assess the action. Suddenly, a swarm of flies passed close overhead, indicating Grengal herself might be nearby. But instead, the insects coalesced into a humanish shape so that one of the Ragnak was unexpectedly behind him. The vile witch hissed, and dark tendrils issued from her fingertips, snaking their way through the air past the undead and into the enemy host. Where the tendrils touched the living, orcs screamed as they shrivelled to dry husks. Then, as quickly as the Ragnak appeared, she was gone, dispersed, with flies buzzing in all directions.

The garrison, bolstered with arriving reinforcements, rapidly pushed back the undead. There was a stone man amongst them, who Demmal charged. As he ran, another prayer strengthened his arm, but before he could deliver a crushing blow, the leader of the Devoted was hit by an extraordinary force from above. It was the most he could do to flail his axe to keep those that would finish him at bay. As Demmal looked up through glazed eyes, he saw the shape of a bull and rider lifting back into the air. A giant vulture came from the side to strike the rider, but the orc was sturdy enough to pull himself upright and remain in the saddle. Flies buzzed about Demmal, again in an intense swarm that pushed all his enemies back except the stone man. The living statue brought a hammer down on Demmal's shoulder and would have smashed his collarbone had Demmal not had the essence of the War God flowing through him. That same divine energy hastened his recovery, so that Demmal staggered back to his feet and an instant later was on the attack. With renewed prayers, he struck at the stone man and others hurrying to support him, growing in stature until he was momentarily giant-like, chopping all those about him to a bloody pulp. Even the stone man was severely damaged and shuffling quickly backwards. Shots from muskets rang out, and above Demmal, the wall exploded, showering him with debris. Ignoring the blast and dust, Fangar, with a contingent of Tomb Guards, ran past to attack the enemy in the buildings. Nearby, Vikas and his hounds were still engrossed in combat, though the skeletons around him were no match for the fierce Rhalec who arrived to bash them aside.

When Demmal turned, this time Grengal stood next to him.

"Why do you dally here, Demmal? I want the Devoted to blockade the citadel. We will finish this army now. Give the order."

Grengal turned, and a swarm of insects emanated from her outstretched arms, joined by other swarms cast by Ragnak witches who coalesced on the wall above. Ancient mummies, the tomb lords of the Dead Wastes, stood with them. The flies became so thick that Demmal could see nothing else, and he waited until the air cleared, and a tangle of fallen soldiers carpeted the road before him. Skeletons, following the flies, poured into the street and side alleys. Except for their rattling bones and the buzz of remaining insects, the noise of battle seemed distant. A spectre flitted past, almost invisible in the daylight. In the lull, Demmal waved to Vikas, and he shouted for Fangar to join him.

Once the keepers descended the steps, they stood amongst the bodies, and more dead rose to their bidding. Mysteriously, there was orange smoke in the sky above Angorok.

The three Devoted hastened through the city's alleys, keeping their bearings by looking up at the looming citadel. They passed the enemy, some of whom paid the barbarians little attention, while those that tried to bar their way felt the War God's anger and did little to delay them. When Demmal burst onto the main thoroughfare leading to the citadel's steps and entrance, he met a host of orcs and men. At their fore, formidable stone men and towering clockwork defenders formed a wide cordon to protect those retreating.

Standing before the portal, ushering the soldiers into the safety of the citadel, Demmal watched Mannace as he pointed and shouted. Not far from the enigmatic leader, Dekon slouched in his war rig, wounded, and receiving attention from a healer. It saddened Demmal that Mannace was his foe, but that was war, and the War God gave no mercy or tolerance for disloyalty. He did, as Grengal instructed him, have a job to do!

Demmal called on his god-gifted strength and released a roar that reverberated between the buildings and filled the sky. At first, the surprised enemy cowered and stepped back, but when they saw it was just three men that confronted them, soldiers charged, and musketmen fired. Answering Demmal's call, ghosts appeared from buildings, and all kinds of spectral warriors hurried from their hiding places. At first, they were just a few, but soon masses attacked from all directions. From alleys, skeletons and zombies poured into the thoroughfare. Amidst the mob, Tomb Guards and Tomb Lords secured sections of the streets, so that the revealed Ragnak could safely unleash their death magic on the desperate crowd. Keepers appeared at the windows of secured buildings, waving their staves and spurring the undead into a ferocious fervour. At their urging, the skeletons swarmed over the barrier of animations.

Sensing the siege was lost, the enemy pulled back, and those nearest the citadel hastened their evacuation into the building. Others ran to join them or withdrew into the city towards the north gate, not looking back at the swarming enemy at their heels.

Demmal felt the intensity of the prayers from priests among the citadel defenders. The devotions prevented the spectres from overwhelming their position. Other retaliatory magic arched towards the undead, exploding amongst their ranks, and dispersing the growing clouds of flies. Seeing more Devoted finally reach the combat, Demmal, Vikas, and Fengar, yelled their battle cries and charged into the fight.

Ducking under the swing of a Keshik dervish, Demmal blasted the woman with a punch of the War God's wrath, sending her body spiralling over the top of the melee. With his axe raised, he charged and shattered a stone man, knocking bowmen and priests back with the aftershock of his prayer. Around him, the fighting was desperate, and Fengar disappeared in a blast of magical fire. Demmal dodged left to avoid the fierce heat from the explosion, joining Vikas in an assault on a priest of war. The devout warrior in his war rig was tall and commanding, with a hammer in his hand that cracked and sparked with spiritual energies. Rays of white light blasted from the weapon at Vikas, but he ducked the magic and swung his axe at the priest's leg, denting the rig and putting his enemy off balance. Dekon took advantage of the diversion by chopping down at the champion's chest armour, his axe-head penetrating deeply into the steel. As their opponent toppled forward, the devoted struck more blows to ensure the war priest would not rise again. Then, finally, they were through the dwindling cordon.

Still, most of the enemy had already escaped into the citadel portal, and it was just the few living that pushed through the closing gap, sacrificing their animated allies who battled on. Mannace was steadfast at the doors, helping people pass through. The leader glanced up, and Demmal saw, by the shock in his expression, that Mannace recognised the barbarian charging towards him. Staying focused on his objective, Demmal bashed aside two retreating soldiers, and he raced towards the narrowing gap in the closing doors. The stunned Marshall of Angorok waited too long before stepping back. Demmal was atop him, axe raised in both hands above his head, staring his counterpart in the eye. At the last second, Demmal leant forward, and he put his elbow into Mannace's chest, sending him reeling backwards. Hands grabbed the leader and pulled him inside the citadel as the doors closed. When they slammed shut, the wood and steel of the portal instantly changed appearance to be like that of the other stonework, sealing the soldiers of Angorok away.

Demmal slammed the flat of his blade against the stone and roared. It was a howl birthed in his gut but haunted by the pain of a lost past. In that moment he hated Grengal. Hated what he had become. When Demmal eventually turned and cast his vision beyond the fighting, it took a moment for his emotions to settle and to take in his surroundings. His army of dead swamped the defiant guardians, striking and grabbing at them, while others spilt into the streets beyond the citadel. Skirmishes abounded with orcs and riflemen as enemy units hastily withdrew toward the northern gate.

Unexpectedly, there was a tremendous crashing sound as a gigantic shape appeared above the houses. With reckless abandon, it kicked skeletons and toppled a building onto a street full of undead. Demmal caught sight of another colossal creature pushing over a bell tower to aid the escape of the fleeing defenders. The Devoted leader quickly called his barbarians back. They did enough this day, and he would not sacrifice them against such an impossible enemy.

As twilight approached, demons, led by their massive generals, smashed their way through the walls and ramps to assault the citadel. Their powerful magics splashed and blasted the fortress-like walls, and they clawed at the stonework to break it apart. However, by midnight, the generals fell back, defeated by the impregnable defence, while their minions smothered it, crawling and seeking a weakness. As Demmal retreated with the Devoted, he wondered about the sense of allying with the demon spawn. Perhaps Grengal hoped their potency would be enough to demolish Angorok's final bastion. His heart felt the terror of those trapped within.

Demmal felt compassion for the handful of orc and human prisoners tied to poles outside the city. Grengal summoned a swarm of flies, a unique few landing on the prisoners to gnaw their way into the screaming men's flesh. Demmal subconsciously placed a hand on his chest, feeling the welts where he once suffered the same horror. He could still feel the creatures alive within him, wriggling and giving him no peace. It was the same diabolic magic that compelled him to serve Grengal. Like his fate, these prisoners would join the ranks of Grengal's servants, assassins, and spies.

As Demmal reflected further, he realised that he served the high keeper not because she chose if he would live or die, but because the Ancient allowed him to preach the War God's doctrine and train the Devoted to the War God's cause. He was proud of the elite troop.

DARKEST HOUR

So many years ago, Tyriah was right; the cities of the Veldaan were a tomb for Mannace and his wardshundres of thousands of people crammed into Angorok's final sanctuary. They were safe, at least while the masonry and enchantments of the citadel and its immense cellars held against their aggressors. But it was a meagre and depressing existence in the dim light and cold chambers. Work continued to increase the space in the lower reaches, and there was a determination amongst the populace and soldiers to continue the Northern fight. Contact with the outside world was possible using the two flying ships teleporting in and out of the citadel's underground port.

Mannace stood in the room with the transparent wall. Two demons, a flyer and a crawler, clung to the exterior stonework, obscuring his vision. Still, he could see past them at the vast horde of demons and still an endless quantity of undead.

He spoke to Elderlin, who stood quietly with Jayne and Uz nearby.

"When will they turn on each other; it seems inevitable. And why do the demons and undead collaborate? Am I such a significant target that they would put aside their fierce hatred to defeat me? It is no secret that the Hells despise each other. So, this alliance is ludicrous."

The Asari shrugged as if he had no answers, but he shared his thoughts anyway. "How do you know that the Hells despise each other? Perhaps that is just hearsay, and we are learning otherwise. Or perhaps the demons and undead are not commanded by the hierarchy of the Hells?"

"You are right, Elderlin. We fought demons and undead before the Mad King's treachery. But not like this."

Mannace pointed at a gigantic demon through the portal. The vile creature stomped amongst the rubble and bellowed at the horde around it.

"I imagine if we went back an Age to when the Gods and Ancients and Hells fought, it might look like this. It is not a battleground for ordinary men."

"Men are not ordinary, Mannace. The world is much bigger than Angorok, and the North and men are far from being defeated. Have faith in your kin and the other races. Have confidence in your technology and industry."

The Asari walked to stand in front of Mannace and meet his gaze.

"What you see out that portal is the same as it was in an Age past. The foe you face has not evolved. It has not advanced its culture or expertise across the millennia. They are powerful, yes, and here and now, they have the victory. But *men* rose from meagre beginnings. Men have learned and explored. Men have colonised and adapted. Look at your technology and think of what it will mean for the future."

Mannace met Elderlin's gaze. He wanted to be inspired by the Asari's words. Elderlin was gently nodding as he spoke.

"Your destiny is what they fear. The destiny to unite the North. You are immortal, Mannace, and you will rise again and again, as many times as needed, until you fulfil your fate. Men and their inventions, ambition, and ego will overcome these relics of the past. One day, the undead, demons, Ancients, and even the gods, will be utterly forgotten."

Elderlin shrugged again. He had no more words to give. Then, in an uncharacteristic show of appreciation, Mannace stepped forward and put his arm around the old Asari, drawing him closer.

"Elderlin, I am glad that I found you. You are the heart of all men. I thank you."

Uz and Jayne behind them shared a glance. As the hierarchy of command became more casual in Angorok, Jayne grew bolder in his conversation.

"What of the dark elves and Rhalec?"

Mannace laughed and turned. He seemed rejuvenated.

"Men, Rhalec, orcs, we will stand together."

As he paused, Mannace realised he had not included the dark elves, and the good humour seemed suddenly lost. Jayne and Mannace shared a long look, leaving much unsaid until Uz lifted his horn to offer a prayer to the Sun God. Then, he looked thoughtfully at the others and bared his yellowish crocodile teeth.

"Let usss pledge honour and unity. The future isss what we make it."

Mannace was half asleep on his bed. Sleeping with so much responsibility and the threat of the demons on his doorstep was hard. The words of Elderlin swirled around in his brain, and he did his utmost to shift his thinking from the present to longer-term plans. It meant coming to terms with his role, his destiny to be a champion for humanity. The thought of it healed some of the angst he was carrying from the disaster at the Mesah Long.

Jayne entered his chamber. That was not strange, but four other dark elves followed him. Mannace immediately reached for the shortsword hidden under a pillow and shifted out of bed to confront his assassins. There was no mystery as to their motives.

"So, this is it. After so many decades, you finally dare to put a blade in me. Why did you wait so long, Jayne?"

One of the elves, possibly eager for the prestige of the kill, raised and aimed his repeating crossbow. As he pulled the trigger, Jayne pushed the assassin's arm, causing a flurry of bolts to strike a line across the wall above Mannace's bed. The bowman coughed blood and collapsed to the floor as Jayne withdrew one of his blades from the elf's side. Jayne quickly raised his second sword to parry as one of the other dark elves sliced viciously at his head. In a heartbeat, Jayne had two of his kin raining cuts and thrusts at him, and it took all his skill to defend as he stepped backwards. However, Mannace was not idle, heaving his bedside cabinet at the assailants, hitting one and throwing both off balance. Jayne used the distraction to his advantage, and he leapt to the attack, impaling one combatant, and stabbing the other twice in his limbs before decapitating the dark elf with a powerful slice. One dark elf was missing, and Jayne glanced at Mannace before disappearing out the door in pursuit.

Later that evening, Mannace, with ten of his rangers, Elderlin, and Uz in tow, made his way to Jayne's private room. They knew he was inside, and two rangers with blades drawn pushed open his door. Two others with crossbows aimed through the open portal. One of them put down his weapon and looked back at Mannace."

"What is this?"

Mannace pushed past the soldiers and looked into the lit room. Jayne was on the floor, his blades cast aside. Crawling over him were spiders the size of a hand, black and furry. Mannace rushed in and began casting the creatures aside, soon helped by the others. The marshall knew from the fate of other elves that these were the spider mother's assassins; efficient and deadly. Uz leant over the still dark elf, glancing up to nod optimistically at Mannace, before starting a chant and lifting his horn towards the heavens. Even away from the light, all in the room could feel the tingle of magic at work, and the cool chamber grew suddenly warmer.

A ranger in the corridor put a boot down upon one of the escaping arachnids, twisting his foot to ensure the job. Before he looked up, a spear appeared through his gut, pushed with a second shove to protrude out his back. A spiderkin, one of Jaal's children, pulled the weapon free, then as suddenly as the creature appeared, it was gone. In its place was the noise of scuttling and shadowy shapes appearing in the corridor. The crossbowmen fired, but within seconds the passage was filled with giant spiders, man-sized, scuttling along the floors, walls, and ceiling. They descended mercilessly and overwhelmed the rangers, webbing them and biting them with poisoned fangs.

A ranger in the room slammed closed the door to Jayne's chamber, just in time. One of the spider's legs was severed as the door locked. Another man pushed a set of drawers across the room to shove against the portal. Elderlin took the initiative.

"Pick up Jayne and follow me."

The wizard cast his hand in a downward motion, and the wall at the back of the chamber melted, creating a hole in the stone large enough for them to pass through. With Elderlin and Mannace leading them, the group did as instructed. They were in the rangers' barracks, and the yells and screams of its inhabitants indicated more skirmishes were breaking out. Stepping into a wide corridor, Elderlin picked a route, hurrying ahead of the others. In the opposite direction, shapes manifested in the gloom. Rangers appeared from a side door, in a state of half-dress. The enemies charged one another.

After running a short distance, Elderlin turned and retreated to the back of the group. With a finger, he leaned down to draw a line across the floor. Then, stepping back and enchanting, flame abruptly erupted from the stone and created a barrier for any pursuers. Next, Elderlin led them down a side passage. He knew these citadel corridors better than anyone, hurrying them away from danger. Twice, the Asari changed course to avoid the sounds of battle. Alarms were ringing, and troops in organised formations responded. Nonetheless, twice they narrowly avoided massive spiders scuttling along the ceilings, and as they neared their destination, the noise of scurrying and carapaces scraping along walls was close behind them.

It was by chance that Mannace's flagship was in dock when the small troop burst into the underground bays. Without hesitation, Elderlin led them aboard. Mannace dallied at the base of the loading ramp, causing Elderlin to turn and speak fiercely to him.

"Mannace, you must leave Angorok, and it is good for the spiders to witness it. They will tell their mistress that you have departed, and she will turn her attention elsewhere. It is dangerous for us all if you remain here."

Mannace reluctantly responded by moving up the plank. When he passed Elderlin, he patted him on the back.

"You are in such a hurry for an old man."

Spiders were entering the docks and scuttling across the walls and ceiling. Rifle and musket shots rang out from the ship marines, while garrison soldiers guarding the port ran to engage the infiltrators.

While Mannace took a moment to ensure Jayne was still alive, which Uz confirmed, Elderlin made his way back to the dock. With a wave of his hand, he cast the boarding ramp aside and called out to the ship's crew.

"Be away. Take the marshall far from here."

The crew responded with shouts, and as Mannace arrived at the ship's rails, instead of looking across at the Asari, he was glaring down upon the city of Viletri. As always, Mannace adapted quickly, and he called for the captain.

"Land in the street before the Temple of Healing. Jayne requires urgent treatment."

The captain, a tall Arenlander, saluted, then hurried to pass the instruction to the navigator. Mannace closed his eyes. It was so foreign to be under this bright sky, and looking down upon the pristine metropolis, he immediately felt he didn't belong here. Then, after a long while, when he heard civilian voices, the marshall opened his eyes. His flagship was causing a commotion as it drew close to the temple entrance, and one of the gigantic guardians at the nearby Temple of War looked menacingly down at the troublemakers. As Mannace helped the unconscious Jayne, he realised that the dark elf had been at his side since the beginning, when Viletri was no more than an ambitious port town. Though he had never considered the aloof bodyguard a close companion, he could not imagine Jayne not being alongside him.

Mannace spent the night at his Viletri residence. There was only a meagre staff, some of whom had never met the marshall, as he hadn't visited his home for many years. Nevertheless, it was nice to be in familiar and comfortable surroundings.

The next day, Mannace was delighted to learn that Jayne was stable, and that Render was also amongst the patients undergoing treatment by the healers. A team of Fesadi were taking care of him, and they would not permit Mannace to enter the private chambers. Althea, who was based in Viletri and still played a part in the centre's management, personally came to see the leader.

"Jayne's recovery will not be quick, Mannace. His paralysis may take weeks to subside to a point where he can rehabilitate. It might be a year or longer before he will be back at your side."

Mannace nodded, "Perhaps when he is able, it is time for Jayne to follow a path of his own shaping. He has earned his freedom from those that would give him orders. But", he added, "He remains in danger while on the Great Continent. Althea, take him to Bracadia, out of reach of those that would see their foul work finished."

"What do you mean, Mannace?"

"Eya, her influence only extends to the shores of this continent. She can use the Ways, and the spiders still have their catacombs near Viletri. So, her assassins will find Jayne here. I am certain of it."

"Hmmm!"

Althea was not one to dally, and she excused herself from the conversation to give orders to her staff. Already, stretcher bearers were making their way to transport the dark elf to Althea's flying ship. When she was satisfied that the task was in hand, Althea returned to Mannace. She confronted him with questions that needed asking.

"Where is the emperor, Mannace?"

Immediately feeling weighed down, Mannace took a seat. The question jolted him back to the importance of unfolding events. At Angorok, he focused on their dire situation. Now, in the peaceful surrounds of Viletri, he was forced to consider the bigger picture. Emotions swelled within him because the events had gone so poorly for them. He looked up at his peer once his mind stopped spinning long enough to gather some initial thoughts.

"Althea, the emperor's party was ambushed and killed at Angorok. The emperor's body was not amongst the Fallen. It disappeared. If he has not surfaced, I assume he is no longer with us."

Seeing Althea's distress, Mannace decided to share his whole story, though much of it was speculation.

"Angorok has been under siege, and only a final stronghold remains. The Bracadian troops all fled towards Colossus to make their way back to Bracadia. Were you aware of that?"

Althea nodded, "The fleet are transporting them. It is a significant undertaking to ferry them all to Bracadia by sea. Where are Jeylan and the flying ships?"

"Demons destroyed Jeylan's fleet. There is no good news, Althea. I expect betrayal from Ahmeda, but I can't yet prove it, so she has been delivered back to Bracadia, where she can do less harm. All the dark elves serve the enemy; I am sure of it, and Jayne is a victim of that, for his duplicity when he saved me. There is an alliance in the North between demons, undead, and spiders. The citadel at Angorok is a sanctuary under siege. It is hard to see a way back from such dire ends."

Althea was thoughtful, and she "humphed" to bolster herself. She was shaking her head when she looked back at Mannace.

"Was it so wise to put Ahmeda back amongst the Bracadians? It seems that you have put her a step ahead of you if she is your enemy!"

Mannace laughed, "Yes. A step ahead of us. The emperor informed me that you were his controller. Is that still the case?"

"Yes. The emperor told me you would be his new general. Is that still so?"

"No. He did not deliver his end. He lost his nerve, and we have lost the North. He was astute, but like all men, he was flawed. He was the first man to ever walk upon these lands, Althea. He came to Angorok with great ambition and stirred the pot, with only mess to show for it."

"Sounds like you have a lot in common!"

This time Mannace's laugh was loud and abrupt, ending with him casting his hands in the air. "What if the emperor is dead or gone, never to return? Why should you or I care about Bracadia?"

"It is not about Bracadia, Mannace. It is about humanity. Are you not proud to be human, to be Viletri born? The emperor has shown us that there is much more to the world than the bloody North. So, get your people out of there; be free of the demons, undead, and spiders."

Mannace listened intently and wanted what Althea offered him, but then his shoulders sagged, and he sighed. With an effort, he straightened himself and stared at Althea.

"You take care of humanity, Althea. The North is my burden, and despite what you may think, we must continue to fight in the North to give humanity its chance. Never forsake Angorok and the North, Althea. It will be at your peril." Mannace smirked, "Like me putting Ahmeda where she can do the greatest harm."

"Let me take care of Ahmeda. I have not been idle, Mannace. I have used the emperor's proclamation to a good end and will manage the news of the emperor's demise. Ahmeda will want the empire to stay united and strong; it is in all our interests."

NO SAFE HAVEN

That night there was a thunderous banging at Mannace's door. Marines guarding Mannace's residence ran to confront the intruder. When they opened the door, a stone man stepped through and yelled for Mannace. Mannace donned his breastplate and grabbed his sword, descending the main staircase to investigate the ruckus.

The stone man was unmistakably cast in the image of Syprus, and Mannace quickly deduced that he inherited this new form. However, the memory did nothing to put him at ease.

"Why are you bashing at my door?"

"Flee, Mannace, out the back, NOW!"

It seemed ludicrous, but he remembered Syprus possessed the advantage of the Oracle's sight, so he reluctantly moved towards the rear exit, glancing back at Syprus, who watched him withdraw.

"Assassins, Mannace, run!"

As a marine closed and barred the front door, the tip of an axe head appeared through it, and Mannace could hear a top-level window smash. The marshall looked down the corridor leading to the back exit. It did not feel right to run, especially out the back and into the dark. Syprus was indeed the Oracle's man, but he knew nothing of tactics. Mannace relied on his gut instinct.

"Into the cellar, now, hurry."

Mannace opened the stout cellar door and waved at the others to follow. The marines quickly responded though it took more coaxing from Mannace before Syprus joined him. There were footsteps upstairs and more splinters flying off the front door. As the small group gathered in the darkness of the cellar, Mannace ran his hand across a lighting strip that brought the blackness to life. They were in an ample room, accompanied by barrels of all sizes and shelves stacked with bottles of wine. The marines seemed expectant that Mannace would reveal other surprises, perhaps a secret exit, but they were disappointed when the leader grabbed a stool and sat down.

"Who are they, Syprus?"

"The Blood Legion. I had a sudden vision and just arrived at Viletri in time."

"Why would the Blood Legion want me dead? They are an old ally. That doesn't make sense."

Voices accompanied the first unsuccessful push on the cellar door, then silence. Finally, after a long time, a soft female voice was heard through the crack at the base of the door.

"Hello sweeties, are you comfortable down there? Are you warm enough?"

The smell of oil became noticeable, and crude liquid slopped down the stairs and onto the stone floor. While Mannace and the marines backed away, Syprus moved forward and up to the door. Casting the bar aside, the stone man pulled open the portal and grabbed at two men tipping tall urns. One reeled back out of Syprus' way, but the other was picked up by the stone man and cast down the passage, banging against the wall and knocking aside legionnaires. Desperately, Syprus kicked the discarded urns, but not before they spilled much of their liquid. It was too slippery to pursue the assassins, and when the woman appeared at the end of the corridor, she threw a torch into the oil. Flames engulfed the hallway and the stairs to the cellar.

As best they could, Mannace and his companions used their cloaks and sacks stored in the basement to smother the oil-fed flames, but they could do little to quell the growing blaze in the building above them. Soon the heat was so intense that they hid behind barrels, and the billowing smoke made them crouch low to the floor. Syprus came down the steps, closing the door behind him, but there was little else he could do to help. Then, the smoke, fire, and cellar timbers all levitated upwards. Through splintered planks in the ceiling, Mannace watched the wreckage of his home implode into a ball of debris, tumbling from the sky to land heavily on the site it had occupied. The remaining cellar timbers snapped, and next to Mannace, a section of mortar and stone crushed two marines. Syprus saved another, by catching a falling beam and bracing it on his shoulder. The action likely saved Mannace from injury, though they were all trapped under a pile of wood and stone.

A ghostly face appeared next to the marshall, then quickly vanished amongst the rubble. Not long after, there was a commotion above. Rays of illumination flickered through the dust and debris, growing until the rays became a flood of daylight and a passage back to safety. City guards scrambled through the ruins to escort the three survivors through the mess and onto the nearby street.

To his astonishment and relief, Mannace saw Kakos at the head of the rescuers, and with them, Deedee and a handful of Legionnaires were under guard. Kakos stepped up to the beleaguered leader, and Mannace could see darkness in the liche's eyes, like portals to oblivion. The undead lord crackled with power, more fearsome than any sorcerer Mannace had ever seen. Mannace could feel Kakos reaching into him, touching his soul, and caressing his mind, taking what he needed. Answers to many questions.

"You fear me."

Mannace did. He felt a suffocating dread, so much so that he could not move nor speak. Words seemed inconsequential. His body went numb. Kakos turned and walked to Deedee.

"Take him, but do not kill him. He did not kill you. I was there when you were his prisoner, Delaria. Bring him back to me in twenty days."

For good measure, the liche addressed others that watched on in awe.

"There will be no disorder in my city. No reckless burning. A price must be paid."

With that said, half of the collected Blood Legionnaires dropped to the ground as if their brains and bodies abruptly stopped working. A comrade reached down to one and then looked up to others, shocked and shaking his head.

"My justice is fair. Go about your business."

Kakos turned, and half walked, half glided, back towards his city halls. Mannace, incapacitated, was dragged away by Deedee and her guards while Syprus looked helplessly on.

Jaal learned from one of his daughters, Vilera, that Mannace escaped Angorok. He did not know if he could trust Vilera or if it was another test of his loyalty to Eya or a game to see what he would do. These women made him fuck and serve, and he swore allegiance to them and the damned Order daily. They were mistaken if they thought him broken, as he did not value life so highly that he would suffer such cruel indignity to exist. Fuck them.

As if that thought awakened him, Jaal left his daughter, making his way through the catacombs, and at just the right spot, stepped deftly into the Ways. Eya would know but fuck her. She would not catch him, for this netherworld was his domain, and he knew it better than any other. But, of course, he could not remain still – the chase was on, and if he took just a moment to pause, they would catch him. If his actions were too predictable, he would become trapped. Jaal would put his blade through his heart before those bitches held him again. He exited onto a bleak grassy plain, running across the tussock and disappearing once more into the Ways. This time he used his speed, the innate skill to slow time, to travel even faster through this wormhole, exiting abruptly in a forest covered in white. Jaal laboured several steps through thick snow and disappeared into the void. When he reappeared, Jaal was in the spider caverns just a day's travel north of Viletri. He smiled.

The grin, however, was premature. A voice from behind berated him.

"You think me so fallible, so easily betrayed?"

"I think you're insane, Eya. Your brain has cracked, and madness leaks forth."

Eya started replying, but Jaal was already back in the Ways, taking paths known and new, running and weaving as if that might help hide his trail. It was only his imagination, but he could feel spider legs on his back and eyes carving hate into his neck. He accelerated faster. This time Jaal arrived on a beach. He did not know where, but he saw fishing boats out to sea. With panicked speed, the dark elf sprinted for the brine, wading into the ocean, and throwing himself into the waves. His mind and head raced as time slowed, swimming until the water was deep, and the swells buoyed him. Looking back, Eya was there, naked, and malevolent in the sun. She watched him, but her magic ended at the shore. At least, that was what Jaal hoped as he turned and swam toward the horizon.

Mannace was stretched and tied length-ways over a large barrel, naked. A stone man, Deedee's helper, held the barrel and pressed a hand on Mannace's head to keep it pinned to the hardwood. There were bruises across the marshall's body, and blood seeped out his arse. Deedee's other helper, a belg slave soldier, was hunched in the corner of the room, his head cramped against the ceiling. The big slave was blessed with the mole men's conditioning, giving him unending patience, and he never questioned his mistress' orders. Also naked, he massaged his massive cock to keep it hard.

Deedee circled Mannace, leaning down to meet his stare.

"Look at all that blood on the floor, sweetie; you'll need to clean that up later. After that, perhaps we take a walk outside. You can wave to your old friends, sweetie. Can you walk, sweetie, or was Gagar too hard on you? He can get a bit over-enthusiastic when lust takes him. Strange that isn't it, sweetie, that despite all that conditioning, deep inside, he is still a man – still a slave to his cock."

Deedee stood and slapped Mannace playfully on the ass, making the marshall flinch. Then, seeing the reaction and knowing how tender her prisoner must be, Deedee leaned to whisper in his ear.

"You miserable fuck. I will cut off your cock, hands, and feet and deliver you alive to that fucking liche. I will leave your tongue so you can lick his rotting balls."

Standing, Deedee added, "Won't that be lovely, sweetie."

Mannace mumbled. He was parched and broken, with little strength even to talk. Deedee went to a water bucket and drew a cup of cooling liquid. She threw it in Mannace's face to shock him to his senses.

"What! What did you say!"

His voice was weak though loud enough this time to be heard.

"I am sorry, Delaria."

"Huh, sorry are you! Sorry to be cast over a barrel with Gagar stretching your arse. What are you sorry about, Mannace?"

"For not pulling your guts out through your cunt."

Deedee snarled. "It's nice that we're talking, sweetie." She nodded to Gagar, who made his way over to them. Mannace seemed to gain some strength, and he spat out embittered words.

"Harder, Gagar. You fuck like a pissy girl."

The locked door to the room clicked and swung open. Kakos entered and glided to the centre of the room, casting his eyes about to evaluate the scene. His face was expressionless, emotionless, as always. Behind him, two city guards entered to stand next to their lord while several Blood Legionnaires skulked in the corridor and peered through the open portal. One shrugged at Deedee, who gave him a damning stare.

"Your time is over, Deedee. Mannace will come with me now."

The Madam's look was almost as dire as the liche's, and she stood her ground defiantly.

"Twenty days, you said. I will have what is due to me."

"You have had six. It is enough. I am no fool, Deedee. Twenty days was never my intent."

Gagar stepped behind Mannace and rested his erect spear on the bound man's arse. The belg moistened the head with saliva, intent on following his orders and ignorant of what played out about him. Deedee backed away from the belg but abruptly turned to the Stone Man, spitting out quick words.

"Crush him."

Suddenly the room seemed alive with light and shapes, some black and menacing. The stone man hurled backwards while Gagar collapsed, lifeless. Deedee froze in place, unable to move. When the light and shapes vanished, the Viletri soldiers hurried to release Mannace from his bonds and held him upright. Kakos approached Deedee, her determined glare replaced with horror. The liche looked into and through her, studying what he saw until satisfied.

"You have a job here. Do it."

The soldiers hauled Mannace away, and Kakos surveyed the residence and its stunned occupants as he slowly passed back through the corridors and exited the main entrance.

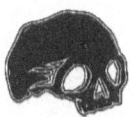

Recently, Kakos made the Viletri City Hall, its great chamber where Mannace first addressed the nations of the Blood Sea, his abode. He conducted all his business from there, and when his busy schedule permitted it, he indulged in his pleasures. Boys in white silk robes stood upon a platform, raising their divine voices in a chorus of pitched melodies. The haunting sounds calmed Kakos and reminded him of who he once was, a man, a living man of principles, optimism, and passion. And this other man before him; he remembered as a leader, somebody he once respected above all others. When Kakos spoke, his tone was even and almost appeasing.

"If I surrender to the music, Mannace, I am human again. I am the same man that stood at your side."

Mannace still lay on the floor, on his back, naked, where the guards dropped him. His voice, though shallow, had returned.

"You are less whiny and more confident. I like you better now."

"Are we friends?"

"Huh, fuck you, Kakos. That bitch drugged me, and I may never stand straight again. Was that friendship to hand me to that angry bitch?"

"Who is whining now, Mannace?"

Mannace managed a small laugh, and for the first time, he rolled awkwardly onto his side, taking time to catch his breath.

"Allies, yes. Have you ever had a friend, Kakos? I don't think so. Trust and respect, that must suffice."

Kakos walked about the room, looking up at the maps painted on the walls, reminiscing, processing. All the while, he soaked up the voices of his treasured choir. Finally, he stopped to stare at Mannace.

"I watched you defile Delaria, and you treated me like furniture as you went about your dirty business as if I were only there when you needed me. Like a chair to sit on. What you did to her was unnecessary. How you treated me is unforgivable."

Mannace frowned, "I elevated you. You possessed everything you wanted. Even when you were dead, I protected you."

"Used me. You are still using me."

Mannace wanted to say more, but unseen hands silenced him. He coughed and returned to lying on his back.

"Mannace, you will depart Viletri and never return here. Hurry, for when the singing stops, you will not find me so reasonable." The intimidating threat accompanied a Hellish glare that reminded Mannace of the monster Kakos was. "Leave now."

"Mrrrgggghhh"

While Mannace tried to talk, invisible hands grabbed him, and he slid across the floor. The massive doors to the council chamber opened, and the unseen forces cast Mannace out the entrance, rolling like a dead body down the stone stairs. His voice returned as the doors slammed shut, shouting through the unbearable pain.

"Fuck you. You freak corpse. Fuck this city and all its fucking nonsense. You ungrateful cunts. Damn you to the fucking Hells. Let the demons and undead devour you. I'll not save you again!"

Amongst the many onlookers, Syprus and Uz were there. The stone man picked Mannace up and cradled him. Then, another familiar face appeared, Gideon the engineer, who wrapped a cloak about the marshall's body before stepping back into the crowd. The flying ship was gone, so there was little choice but to leave through the city gate, past the onlookers, and trudge amongst the deep snow surrounding the metropolis. While Uz placed a spiritual hand upon Mannace to put warmth back into his body, Syprus offered some small hope.

"The Oracle, and The Light, will give you sanctuary and salvation, my friend."

PART FIVE:

The Races

THE BLUE LANDS

Titus Kane, Althea Kane's husband, seconded one hundred Viletri guards and left his position as Viletri's military commander to assume the role of his wife's protector. It gave him purpose and a way for them to spend time together. The Viletri elders were married for over eighteen hundred years and still found comfort and pleasure in each other's company. Eight stone men were among the assigned guards, with the best auxiliaries. Included was an animator controlling five steel workers, an orc shaman skilled at cloaking, three brula scouts, a decorated war priest with several acolytes, a team of Fesadi menders, and an experienced battle mage. The soldiers carried shields and hammers as their primary weapons, as well as a variety of secondary arms such as shard guns or repeating crossbows. All wore their Viletri colours and polished dwarf-crafted armour with great pride. The unit was an elite force, exuding confidence.

Althea seconded one of the few remaining flying ships in Arenland. As she disembarked before the emperor's palace with Titus and her guards, Bracadian riflemen rushed from the castle, forming units to barricade them. Responding quickly, Titus issued commands, deploying the dwarven shield disks that would protect them from bullets if combat ensued. Althea sent a messenger forward with papers to show the Bracadian commander, and when the man finished reading the documents, he bowed in acknowledgement of Althea's authority. However, the reduction in tension was short-lived as Ahmeda emerged from the palace with her loyal priests and acolytes in tow. Perhaps more than three hundred robed men marched at the priestess' side, with their dark armour and black rifles ending in long glistening bayonets. Most wore pistols at their side, and some sported thin, pointed swords with a sinister gleam to their blades. Althea knew that Ahmeda groomed the War God's faithful in Bracadia, but she hadn't witnessed his chosen soldiers. The controller turned to her husband.

"Arrogant bullies, like their mistress. Nonsense!"

Ahmeda walked halfway between the two forces and stopped. Althea bravely walked out to meet her, folding her arms, and giving the priestess her most venomous glare. Then, unexpectedly for Ahmeda, Morgan Cain descended from the sky and alighted next to them. He stepped to be by Althea's side, an action that declared his allegiance and made Ahmeda shift uncomfortably. Her reaction showed that while the priestess considered Althea no threat, Morgan was a dangerous adversary.

Althea spoke in a soft voice so that the distance from the troops made it a private conversation.

"I will speak plainly, Ahmeda. We must continue the emperor's work. In the emperor's absence, I will control his affairs. Morgan will command Bracadia's military. But, of course, you will serve your emperor and your god as you see fit, in the empire's best interests."

"I see fit to assume the throne until the emperor returns. I stood at his side as an equal and knew his mind. He would want me to rule in his absence."

Althea quickly lost her patience, "I have spoken with Mannace, and your hands are dirty, bloody even, Ahmeda. Your allegiance is not with the empire. You are not fit to lead!"

The high priestess pushed out her chest and looked down her nose at her accusers. She was commanding and powerful and well suited to the mantle of Empress. Here in the Blue Land, with the loyalty of the palace divisions, she had reason to be confident.

Not to be perturbed, Althea poked the dark elf in the breast with her finger, then a second time for good measure. "Don't get haughty with me, Ahmeda. I know more than one Shaman who can look into your soul to find the truth. We have one aboard. Shall I send for him?"

The dark elf's eyes narrowed, and the power of her gaze made Althea momentarily choke. She coughed and recovered but still breathed heavily, looking faint. The high priestess kept her eyes locked on the controller's, and casually her left hand lifted higher. Then, breathing in deeply, the priestess opened her black heart to draw on her powers.

There was a resounding crack as Morgan lurched forward, his head colliding forcefully with Ahmeda's. The high priestess turned at the last moment to take the impact to her forehead, which jolted her backwards. Spinning once, she tumbled unconscious and bleeding to the ground. All around them, soldiers raised shields or pointed their weapons. Because they knew Morgan as well as Ahmeda, most were confused. Only the War God's faithful rushed to their leader's aid. Morgan and Althea stepped back to let them collect her up and rush her away. As they were doing so, Morgan raised himself to look down on the crowd.

"Bracadians, this is Althea Kane. She carries papers from the emperor that I endorse, that she is to be obeyed. Papers were also sent to the Blue Lands and all the governed provinces that Althea Kane is to be obeyed. I will stand by her side to see that Althea Kane is obeyed."

Morgan hovered closer to the Imperial troops, purposefully surveying them. Most lowered their weapons to meet his stare and listen.

"The emperor's whereabouts are unknown. Until his return, Althea Kane will govern Bracadia from the Blue Lands. Our armies return from war in the east. They have fought demons and the living dead. Be proud of your soldiers. Glory to the blue land, GLORY TO BRACADIA!"

There was a loud cheer, and several riflemen shot into the air. Amidst the commotion, the Bracadian commander came to stand before Althea, saluting.

"At your service, Althea Kane."

In a lower voice, he added, "Is the emperor alive?"

"I do not know, Commander. Let us hope so."

"Indeed, the emperor is the empire, Althea Kane."

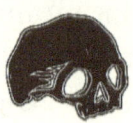

While Althea settled into the business of governing Bracadia, it was Morgan to whom the people and their governors rallied. Some called him The Bracadian and revered his miraculous form and flight. To them, he was the ambassador and voice of the emperor. Morgan, however, did not want the fame, though he used it to inspire loyalty where there was doubt and fear. After leaving Althea to rule, it was some time before he returned to the Blue Lands, and it was Ahmeda he visited before Althea. The priestess was at her War God's barracks beneath the emperor's palace. He spent time with the priestess and emperor over the last decades, leaving him with many questions.

"Why would you betray the emperor, Ahmeda? He adored you. You had everything."

"I do not need a man, Morgan. Not for love or to give me what he thinks I need."

"He served your purpose. He embraced the War God's doctrine. What do you have to gain by his demise?"

"The emperor is missing, Morgan. I do not know where he is. He made a poor choice to align with Mannace and interfere in politics, which he does not understand. His place was here in the Blue Lands, not in the North. He meddled where he was not welcome and paid the price."

Ahmeda put a hand to her head where Morgan had bashed her. Morgan could see it was still very sensitive from the large bruise and her flinch.

"You would have killed Althea, removed her from the game. It would have been a mistake. Instead, she will keep the empire whole, strengthen its many parts, and move it forward."

"She poked me, Morgan. Why do you think she did that? What do you see? I see a clever woman who wanted you to rescue her. Did you rescue her, Morgan? She made you strike me, did she not? You are blind, Morgan, ill-equipped for these games."

"Will you stay here or return to the North?"

"I never wanted to be in the North! It was the emperor that insisted I be there at his side. It was ignorance on his part to think that the world is as simple as the Blue Lands."

Morgan shrugged, "I will stay here for a time to help Althea and protect her from you. Ahmeda, I care enough about Bracadia to keep it safe from your dark mischief. The empire would fall to chaos if you held the throne."

"I am the voice and hand of God, Morgan. Bracadia will serve the War God's purpose whether I am on the throne or not. I will be its general, not Mannace, and certainly not you. All those years, the emperor could not see what he already had. He did not understand what can be accomplished through absolute faith and conviction."

"He did not advocate your ways. He was not prepared to embrace the darkness."

"That is ignorant, Morgan. The darkness is the strength to do what must be done. The emperor was weak. He did not have that dark part of him to achieve his ambition. I will prepare Bracadia for war and lead the faithful to conquer the world. Let Althea be the light and let me be the dark. You can do that, Morgan, stand between the light and the dark. You know the wisdom of what I say. Bracadia has no heart, no purpose. I will give it that, not Althea!"

Morgan was absentmindedly nodding. Then he looked hard at the high priestess to assess her resolve.

"To do that, I will have to take the throne. Until the emperor returns."

"The Bracadians will follow you, Morgan. They revere you."

"Can I trust you, Ahmeda?"

"I value order, Morgan, and hierarchy. You know this to be true. Allow me to be the darkness that Bracadia needs!"

Seeing that Morgan was still deliberating, Ahmeda, although it irked her, knew how to convince the metal man.

"Look at Mannace, who you hold in such high esteem. Is he not both darkness and light? Is the strength you see in him, not the same strength you would want for Bracadia? Does a man not have two hands; one to hold out in friendship, the other, a fist to smite down his foes."

Althea did not appreciate how vast the empire was until she sat at its centre, confronted by the daily challenges of its governance. She controlled an army of staff and seconded Fitius' clerks to help execute her orders, commissioning buildings, recruiting specialists, and convening diplomatic meetings or coalitions. With the vast distances needed to be travelled, even with the flying ship, executing the first stages of her plan would be an endeavour spanning many years. The controller spent time with governors or their lackeys, who travelled to the Blue Lands to meet Althea, make proposals, and leverage the technologies of the Eastern Colonies. They all departed knowing they gained in the bargaining, and Althea grew in confidence as she collected new allies.

Likewise, Ahmeda nurtured her networks, with temples and barracks in many lands. As soldiers returned home from the East, they brought stories of unnatural creatures and bore witness to the powers of the War God. The belief was fanatical amongst many of those returning, pledging their loyalty and souls to the War God's safe keeping. The War God's blessings and protection were a rich reward through the power of prayer. Ahmeda travelled, recruiting to her order, sharing the divine doctrine, and where necessary, she was the threat of violence where governors doubted the new regime. But, as yet she was not required to be the executioner.

Morgan Cain remained the ambassador, the voice of the emperor and self-appointed ward over the empire's throne. Like Ahmeda, Morgan preferred travelling to meet with governors on their home ground. It gave him a better sense of their culture and traditions, which helped him to form stronger bonds. To the people, Morgan seemed celestial, a being to rise above others. Unlike the reclusive emperor, the man of black metal flecked with blue was a leader they could see and admire. His return visits became a celebration time in the Bracadian empire's capitals. At his side, Symin was Morgan's messenger and aide. The young prodigy was too shy to take on the mantle of a diplomat. Still, he was becoming confident to relay commands, and he had a presence of sorts in that he was aloof and indifferent to rank, even when confronted by the most imposing of governors. This irreverence gave him an air of authority.

THE SPIDERS

The Fen felt safest within the Tangle. However, it was worrisome to them how quickly the spiders spread through the forest of the hand and that demons infested the woodland. Thankfully the monsters seldom crossed the borders into the lands of the Fen. Therefore, it was unexpected and horrific when giant spiders suddenly swarmed through the trees above the Hodoogo tribe, settling menacingly in the high branches. Below them, the dark druid, Roanna, helped the men to gather and protect their families. She moved the forest to shelter them with waving branches and layers of thick, thorny vines. As always, a Ra Anu scuttled by her side. The petite doe fed the druid's magic, keeping the black spiders at bay.

Eya appeared, well beyond the defence, staring at Roanna across the distance. The spider mother walked closer, careful not to trip on tree roots, then waved for the dark druid to join her. Roanna stroked the neck of the Ra Anu, commanding the creature to stay. Then with a deep, fortifying breath, she boldly strode toward the naked Eya until they were only an arm's length apart. Eya's bare form betrayed none of her significant powers, but the dark druid could sense ancient, primal forces within the spider mother's sleek frame.

"Leave the Fen. They are no threat to you."

"I have protected the Fen, Roanna. How do you think they have survived when surrounded by demons and my children? They live by my mercy."

Roanna immediately wanted to ask why, but in her gut, she already knew the answer, making her shiver. Eya expounded anyway.

"The Fen are under your protection, Roanna, are they not? And you are of the Order as your mother has explained to you. The Order has rules, Roanna, and I honour that in keeping the darkness from consuming these primitive people. I also honour the loyalty shown by your father, Jaal, and your mother, Ahmeda. The Order is family, Roanna."

Roanna could find no words. So instead, she removed her robe, letting it fall to the earth and leaving her naked. The dark druid was stunning like her mother, proud, defiant. It was a gesture to meet the spider mother on equal terms, a statement that she, too, was more than she seemed.

Eya altered her stance, turning side-on to the druid. While it was not magic, the forest about them also shifted a half step, and wherever there was a shadow, more spiders of all types and sizes revealed themselves. They watched Roanna intently, their predatory eyes searching for weakness.

"I will be blunt. Acknowledge your place in the Order, in my service. Else the Fen will die."

Roanna remained stationary, her eyes darting between the creatures that watched her. Internally, she was rehearsing her next actions to defend and attack. She forgot the Fen, letting her darkness prepare her.

As if sensing the druid's nature, Eya smiled.

"Yes, embrace the darkness. Embrace your roots, Roanna, and know *your* people.

Still smiling, Eya turned back to face the druid.

"Did you know the elves have departed the lands? Not just at The Hand, but all lands. They travel North, led by a calling. But you do not have that urge, Roanna, for you are not of the elves. You are of the shadow, like your mother and like your father. The dark elves flock to me, Roanna. Your mother, Ahmeda, led them here. Know your race, Roanna. Know your place in the Order, Roanna. The Order is who you are. The dark elves are your tribe."

Vilera descended cautiously from the shadowy canopy, landing near her mother and half-sister. As the spiderkin looked sternly at the druid, Eya saw a flicker of doubt cross Roanna's face.

"You are sister to the spiderkin, Roanna. Vilera has always been loyal to you. Join your sister now and come with us. The Fen will be safe, I promise it, and you may return to them later. I will consider them yours. Teach them the Order, and they will have my protection."

At last, Roanna found her words, "Why am I important to you?"

"Because you are significant, Roanna. I watched you defend the gorge against the demons. It was a revelation to witness your spell weaving. I aided you then, too, remember? And know that you carry my blood as well as Jaal's and Ahmeda's. I want you by my side."

Roanna stepped over her robe and around Eya. The dark druid walked to where she first saw Eya appear, then turned to the spider mother, who was still intently observing her.

"I *will* join you in return for the Fen's safety."

Roanna's shifting eyes told Eya a different story: her cooperation had little to do with the pitiful Fen, but she nodded to maintain the facade. That said, Roanna stepped into the Ways through the portal Eya left open.

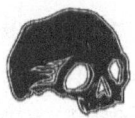

Semril was assigned to protect Roanna, and the dark druid accepted his assistance. Though she was capable of defending herself, it seemed wise to be guided through the lair of the spider mother, and it made sense to have a minder until the denizens of Eya's domain were familiar with their latest addition. As she travelled the subterranean tunnels, Roanna was surprised that the catacombs beneath The Hand were so extensive, and some locations were spectacular.

Descending into the very depths of the realm, the two dark elves stood on a stony shore, looking across an underground lake. Glowing bugs gave the grotto an eerie glow, and fish with lights on stalks in front of their flat heads appeared and disappeared in the deep water.

"Semril, how did you come to follow the spider mother?"

"I came to The Hand with Jaal. I served in the Blood Legion, and we needed Eya's help to travel the Ways. Eya compelled me to stay."

"What do you do here?"

The dark elf was behind Roanna, and he put a hand on her shoulder, surprising but not alarming her. When she seemed comfortable with the contact, Semril moved his fingers around the druid's neck, massaging, and he ran his other hand down her side, across her arse. Then, he lightly gripped the soft flesh where her ass became her purse, boldly massaging there too. Gaining in confidence, he replaced the fingers about Roanna's neck with his lips, kissing her gently. In response, the dark druid turned, tentatively putting her lips against his. She was inexperienced, but Semril's masculine touch lit a fire within, one that Roanna hadn't known existed. Instinctively, she closed her eyes and let her primal urges and magic take control.

As an elemental wind gusted around them, Semril lifted Roanna's robe over her head, tossing it behind, and pulled her close. With one hand, he unfastened his belt, pushing his leather pants down to his thighs. Such was the force of the surrounding gale that he tightened his arms around Roanna to prevent her from flying away. Gripping her long hair in one hand, Semril squeezed her flesh with the other. His cock hard, the bodyguard bent his knees, then guided his spear into Roanna's moist purse. Leaning closer, the druid's legs wrapped around Semril's thighs, and her fingernails stabbed cruelly into his back and shoulders. On such unsteady ground, Semril might easily have lost his balance and fallen, yet there was an aspect to the wind that lifted him, holding him above the pebble beach.

Roanna's purse possessed a life of its own, pulling him in with its magic, fiercely gripping his spear, pulsating with wild, erotic energies. Semril closed his eyes and let his spirit merge with the druid's enchantment, trusting that she would protect them both. Clutching Roanna even tighter and embraced by the wind, Semril used all of his strength to pull back his cock, thrusting hard and then again with more force. It sparked wild sensations throughout his body, and the dark elf felt the thrill of the friction ripple through Roanna, her screeching piercing the noise of the whipping gale. As well as her fierce cunt, Semril sensed her skin against his, gliding over his body like a snake. He fucked her hard, brutally, losing himself in the untamed madness of their joining.

Later as they lay exhausted on the rocks, Semril held his thumb in Roanna's purse, gently stroking her hair with his fingers. He enjoyed the perfect shape of her legs, which he kissed, and the sensual view across a tight stomach and pert breasts. She looked back at him questioningly. His response shocked her.

"You are perfectly formed like your mother. You are a better fuck."

Taken aback, Roanna was quiet for a time before raising herself slightly on her elbows.

"How so?"

"Your magic is wild. You gave everything, and my cock was on fire from start to end, like I have never experienced. Your mother is demanding and selfish. I have fucked all the matriarchs with all their powers and tricks. Eya has the tightest cunt, but Saska is the best of them, raw and insatiable. Though not as satisfying as you."

"Should I be grateful that you find me the best? What is your game, Semril?"

"No games. We are dark elves; we fight hard, and we fuck harder. That is life."

THE DWARVES

Logthar brought Elderlin's message to the BruEkNa. When she finished her conversation with the stone master, who quickly departed, Logthar read it to her.

"The nation of Angorok has fallen. We, the last of men that once called Veldaan, or Islan, or the Sarang, or the Young Kingdoms, home, are trapped within the citadel. Demons and the dead surround us. The North is lost. We can no longer be your eyes nor ward. Be warned."

The BruEkNa seemed unfazed. Logthar knew she shared no empathy for the plight of men.

"You talk with these men, Logthar. Are they truly defeated?"

"No, not utterly. They may survive to reclaim their lands when the demons and undead are gone. Men are resilient, BruEkNa, and persistent. They have a port within the citadel for their flying ships, so they are not cut off from the world. Will we aid them?"

"No, Logthar. We have paid our debt. We have no business with these men."

"What of the Bracadians, BruEkNa? Will we trade with them?"

The BruEkNa stood with her hands clasped behind her back, thoughtful. Against her better judgement, she liked Morgan Cain, perhaps because he was not of human flesh, and she had promised him emissaries. But that was before he also requested aid for the men of Angorok.

"The blood of men is poison, Logthar, a curse. The grey dwarves mixed blood with men and now bear that same affliction: you will die like the mortals. Should we invite such folly into our realm?"

"Let the grey dwarves trade with men, BruEkNa. You have seen the benefit of their invention."

"Logthar, the KinRa seek to purge the grey dwarves. Only my hand stays them. They say the curse of the mortals, which is also the curse of the grey dwarves, will infect the true dwarves. SinKayLas believes if left to fester, our race will decline."

"Let me take the grey dwarves back to the Iron Halls. Many will travel from there to other places, to homes they left to answer your summons. They came to fight in your armies. If they leave, their blood will not mix with the true dwarves."

After another period of quiet deliberation, the BruEkNa made a bold decision.

"Tell the metal man, Morgain Cain, that his emissaries will be received at KragKraka, on the mountain. Your grey dwarves will occupy that fortress and be intermediaries. Then, take the rest of your people back to the Iron Halls. All must depart, Logthar, else the KinRa will act against them, with good reason."

"Yes, BruEkNa. It will be done."

As a final caution, the BruEkNa added, "I trust you only of your kin to enter the realm, Logthar, and no human shall set foot in the mountains. Only the man of metal may accompany you."

"What of Morgan Cain's messenger, the young man of metal, Symin?"

"He too may enter. But no others."

"Yes, BruEkNa. Your word is law."

It was not as simple as Logthar stated for the grey dwarves and others that were not of the true dwarves to return to the lands of men. The city guards killed the first to arrive at Viletri. They held no fondness for the kin that besieged their city. In Arenland, those returning to their mines found the claims were taken by others, with the authorities showing no sympathy for their plight. At least in the city of Ostoik, the dwarves were not shunned, though they would have no easy task of re-establishing themselves. Some of the more adventurous purchased passage from Ostoik to Bracadia, where Logthar informed them their skills would be in high demand.

Fergis, a rotund and jovial dwarf, made his way to a tavern at the docks where seamen congregated. The dwarf was legendary for his feats of naval engineering, though more for their novelty than worth. In the modern society that Arenland had become, with ships of steel and others that sailed the skies, he was more an oddity than ever. But at least there was one familiar face amongst the sailors.

"Kraken, you dog. Where be your ship and crew? Do you have work for an old hand?"

"Always for you, Fergis." Kraken laughed, "You may be just the pirate I need."

Fergis looked around him. Only Kraken would be so bold as to shout out piracy in the port where the Arenlanders, even the Aren sailors, were very serious people.

"By Ramthos' bollocks, you are trouble, old man. You are looking at an honest dwarf seeking fair pay!"

"An honest pirate it is then! It is Ramthos that has sent me, Fergis."

"So, you are answerable to the Sea God himself now. Your brains are full of brine, Kraken. Madness has you in its grasp."

"We will make a good team then, Fergis. Two old maddies in search of a mad king."

"Where is your ship?"

Kraken smiled broadly, "It will be here very soon. I hope you have all your gear with you."

As if the timing were rehearsed, there was a sudden commotion and shouting outside. Kraken hastily rose from his stool, pulling Fergis along, joined by the other sailors who tossed aside their drinks to grab their kit. As Fergis followed them out the door, netting hung from the sky that the sailors leapt at, scrambling deftly upwards. Fergis barely grasped the rope when it lifted him high into the air. As he looked down, to his horror, the city of Ostoik shrunk away, then suddenly disappeared, to be replaced by an endless ocean.

"Damn you, Kraken, put me back. I'll not be part of your bloody scheming."

When the other sailors were aboard the flying ship, they hauled on the net until Fergis appeared at the side, then strong hands yanked him over the railings. As he looked about, the dwarf could see a couple of other familiar faces; old pirates from Urgar's crew, and the dark elf, Jaal, who Urgar once befriended. He returned a nod from the elf and then made his way to the captain's quarters, where Kraken was already making himself at home.

"What the Hells, Kraken. What are you doing?"

"Whatever I want, Fergis. Do you like my new acquisition?"

"Who the fuck did you steal it from? It looks fancy, like some rich bastard's boat. Are you insane?"

"Worse, I'm bored. Pirating isn't the fun it used to be. But this adventure won't be dull, Fergis. So, relax. What are you afraid of?"

The dwarf grunted and eyed Kraken with deep suspicion, "Fuck you!"

EaJa-KulAmani, BruEkNa of the true dwarves, leaned forward from her throne, listening intently to GarRamMon, her mastersmith. RuMar, commander of the VengTan-AsTenRey, the famous engineers, was close by. As much as the mastersmith was proud of his team's accomplishments, little of it was what the BruEkNa wanted to hear. She raised her hand to end the chatter.

"GarRamMon, I want solutions that I can use today. If the demons were banging on the entrance to your halls, what would you do? What devices would turn them back? How would you stop their magic? How would you defend your domain? The KinRa turned the demons back, but the Legions of Hell regather their strength at the Rift, and they will return prepared. Arm our generals, protect our kin!"

The mastersmith was silent. He raised his hands as if he might reveal a master plan, then put them down again as if defeated. RuMar shrugged too, but unlike his peer, his eyebrows lifted, and he started a new line of conversation.

"They don't abide water. It kills them outright."

GarRamMon shook his head.

"How would that work, RuMar? There is little water when they go deep. None if they draw closer to the core."

"There is steam or ice."

"I can work with steam. Logthar has talked about the designs of men, where they used steam to power their contraptions. It will take time to investigate, and we are already learning the clockwork of the grey dwarves. But stone and steel, the old ways have their value too."

The BruEkNa was growing impatient, though the mastersmith seemed oblivious to her huffs and reddening cheeks. He seemed shocked when she spoke down at him.

"Enough! Did you not hear me! They are beating down your door, and you would study and experiment. Enough! I need action. Bring me designs in two days of what you will build for me. Dwarves will die while you procrastinate!"

EaJa-KulAmani turned to RuMar.

"RuMar, brains not steel, will keep the IceSleepers and Core safe. Work with the mastersmith to plan a new defence. You will have all the engineers and workers you need. Let us fight a different kind of war against these demons. Against the Hells, the price paid in dwarven flesh is too high. I trust you, RuMar, to help our warriors and people and find us better ways. Do this for me, and you will have a place at my side."

The last comment took both dwarves aback, and RuMar proudly puffed out his chest.

"The Hells will break upon our defences, BruEkNa. I will keep our people safe." Inflated by the confidence the BruEkNa showed him, RuMar put a hand on the mastersmith's shoulder to guide him back towards his halls. "Come, GarRamMon, summon your chief artisans. You and I have work to do."

THE FESADI

Render did not expect the lands of the Fesadi to be so lush and full of life. Where most populations would lay their footprint over the land to raise their civilization, the gentle Fesadi integrated into their environment, living alongside nature. The Fesadi were a content people; satisfied, generous and kind-natured to the point that their compliance irritated Render. They agreed with everything he said and gave him everything he asked for, without question. It made the sorcerer feel like a rat in a chicken coup, in the shady corner of a sunlit yard. Unfortunately, Althea ordered the menders to bring him here until he was fully healed and rested. Staying at Viletri was not safe for him or those that harboured him. Such was the price for defeat in the North and to have such powerful, far-reaching enemies.

Render ran his good hand down his left side, where the flesh on his arms and leg was replaced with tiny, interwoven vines. He knew from the experience of having a finger repaired that the rejuvenation would be no different in functionality to the missing meat and bone. It still felt like wickerwork to touch, and it would never look human. Amongst the Fesadi populations were men and women made entirely from the vines, transitioning from their mortal bodies to a form that significantly extended their life. Render moved stiffly, relying on the mender's concoctions to dull the intense pain. The discomfort and drugs interfered with his magic. But not so much that it prevented his experiments.

Render held captive the souls of eight Belarch in a jewel he carried. It was a dangerous cargo that would bring disaster if the treasure were damaged and the powerful Belarch escaped. The sorcerer also possessed the half-flask of goo that Mannace gave him, called the Essence of Life. Apart from that, the sorcerer retained only his accumulated knowledge and keen intellect. He liked that simplicity, and it seemed a luxury to focus his attention on just one or two things.

The Essence of Life was a rare treasure that he used half of to animate the behemoth corpse at Tarnac, but in many ways, that was a terrible waste of the artefact. For someone like Render, who dedicated much of his time to establishing life-magic disciplines such as animation and technomancy, this odd substance held many secrets and codes to expand his understanding of creation.

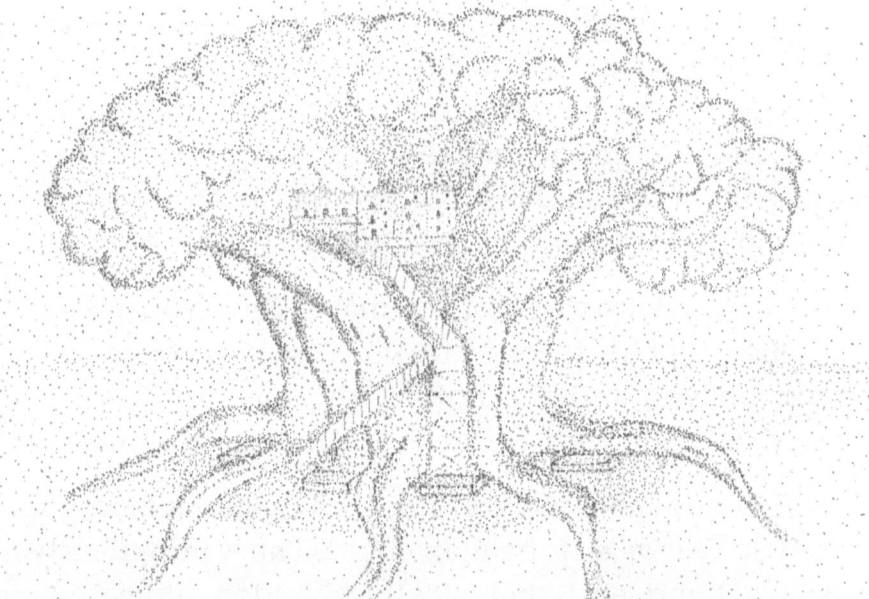

Render was introduced to a tree adored by the Fesadi. It was considered sacred, but for many decades it was slowly dying. Its tremendous age was showing in the peeling bark and crumpled leaves. Carved on the tree's enormous trunk were the names of the first Fesadi settlers, and high above, expansive boughs reached over the central buildings of the royal zoo. It was a treasured centrepiece of Fesadi society. Would the Essence of Life be enough to restore the magnificent tree, or was there a way he could use the soul of a Belarch to give the tree immortal magic? These questions enthralled Render, who already contemplated new ideas and experiments.

After many years alongside the Fallen, it was restful to be away from the cult and the demonic dreamers. Even Fek was absent since Render secretly departed the Great Continent.

During his convalescence, Render received unexpected visitors. Mannace, Uz, and Syprus, in his stone form, came to Render at the zoo, and he took them aside to a park where they could sit and talk privately. There was no friendship between the sorcerer and the Oracle's priest, and even in this tranquil place, Render felt his blood rise.

"Why are you with this fool, Mannace? Have you not put up with enough of his hokum? Do you forget the false destiny he put on you and the failure, the torture, of the past decade? Be done with this hack and his false promises."

Syprus would have scowled had he a human frame, but he glared as best as a stone man could. Then, indignantly he raised a hand and theatrically shielded himself from Render's insolence.

"You are not a true immortal, wizard. You do not understand patience or the balancing nature of time. A path may bend and dip before it ascends and is straight again. Destiny will be fulfilled."

"Mannace, are you so weak of mind to be tricked twice by this drivel? The future is what you make it. Better you have a sword in hand and strength of mind to take your destiny as you have always done. Do not give this priest or his oracle any credit for your achievements."

Syprus quickly answered for Mannace again, "Magic is not miracles, clever is not wisdom; you are a jester with a big stick, waving it around like you are the divine one. A wise man ..."

"ENOUGH!"

Mannace was intimidating as he puffed out his chest and asserted himself over his colleagues. Baffled by human interactions, Xu turned his back on the group and wandered off to bask in the warm sun and meditate. Meanwhile, Mannace glared at the two that remained.

"The Oracle has its uses, Render. It guided me here to find you. I have experienced other dreams too, and they have shown me that we have more to do in the North. We have nations to lead, you and me. You will command from Tarnac, I have seen it, and I will rise again as Marshall of Angorok. Our people remain defiant against the enemy and need our leadership."

Render seated himself on a park bench, sitting back as if relaxing. He knew enough of Mannace's character not to challenge him on his beliefs, but that did not mean he would be quick to jump on his wagon.

"The fallen are capable of caring for themselves. I will rejoin them when the time suits me. But Mannace, it is a gift to have this time away from the North. Why are you so eager to return?"

When Mannace hesitated in responding, Render pushed forward his argument, "Are you not of more use to those in Angorok if you are free to build your alliances and gather your strength? I understand what has happened in the North. Did you know that Althea, Morgan, and Ahmeda rule in Bracadia?"

Mannace did not know that, and his eyebrows were raised, followed by a frown.

"Ahmeda cannot be trusted. There is an alliance working against us!"

"The spider mother, Saska, Ahmeda, and another woman who is perhaps the most powerful. They aided me in defeating Churgwarthos and his Belarch. I would be dead and cast into oblivion if not for them. It makes you wonder who your friends are."

"Why did they not kill you after Churgwarthos was vanquished?"

Render shrugged, "Because I escaped."

Mannace nodded, "A good thing you did. Better dead than caught in those bitches' grasp. They bring darkness to the North."

"They work within the darkness, Mannace. They take their opportunities and play the game the same as we do. And remember, I am of the darkness, and I have a hand in the Four Hells to boot."

"You are not of their *Order*, my friend. It is an alliance built in the time of the Ancients and is a means for the Ancients to assert themselves upon the mortal races. Jaal is a part of it. I no longer trust him."

Render suddenly lost his temper, "Open your mind, Mannace! Jaal started this journey with us, and he will finish it with us. He has always been a loyal friend, always there when most needed."

"He serves many masters!"

"He has his path, but he has never forsaken us. Never!"

Taking a moment to calm down and relax back into his seat, Render changed the topic to more practical matters.

"You have been hiding in Angorok for too long, and your world is too small. Perhaps your problems will not appear insurmountable when you step back and see Angorok and the war in the North for what it is."

"And what is that?"

"A spec in space and time, my friend. It is one piece in a game. Have you forgotten all the other pieces? The Eastern Colonies are without a governor, Mannace."

"I left that behind, Render, and have no desire to be a Bracadian governor. I am satisfied to have Angorok as mine alone and to be marshall in the North."

"And how is that narrow thinking helping those you would protect? How will you win the North from the basement of your citadel!"

Syprus stunned everybody when he interjected, "The wizard is right. You must rise before Angorok rises. To champion light, you cannot hide in the dark."

Mannace lowered himself to the grass and lay down, looking up at the light as if he might draw wisdom from it.

After a time, he closed his eyes and enjoyed the warmth of the sun on his face. He cleared his mind, happy to be reunited with Render and satisfied to enjoy the company. It was a long journey to reach the Fesadi homeland, and Mannace intended to stay at least a few days, so there would be ample time for further talks. As he relaxed, he looked up at Render and had the final word.

"I am glad to see you so well, my friend."

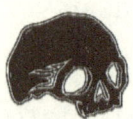

"How do we find the Mad King? I need *The Bell* to fulfil a promise. The artefact can do the impossible, Render. It can change the fates that have befallen us. It will aid us in forging a new future."

Render looked up from his incanting. He hated to be interrupted, but Mannace's question captured his interest. The sorcerer was facing the trunk of the ancestral tree, and he asked Mannace to look up, taking in the magnificence of the towering wood and foliage. It still appeared to be dying. Mannace was momentarily distracted by Render's work.

"Are you making an undead tree, Render?"

"Hells no!" But as the sorcerer pondered, he changed his answer, "Perhaps a little. There is new life in its old form: sentience and magic. The Fesadi will be happy to see their tree restored, but they would curse me for knowing the how of it."

The sorcerer laughed, "It is like the new flesh they gave me. I would never ask to be part plant, Mannace, but it is a means to an end. Only the Fesadi could have restored me to full function. So, this work I do now to revive their tree is payment and retribution. Their mending is so righteous as if it is superior to any magic. Well, now my magic can heal what they cannot. Fuck them, eh, my friend."

Mannace peered sideways at the sorcerer, and lines creased his forehead.

"There is madness in you to waste your time on a tree for such pettiness."

"Huh, you underestimate me, Mannace. Do you know me so poorly to think the tree serves no purpose? What is your plan to find your Mad King?"

Mannace was silent. His eyes moved from side to side as he put his mind to work on the sorcerer's riddle, but he could not connect the tree and its magic to his quest. Render met the marshall's gaze, then put a hand on his shoulder. He placed his other hand against the bark of the mighty bore. Instantaneously the world went dark, and both men were in blackness. There was enough ambient light that after a short time, Mannace could sense the earth beneath his feet, piled with bones. However, nothing here seemed natural. Just as suddenly they were back at the tree, and Render put both his hands at his side, twitching his fingers.

"The fourth Hell; the realm of the dead. I have made a portal connecting with Viletri, Tarnac, Vlustoven, my tower near the Valley of Agony, and Adash. I will have Adash back one day, Mannace."

Mannace's senses were still reeling, and he felt his gut churning. He considered many questions but focused on the challenge in front of him.

"How will this help us find the Mad King?"

"I will work on that, my friend. I will speak with the souls of the Fallen, and we will travel the paths of the dead. Are you afraid, Mannace?"

"Fuck you. Should I be afraid? You are a danger to us all, Render."

The sorcerer laughed again. A perilous glint in the sorcerer's eye added to Mannace's reservations, but despite any misgivings, the big man placed a hand on Render's arm.

"It is you that scares me, Render, not the bloody dead. But I trust you and will follow you through the Four Hells and beyond if it gets me what I want."

THE HELLS

Saska fawned over the enamoured war leader. Demmal, a mighty champion and wise priest, proved as weak as any other man for the seductress' lure. The War God did not protect him. In fact, divine energies fed his hunger to fuck such a spectacular creature. He had watched Saska when she lived with Jaal in Viletri, always envious of the dark elf's luck. Now, in the presence of Grendal and four keepers, he was prepared to lay the demoness across the table and release his fury against her loins. At the door to the room, two of Demmal's soldiers, the Devoted, looked on in amusement.

"Saska, enough!"

Grengal's voice and latent magic blew like a breeze across the gathering, ruffling cloaks and blowing back Demmal's unbound hair. The breeze carried away much of the yearning that consumed the war leader, but he remained confused, unsure who he might support if the discussion between Saska and Grendal went poorly. In his miasma, he forgot or didn't care that Grendal held his life in her hands.

"Your demons are making no progress against the citadel, and they have become a nuisance. Tell the generals to take their armies north."

Saska let out an involuntary laugh and pushed herself up against Demmal. She touched his cheek intimately while her other palm slipped past his trouser belt to tease the leader's manhood. Then, she turned her head to face Grengal.

"I no control generals. Easy to encourage attack Angorok, but not want to leave. Let them finish work."

"That is not what we agreed, Saska. Angorok will be mine."

Saska pulled her hand out of Demmal's trousers and gave the Ancient her focus, looking at her intently. Demmal, not wanting Saska's attention to stop, grabbed the seductress' arm. Ruthlessly, Saska spun and put her knee to Demmal's groin, sending him staggering backwards. Bent over but staring up at Saska, the leader of the chosen appeared in pain and even more confused. The demoness stepped away from him and towards Grengal.

"Why you care Angorok?"

For a moment, Grengal became the swarm, enough to trick the eye and be a reminder that the Ancient was much more than she seemed. It moved her a fraction closer to Saska and left a buzz about the chamber as flies circled about and landed on their mistress, amalgamating into her form.

"Send the demons south to the Rift then, to join their kin and purge the dwarves. Tell them to seek the Core. That will feed their greed."

Grengal's tone was commanding. Saska knew nothing of the dwarves or the Core, so she tilted her head as if thinking and absentmindedly ran her hand across the sweat between her breasts.

"I control only horde, my flyers. I tell the generals go south. They decide."

Again, Grengal seemed to expand and contract back to her human form. In doing so, more flies escaped before circling and returning dutifully to their mother. She leaned in close to the seductress, looking deeply into her eyes.

"Remember your rank in the Order. When I restore Order in the North, *all* will know their place."

Saska was fearless in returning the stare, defiant in her stance, yet not bold enough to contradict Grengal's words. Not here, where Grengal was dominant and had her lackeys. Behind Saska, Demmal was writhing on the floor, but it was another's magic that gripped him, not hers. The Seductress looked down at the war leader as she passed by him towards the exit. Now that her lust lessened, Demmal looked old, unappealing as his face contorted with agony.

In contrast, one of the Devoted at the door was young and powerfully muscular, with wickedness in his eyes that she liked. It took only a smile, and a slight caress of his soul, for the man to abandon his post and follow her. While Demmal was essential to the ancient, Saska knew that Grengal would not deny her this lesser gift.

Demmal stood before his mistress. His head was bowed, embarrassed by how easily Saska controlled him. The war leader's mind was still reeling from the pain Grengal unleashed upon him, and inside his chest, the flies were active, making him flinch involuntarily. The ancient chastised him and was quietly considering her next words.

"Should I take your cock and balls?"

It was a serious question.

"I will pray to the War God, mistress, to have the strength to resist. Next time I will be prepared."

Grengal cast her glare at Demmal to test his mettle while she silently contemplated carrying out her threat. Finally, after long deliberation, the Ancient appeared to relax, changing the topic of their conversation.

"It was a mistake to ally with the demons. We will never be rid of them. Your advice has put us in a poor predicament."

"We have seen off the Bracadians and the colossi. Without the threat of the demon generals, the colossi would have scattered our forces. We have no means to defeat them."

"And the demons and their generals. What happens when they turn on us? Can we vanquish them?"

"They are flesh. The demons *can* be defeated."

"Your girlfriend will send them south to the Rift. She has more influence than she wants us to know. You could learn from her."

Demmal's brow furled, and his nostrils flared.

"That bitch is a friend to no man. Nor to you, Grengal. She has no loyalty to the Order or even the darkness. She is a child of the Hells, serving only them and herself."

"Is that so? You do not have the vision, Demmal. You only see with your eyes and in the present for all your divine craft. If Saska were disloyal, I would know it. Perhaps she is more dedicated than you, who follow because I enslaved you."

"Free me then of your flies, and you will know the depth or falseness of my loyalty. But understand that I serve the

War God first, then you, and then the men I command, the Devoted. It is the way of the priesthood and more compelling than any threats or flattery. I serve because it is my code."

"Do you still serve the enemy? The man called Mannace?"

Grengal seemed curious, leaning in to encourage an honest answer. Demmal knew he was trapped; it was not his character to lie or even conceal the truth.

"I swore oaths of loyalty to that man. I served him as I serve you, as war leader in the North. I served him because he possessed a vision and an eagerness to learn. He united the people, and he honoured the God of War."

"Do I not have a vision, Demmal?"

"Not that you have shared, Mistress."

"Huh, you should do your job then. Do what you are told."

Demmal was frowning. He found it hard to talk to the Ancient as if they spoke an entirely different language. It felt like he should be saying more.

"I obey, Mistress."

Grengal looked at him sideways, like she was also dissatisfied with their understanding. Then, after a long silence, she spoke more decisively.

"Pull our army further back from Angorok. We do not want to be in the path of the demons if they depart the city."

"Yes, Mistress."

"Is that all you have to say?"

The war leader shifted uneasily.

"Yes, Mistress."

Grengal pulled back her shoulder, her steely glare returning. Flies were buzzing in the air, and one was walking across Grengal's face as she spoke. Her words were soft yet threatening.

"Do not embarrass me again, Demmal. Do not outlive your usefulness."

The demons oppressed Angorok, destroying everything that the undead left standing. Only the citadel, with its potent enchantments, stood defiant amongst the rubble. Even the once mighty city walls were toppled by the enormous brutes, with few sections standing as a reminder of the formidable defence.

As Grengal watched from a distance, she could not tell whether it was Saska's influence or the demon general's choice. Still, there was a shift in motivation amongst the armies of Hell, and gradually the demonic horde moved away from the city. The masses meandered south across the expansive Veldaan. There were meagre pickings for the bloodthirsty fiends, who encountered only ruins and lifeless prairies. This ravaged landscape was already picked over by forerunners of their kin and the wandering dead. Not that it mattered, theirs was hunger that waited millennia to be satiated, and amongst the legions of the abyss, only the generals possessed any concept of space and time.

When the demons arrived at The Rift, they were met by their kin. Hell-spawn of all types were resident in the deep crevices and hunted in packs for any vestiges of life. Generals amongst those at The Rift confronted the newcomers, roaring and stomping, sometimes pushing up against one another. It always ended in dominance and submission, establishing their demonic hierarchy. When gathered together, their numbers were vast, content for the moment to find shadow in the depths and wait.

A flying ship appeared within the abyss, where the light of day was but a spec high above. In this monstrous cavern, the Rift walls were covered in demons who clung to the cold stone. Many shifted and resettled at the ship's appearance, while several flyers launched themselves to circle the imposter's vessel. On deck, at the prow, Saska stood with eyes closed. She could sense the shared presence of tens of thousands of her kin. Below her, one of the generals added to the collective awareness, dominant over the others, yet Saska easily bent the creature to her will. She controlled all their thoughts, and she spoke with the habit of words to reinforce her mandate.

"Gather. Wait. I Saska, queen. Obey me."

Of the demons in the living world, there was only the guardian of the portal between worlds that Saska could not influence. Like her, the guardian served just one master, from the Abyss itself. The voice of the master came to her infrequently and was often indistinct between worlds, but it gave instruction, and for now, Saska was obedient. Command came naturally to the seductress. However, she was no general or tactician. That did not interest her, and her plan to lure Demmal to her service had failed. Where was Jaal when he might be of use? The thought distracted her. Absentmindedly, the demoness ran her hand across her stomach and down to her purse, massaging the long lips and using a finger to feel the softness inside. Jaal was the best of her lovers, but her connection and loyalty to him made her weak. Why should she be beholden to one when there were so many? So many cocks to fuck and souls to drink.

THE ELVES

It was a great advantage to have the flying ship, and from her high perch, Casteel witnessed the migration of elves. As she passed over the ocean and then the land, there were small armadas of ships far below, then caravans trekking north across a great arboreal continent. On reaching the coast, a large city with farms and lands sown in crops indicated a human colony. To avoid unwanted drama, Casteel was reluctant to make contact with men or elves. Instead, the Blood Legion crew resupplied their hold from remote rivers and sent hunters for food. Athose did his utmost to establish himself amongst the legionnaires, but even Rey and Argo remained distant. They were friendly but not the same camaraderie he previously enjoyed. Casteel went to him when he was alone on the deck.

"Why are you so glum, Athose?"

The young elf was not so foolish to state that he missed the simple life of a legionnaire. Instead, he surprised Casteel with much deeper thinking.

"Why now? Why are the elves all drawn North, and for what purpose? Perhaps a seed was planted at their creation, so all the elves would come together at the right time. What reason might deserve such a patient plan? Who would have such patience?"

Casteel smiled and huffed in a way that was a half-laugh.

"You are amusing, Athose, with so many questions."

"How many elves do you think there are? Is it just the wild elves and the Alani, or are there many other elves from other distant shores?"

"There is the Merrin, who live on the Great Continent, and the dark elves. We will find out soon enough who is at the destination. Why do you ask these questions?"

"We could look at our feet, Casteel, and wonder why our nails grow. Or we can look up and be curious about important things that affect us. We can walk with our eyes closed or lift our heads and look ahead to know what our future might hold."

Again, Casteel laughed, "Is that what your Mad King told you?!"

"Yes, it is. Is it such bad advice to use your brains and question what you see? I know why the legionnaires don't like me, Casteel. I am not a follower anymore. I lead!"

Casteel was silent for a while, staring at Athose, then up to the heavens where the young elf was watching the wyverns that travelled with him. When she returned her gaze, she had a stern expression.

"It is good that you have questions, but wisdom does not come from curiosity or reasoning. Wisdom comes from a much more profound place, Athose. You may figure things out, even be a master of the game like your Mad King. But will you make the right choices? Will your decisions benefit the light, or embrace darkness?"

Athose was attentive. His willingness to listen restored some of Casteel's faith in him, so she continued.

"There is a part of you, Athose, that knows what is right and will lead you towards the light. It is that sense of what is just. It is the intuition to show caution or to rush in. It is the part of you that knows your best future and will guide you toward it. Do you know what I mean, Athose?"

The young elf's frown showed that he was having trouble with the concept, which was not surprising to Casteel. The response, however, was not what she expected.

"When I close my eyes, when I am near to sleeping, briefly, I can hear a voice. It is the inner me, and it guides me. Because it is me, I listen to it. Is that intuition, Casteel? Am I right to listen to the voice?"

The leader of the Blood Legion raised her brow and took a deep breath. She was going to scold Athose for making fun of her, but when meeting his stare, she could tell his sincerity. Casteel closed her eyes to clear her mind, letting her own wisdom guide her.

"Athose, Alani parents direct their children to understand mind, body, and spirit. They encourage mastery of oneself above all other things. I will teach you the spirit warrior."

"I am not a child, nor are you my mother, Casteel."

"Then don't act like a child."

"Learning is done through living and experiences, Casteel. Follow your nose, and the future will unfold."

"Follow your wisdom," Casteel corrected him. The two elves stared at one another, then returned to looking up at the distant wyverns.

"They are magnificent. I don't know why they follow me."

"Others are taking care of you, Athose, until you can care for yourself. You are special. Anybody with *wisdom* can see it. What that means, only the Fates and the future will reveal."

Athose shrugged. "I am bored of this trip and conversation. It will not be soon enough that we arrive at our destination."

The insult earned the young elf a fierce glower as Casteel stood to face him.

"Young brat, how dare you disrespect me. Arrogance is unwelcome here. Unwelcome anywhere!"

There was a flicker in Athose's glare as he momentarily looked away, then returned the gaze even more defiantly. Casteel could see why others were giving Athose distance, but rather than be angry, she pitied the boy.

"War and loss and responsibility. You can't handle that yet, not as a boy. You do not have it, Athose, the wisdom to lead. The Fates have sent you down a path you are not ready to take when all you have to counsel you is a mad king and a voice in your head."

Casteel carried fond memories of the younger Athose, enough to show him some compassion even if he didn't deserve it.

"It is not my role to be your parent. So where is Jaal when he is needed?"

Seeing Athose flinch, Casteel held her tongue, quickly remembering that any mention of Jaal was a slap for her young ward. So instead, she imparted simple advice, "Humble yourself, Athose. Listen. Show respect."

Athose shrugged uncomfortably. When he looked like he might speak, he drew a deep breath and quickly shook his head. After holding their gaze a little longer, both elves turned, and Casteel headed below deck. Athose moved to a place by himself at the stern, looking down on the great forest below. Then, when he was sure nobody was looking, he ran his sleeve across his eyes.

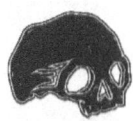

The terrain beneath them was changing. As the *Gull* moved further inland, rocky crags appeared out of the forest, becoming more prominent, until, after another day of travel, the bluffs dominated the landscape. Long ridges, cliffs, and canyons bespoke a landscape once in turmoil, perhaps a battleground of the gods, bearing countless ancient scars. Casteel's musings were interrupted by a lookout who put aside his viewing scope and called for the navigator to swing starboard. Soon Casteel saw what had gotten the man so excited. Along one valley was a long procession of travellers that Casteel presumed must be elves, moving in the same direction as they did. At a distance, they appeared colourfully dressed, so they were not of the Fogmir, and as the *Gull* continued in the same direction, it was clear by their multitudes that they were not Alani either. It was hard to determine how many there might be among the trees, but Casteel guessed tens of thousands. She turned to Rey, who was peering over the boat's rail.

"I am excited, Rey, to learn why the elves are pulled to this single destination. All elves, Rey. I am anxious, though, that life will forever change. What destiny awaits us?"

Pulling back his shoulders to strengthen his resolve, Rey boldly asked Casteel a question on many of the crew's lips. His tone was serious.

"What of those aboard that are not elves? What are your plans for the Legion?"

Casteel turned to face the belg. She looked about the deck at others, all doing their jobs or relaxing in the sun. She took a deep breath to brace herself, then looked up to meet Rey's gaze.

"You will lead the Legion, Rey. You will take the ship and return to the North. Take your orders from Mannace."

After another deep breath, Casteel put her hand on the belg's chest, pressing hard with her palm as if to cement their connection, before stepping back to meet his stare.

"You are wise, Rey. I trust you to care for the Legion and keep them true to purpose. They will honour you. You will take charge immediately to do what is needed when the time is right."

Rey stayed steely-eyed. He let out the breath he was holding.

"Casteel, if I am in charge, I will set this ship down now, and you can journey with your kin by land. I do not trust that we will have the option to turn back when we arrive at your destination. Your gut pulls you forward. My gut tells me to run. This is elf business, and others will not be welcome."

Casteel shifted her gaze and moved to the rail. She glanced up at Rey, whose stare remained fixed upon her. Below, the elves wound their way across the unfriendly terrain. Having thought about this many nights as they journeyed, Casteel already knew her mind; she would not put others in peril.

"Set us down, Rey. You are right to raise these concerns. I will fetch Athose, and we will gather our belongings."

Staying composed, Casteel reached out a hand to grip the belg's wrist.

"At least I will take the boy, so he will no longer be a nuisance."

Rey laughed. It was a generous laugh befitting a kind soul. He put his free hand over Casteel's.

"Look after him, Casteel. He needs words to guide him. That is, if his pointy ears are working. I will take care of this lot and make you proud."

Before Casteel could share more, Rey gave her a gentle push, enough to unbalance her, while he turned to stomp across the deck. The appointed commander took a deep breath as he paced, using it to bark out his orders.

"You lot, clean up that mess. Agro, you git, get off there. I'm in charge now, ladies, best show some respect."

Agro, who was balancing on the deck rail, was cocky as Rey approached until the big warrior walloped the orc across his shins, causing him to summersault and barely catch himself before plummeting off the ship's side. Another legionnaire helped hoist Agro back to safety. Rey loomed over him.

"Put out the colours. Prepare for landing."

The Fianti were a pragmatic people, factual and precise. They followed a strict hierarchy, and Casteel was not permitted to meet with their queen. She was, however, entitled to an audience with their military commander, the Eganji. After a day of travel through the wilderness, at night, Casteel, Athose, and Yuriki sat across a campfire from the Eganji. As guests, they were fed, eating in silence as was the Fianti's custom.

Yuriki, her stomach quickly filled, offered Athose half of the meaty stew, which he readily accepted. Though not elven, Yuriki resembled an elf more than a human, and for now, the Fianti's curiosity made her welcome. Sitting next to Athose, she ran her palm up and down his back. Even in the company of the eganji, she nestled intimately into his side. Athose seemed not to notice, consumed in private thoughts as they ate.

After they finished dinner and the companions washed from bowls bought by soldiers, the eganji asked questions in his broad accent, and Casteel readily relayed what information she knew. She spoke of the Alani, the wild elves of the Forgmir, and the little information she possessed of the Merin. When pressed for more detail, Casteel described the Eastern Colonies, the South now occupied by the dwarves, and the chaos in the North. The eganji was especially interested in the North and its history, so Casteel shared everything she considered would be of interest. It was late before she could ask her questions, and their time was almost up. The history of the Fianti was not crucial to her, so she focused on what lay ahead.

"Do you know where we are headed? What pulls us to our destination?"

The eganji seemed surprised that Casteel did not know. He sat back and eyed Casteel suspiciously.

"In Alani society, the Elder Council are guardians of the past. Some might know the origins of the elves and our most ancient lore, but they do not share it. They are trusted to guide the Alani in everything, and they have said it is time to travel. So, the Alani and the younger elven nations answer the call. Are we wrong to make this journey?"

"No, all elves must answer the Siren's call. All will gather."

"Who are the Sirens?"

"Servants of the Father. We are all servants of the Father."

The eganji was tall and robust, befitting his role, with piercing eyes looking deep into Casteel. She sensed his curiosity, but she also perceived judgement as if she were inferior. She would not accept such arrogance.

"Why do you look down at me? Do I not deserve respect?"

Her counterpart shook his head as if to dismiss Casteel's challenge. He stood, so she did the same.

"How can the Alani serve the father if they do not know him? How can you live so long yet march to the gathering in ignorance? I do not understand!"

When it looked like the eganji would turn and leave, desperate to know more, Casteel threw another question to keep his interest.

"The dark elves do not feel the summons. Why is that?"

The eganji looked down at Casteel, and his menacing tone reinforced the judgement Casteel had already perceived.

"Elves of the shadow are an abomination to be eradicated. They are not of the father's image. They are vengeful, serving only the mother."

The word mother was spat from the commander's mouth with such hatred that Casteel was shocked. For such a passionless people as the Fianti first seemed, now the eganji was fiercely animated. He addressed Casteel with unexpected vigour, making her fearful for herself and her wards.

"When the father subdued the mother, he laid his seed in the vessel and spawned the immortal race of elves. He made us in his image so that we would rise above others and serve in his name."

With a finger pointed at Casteel, he reinforced his message by stepping around the fire and leaning over his guests.

"Your ignorance is unforgivable! That you would know these dark elves and not cleanse their stain from the land is a sin against the father! Let us hope your council has more wisdom, else your Alani will reveal themselves to be fools!"

Shaking his head, the eganji stormed off. Casteel was stunned, as was Yuriki. Athose, though, smirked, continuing to finish his stew.

"Orcs are far more pleasant. It's hard to like elves."

Casteel was afire with emotions, incredulous at the young elf's calmness.

"It's easy to be smart when you have only yourself to care for."

PART SIX:

The Bell

SANCTUARY

Kraken relaxed into his chair. The craft they liberated from the Arenlanders was a luxury vessel, and the pirate watched Fergis and Jaal sink into comfy seats. Fergis tossed a cushion aside and bounced up and down to test the springs.

"Bah, do these Arenlanders have nothing better to do than to invent ways to be lazy? Better to sit on a bloody rock. A rough bastard stone so cold it'll freeze your bollocks off. That'll get you up and doing something bloody useful. Waste of bloody time, bloody Arenlanders."

Despite his complaining, Fergis eventually relaxed, throwing one leg over the armrest, and leaning into a cushion he snatched from a vacant chair.

Jaal appeared perturbed or pissed off. Kraken needed to know which it was.

"What's up your arse? Thought you'd be happy to be heading for distant shores."

Jaal was not in the mood for a conversation and looked disdainfully down his nose at his present company. That just made them smirk, which in turn caused the dark elf to shake his head.

"I'll be happier when we've passed over the North. It's a poor choice of route."

"Well, the navigator has only been as far as Skon, so you know how that works. We have to do it hard from here. He's a fast one, though, faster than when I travelled to Bracadia. Now that was a bloody adventure. That bitch of yours lad, she's a mad one."

Jaal was quick to talk over Kraken. There was passion in his tone, "You have no idea, Kraken, how mad that bitch is, and the others. If you understood the danger we are in travelling across the North, you would shit in your pants."

The pirate laughed. Fergis seemed confused, while Kraken remained unflappable.

"Seems like your problem, lad. I've got no grudge against the woman. We're keeping her as high as we can, so what else can we do? You worry too much. Ramthos protects us."

"Fucking gods, are you happy to be a pawn in their games? For Hell's sake, Kraken, you are smarter than that."

Suddenly serious, Kraken responded, "I'd be long dead if I didn't have faith. Ramthos is no ghost, Jaal. He is real, and he is with us as we travel. He will pilot us to where we need to be. Embrace that. Embrace him; it will cost you nothing."

"There is always a cost."

Again, Kraken laughed, but it seemed more introspective. After a moment, he rallied his resolve.

"It's more like repaying a debt. Whatever! You can face the world yourself if that's your choice. I'll take Ramthos' blessings and not be quakin' in my boots like some homesick brat! Faith in Ramthos will put steel in your spine – freedom to do as you choose, to cast your ambition beyond the horizon and not fear consequences. That's true freedom. But, Jaal, it's your business."

Most days, Jaal was unflappable too, but he felt like prey, and there would be no sleep for him until they were past the land and the sea was beneath them. He absentmindedly checked the blade at this belt. His nervousness was palpable. Kraken smiled, and when he spoke, he was theatrical in his hand movements, putting his wrists together and flapping them like a bird.

"When the gulls cry, they cry for thee. To the sea. Quickly, to the briny sea. Set your course to the unknown and be free. Be free!"

Jaal was incensed, "What the fuck does that mean, you mad old bastard?"

"Don't let your fears trip you up and keep you from your destiny. Keep moving forward. We have tricky business ahead, Jaal. You will need your full wits."

He saved them, this man with no name, from the vicious Surg-Ta. The Ben-Jar thought themselves safe from the Red horde on their islands, behind their towering ancient walls. But the Surg-Ta came on massive rafts and floating fortresses and laid siege to the island cities. They were intent on overwhelming and enslaving the Ben-Jar, as they did to all others they encountered. The man with no name vanquished them by summoning the beast from the depths and setting it loose upon the enemy. The Surg-Ta, always a relentless opponent, were sure to return.

The Mad King walked along the sea wall as he did each morning. Qi was one of the smallest islands, and he usually completed the loop by the time the islanders opened their markets and began their day. From the high vantage, he enjoyed watching the orange sunrise over the calm waters, the view of the many other islands, and the distant mainland. It was such strange geography, this collection of islands in such deep waters, like the peaks of submerged mountains, reaching up to take a breath of air. The houses of the Ben-Jar were all made of the same orange clay. They appeared on every piece of available land, except where the slopes of the rocky isles were impossibly steep. Before the Surg-Ta vanquished the mainland, the Ben-Jar were traders, enjoying great prosperity. Now they fished and scavenged. While still a proud, capable people, they lived a meagre existence.

Though Qi was small compared to its neighbours, it boasted a good-sized harbour and was the only city with a tall and wide sea gate to accommodate the monstrous Ark. The Ark was a dominating presence in the port and housed the Mad King and his retinue.

Today, Ultan, Karnate of Qi, walked alongside the King. The karnate governed the island, and he was interested in everything this foreign man could tell him about distant places. Now he shook his head.

"It was told to us over generations that the sea was boundless. That to go beyond the horizon was perilous, and those that tried did not return. We are great travellers, but always land must be in sight. We will be lost forever if we are lost to the land."

"Ultan, there are many other lands, and traders move between them. Traders are forever exploring. More than anything, greed is a tremendous motivator."

Ultan smiled at the nature of men, not dissimilar amongst the islands. The Mad King stopped to face him.

"I wanted to be away from those distant lands, so I sailed into the unknown and here I am, with the Ben-Jar. It is restful here."

The karnate was surprised.

"The Surg-Ta will give us no rest, no peace. You saw their fortresses upon the ocean. There is no effort they won't take to meet their desire for conquest."

The ordinarily stoic Mad King was suddenly exasperated, "Then learn from that. What will the Ben-Jar do? What will you do? Will you sit and complain and wait for the Surg-Ta to return?"

Ultan seemed taken aback and confused, which frustrated the King.

"Your people are lost. How will you lead them, Ultan? You are an intelligent man. How will the karnates reclaim their greatness?"

The noble straightened, regaining his authority. He was not used to being talked down to, and he was agitated now as he returned the Mad King's stare.

"You will lend me your ship, and I will travel upon the sea to these other lands. You will be a guest in the palace until my return. Take all the rest you need."

"What of the other karnates? Will they rest while you labour? Will you save them all?"

"They can save themselves!" was the quick response. The Mad King knew they were rivals, not to be trusted if Ultan were to depart for an extended time. The King carried a bemused smirk, though Ultan was too roused to notice, sharing his quickly evolving thoughts.

"The other karnates will join me. It is a task that must be done together. I know how they think, and ultimately they will not want to be absent when we discover new ports and sign new agreements."

"What of the Surg-Ta?"

Ultan's eyes darted about as his mind raced. The Mad King made it easy for him.

"I will protect the Ben-Jar from the Surg-Ta. I am just one man, but I have the Kraken. And to maintain the peace between the islands, I have the colossus. Tell the karnates that. Tell them I will keep the Ben-Jar safe while they travel to save their people. I make that promise to you now, Ultan."

It was a lot for Ultan to consider. He drew a deep breath and moved ahead of the King to resume their pacing along the wall. It was possibly a step too far, but the Mad King could not help but add.

"Where I come from, people call me The King. I know it's not a term used here, but perhaps it is a way I could be addressed."

Ultan paused to turn his head and say, "Yes". After that, the rest of the walk was in thoughtful silence.

The palace was far more comfortable than the ship. In better times, the court, though small, was expensively furnished, but with the insurgence of the Surg-Ta, luxury items were in short supply, and the famous wealth of the Ben-Jar was evaporating. At his order, the slaves that remained with the king restored the palace to a sparkling state. Their continuous industry gave a renewed sense of purpose to people in the city and those visiting from other islands. When the karnates departed on the Ark, many of the Mad King's entourage went with them to crew and power the massive ship. Most of the mole men stayed, starting work on the Surg-Ta prisoners. The Surg-Ta were fierce men, closed-mouthed when asked any questions. The king expected they would soon bow at his feet once the mole men conditioned and repurposed them, readily sharing any information.

The High Satar, who purposefully stayed at an inn on the far side of the city island, came to visit. Despite all the time that had passed since fleeing the North, his brother's animosity was still apparent in every word.

"What is your purpose, *brother*? What *game* are you playing now?"

The Mad King was unperturbed by the harsh tone. "Does it matter? We needed to be away from the North. So, this sanctuary is our new beginning?"

The High Satar inspected some heirlooms on pedestals along the corridor where they stood. He didn't seem impressed.

"I didn't ask for a new beginning. I was happy with my life until you put what I built to ruin and dragged me away. These islands, this place, has no soul. It is dead, awaiting its funeral."

The description made the king smile. He, too, missed the drama of the North, and as sophisticated as the Ben-Jar considered themselves, their lives and civilisation were trivial. He would not concede any error in judgement, however.

"Imbor, do you really miss it? A bright light to attract fools. Of course, it became more interesting when it fell into the Abyss."

The High Satar couldn't help but snigger. He did not miss Imbor, though the eternal priesthood he established was also lost to him. That was unforgivable, wiping the smile from his face.

"I never messed with your plans, brother. You ruined mine."

"Bah, sitting in your garden on your hill. I was embarrassed for you. You are better here, where you are bored. It will make you think of possibilities. It will drive you to do new things. Things that will shape the Age and never be forgotten."

There was a slight shake of the head. Absentmindedly, the High Satar continued to inspect the ornaments rather than meet the king's gaze.

"And you. Are you bored? What chaos are you conjuring? What will you do?"

The king quickly retorted, "What will *we* do, brother? There is only us, remember that."

PATHS OF THE DEAD

Render, Mannace, Xu, and Syprus held hands as they stepped into the darkness at the base of the ancient Fesadi tree, disappearing one by one into its shadow. When they reappeared, they were at the Sorcerer's residence in Viletri, in the basement beneath his holdings. Mannace was not happy to learn of their location.

"By the Hells, Render, would you put us in the clutches of that fucking liche? Get us away from here."

"Patience, Mannace, Kakos will not come to this place. There are wards to keep the dead away. Wait while I collect what I need."

When Render returned, there was a man with him, handsome and fit with a pack of goods strapped across his back. Mannace remembered him as one of the Guardian Chosen, upon whose death his soul would bind to the remaining idle statue guarding Viletri. The blonde man looked up with his steely blue eyes.

"Mannace, sir."

"Kole, you have grown to be a man since I last saw you. Render, why is Kole here?"

"He has travelled the paths of the dead with me before. He is strong, and sometimes I transport things between my holdings through the paths of the dead. He is fearless, a rare trait. And smart, perhaps even rarer."

Mannace paced anxiously while Uz and Syprus waited in silence.

When the group held hands and entered the shadow again, they were in a darker place. Render turned to face the others.

"These are older paths. You can let go of each other but dare not wander off. As I explained, the path will take us to the person we seek. There is no time here. It is the past and present merged into one. Follow me."

About them was darkness, or on closer inspection, a void. As the companions walked, it was on no path that could be seen, but it gave the sense of travelling. Nobody spoke. It was too hard to focus on words, construct sentences, or even think. Soon, there was the momentum forward, but nothing else. At the fore, Render remained vigilant. Unlike the others, his eyes darted about, watching, ready for any dangers. He dared not educate his companions just how risky this business was.

It had never happened to Render, but a floor was manifesting beneath his feet. Walls appeared from the nothingness about them, and he was suddenly walking a corridor. The others continued close behind, tranced and seemingly unaware of the odd transformation. Ahead, the passage opened into a room. It was not possible to stop or proceed with more care. Not that this was real. Render sensed no magic to it, not even the tingle of death.

As they moved into the room, its dimensions expanded to be a magnificent arena bigger than the stadium at Colossus. The companions' momentum ceased for the moment, and Render stood stationary, the others merely shadowing behind him, trapped at the stadium's centre. Then, above the amphitheatre, a face abruptly filled the sky, piercing yellow eyes staring down upon the sorcerer. It was a porcelain, cracked, possibly feminine face. To the right of Render, Kakos stood staring at him. Spectators were filling the arena seats, ghostly figures, silent and watchful.

A voice, definitely feminine and time-worn, boomed from the sky.

"Thief. Trespasser."

Render choked on his own breath, coughing harshly, not permitted words to respond. This encounter was a reckoning. Kakos smiled at his discomfort.

"Give me a soul. And I will permit you to complete your journey."

Following the proclamation, Kakos seemed less happy, so Render assumed he might have an escape. Without conscience, he pointed to the shadow he knew to be Syprus.

"No."

He pointed towards Kole. Perhaps the chosen guardian was a prize, but again the voice uttered "No."

Render skipped past Xu, who he expected was of little value, and reluctantly pointed to Mannace. Mannace, who the Oracle and fates held so precious. The sorcerer's breathing was laboured, struggling for even the slightest gasp, and his mind was increasingly dizzy.

"No."

Suffocating, Render put a hand to his chest. Desperately, he patted himself to make his offering clear. Suddenly, the sorcerer caught a breath, and as he sucked in air, his mind rapidly cleared. Render looked up to the imagined sky. The yellow eyes staring back at him showed no emotion. In contrast, Kakos to the side was grinning once more.

"I accept your offer. Travel now, my disciple."

With that said, the illusion and even Kakos were gone, and the party continued their momentum forward. However, the void was not empty as it had been, and ghostly whisps appeared and disappeared from the nothingness. They seemed curious to Render, at least not the angry phantoms he dreaded might ambush their passage. He understood enough of the domain of the dead to remain fearful, but he struck a deal with their goddess and was still alive. It was likely that, for now, she did not want him dead.

As they exited the paths, it was daytime. Render, used to the long trek through the darkness, shielded his eyes from the harsh sunlight. The others, for whom time in the domain of the dead stopped, thought the travel to be instantaneous. Xu reached up to the sun and gave a blessing in his rhalec language. Then in the common tongue, he addressed the others.

"Let'sss hope they are a friendly peoplessss."

Around them was a market, busy with customers who, upon the companion's sudden appearance, were backing off, yelling, and pointing. Amongst them, soldiers in armour rallied with swords drawn. There were just a few, but it was likely that soon many more would follow. As Mannace looked about, Render had already disappeared. That was good; the sorcerer would rescue them if they got into trouble. With hands raised to show his peaceful intent, Mannace called to one of the guards.

"I am Mannace, Marshall of Angorok. Take us to the king."

Mannace felt the blood rushing through his veins. In the past, he had considered the Mad King an ally, somebody he admired. But the king put Mannace's destiny to ruin, which was a torture he could not forgive. He didn't know how he would act if the king were before him.

Significant time passed before an officer, backed by a sizable contingent of garrison troops, took command of the situation. Without an explanation, they led the trio through the city to an inn, ushering them inside. Guards stood at the doors and in the surrounding streets, so it was unclear if they were guests or prisoners. At least it was a comfortable lodging. Mannace, who felt exhausted, lounged in the common area. As he began to relax, the Mad King entered the room. At least, that was what Mannace thought at first, but he soon realised it was a man who resembled the Mad King rather than the man himself.

The men stared at one another. Their clothing and appearance made it clear that neither fitted this city nor region and that there was potentially more to this encounter than chance. The High Satar was the first to speak.

"You thought I was somebody else. My brother, I imagine. There are guards at the door, so your relationship with him is not one of trust. Though you are alive, so he has a purpose in keeping you. He put you here with me. Why is that, do you think?"

"A game."

"I expect so."

The High Satar sat in a chair facing the visitor. "You carry upon your being a great weight. The hopes of men. The Fates gravitate to you, and I can sense their presence." Then, appearing smug, he added, "Welcome Mannace, to the islands of the Ben-Jar, to the city of Qi. Why have you come all this way? To kill my brother, I expect. To exact your revenge?"

Mannace could see that the similarity in this Mad King's brother went further than looks, but he bore no patience for games. He preferred truth.

"I am here for the Bell. If you are smart enough to guess my name, you must surely know my purpose."

"I might have guessed it. But would revenge not also be paramount? You have every reason to hate my brother."

The High Satar was a little too eager, and Mannace became more circumspect. He was still undecided if he would kill the king or not. His inner conflict was distracting, and Mannace felt his thoughts might be transparent from the thin smile on the brother's face. Indeed, the brother responded.

"He gives me the same torment. Why is it so hard to run a blade through his twisted heart for what he has done?"

It was a conundrum that captured Mannace's interest. His gut knew the answer, and for some uncanny reason, Mannace trusted this man enough to share it.

"Because it is rare to find a man like the Mad King. We strive to achieve our destinies, but for him, the world bends easily at every turn. How he has avoided death is a mystery to me."

The High Satar added his thoughts to Mannace's thinking.

"Vestig Gozer would kill him. He would not delay his strike. Vestig would crush his skull with his boot to ensure his work, then have the body incinerated. Why is it so simple for Vestig, yet hard for you? He betrayed you."

Though Mannace was not a player of games, he was astute enough to see that the brothers were indeed alike.

"I see where this conversation will take us. If you want your brother dead, do it yourself."

The High Satar leaned back in his chair, reflective, allowing quiet to fill the room.

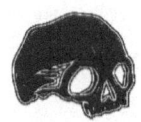

FELLOWSHIP

While walking the streets unseen at night, Render sensed another wizard nearby, Maresh. Maresh once served Render as an underling, though only for a short while, working alongside the sea mage at Viletri. Though decades eroded the memory, it was a sufficient association for Render to have marked the mage so that he could now detect his presence and even lure him to his location. He cast a subtle compulsion.

Render stayed hidden on the edge of near-space until the mage and his companions were close enough to make out their faces. They approached down a quiet alley, carefully surveying the next street before Maresh slunk closer to the wizard's location. Grasping a hammer, Maresh was incanting with his other hand but uncovering nothing. An even more unexpected turn of events was catching a glimpse of Jaal in the shadows. Seeing his friend in this city was beyond a fluke, and Render did not trust such luck. So far from familiar lands, the coincidence was a blatant manipulation of events. Instead of revealing himself to Maresh or Jaal, Render slunk away, ending the compulsion so that Maresh would continue his business.

The sorcerer recognised pirates when he saw them, a motley, undisciplined bunch. But why did Jaal keep such company, and why here? Who pulled the strings so he, Mannace, and Jaal were at this same place at this time?

As Render looked back to watch the pirates move to another alley, well behind them a figure followed, scampering like a rat in the dark. A mole man, the Mad King's spy. Seeing one on Jaal's trail was a concern, and he withdrew to a safer distance as the Dragu possessed senses well beyond that of men. The presence of the Dragu made Render more cautious in his exploration.

Jaal and Kraken leaned closer to Maresh to hear what the mage detected. Behind them, Fergis and a handful of other pirates kept vigil over the port and streets. When Maresh was sure of his findings, he whispered to the others.

"There is magic in the harbour as if something is secreted within its depths."

Kraken nodded, "That will be the bell."

"Not the bell", Jaal added quickly. "The bell has no magic, at least not that a mage would find. I heard Render say that. It was *peculiar* to him."

"Then what is it?" retorted the mage, raising his voice in annoyance.

Jaal held a finger to his lip to remind him to be quiet, "A colossus perhaps, to carry and guard the bell. Or something new, not of the Mad King's making."

Kraken was excited and patted Maresh on the arm to enthuse him. "Ok, lad, get it out. Let's have a good look at it."

Maresh returned a stare as if Kraken were mad. "It might not be the bell."

"It's the bell, lad. Trust me on this. I know it's the bell. So, get it out of there."

Maresh shrugged, "How the Hells would I do that? And what if it's a bloody colossus? Do you have a plan for that?"

"Yes", Kraken glanced at Jaal. "He's the bloody master of colossus." Jaal returned a blank stare. It was true that the dark elf previously commanded the creatures, but not above the influence of the Mad King, who shared a more profound understanding with them. Kraken knew his mind, "We need to do this before it gets light. Do what you need to do. Do it now!"

"What is your hurry when we have time?" Jaal's tone was blunt. "You have been patient to get here. Think this through."

"My senses tell me we are out of time, Jaal. Thievery and knowing when to run; that's my talent. Let others have patience. It will put them behind us, wondering what happened. There is no better time to act than now." Kraken turned back to the mage, "Get the bloody bell out of the harbour and onto this wharf."

Fergis approached, flapping his hands for them to keep their voices down. Kraken turned to him, "Fetch the ship, Fergis, take Alli and Jinj and bring the ship to the harbour before dawn. Get ropes ready to haul the bell. We'll pull her free from the damn harbour if we have to. Get those bloody stumps you call legs moving."

Kraken saved some final words for Jaal.

"Ramthos led us here. Ramthos will see us free from here too. Have faith, Jaal. Get on board, quickly lad, or you'll bloody drown."

Jaal was surprised when he walked up the palace steps to see the Mad King at the door, standing in the dawn's early sun, waiting for him. The King ushered him in, and together, the pair made their way to a comfortable chamber where they sat and were brought water by a slave. Jaal didn't know how much the king knew of his association with the pirates or their business, so he remained silent until his old acquaintance spoke.

"Tell me about the mother of spiders."

It wasn't the topic Jaal expected, but it brought the tension of his situation back to the fore. He sneered before answering.

"She is asserting herself in the North. A dark alliance. A sisterhood. Saska and Ahmeda, with Eya to lead them. They will bring the North to its knees. I will never go back there."

The Mad King made his assumptions, "So, you and I, we are both exiles then?"

"Perhaps. They have come for the bell."

The Mad King was interested, "Who?"

"You tell me?"

It was the Mad King's turn to smirk. Perhaps he knew more than his visitor.

"They are all here; your pirates in the night, Mannace is resting at an inn, Render lurking somewhere in the shadows. You would gang up and rob me. Kill me, perhaps. Is that why you are here, Jaal? It is your job to kill *me*?"

Jaal kept a straight face. "I *should* kill you."

Both men were silent, eyes locked.

The Mad King relaxed, and half turned away from the dark elf, refilling his glass from a decanter left on the table. "Did you know I have a brother?"

Jaal didn't, so he shrugged his shoulders. "And?"

"And ... he is here too. A reunion of family and friends."

"Let them have the bell. Be free of the lands you left behind and their drama. Does the bell serve any purpose here, away from the North? Do you want all these problems on your doorstep?"

The Mad King was curious, "Why do you care? Did I not help you to be free of your shackles? Are you not able to follow your path and not be concerned about the ambition of Mannace or these *pirates*?"

The last word was spat out with disdain as if the king looked down on them. He judged Jaal as well for his association with such lowly men.

"You will regret that slur. They are the pirates that stole your bell from under your nose."

"That cannot be. I have the pirate ship. Do you think I would let thieves make a fool of me, whether I need the bell or not? Go and see for yourself; the Dragu have it, and the crew, in their *capable* care."

Jaal sat upright and addressed the king more formally, so he would understand that the game was over, and he was not jesting.

"I watched them extract the bell. I played a part in their plans. You know I command the colossi. And you know that Render is powerful, and they have a sea mage. But, of course, magic played a significant part. They are gone, and Mannace with them."

Holding his stare, Jaal added, "I am here for the pirate crew. You will give them to me."

The King was visibly agitated. He placed his glass on the table with a bang, so the remnant of water splashed over his wrist.

"There are consequences for stealing from me!"

"There are consequences to setting demons loose upon the world! You are lucky that they took the bell and left you alive. I am not here to kill you unless you deny what I ask."

The Mad King's stare was daggers, piercing Jaal's dark heart. Nevertheless, Jaal remained calm, knowing that he could easily carry out his threat, and despite their past relations, Jaal would be merciless if needed. The king eventually relaxed back into his seat, and with great effort, he regained his composure.

"And what will you do after the pirate's release, Jaal?"

"I will stay here with you. I will take the flying ship if I need to return to the North."

At that moment, the High Satar appeared at the door. He was surprised to see Jaal, not understanding who this dark elf was or his purpose. Nevertheless, he carried an urgent message to pass on.

"Your guests are no longer at the inn. I thought you should know."

The Mad King sagged noticeably, the news giving evidence to Jaal's claims, but the leader quickly straightened, and this time, he spoke with his usual authority. There was a hint of anger in his voice as well as determination.

"Brother, this is Jaal, an old friend. He will be joining us."

THE SURG-TA

The Mad King, his brother, and Jaal, sat around a small table in the captain's cabin. The Mad King's staff crewed the flying ship, and of the captured pirates, only Fergis was aboard. Jaal enjoyed an old association with the dwarf when he often sailed upon Urgar's mercenary craft, and it suited Jaal to keep the inventive engineer around. To prove his worth, Fergis helped to keep the boilers and other ship machinery working. The few other freed prisoners were put on a shallow hulled boat and left to the sea.

As they chatted, Jaal posed a question to the Mad King.

"I spoke to an elf, who told me you were a *Dark Light*. He wouldn't explain it, so what does it mean?"

"It means he is a menace, a damned nuisance to all he encounters."

The Mad King ignored the High Satar, shaking his head at the old priest's insult. Instead, he faced Jaal, doing his best to keep his brother out of view.

"You too bear that mark, and your son, Athose. It is a term for those that shape their destiny, which others follow."

When the High Satar looked as if he might talk over the top of the conversation, the Mad King put his palm up to stop him and hurried his explanation, "Mortals are drawn to light. The elves, in their ignorance, follow such a beacon and would make others choose that same path to protect their interests. But, for those who choose an independent path or cross many paths, the elves see it as a challenge to their purpose. A risk to their way of life."

The Mad King seemed satisfied and leaned back to let the High Satar have a say. The priest took a moment to gather his thoughts.

"Yes, what you say is true, but there is more to it. The light pursued by the elves, and some men, is divine. It is their god. They believe other beacons lead away from God, away from truth and grace. In the case of a dark light, they consider that oblivion is the destination. My brother here is a good example, don't you think, of ungodliness and peril, a beacon leading to oblivion."

Jaal shook his head, "I serve darkness. It affords me the strength to do what must be done. Darkness is needed as much as light, perhaps more."

The High Satar, who led the eternal order, lifted his head, and raised his voice as if he were giving a sermon.

"Man must have authority over the gods, light and darkness, the Hells, the wilds, the sea. In all cases, man must be the master. Man must be in control."

"Man is able", retorted the king. "I do not need gods to serve or be served. Ignore the gods, and they will cease to exist."

"Can you ignore day and night, brother? Do you not cast a shadow? And even you, brother, have a soul, a divine gift. Yes, you, least of men, who set the Hells loose upon the North. A dark light indeed."

Jaal's head was spinning. The sudden religious debate was beyond his simple reference, and pragmatically, he needed only to know about the darkness. It was enough; sometimes, the darkness alone consumed him. Jaal turned to the king.

"I envy your position. It is so simple to be godless."

It was night, and their destination became apparent by the tens of thousands of campfires dotting the terrain below. Despite their arrival, the Mad King ordered the flying ship to remain stationary, and it was not until morning that they descended. With a single Dragu to accompany him, the Mad King fearlessly set down amongst the Surg-Ta. They gathered, these fierce men, to watch the descent, and now their general approached on his chariot. He pulled the horses to a stop and looked down at his visitors, a visage of anger etched on his features, with fierce eyes to match. From the prisoners captured by the Ben-Jar, the Mad King understood some things about the Surg-Ta and their warlike ways. Enough to be direct.

"I have come to give you the Ben-Jar, and to show you richer lands."

When the leader sniggered, the Mad King stepped closer to the chariot, "The next time the rafts of the Surg-Ta approach the island cities of the Ben-Jar, the monster from the sea will be gone. You will have your conquest."

"What richer lands? What lands can you show the Surg-Ta, that we cannot already reach? The world submits to the Red Horde."

"Only the world you know. Unless I reveal them, there are lands outside your reach."

"You lie. The horde touches all lands."

"Come aboard my ship, and I will show you. Then, before the day's end, I will return you to your camp, and you will be wiser. This is my gift to you."

The general eyed the king suspiciously. Still, he stepped from the chariot and stood before the king, driven by compulsion, as were all the Surg-Ta, to march and to conquer.

"Show me these lands."

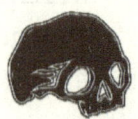

Jaal was incredulous. As much as he was concerned for his safety as they appeared, first over Angorok, then Skon, then high above Antigoth, he was more shocked by the Mad King's actions. The king revealed parts of the Bracadian mainland as the tour progressed. The navigator was experienced and able to traverse many lands, and the general of the Surg-Ta was astounded by what he witnessed. Jaal watched him hungrily conversing with the Mad King as they surveyed the vast territories from the ship's prow.

When the king passed by Jaal, he observed the disapproving look on the dark elf's face and stopped to address him.

"They should have let me be. Did you think I would let them steal from me and there not be repercussions?"

Abruptly, the Mad King saw the danger, the conflict of loyalties etched in Jaal's long frown and hateful glare. A Dragu lurked nearby, sensitive to the tension, another warning of what might follow if he left Jaal to brood. The Mad King brought his attention to the situation and placed a hand on Jaal's shoulder.

"Jaal, what of *your* revenge? You are a castaway, too, fearful of returning to the North. Eya humiliated you. Will you roll on your back or stand tall and strike? Are you equal to this challenge, Jaal? Are you Eya's pawn, or will you craft your own game?"

Jaal seemed uncertain, his eyes darting about, giving away his confusion. Finally, it was enough for the king to confidently step away, and even the Dragu moved on. After a short while, Jaal shifted to the bow and joined the Surg-Ta and king as they made their plans. He took a dagger from his belt, and with a determined thrust, Jaal jabbed the blade into the top railing to get their attention.

"As I serve the darkness, I swear, The Order will be mine."

While the Surg-Ta general was surprised, the king, who understood the bold declaration, drew a thin smile.

DRAGON

Render returned the adventurers safely to the Fesadi tree. Though little time passed, they all looked and felt like they had journeyed a vast distance. Render was noticeably fatigued.

"Why are we so exhausted, Render?" Mannace stared at the sorcerer, but his friend was too weary to reply, indicating with a meek wave of his hand that they should all rest. The colossus was with them, towering above the other travellers and clasping the prized bell. Nearby, Fesadi gathered and pointed up at the immense being. Ignoring the commotion, Render lay down on his back, drawing deep breaths. Showing concern, Uz leaned over him, casting a blessing so that the sorcerer was glowing as sunlight soaked into him. His breathing relaxed.

Nearby, Kraken and Kole examined a zoo compound where deer-like creatures bounced and frolicked. Kole put down the backpack he carried, sitting on it to relieve his sore legs while he watched the beasts dance. Defying his age, Kraken was already moving to another enclosure, more energised than his companions and eager to explore the spectacular menagerie.

One of the Fesadi king's sons came to usher the people back and give the travellers their privacy. He brought healers that tended to their tiredness. Soon, only Render slept while the others moved about. Prince Urgust, a proficient healer himself, knelt next to the sorcerer and placed a cloth soaked in oils on Render's brow. He wiped away the excess fluid to protect his patient's eyes and then put colourful, pebble-sized stones around Render's sleeping body. A large sapphire was set above the head, reflecting blue light against the base of the great tree.

Mannace seemed impatient, "Is he right, Urgust? When can he travel?"

"We will take him to the temple when he is rested enough to walk. He should mend there until he fully recovers. It will take time. I cannot say how long, but you can tell by his look that he has endured a great ordeal."

Mannace could see it too, now that Urgust drew his attention to it. "He has aged!"

The prince nodded, though he could not expound further on his observations, "Perhaps the sorcerer will share his experience when he is well enough to converse."

"I don't have time for that."

In truth, Mannace didn't know why he felt so rushed, but his gut told him to hurry. "I will leave him in your good care."

Mannace was apprehensive as he unloaded the bell at Zetarach's busy port. He dared not bring the colossus to this place, unsure if the creature would cooperate if he understood Manance's intent. So instead, rhalec priests and their initiates gathered to place the great artefact onto a sledge and drag it through the streets and catacombs towards Atek's lair. At Mannace's side, Uz was excited.

"You have stayed true to your word, Mannassss. Atek will reward you for your endeavoursss."

Mannace shrugged as if the reward were not important to him. Behind Mannace, Kraken seemed agitated as he watched the Rhalec move away with the bell.

"I must have that bell back, Mannace. I don't like the feel of this. How can you be sure of your plan?"

Again, Mannace shrugged, "Have you ever seen a dragon, Kraken?"

"No, I have bloody not, nor do I ever want to. Are you messing with me, Mannace? What bloody madness are you suggesting?"

"That Atek is the dragon, Kraken. I have been in her presence but have not seen her. The bell will restore her into this world, and we will soon know the truth."

Kraken was dumbfounded, "Why would you take such a gamble to revive a monster that could easily vanquish you and destroy what you have built?"

"Your namesake, the Kraken, was restored. The colossi are revived. Did the world end when they were set free?"

"No, but a bloody dragon? You have not thought this through. I would not have aided you to come here had I known."

Mannace laughed. He looked Kraken in the eye.

"I know. But it is the time for truth, and when we finish here, I will return the bell to you and not question your purpose. Look at us, Kraken; neither has much to lose."

Kraken smiled at that and nodded, "Seems fair. I hope Atek shares your view and doesn't make a snack of us both. Bloody dragon, are you serious, Mannace!?"

"I am sure of it."

It was strange timing, but a question came into Mannace's head, and he realized he might not have another opportunity to ask it.

"Kraken, how did you know my father?"

"Your father and I shared a passion for a beautiful woman."

The answer came much quicker than both were expecting, as if it had been at the top of Kraken's mind, waiting impatiently for the opportunity to escape. But once released, a flood of words was unbound.

"We were best of mates, Vertov and I, and at first, it was a game to bed such a pretty creature. The three of us even shared a bed, but he loved her, the fool, and she chose me." Kraken huffed. "Me, a rogue. I am no lover, Mannace. I didn't want the love of a woman, so I chose the sea. I always choose the sea and I left on a ship to rid myself of such drama. Your father, he fled too, on foot, and never returned. I don't understand it, to be a slave for bloody *love*. It is a monster in disguise, set to ambush men in the night and rip out their hearts with its claws. It was like that for your father, stabbed in the bloody heart, and he blamed me for his wounds. Stupid, over a pretty face and warm purse. His ego took the blow hardest if you ask me. I swear it by Ramthos. That's how I see it!"

Uz, who was behind Kraken, surprised both men by stepping forward to interrupt their private conversation.

"Only the godsss warrant love. It isss our role to ssserve. Ssservice to the deitiesss, or your light, or to Ramthosss of the Sssea. Love of the godsss is everything. It isss sssacrificcce and reward. Love of othersss, or of thingsss, or of ssself, will take many pathsss, but all lead to the abyssss."

377

"The abyssss," echoed Mannace, happy to be distracted from Kraken's explanation. He had no more capacity for drama.

"What of Atek," retorted Kraken, "Is your dragon a God?"

"Atek is firssst in Order."

"What does that mean?" Kraken appeared annoyed by the Rhalec's response. It was Mannace, though, that explained.

"Atek is one of the Ancients. Is that not so, Uz?"

"Yesss. We ssserve."

Kraken was not at all interested in politics. He wanted only one thing, "Will I get the bell back, Uz?"

This time, nobody answered him.

The city of Zetarach shook. At first, there was a rumble beneath the earth. Then the ground moved gently. At least that's how it appeared at first, but the seemingly calm movement was enough to force the Rhalec to their knees, and in places, ancient towers tumbled. Civilians scurried or crawled for safety as the shaking intensified. Everywhere, structures collapsed, and the screech of the terrified or wounded bespoke the horror of those caught within. When the violence abated, Mannace and Uz joined others who ran to the rubble to help the trapped and hurt.

Kraken hastily retreated to the ship, where a remnant of his crew took charge and prepared the sails.

"When they bring the bell, we will be away from this place. With haste, lads, this bloody forest is cursed. We shall put distance between it and us. The sea is calling. Ramthos is waiting."

It was not until late at night that the priests finally reappeared, chanting as they dragged the bell. Keeping to their word, the Rhalec loaded the artifact onto the sailing ship's deck, and Kraken wasted no time casting the boat free. As the vessel pulled away from the dock, holding a flask of liquor high in salute, Kraken shouted back into the darkness.

"Good luck to you, son of Vertov. May Ramthos guide you in your adventures. May your light protect you from the beast."

RETURN TO ANGOROK

Elderlin guided Mannace from the inner port to his new quarters. Unfortunately, during the skirmishers with the spiders, the wizards purposefully collapsed many of the citadel's corridors, and Mannace's rooms were amongst those destroyed in the conflict. The Librarian explained more as they progressed through the passages.

"It was a close thing when the spiders came in large numbers. UnRey, the true dwarf, saved us. It was his elemental magic that trapped and buried the attackers. All the Ways are blocked. We are certain of it, enough to rebuild where we can and expand further into the depths."

Elderlin took a deep breath, turning to face Mannace, who was following behind.

"Angorok is no longer besieged, but we dare not venture into the Veldaan." With a smirk, the librarian added, "You won't believe it, but Skon remains defiant. The Blood Legion operates from there, and the belg, Rey, leads them. Otherwise, the lands from the Veldaan through to Amon Murn are deserted but for the damned or the dead."

Turning back to lead the way, Elderlin raised a point at the fore of many minds, "You were gone for a long time, Mannace. Even I doubted that you would return. Some who were once loyal have departed on the flying ships in your absence. They are desperate to feel the sun on their faces, and others leave for a better life."

"But others stayed," was Mannace's quick response. "You stayed. Who, with a sane mind, would remain in this bunker, in the gloom and confronted by horrors, Elderlin?"

The Asari knew the marshall well enough to answer the question, "Only the most loyal. Only the most determined, Mannace, and those who choose a life less ordinary."

"Well said, my friend. Less ordinary indeed."

The following day, Mannace made his way to the war room. Figurines were idle around the edges of the central table or on cabinets nearby, all covered in dust. The gloom was cold and depressing, with empty fireplaces and a single light strip for illumination. It surprised the Marshall of Angorok that Elderlin would let these rooms fall to such a depressed state. But, at his summons, clerks were arriving.

"Gimbel, get some more lighting and put wood on the fires. Hundi, help Gimble and fetch brooms. All of you, for Hell's sake, get this place to a proper state."

Mannace grabbed one of the clerks by the arm, looking him up and down.

"Where is your uniform?"

"Where is your's, Marshall?"

"Huh, since when do I answer to you, Jarid? Did the Hells come and take away your respect?"

The clerk seemed determined, and he shook Mannace's arm away, "The Hells did come; the dead, and the swarm, and where were you, Marshall, while we fought in the dark? Clean your own bloody mess!"

Mannace swung his arm, catching Jarid hard on the collar, up-ending him so that the clerk landed painfully on his arse. The marshall leaned over his stunned subordinate.

"Hold your tongue and do as I say!" Then, addressing his wider audience of clerks, Mannace raised his voice so that it boomed through the hall and corridors, "All of you, get to work. We are at the heart of the world, of history, past *and* future. It began here, don't ever forget that. Would you rather push paper for a bureaucrat in Yanth, or are you proud to forge destiny here in Angorok? Enough of hiding in the dark! Tomorrow, we rebuild the North. Our North!"

Mannace helped Jarid to stand, and the clerk scurried to make himself useful. For the first time in a long time, Mannace felt invigorated, as if he might, in fact, sally forth and have the North at his feet.

By nightfall, the war room was a hive of activity. One of Elderlin's apprentices assisted in lighting the hall with a ball of luminescence shining down from the high ceiling. Unfortunately, it was too bright, so those entering the room held their heads down until they adjusted to its brilliance. The war room remained chill as the fires were unusable without outlets for the smoke, so the gathered officers wore woollen shirts or thick furs. Clerks placed figurines on the table, all at the city of Angororok or Skon, to represent the troops loyally allied to Mannace.

"It's a beginning," Mannace said to those close to him. Then he raised his voice to be heard by all those gathered. "We have proven that we cannot be dislodged, nor defeated. Our enemy does not have our resolve. Nor do they have the mettle of the men of Angorok to grab and firmly hold the North. That is our destiny, men. From this new beginning, we will rise to be masters of the North. I pledge to you, the Light, and the men of Angorok ..."

Mannace slowly scanned the room to meet the gaze of all present.

"...The North will be ours!"

There was enthusiasm in the room. Mannace could see that the officers wanted to believe in his words. Genuinely, while he couldn't explain it, Mannace felt in his gut that this was the time to claim the North, more so than when he led the vast armies of the South before the Hells opened their gates and set their foul hordes upon the lands. While those events broke him, he now saw them as the prelude to greatness. As Marshall of Angorok, surrounded by men and allies he trusted, Mannace finally understood and embraced his immortality. In time, the North would be his. This Age would serve him.

"We are blind. We must open our eyes and cast our gaze wide. Then, we will have the sun on our faces and our feet on the grass."

His audience raised their shoulders and puffed their chests. Mannace's words reminded them how trapped they were beneath the citadel of Angorok. They all yearned to embrace the daylight. Finally, one officer spoke, "Yes, Marshall. Let us be free of this prison! We have survived the hordes, and they will rue their unfinished business. We will rise. The North will be ours."

Later that evening, Mannace sat alone in an alcove, resting in his favourite chair, while absentmindedly turning over the figurine of a soldier in his hand. There were footsteps in the war room. It was unusual for anybody to be here this late, so Mannace cautiously raised himself from his seat and peered through the alcove arch. A man standing at the far end of the war table stared back. He likewise turned over a figurine in his hand, placing it back on the table's edge. In the dim light, Mannace thought his eyes might be playing tricks on him. Was this the emperor's ghost?

Mannace asked, "Are you dead?"

Jesephine rested her chin on the admiral's shoulder. With one hand, she moved a finger under his shirt and across his chest, circling his nipple. Her other hand slipped past his belt and took a firm grip of the admiral's rising spear. He was used to her seductive ways and yearned for the erotic touch. He lost his thoughts in anticipation of the sex that would follow. Together they watched the spiderkin and dark elves issuing the navigators orders, working on small activities to get them used to following instructions. It was obvious that some of the navigators resisted being controlled. Still, because of their naïve natures or slave conditioning, most accepted their new circumstances and complied with whatever was asked. Staronis didn't care. He was comfortable with his betrayal and satisfied to resign his authority and give himself entirely to a decadent lifestyle. The pleasure he experienced with Jesephine made him doubt what he ever found important in the emperor's service. At this moment, it contented him to be amongst Eya's entourage, with Jesephine's hand around his cock.

Eya entered the underground chamber from a side tunnel. Two dark elves with swords drawn kept vigil at her side, suspicious of anybody that came close and pointing their weapons to keep everybody at a safe distance. Even other dark elves gave them ground. Staronis immediately noticed Eya's nakedness, though his passion extended only to Jesephine, who continued to ply him with her seductive handwork.

A slave to his rising passion, the admiral turned, pressing Jesephine back against a rock pillar. Loosening his belt to let his pants fall to his ankles, Staronis freed one foot so that he could widen his stance. With his other arm, he lifted Jesephine's leg to expose her purse beneath her dress. Her soft hair and tender lips made him draw a deep breath, and he wasted no time pushing his hard cock against the inviting flesh. More than anything, he enjoyed the anticipation of entry, savouring the slight resistance, then the smooth, slippery penetration. He withdrew and repeated the sensual action, slower to embrace the sensations.

Eya stood beside him, looking Jesephine in the eye. Staronis had no mind but to satisfy his passion and to bring Jesephine that same pleasure. He would have kissed her sweet mouth, but Jesephine held him back with an extended palm so that she could maintain eye contact with the spider mother. As always, Eya's look was severe.

"The Bracadians have arrived. I need the admiral for the negotiations. You will come too, Jesephine. Your influence is required. Are you prepared?"

Jesephine moved her gaze to Staronis, "Fuck me harder." To Eya, Jesephine turned back and smiled, understanding her worth and not seeing the need to bow to the Ancients' demands. Eya moved a step closer, looking down at their sex as Staronis quickened his pace. Eya was amused at the admiral's urgent expression.

"Quicker. You have tasks to attend to." The spider mother glared at Jesephine, relaying that same order with her eyes. When the seductress failed to acknowledge her, Eya reached down, and there was a surge of power as she gripped the admiral, who immediately climaxed and screamed. Jesephine staggered back, her legs buckling, bringing her to her knees.

Eya moved between the two, so the dazed admiral shuffled to widen the gap. "Come with me, now!"

Together the trio and guards marched through passages before arriving at a room with a platform at its centre. The wooden structure sported a navigation stone in one corner, with a navigator and two dark elves standing close. Also on the platform were men who appeared to be traders. Around them were sacks and crates. Dekon Ruel stepped from the platform to the earth, striding to where Eya waited.

"Mother. Their leader is Regano Farquo. He was nervous about travelling here and dislikes the underground, but greed gives him courage. He will calm when he sees gold."

"It is not for me to talk with these Bracadians. Staronis will establish trade in what we need. Admiral, is everything in hand?"

"Yes," was the quick response. Staronis seemed stern and official, his returned self. He stared at the Bracadians, who mostly had eyes on Eya. Then, straightening his shirt, the admiral strode towards them, with Jesephine trailing behind. Eya turned to Dekon, who stood tall and proud, perhaps defiant.

"Tell Ahmeda to return here, Dekon. I want her at my side."

"She cannot return from Bracadia, Mother. I will stay. I will be fist and blade."

"No! She must return. I command it. Tell her there will be consequences for disobedience."

Dekon huffed, but he kept his thoughts private. Instead, he nodded obediently and backed away, turning, and striding to where the Bracadians were talking with the admiral. When Dekon looked back, Eya was already gone.

CIRCLES OF DARKNESS

"This will be our circle." Eya's tone was stern, her eyes malevolent. "Roanna will join us."

Grengal looked down her nose at the young dark elf. It was evident in her frown that she disagreed with Roanna's inclusion.

"Why this girl? What does she bring? The circle is not a trivial matter. Where is Ahmeda? What game are you playing, Eya?"

"Are you so blind, Grengal, that your vision is only in the present? Explore the potential. Sift through the possibilities, and you will understand."

Grengal shook her head. As she did so, flies lifted out of her hair and buzzed around the group before disappearing into the darkness. Saska laughed at the insects, swatting one away, earning her the disapproving stare of the others.

"Our business is serious." Eya looked coolly at the succubus. "Darkness binds us. The darkness does not suffer foolishness."

Saska smirked, returning the Ancient's stare. "You bait trap with daughter, but prey flown."

Eya ignored the accusation. Instead, she held her hands out so that Saska, Grengal, and Roanna all reached out to link first physically. Then, as the darkness flowed through them, they connected more profoundly. Roanna, who had never experienced the ritual or touched upon the essence of the Ancients, gasped, which made Saska laugh again. Silence followed. For an extended period, the circle continued to meld their power, and when they finally concluded, Grengal lifted her head to speak.

"Wild magic, such untamed energies. It will serve this circle well. I understand your choice, Eya."

Eya gave a satisfied nod while Roanna, who possessed a stunned look, held her hands to the fore, staring at her fingertips. "I did not know the currents could run so deep or strong."

The others looked at her. Even Saska was serious now. However, Eya was responsible for the dark elf's education.

"The darkness is nothing and everything. Within the darkness, we can be many or one."

"I am all of you."

At that realization, though it was a novice understanding, Eya smiled. Grengal huffed.

"What is our purpose?"

Grengal asked the question to break the miasma and bring them back to their business. She did not wait for others to answer. Instead, she was firm in her view, "The North is broken. It must be reforged to our design."

Before the others could speak, she made her claims, "I will have the Markhon and everything east of that. Regnorak and Altair resist, but they will break. There is the pit at Imbor, the portal between worlds. I will need the help of this circle to close it."

Saska huffed. "Pit remains open. Serves purpose. No close."

"It is an abomination, and it will be closed. The Hells have their politics, and those defeated will return for revenge. Not for the first time."

"I of Hells. Dead of Hells. Nonsense."

Eya was pragmatic, "We do not have the means to close the pit. Not today."

Grengal raised herself in response, pulling back her shoulders and growing noticeably taller. Flies buzzed through the air. The ancient looked down on the others.

"My army of the dead are of this land. They serve the darkness, not the Hells. As do we of this circle." Her fierce stare targeted Saska, who drew closer to the Ancient and dragged a finger seductively from Grengal's shoulder, across her breast and down to her thigh.

"I of Hells. I of Order. I of Darkness."

The spider mother was firm in bringing Saska back into line. "Second in Order. Do not forget your place. Else you will learn to fear the darkness, and every shadow will be your assassin."

The succubus remained defiant., "Where Jaal. Where Ahmeda. Who ..."

"ENOUGH!"

Eya's voice consumed all the space about them. Eyes suddenly stared from every shadow, as if the spider swarm surrounded them and was a moment away from overpowering and devouring its prey. Just as suddenly, Grengal fragmented into a mass of flies that vanished into the night, reappearing when Eya's wrath subsided. The Ancient coalesced at a safer distance, staring at Eya maliciously.

"I do not tolerate such disobedience in my Order. You allow too much freedom."

The Spider mother took a step back as if the words were a blow, "The circle is our strength. What do you bring?"

All women stood silent for a time. Finally, Eya spoke in a more level tone.

"The lands west of the Markhon, I will have."

Grengal was still solemn but nodded. "So be it. The North is divided. Darkness binds us."

"Lift her now!"

On the Admiral's order, Engis drew on the combined power of all three gridstones embedded in the base of the giant tree. Then, through the navigation stone, reaching into the earth, the young navigator lifted the land, as enormous a space as he could imagine. With his eyes closed, he felt the ground shaking beneath his feet, but he also sensed an upward movement that he controlled with familiar precision and grace. The admiral's hand was on his shoulder, gripping him to keep him balanced and motivated.

Far away on a hill, Eya observed with satisfaction as a vast chunk of the landscape levitated skyward. It was strangely bowl-shaped, though great clumps of dirt continued to crumble from the base and crash into the crater that was left. On the edge of the rising mass, more pieces of rock and some of the giant trees fell away, tumbling through the air. Eya was proud of her achievement. She could not recall any other Ancient accomplishing such a feat.

"The North will feel my wrath."

Dekon was not convinced, pragmatic in his concern, "It is vulnerable. It relies on the navigator to move it. How hard is it to kill one man?"

When Eya was unmoved, the war priest felt compelled to add, "The God of War will not see the valour in such a weapon. He will oppose it."

Eya was still captivated by the floating island. Her tone was dismissive, "Ahmeda would take this rock and use it to scrape Angorok from the Earth. Why is your thinking so limited? Being around humans is a curse, Dekon. Help your people to remember what it is to be of shadow. You defeat yourself before your sword is even raised."

Dekon fell silent, his head bowed and his eyes busy in thought.

Roanna, who also stood at the Ancient's side, could see the inner turmoil Eya's words stirred in the high priest. In truth, she was even less impressed with Eya's perceived triumph. To the dark druid, the destruction of The Hand was a horrible reminder that her adoptive people were defeated and fled. She should have a more profound sentiment, but she realized another truth: the darkness freed her from the little remorse she felt toward her adopted kin.

The Ra Anu was the child of Fengal, and if she regretted one thing, it was the risk that by joining the dark elves, her bond with the doe was broken. In that moment of fleeting thought, Roanna turned and strode purposefully down the slope and through the trees, immediately compelled to travel to the Tangle and seek the Ra Anu. Saska demonstrated that she could be part of the Order and the circle and still follow her chosen path. Roanna admired the demon's fearlessness. The Fen, the Ra Anu, the forest – were still things she held to be important. After being in the Ancients' presence and sharing with the circle, she realized that she must claim these things as her dominion.

Roanna quickened her pace.

Demmal frowned as he read Grengal's rough scrawl. She was specific in her orders to withdraw the horde into Amon Murn and conquer Regnorak and then Altair. Even Churgwarthos had left Regnorak alone, with its towering defences and monstrous guardians. It was the final bastion of the old North, and more than anything, Demmal felt sadness to eradicate the last vestiges of a once proud nation. Grengal's dominion was the dead, and her Order would be a regime of servitude and oppression. It made the general of the Devoted question why he clung so desperately to life when the cost was far more precious.

Yet the War God was with him. Surely that meant that he and the Devoted served a higher purpose. As Demmal pondered, one of the keepers approached with a colourful entourage of guards. Expecting drama, Demmal was not disappointed.

"General, the horde is sluggish. They have not fed for some time."

"We will return to Amon Murn."

The man with the problem was agitated, pointing his staff at Demmal, his tone turning malicious, "How will it help feed the horde, to return to that barren land?"

Demmal lost his patience. Stepping forward, with a heavy slap, he knocked the keeper sideways. The man's guards raised their spears, but none were so foolish as to challenge the Devoted leader.

"Don't burden me with your problems. Let the dead feed upon themselves."

With more thought, Demmal added, "We will journey to Altair. Let them feast there if they can find any life in the cold."

"The stronghold of the giants. Can we not leave them in peace?"

The man's arrogant tone was gone, humbled by Demmal's strike, and reminded of his place in Grengal's hierarchy.

"It is a bastion that we will overcome. The giants and refugees they harbour will yield or fall. Regnorak will follow."

Not waiting for a response, Demmal turned and strode towards the Devoted camp. It was time to get the horde moving.

THE BRACADIAN

The basement floor was wet, and Althea watched her step so as not to slip. A burst of steam puffed out of the machine next to her and spilt across the stone tiles. As it evaporated into the air, it left a lingering scent of heated dampness. All about her, large machines whirred, their clockwork mechanisms clanking. The noise of steam passing through pipes made the machinery seem alive. Symin, who stood next to the controller, was distracted by a device she had gifted him.

"Do you like it, Symin?"

The fact that the young man did not respond answered the question. Instead, Symin manipulated the gadget, changing its shape and revealing new mechanisms.

"It is a marvel. A clockmaker in Antigoth crafted it; I believe it has some magetech properties. The artisan crafted it as a toy, but I could see the greater potential. It will help you calm yourself and occupy your busy brain."

Althea climbed a set of stairs and exited through a portal that two engineers flanked. They bowed before sealing the doors behind Symin, who absentmindedly followed. Crossing the road, Althea joined a group of officials waiting for her. Together, they all stared back at the completed construction. The chief engineer seemed impatient.

"Well, is it what you wanted?"

"It is magnificent, our first university hospital. It will change lives. It will spark an exciting future."

All the stonework on the five-storied building was pristine with its white finish. At the windows, bright crystals radiated a brilliance of colour so that the edifice sparkled like a jewel. Althea soaked it all in. The chief engineer offered a different perspective.

"It doesn't look like much from the outside, but it's got bones of steel, and the steam and tech work is unparalleled. We could go bigger for the next one, at least three more stories, and there are improvements to be made to the pipework. The next one will be quieter for sure."

"You build them, Gideon, and I will fill them."

The inspection brought many concepts together for Althea, and she shared her thoughts with the group.

"What we have constructed here in this city, every other city in Bracadia will want. The teachings at this place of learning will spark competition and innovation as they did across the Blood Sea. If you return to this place in thirty years, the city will have risen to match what you have built today. Be very proud indeed, gentlemen and ladies, of what you have achieved."

Titus waved from a distance. The gesture served no apparent purpose, except it made Althea aware that she was running to a tight schedule. The controller turned back to her audience.

"Whatever resources you need are at your disposal. Let me know how I can assist. When I have time, I will bring the governors here. After they have seen your work, expect each of them to be in your ear, to make them your top priority."

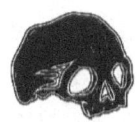

Atrula D'Austini, governor of Dreban, was not happy to have Saska as a visitor to the palace. The succubus took no precautions to disguise herself, and she had already enamoured two of her husbands. The useless men followed Saska around like they were her pets, forgetting their purpose. The consequences for their weakness would be severe. Atrula pulled Ahmeda aside into a private chamber, needing an explanation.

"Why bring that creature here!?"

"She came of her own accord. My dealings are with the admiral, but this is a great boon, Atrula. Saska has the power to make you immortal. See for yourself that the admiral is younger. That is because he has Jesephine at his side, Saska's apprentice."

"What!" the governor seemed shocked, "What do you mean?"

"Those that serve her gain some of her innate gifts. Beauty and immortality."

Ahmeda let the concept sink in, knowing the temptation would immediately hook Atrula. For all that the governor was clever and ambitious, vanity was her weakness, and the lure of beauty with immortality would be too great a prize.

"I will not serve the succubus. Is there another way?"

The high priestess shrugged, "Perhaps."

"Don't tease me, Ahmeda. You know with me that it's best to get to the point. What is it that you want?"

The high priestess met the governor's stare. Atrula appeared determined, and Ahmeda already trusted her enough to be frank. With Atrula, she did not need to be delicate.

"I serve the Darkness. The War God is of the Darkness. The Order, of which I am part, serves the Darkness. Saska, though a servant of the Hells, also serves the Darkness. Join us in this service, Atrula, and immortality is within your reach."

Atrula remained silent, staring intensely to encourage the high priestess to say more.

"Under the shadow, we do what must be done. Do you not already value dominion and order? You possess zeal and cunning. Darkness abounds in you; set it free and discover who you can be."

The pause of silence quickly became deafening. The weight of it spurred Ahmeda to share even more.

"Join in a circle with myself and Saska. Jesephine too. There is unity and power in a circle, Atrula, and you will benefit from the gifts Saska can offer. The circle is a sisterhood; a bond eternal and not lightly offered."

It was Ahmeda's turn to be surprised, though she should not have forgotten how quickly Atrula's mind grasped the present and future. Already the governor was conceiving new plans.

"I have an apprentice, as Saska does. My apprentice will join the circle."

"Perhaps."

"It will be so, Ahmeda. I do not give myself in part to any endeavour."

"Who?"

"Blackbird. She is special. I will prepare her."

Ahmeda seemed displeased, and she took a long time to respond. But eventually, she looked intently at the governor and gave her answer.

"I owe you a debt. Tonight, I consider that debt paid."

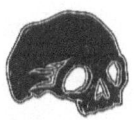

The Charikon capital of Ugol spread out over the barren landscape below. The towering clay spires were unchanged since Morgan's last visit. It was a fond memory of life when it was still simple. Now he carried the burden of great responsibility. However, this was not a diplomatic visit, and he possessed no agenda other than to ease his heart.

Landing in the market square caused a raucous that Morgan ignored, though he glimpsed soldiers pointing and rushing away to notify officials. The added weight of their inevitable questions and demands slumped his shoulders, and it took all his fortitude not to return to the skies. But, at least for a few moments, he would do something for himself and not for the benefit of others.

Thankfully, Arta was at her residence, and with a huff, the burly woman ordered her bodyguards to let the man of metal through her door. He stood while she relaxed into a comfortable chair. Then in the awkward silence to follow, Morgan reluctantly sat, though it served him no purpose. Arta's glare was fierce.

"Well!"

"Well, what?"

"What the Hells is the stand-in emperor doing sitting in a chair in my house? You make my life hard, Morgan. So, what do you want!"

"Can't I just have a moment's peace, Arta?"

"If you wanted peace, why kill the emperor and take his place?"

"I didn't kill the emperor. Is that what they are saying!"

"No. I said it. I just wanted to know. Where the Hells is he then?"

Morgan would have closed his eyes if they had lids. Instead, he looked down and imagined drawing a deep breath. It calmed him.

"Nobody knows. Until he returns, Bracadia will hold firm."

"Seems to me like you have the top job, Morgan. What's that like then?"

"It's bloody hard. What kind of question is that?"

"What am I meant to ask? Do you want me, Morgan? Is that why you have returned? You want some of this?"

Arta lifted her large breasts and let them sag back against her chest, showing her age. Morgan lost his words, so Arta answered, "You don't have a cock, so I'm not sure what use you would be."

Morgan smiled and relaxed for the first time in an age. Arta could see the change in his demeanour, so she purposefully smirked and settled back into her chair.

"Why are you here, Morgan?"

"To remind me who I am."

"Just so you know, if you had a cock, I would let you fuck me."

Morgan laughed. It was a release he desperately needed, and when there was a demanding knock on the door, he got up to answer it.

"Leave me in peace. I will be out in my own time."

When he returned, the old friends sat in silence. It was Morgan that resurrected the conversation.

"How is business?"

"Why do you care how's my business? It's none of your business is what it is."

"I don't care, honestly. I just wanted to see you, Arta. I wanted to know that you're still here, alive."

"I'm alive." Then, with a smirk, Arta added, "And Mannace, is that pig's arse still alive?"

"Yes, just. He is still an arse."

Now they both laughed. Morgan, however, was suddenly serious, leaning forward.

"The emperor will not return. That is a lie to stop the panic. I must decide if I will leave or if I will rule."

Not taken aback, Arta stated the obvious, "If you don't rule, who will? Anyway, where would you go? You are always leaving, Morgan. Why don't you stay and be useful? You would make a better emperor than most. Seriously, you are such a whiner – do you hear yourself!?"

Arta could tell that inside the invulnerable metal frame, there was a fragile man, procrastinating. It made her instantly angry.

"Fuck off, Morgan. You cannot hide here. I'm not going to give you a bloody cuddle and tell you it will all be bloody right. Don't be a damned child for Hell's sake – you have a bloody empire to run."

Morgan laughed.

"I visited the Oracle at Viletri.

There was a pause, making Arta impatient.

"And ..."

"I had a dream, Arta, that started with me as emperor."

Now Morgan sighed. The vision was the crux of his dilemma.

"If I am emperor, then I fear the rest of my dream must also be true!"

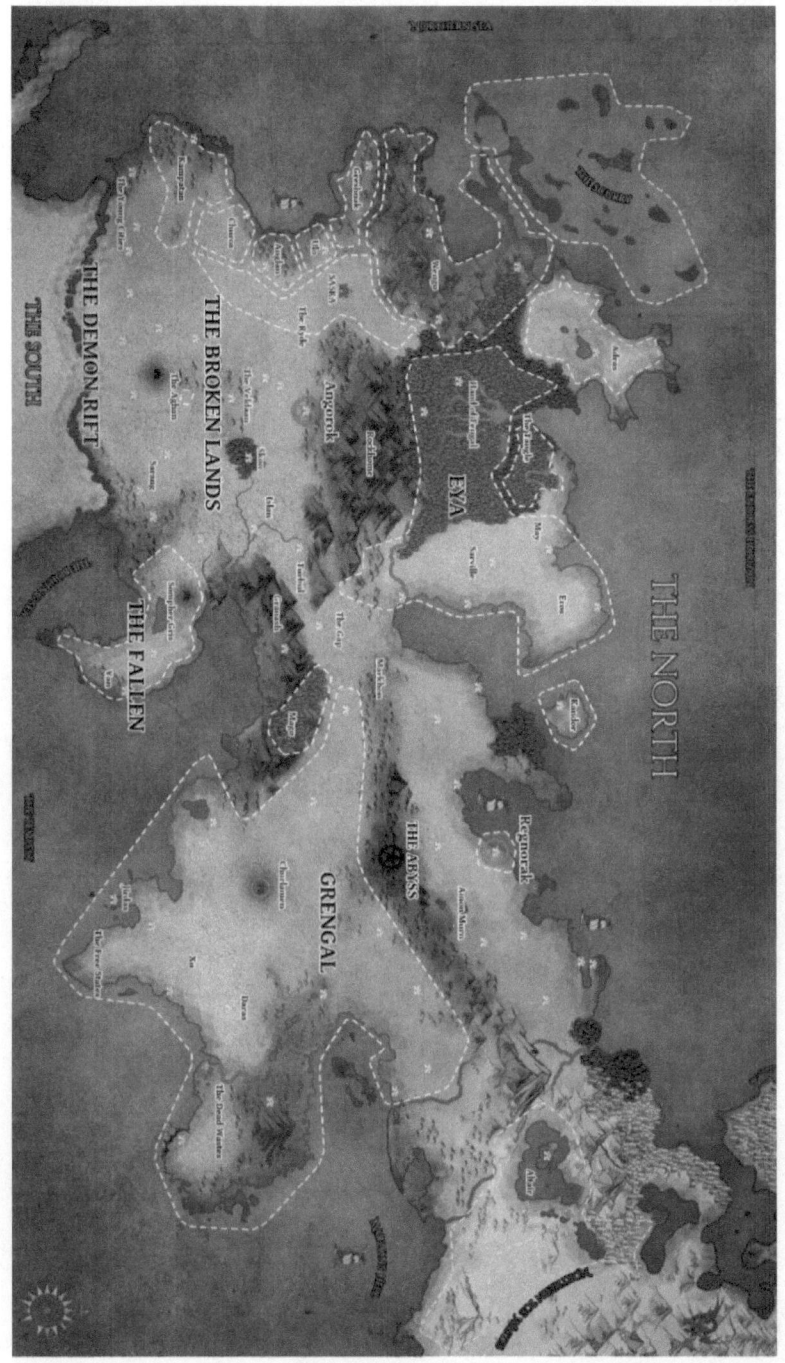

Immortals Book 4: The Dark Light

Year one hundred and eleven of the New Age was an auspicious date. The Doctrine of War decreed a time of reckoning, while the Eternal Priesthood declared it the Unseen Year. In the tumultuous North, forces of darkness and light both claimed the Age, while in the south and west, the burgeoning empire of Bracadia held the period sacred as a time of humanity.

But games were afoot, and the Surg-Ta cruelly usurped all their predictions. Like a great tide surging from the distant east, the Red Horde flooded the coasts, disembarking armies wherever their fleets collided with the land. Fierce and uncompromising, the Surg-Ta's ambition was infinite, and the War God's reckoning was suddenly imminent.

Would Mannace, ordained by the light, be the hero to save them? In the past, his spark ignited collaboration and innovation, again so desperately needed. Yet why should he care when the world so pitilessly spurned him, abandoning him to marshal the North alone?

Might Render, steeped in dark sorcery, be enough to strike terror into the brutal invaders? Did he possess means beyond that of mortal men to resist the Surg-Ta? In such desperate circumstances, was darkness the unlikely champion to save humanity? Or would it be in the shadow's interest to let humanity fail?

Jaal, a dark light, crosses all their fates. Will his influence be vital, or does he foolishly risk everything by interfering? Perhaps in this utmost of trials, he is the one to usurp destiny and recast the Age.

Ancient masters, rising gods, advancing technology, dark circles, a mad king, a shattered North! The three companions confront a hostile realm of broken factions and tattered alliances. Nations stand apart, unready to resist the Red horde or unify even when faced with impending ruin.

About the Author:
Andrew Wratten

I am a proud Kiwi, living in sunny Australia, with my beautiful Nigerian wife, Tessy, and our six amazing children. Family and friends mean everything ... and good food of course, and dogs, and embarrassingly, reality TV.

One day on the train to work, I took my fantasy daydream and boldly typed my first paragraphs. Since that time, I remain amazed at how the words reveal themselves and the tales evolve.

It is a wonderful process to shape a story, witnessing the plot unfold, unexpectedly twist, and surprise even me in its audacious conclusion.

The story belongs to the characters in it, and it is my job to help them be heard, understood, and celebrated for all their glorious traits and flaws. I am indeed a puppet of the Mad King, and like all the others in my books, I am dancing to his manic tune.

I hope others enjoy the characters, their triumphs, and their misadventures, as much as I do.

www.ingramcontent.com/pod-product-compliance
Lightning Source LLC
Chambersburg PA
CBHW020248120726
47904CB00001B/131